DEAD MEN AND BROKEN HEARTS

DEAD MEN AND BROKEN HEARTS

CRAIG RUSSELL

Quercus

First published in Great Britain in 2012 by

Quercus
55 Baker Street
7th Floor, South Block
London W1U 8EW

A CIP catalogue record for this book is available
from the British Library

HB ISBN 978 0 85738 184 2
TPB ISBN 978 0 85738 183 5

10 9 8 7 6 5 4 3 2 1

Typeset by Ellipsis Digital Limited, Glasgow
Printed and bound in Great Britain by Clays Ltd, St Ives plc

For Wendy

CHAPTER ONE

'Who, where or what is "Tanglewood"?'

It was a simple question and, given the circumstances, an entirely reasonable and necessary one. Neither I nor my soon-to-be-client were filled with dread at my utterance of those six innocent words.

The thing is, though, we should have been.

Nineteen Fifty-six, the year that was winding up, may have been a bad year for the British Empire but had, for me, been a good one business-wise. Not as lucrative as some of its predecessors, admittedly, but for the first time in years the buck I was turning was completely honest. It had been a full thirteen months since I had done any work for any one of the Three Kings, Glasgow Underworld's answer to Caesar, Pompey and Crassus, and I hadn't gotten into any real tangles.

The last tangle, however, had ended in a way that could have had me stretching a length of hangman's hemp. An experience like that increased the appeal of the straight and narrow.

Since then, I had decided to keep a profile that was as legitimate as it was low. Most of the work I now did was gathering evidence for divorce cases, security work, or snooping about for companies or lawyers. Divorce in 1950s Scotland was a protracted, painful and Rhadamanthine process; meaning it offered a great opportunity for turning a profit. I had taken help on full time: Archie McClelland, the ex-City of Glasgow Police beat man, who did most of the court work for me. Courtrooms made me nervous, especially when some smart-ass lawyer started to call into question my credentials as a witness. Some things don't bear a great deal of scrutiny. My past was definitely one of them.

The most important thing was that it had been quite a while since I'd found myself wrestling with a thug, looking down a gun barrel or fending off some Teddy Boy armed with a tyre lever, knuckleduster or switchblade. That was one thing I could say about divorce cases: bursting in on unfaithful husbands *in flagrante* with their secretaries meant that the only weapons you tended to find being waved in your direction pretty rapidly lost their ability to bruise.

'I don't know,' Pamela Ellis said in answer to my question. 'I don't even know if Tanglewood is a who, a where, or a what.'

'But you overheard him say it, so you must have heard it in the context of a sentence, something to give us a clue.'

'All I heard Andrew say was the word "Tanglewood". He was on the telephone and I heard him say "Got it. Tanglewood." Then the person at the other end of the line must have been speaking – for quite a time – and then Andrew just said "okay" and hung up the receiver.'

'And then he went out?'

'Then he went out. He left a note on the hall table, by the telephone, saying he had been called out to a customer and he wouldn't be back until very late, and that he would get something to eat while he was out.'

'And you were where?'

'In the lounge,' she said. They had lounges in Bearsden. Not parlours or living rooms; lounges. 'I had come back early and he didn't know I was in the house. He came in through the front door, made the call on the hall telephone, then left again.'

I leaned back in my chair. Pamela Ellis was a woman loitering uncertainly on the threshold of middle age, as if undecided whether she should simply surrender to the thickening of waist and hip and answer the call of tweed and stout shoes. It was clear that she had once been pretty, and was still a handsome woman, but there was a weariness that seemed to hang about her. She had called into my third-floor office in Gordon Street without having first made an appointment. It was the kind of thing that I decided I should discourage by telling my secretary to send away anyone who turned up without an appointment. But I'd have to start by hiring a secretary.

'And he came back when?'

'Late. I stayed up for him and he didn't get back till eleven. He'd been gone for over five hours.'

'And how was he with you when he got home?'

'Fine. Well, you wouldn't expect him to be anything else.'

'And you were fine with him?'

'I tried to be as normal as possible . . . You know, as if I didn't suspect anything.'

'We don't know yet that there *is* anything to suspect. Did he offer any further explanation for where he had been?'

'He said it had had something to do with work. Someone needing an estimate. That's what he's been saying about all the times he disappears: that it's to do with work.'

'You do know, Mrs Ellis, that there is every chance that it is all exactly as innocent as that?'

'I know. I want to believe that . . . and it really could be business. It's just that he's been so strange lately. Usually, when he gets home from work, he just relaxes. Sits and chats with me. I mean, demolition isn't the kind of business you do out of office hours. The customers Andrew usually deals with are councils or building firms needing a site cleared. And he has salesmen to deal with most of that side of things anyway. But it's not just him going out in the evening at short notice that's worrying me, it's the way he is when he's at home, too; the way he's withdrawn into himself. When he isn't out, he's so quiet. Sometimes he just sits for an hour, staring at the fire and saying nothing. It's just not like him. He has this shed, you see, in the garden. He used to spend hours there, tinkering with stuff. If ever I go into it to borrow something, I always forget to lock the shed behind me. Andrew is always giving me rows about that, but now he's hardly in there. Just sits moping by the fire. The other thing is that I can't find any notes.'

'Notes?'

'Andrew is incredibly organized. Actually, that's not true ... he's terribly *dis*organized and forgetful, so he writes everything down. Makes notes about everything – every meeting, every new client's name, every appointment time or figure quoted. He uses notebooks mainly, but I'm always finding notes on scraps of paper. You see, that's the thing ... there's nothing about these meetings and there's never been any note referring to "Tanglewood". I'm telling you, Mr Lennox, the fact that he is making such an effort *not* to put anything down is suspicious in its own right.'

'When he goes out, is it always for five or six hours?'

'Not always. Sometimes he's only gone an hour. Other times it's five hours. It never seems to be anything in between. There is one odd thing, though, about the longer disappearances ...'

'Oh?'

'He takes a pair of heavy boots with him. I mean, he often takes wellington boots with him if he's visiting a site, but not his heavy boots.'

I nodded, taking it all in. 'Is there anything that you can think of that might be bothering him?' I asked. 'Preying on his mind?'

'No, nothing that I can think of. He's annoyed about all of this carry-on in Hungary at the moment. He listens to the news and it seems to make him worse, but there's something more than that going on in his head.'

'I think it's safe to say that annoyance at current affairs doesn't explain his behaviour being quite so odd,' I said.

'No. It doesn't. Nothing does.'

'So that's why you suspect it could be another woman?'

She shrugged. 'I just don't know. I can't think what else it could be.'

'Listen, Mrs Ellis . . . far be it from me to try to talk you out of giving me work, but before you do hire me, you've got to think about where this may lead you. Let's say your husband *is* carrying on an affair with another woman and we manage to prove that . . . what then? Do you want to divorce your husband if we prove he's been unfaithful? It's a messy, unpleasant business.'

'You can take it to a divorce case?' she asked, perplexed. She clearly had not thought the process through to its natural conclusion.

'I can recommend a lawyer and I – or at least my associate, Mr Archibald McClelland – can appear in court to provide evidence of infidelity, should we find it. My point is that it is a huge step to take – and a difficult one. Sometimes, I'm afraid to say, ignorance really can be bliss. If you want to walk away from this now, I would fully understand.'

I always gave clients this opportunity to consider their options. Of those options, divorce was the toughest and messiest one. Divorce in Britain generally was a difficult and sordid affair, and particularly so in staunchly Presbyterian Scotland. At the end of the war, the divorce rate had rocketed, reaching an all-time record in Forty-seven. It was all the sad result of men coming back broken or bitter or altered and dropped straight back into a society that no longer made much sense to them. Sometimes there would be evidence – often living, breathing, nappy-wearing evidence – of a wife's infidelity.

Ten years after the war was over, it was still claiming casualties, but casualties of battles fought in the divorce courts. I had a theory about it all – as I tended to have about most things. The Great Lennox Theory of Divorce Law was that the government and the law lords went out of their way not to modernize divorce laws that were woefully in need of reform; and the reason for their reluctance to make the process easier was some deep fear that the very fabric of British society was in danger of coming apart. They should have come to Glasgow, I had often thought, to see how threadbare and tattered that fabric was at the best of times.

Pamela Ellis thought about what I had said for a moment, frowning. Then, decisively, she said, 'No. No, Mr Lennox, I need to know. I don't know what I'll do if you find anything. Maybe I'll just confront him about it. Or maybe I'll not say anything. But at least I'll know. At least I'll have found out for sure.'

I smiled. 'That's your decision, Mrs Ellis. Can you tell me some more about your husband, please? Personal history, habits ... anything that might help me build a picture of Andrew Ellis.'

'Oh, I don't know ... Andrew's an ordinary kind of man, really. Someone I've always felt, well, *comfortable* with. I mean, that's partly why I find his behaviour of late so disturbing. It's so unlike him to be anything other than ordinary. He doesn't smoke, doesn't drink much ... he's not much of a one for the pub. Work is everything to him. That and his home life ...' She choked on the last part and clearly struggled to keep a lid on her emotions. But she managed. Ten years of living in Scotland had shown me the Scots were world champions at keeping a lid on emotions.

'Do you have any children?'

She shook her head. 'We tried, but we can't.'

'What about work?' I asked. 'How did Mr Ellis get into the demolition business?'

'He was in the RAOC and then the Royal Engineers during the war. Bomb disposal to start with then demolition. Andrew always said that he spent half his time stopping things blowing up and then the other half making them blow up.'

'Officer?'

'NCO. He was a volunteer. He had been exempt from the call-up, but he wanted to serve so he volunteered.'

'Because he was in a reserved occupation?' I asked. A lot of Glaswegians had dodged the bullet of wartime conscription, sometimes more than metaphorically, because they worked in essential industries such as the shipyards or munitions.

'No. No it wasn't that. Andrew had to go through all of these panels and interviews when it came out about his family background.'

'I'm sorry, what do you mean, "family background"?'

'Andrew's parents were Hungarian,' she explained. 'They changed their name to Ellis from *Elès*. They came over after the

Great War. That's why he was so upset about all of this trouble in Hungary. Andrew has never thought of himself as anything other than a Glaswegian, a Scot. But when he volunteered to serve his country, he suddenly found himself being treated as a foreigner. Worse than that, they treated him as a potential enemy alien because Hungary was an Axis power.'

'But he got in.'

'Only by volunteering to train for bomb disposal. It was dangerous work and there was a shortage of volunteers.'

'I can imagine . . .' I said. I had myself had an encounter with a German grenade that had been some way distant, and with one of my men between me and it. The long-term result of this confrontation had been the faint web of pale scars on my right cheek, still visible every morning in the shaving mirror. The bomb boys got a lot more up close and intimate with munitions than I had been and it took a special kind of cool. Or stupidity. 'And after the war he set up business using the skills he'd learned?' I asked.

'After he was demobbed, Andrew went to work for Hall's Demolitions. That's where I met him. I worked in the office, you see. He went straight in as an ordnance handler because of his war experience and was team boss in no time. But then, when old man Hall died, Andrew couldn't work with his son so he went out on his own.'

'And you went with him?'

'I did all the paperwork when the business was small. I left when the business became established and we took on staff.'

'I'm sorry, Mrs Ellis, but I have to ask: has your husband had any affairs in the past, or behaved with women in a way that has caused you concern?'

'Never.'

'So why now?'

'Like I told you, he's changed. He's different . . . *preoccupied*, I suppose, like there's something weighing on his mind. Almost like he's haunted.'

I nodded. Haunted was a look that a lot of men who'd been in the war had. But it didn't tend to be something that came on suddenly a decade later, like delayed shock.

'Could he be worried about the business?'

She shook her head. 'No, business has been good. Andrew's got a lot of contracts from the Corporation. You know, clearing slums for new flats.'

'I guess it's a boom time for that . . .' I said, and grinned. She either didn't get the gag or chose not to, which I couldn't blame her for – it was a pretty lame gag. But I did see that there would be a lot of demolition work available: Glasgow Corporation was in the process of blasting more Glaswegian real estate out of existence than the Luftwaffe had managed. The Future, apparently, was High-Rise. Hundreds of Glaswegian families now stood staring in slack-jawed amazement at toilets that they didn't need to go *outside* to use. And that they didn't need to share with five other families.

'Could he be worried about something else? You don't think there could be some kind of medical concern that he's not telling you about?'

'I doubt it. Andrew's one of the healthiest people I know.'

'I see,' I said, and tried to work out how relative that statement was in Glasgow. I had grown to have a deep affection for Glaswegians, but remained confused by their lemming-like attitude to diet, cigarettes and booze. I was witness to a million slow-motion suicides by lard. 'Well, I suggest that we keep tabs on your husband for a while, Mrs Ellis. May I 'phone you at home to keep you informed?'

She scribbled down a number with a tiny green pencil in a tiny green notebook, tore out a page and passed it to me. 'Please, Mr Lennox, make sure you only call when Andrew is at work.'

'Of course. I will need a reasonably up-to-date—'

She anticipated my request by taking a photograph from her handbag and handing it to me. The dark-haired man in the picture had pale-coloured eyes, a strong jaw and the type of regular, well-proportioned features that should have made him handsome but instead somehow made him anonymous. Bland, almost. His look was not typical for Glasgow, but he was not the handlebar-moustachioed Magyar I had started to imagine. The main impression I got from the photograph was that this was the kind of face most people would take as that of a pleasant, honest man. But I had learned not to take honesty at face value.

Thanking her for the picture, I then questioned her further about her husband's routine: the usual times he came home or went out, and so on. I took down the addresses of his business premises, his golf club, the number of his car. I dressed up with professional procedure the patent impertinence of snooping into another human being's private life.

When we were finished I thanked Mrs Ellis and she thanked me and I walked her out into the stairwell. She thanked me once more and said goodbye. As she did so, she failed to hide the resentment and hatred in her eyes. At the end of it all, I was the man who, with a single bright, hard truth, could bring her marriage to an end.

Divorce work.

Sometimes I missed the plain honesty of gangsters, thugs and back-alley dealings.

CHAPTER TWO

I got out of bed, crossed to the window and opened the curtains. It was raining heavily on Glasgow. I tried to contain my shock.

I had recently read a short story by an American science fiction writer about space travellers stranded on a planet where it never stopped raining and who, unless they found 'sun domes', were driven to insanity and murder by the endless precipitation thundering down on them. I wondered if the author had ever spent a Bank Holiday long weekend in the West of Scotland.

'Do you want a cigarette?' I asked, looking out at a dull, rainy late-October Glasgow that looked pretty much the same as a dull, rainy early-August Glasgow. The seasons were mitigated here: by the Gulf Stream and by the sooty blanket of smoke belched out by the city's tenements and heavy industry. Glasgow did not have a four-season climate. Unless you counted those times when we got all four seasons in one day.

Fiona White, my landlady for three years and lover for one, eased herself up onto her elbows, allowing the bed sheet to slip from her breasts before recovering it and them. She shook her head. She smoked rarely these days. Or smiled.

'I'd better go. Back downstairs. The girls will be home in half-an-hour.' Her daughters, Elspeth and Margaret, were due to return from school. This had become an afternoon ritual for us every Tuesday and Thursday: an hour stolen behind drawn curtains. Fiona looked tired and her voice was dull: her passion spent and that hint of guilt or sadness or both that I had increasingly noticed in her tone. Fiona White was unlike almost all of the women I'd been with. For her, sex was something that belonged only within marriage; and that was exactly the way it had been for her until the German Navy had intervened and sent her husband to the bottom of the Atlantic, condemning Fiona to a life of stretched means and lonely evenings contemplating over too many sherries a future stripped bare of its promise.

Then I had come along.

As a way of trying to make far-apart ends meet, Fiona White had converted the family home on Great Western Road into two dwellings: upper and lower apartments accessed through the same front door. I had taken the upper flat. True, initially the attraction had been as much to landlady as accommodations, but I had remained respectful and had made no move on her. This was something that, at the time, had perplexed me. It reeked of rectitude and morality, character traits that I long assumed had gone missing-in-action during my war service.

My intentions towards women had not, it had to be said, been noted for their nobility. But Fiona White seemed to bring out an older me – or younger me, depending on how you looked at it. A pre-War, pre-Glasgow, pre-Fucked-Up me.

Thing was, I didn't know what kind of Fiona White I brought out in her.

'Are you okay?' I asked.

'I'm fine,' she said, but in a tone that didn't put my mind much at ease. She got up and began to dress. I watched her. She had the Celtic dark auburn hair and green eyes that you saw a lot of in Glasgow, but her high cheekbones and firm jaw spoke of some other history. She was slim, and of late I had thought perhaps a little too slim, but what upholstery there was was in all the right places.

'Don't stand at the window without a shirt on,' she admonished me. That was the tenor of our relationship; out of view and behind closed curtains.

I sighed and came away from the view of the wet and grey Glasgow weekday afternoon and sat on the edge of the bed, pulling on my shirt: pale blue with a faint gold stripe, French cuffs. My taste for expensive tailoring was, I knew, something Fiona both appreciated and resented. Another sign of her good old-fashioned, deeply-embedded, Calvinism. Not that I was complaining about all of that pent-up repression: what had surprised me – overwhelmed me – about Fiona was that taking her to bed had been like removing a high-pressure lid. Explosive.

But there again, our relationship had been full of surprises: like the way I had come to feel about her. Something nauseatingly honourable and deep. And I had tried so hard to keep all of my dealings with women as superficial and unembellished as possible.

As a culture, Scotland might have been more sexually repressed than a monastery with a view of a nudist beach, but I had, it had to be said, enjoyed a staggering amount of success with the opposite sex during my time in Glasgow. I put it down largely to the lack of sophisticated competition, the average Scotsman's concept of foreplay generally being: 'Come here a minute and grab hold of this . . .'

'Will you be eating downstairs tonight?' she asked me, becoming my landlady once more.

'Are you *sure* you're all right? You look tired.' And she did.

Her face was paler than usual and there were shadows beneath the green eyes.

'I told you, I'm fine.' She forced a smile. 'Do I set a place for you?' It had become the custom for me to join Fiona and her daughters for the evening meal most days.

'No, not tonight,' I said. 'I've got a job on. Following a wandering husband. I'll probably be late.'

She nodded, and finished getting dressed.

'Do you want me to make up some sandwiches and a flask for you?'

'That would be fine, thanks, Fiona,' I said with a smile even more forced than hers. Nothing illustrated the chasm that still existed between us more than her asking me if I wanted sandwiches and a flask. Fiona did not seem to be able to distinguish the role of enquiry agent from that of a night-watchman. She perhaps had a point.

She turned and headed out towards the landing. I took her by the elbow and turned her around, kissing her on the lips. She responded. Just.

'Don't tell me my irrepressible boyish Canadian charm is fading . . .' I said.

'Lennox,' she said, easing herself back from me. 'We can't go on like this. It's not right.'

'What's not right about it?' I let her go. 'I thought you were happy.'

She cast a glance towards the bed we had shared until a few minutes before.

'This isn't me, Lennox. I can't be the kind of woman you're used to.'

'What the hell is that supposed to mean?' I protested, although I knew exactly what she meant.

Her look hardened. 'Please do not swear at me. That's something else I'm not used to. What I'm saying is that this isn't right. It's not right for me. I never wanted to end up . . .' She left the thought hanging in a silence that stretched longer than it should.

'You know how I feel about you,' I protested.

'Do I?'

I let her go. 'What is this all about? What is it you want from me?'

'Nothing, Lennox. Absolutely nothing.' The expression in her face now stone-hewn. 'I'll get your sandwiches ready.'

Archie McClelland had the kind of face that Bassett hounds, undertakers and professional mourners would probably have described as unnecessarily lugubrious. A lanky six-foot three, Archie was tall for anywhere, which meant he was a giant in Glasgow, and he compensated for his height by perpetually stooping. He even stooped sitting down, as I could see through the rectangle of rear window of his ten-year-old Morris Eight as I pulled up behind it.

Archie had parked at the corner of the street, far enough from the Ellis home as not to be seen from the windows. He popped open the passenger door as I approached and I slid in next to him.

'How's it going?' I asked. The gaze he turned on me was so doleful that I felt myself beginning to sink into clinical depression.

'Dynamite came home straight from the office and hasn't set foot outside since.'

'Dynamite?'

Archie nodded his large high-domed head, his bald pate fringed with an unkempt horseshoe of black hair. 'Dynamite

Andy the demolitions man. I have christened the subject of our surveillance thus.'

'Thus?'

'Thus.'

'Do you often come up with nicknames for people?'

'I find it does something to ease the mind-numbing tedium of my employment by you.'

'I see. You could just get another job,' I said.

'I would miss the sparkle of our chats,' he replied. Archie's dry wit had probably been the undoing of his police career. That and his brains. A surfeit of wit and intelligence was an encumbrance in the police, particularly when it highlighted the deficit of both amongst your superiors. What had finished his career for once and for all, however, had been a fall through a factory roof while chasing burglars. That had not been one of his brightest moments.

'You get on home, Archie,' I said. 'I'll take over. If lover-boy doesn't go out by nine-thirty or ten, I'll pack it in myself for the night.'

'I bet Humpty Go-cart doesn't worry about getting home for his jim-jams and Ovaltine. As a private eye you don't set the example I had hoped for.' He nodded a pale brow in the direction of the Ellis residence. 'D'you think our chum is up to some kind of marital malarkey?'

'Most likely.'

'Doesn't look the type to me, whatever the type is. At least from a distance. And if he has a fancy woman on the side, then she's not exactly putting a spring in his step.'

'What makes you say that?'

'He doesn't look a cheery chappy, that's all. Just an impression I get.'

'Well, we'll find out in time, hopefully.' I opened the car door. 'I'll see you later.'

Archie gave an American-style salute.

I was just about to go when a thought made me lean back into the car. 'Tell me, Archie, you wouldn't have a nickname for me, by any chance?'

'No sir,' he said. 'That would be disrespectful. No references to lumberjacking whatsoever.'

After Archie left, I moved my Austin Atlantic forward a few feet and filled the space vacated by his car. I sat for an hour as, with increasing frequency, greasy globs of rain smeared the windshield and made stars out of the streetlamps. I switched on the radio and listened to the baneful baying of a dying dinosaur: the death throes of the British Empire. The news was full of Britain's humiliation as its last, fumbling attempt to remain at the centre of the world stage – its intervention in the Suez Crisis – stumbled on. And while one empire was dying another was flexing youthful muscles: Suez competed for radio time with the latest on the Hungarian Uprising. It was an inspiring beacon of hope in the gloom of Soviet domination, apparently. It was just unfortunate that the West chose to look the other way. Oh, Brave New World . . .

I drank some of the tea Fiona had made up for me; it tasted odd and tinny from the vacuum flask but at least it was hot. The Glasgow climate decided to lighten my mood by turning the tap up on the rain, which now drummed angrily on the roof of my Atlantic. It was going to be a long, damp night. I decided it was far too inclement for adultery and that I would maybe head home earlier than planned. But then, at a quarter before nine, the dark was split by the light from the Ellis's front door and I saw a tall figure, hatted, raincoated and stooped against the downpour, dash out and around the side of the house where, I knew, the garage held the family car.

Obviously the demolition business was good; the car that pulled out of the drive and onto the street was a maroon-coloured Daimler Conquest. Registration number PFF 119: the same number Pamela Ellis had given me and I had written into my notebook.

'Whoever your squeeze is, I hope she's worth it, bud,' I said through the windshield and the rain, waiting until the Daimler had reached the corner when, without switching on my lights, I pulled out from the kerb and started to follow him.

CHAPTER THREE

One of the strange things about being an enquiry agent – a life into which I had carelessly stumbled – was that it was one of the few occupations that gave you a licence to be a voyeur. I considered my profession as sitting square centre between that of the anthropologist and that of the Peeping Tom. I was paid to watch individuals without them knowing they were being watched, and that gave me an insight, literally, into how some people lived their lives. There was nothing improper about the gratification it gave me: it wasn't spying on the intimate, the furtive or the sordid moments that I enjoyed, it was the simple observation of the tiny details, the way someone behaved when they thought they were alone and unobserved; the small personal rituals that exposed the real person.

A Sauchiehall Street store – one of the big ones where the sales clerks acted superior despite the fact that they worked in a store – had once asked me to watch a female counter clerk whom they suspected of having pilfered from the till. It was strictly the smallest of small-time theft – a sixpence here and a shilling there – but over the months it had added up to a tidy sum.

I had followed the woman, too old to have been called a shop girl and too young to be called a spinster, through her dull ritual of work and home, spying on her from behind clothes rails while she took payments and totalled takings; sitting in my car outside her tenement flat while she spent empty evenings and days off at home. I had gotten the idea that the store manager was looking to make some kind of example of her: a warning to others that theft would always be found out and punished. The store certainly had to pay out ten times as much to keep me and Archie on her tail as the alleged larceny was costing them.

It eventually became clear that we were backing a loser: we could find no evidence that she was taking from the cash till.

Then, one Saturday off work, she took the morning train to Edinburgh Waverley. I had followed her onto the train and stood within range at the far end of the third class-carriage corridor. She was a frumpy type, always dressed in grey and a difficult surveillance subject because she seemed instantly to merge into any crowd. One advantage I had, however, was that she clearly had no idea she was being followed and never once checked over her shoulder.

It was when we arrived in Edinburgh that I realized the store had been right about her. This woman, whose rituals and routines were as dull and ordinary as it was possible to be, had disembarked and then done something that was not at all dull and very out-of-the-ordinary: she had retrieved a suitcase from a left-luggage locker at Waverley and disappeared into the ladies' toilets. While I waited for her to re-emerge from the ladies', I took a note of the locker number and then positioned myself where I could watch the washroom door without the attendant suspecting I was some kind of pervert.

I nearly missed her. If she had not been carrying the same suitcase and had not returned it to the locker, then I would not have recognized her as the same woman. It wasn't that she had transformed herself from frumpy spinster to dazzling starlet; but she had donned an expensive and fashionable suit and high heels, had applied make-up to the otherwise perpetually naked face. The Glasgow shop attendant had become the image of a wealthy if unexceptional middle-class Edinburgh housewife. The suit she was wearing was clearly a label that a store clerkess could never aspire to, and I had realized instantly that I was looking at where the pilfered two-bobs and half-crowns had gone. It must have taken her years: years of watching women buy from her clothes she could never aspire to wear herself; years of constant reminding that everyone had a place and her place was behind the counter, not in front of it.

I realized that I could have confronted her there and then; that I could have demanded to know how she had managed to pay for the clothes, the shoes, the handbag, but there was something about what I had witnessed – its bizarre surreality – that made me want to watch her a little longer. My guess had been that this was all about a man and I decided to bide my time to see whom she met.

I had followed her on foot across Princes Street to a typically Edinburgh, typically snooty tearoom-cum-restaurant four floors up with a view of Edinburgh Castle. She ordered from a waitress who clearly knew her from previous visits and she sat contentedly eating scones, drinking tea and looking out across Princes Street Gardens to the castle. I knew then that there was no male companion, no secret tryst with a partner in crime or adultery. There was a peace and contentment about her that was fascinating and I knew I was watching her enjoy the single, complete, indivisible object of her larceny. This was what she had stolen for. It made absolutely no sense and it made absolutely perfect sense.

I followed her from the tearoom. She window-shopped, she browsed, she strolled, but didn't buy anything. Then, after two hours, she returned to the railway station, picked up the suitcase and performed her transformation in reverse. We both caught the same train back to Glasgow but I made no effort to keep tabs on her; I had seen all I needed to see.

Like I said, it was the oddest thing about my job: to be able to look into the corners of people's lives and see what they thought no one else could ever be party to.

The funny thing was that when it came to making my report to the store, I didn't include the details of her trip to Edinburgh. I didn't tell anyone about it. It wasn't that I lied to my client: I gave a full account of the observation Archie and I had carried out and the fact that we had found no direct evidence of theft or even discrepancies in the till receipts. I don't really know why I kept a secret for someone who didn't know I was keeping it. Maybe it was because I could understand why someone would go to such great lengths to be, for a few hours once every month or so, someone completely different.

And now I found myself observing another life.

I followed the Daimler at as great a distance as I could risk without losing it in the dark and the rain. Andrew Ellis drove out of Bearsden, and towards the city centre through Maryhill. Maryhill was the kind of place you drove through. Without stopping if you had any sense. It was a tough neighbourhood where a squabble over a spilt pint of beer could cost you an eye, a lung or your life, yet run-down Maryhill sat shoulder-to-shoulder with prosperous Bearsden; opposite ends of the Glasgow social spectrum squeezed together. I dare say the city fathers had had it in mind to make the commute to work easier for burglars.

Ellis took a left off Maryhill Road and an alarm bell began to ring in my head. Not that there was anything wrong with his road skills, it was just that driving a Daimler into Maryhill was kind of like a Christian standing in the middle of the Colosseum and banging a dinner gong in the direction of the lions. I followed him in, not without trepidation. He took another left, then another, and a third that took him back out onto Maryhill Road. I let him take the last turn without following him, instead driving deeper into darkest Maryhill.

Now the alarm bells in my head were deafening. I had peeled off from his tail when he took the last left because his little manoeuvre had clearly been to check if the headlights in his rear-view mirror were there by coincidence or by design. It was a pretty fancy move for a run-of-the-mill Glasgow businessman to pull, even if he *was* on his way to see his piece of skirt on the side.

I pulled up at the kerb to give Ellis a few minutes before trying to catch sight of him again, although that was unlikely and probably unadvisable if he was on the lookout for a tail.

Mine was the only car in a grey-black tenement-lined street that had the picturesque charm of an abattoir yard. The gloom was punctuated every twenty yards or so by the insipid sodium glow of a streetlamp and I noticed, three standards down, a knot of youths in Teddy Boy gear gathered around the lamp-post, smoking cigarettes with the expected dull indolence of adolescence. They turned their attention to the car, exchanged a few words and started to move in my direction. I decided now was maybe a good time to move on, in pretty much the same way as a wagon full of settlers in Cooke's Canyon, on seeing

Apaches silhouetted against the hilltops, would have decided it was a good time to move on.

Despite patriotic chest-beating to the contrary, British engineering was not, it had to be said, a wonderful thing. Why the design and construction of an even moderately reliable automobile lay beyond the nation that had come up with the Industrial Revolution was a puzzle that I found myself addressing, in slightly more colourful language, as my Atlantic stalled in the middle of the three-point turn, leaving me stranded and straddling the cobbled street.

I glanced, as casually as I could, towards the advancing Teddy Boys. Five of them. I could handle myself pretty well – a little too well, to be honest – but the arithmetic was against me. As I slipped the column shift into neutral, turned the key off then on again, and stabbed with my thumb at the starter button on the dash, an image flashed through my mind of my scalp adorning the mantelpiece of a Maryhill tenement while the residents whooped and pow-wow-danced around the coal scuttle.

The Atlantic wheezed rhythmically, threatened to cough into life, but spluttered to a stall. I repeated the procedure, aware that the gang of young thugs was almost at my door. This time the engine caught. I put the car into gear and gave it some gas. Time to go.

The engine died again.

There was a tapping on the window. A long face with small eyes and bad skin was leaned in towards the glass. He sported a Teddy quiff that clearly needed more grease to maintain than the average ten-axle freight locomotive. I was outnumbered, I had no sap or any other kind of weapon with me. I decided to play nice, for the moment. I rolled down my window.

'Nice motor, pal . . .' The Teddy Boy's small eyes glittered hard as he spoke without removing the minuscule stub of a still glowing roll-up from his almost lipless mouth.

'Thanks,' I said.

'Austin Atlantic A90, isn't it?'

'That's right,' I said. I noticed the others nodded approvingly at his superior knowledge.

'Aye . . . that's what I reckoned. I thought they was all for export to the Yanks.'

'No . . . not all of them. I picked this one up in Glasgow. Second hand.'

'You a Yank?' he said, frowning at my accent in a way I didn't like.

'American? No. I'm Canadian.'

'Canadian?' He turned to his pals. 'Hear that? He's a Canadian . . .' Then to me. 'I got an uncle and cousins in Canada . . .'

'Hasn't everyone?' I quipped. It was something that came up a lot when people found out I was a Canuck. Almost everyone in Glasgow had a relative who'd recently emigrated to Canada. Since the war, Glasgow had been haemorrhaging people and there were regularly round-the-block queues of hopeful would-be-immigrants outside the Canadian High Commission in Woodlands Terrace. As I smiled at my Teddy Boy chum and took in the grimy, wet gloom of a Maryhill street, I could understand the appeal of the Prairies.

The chief Ted leaned his head in through the window. It made him vulnerable and I considered making my move there and then. Taking him out would reduce the odds against me and, because he was clearly the leader, it might make the others less sure of themselves.

And in this kind of dance party, being sure of yourself was everything.

'Do you know what your problem is, pal?' he asked me.

I sighed. 'Let me guess, you're going to tell me.'

'Okay boys,' he called over his shoulder. 'You know what to do . . .'

Party time.

I put my hand on the door handle. I intended to slam him hard with the door and get out into the open where I'd be free to move. For as long as I was capable of moving. I noticed that his little gang had all moved around to the back of the car, leaving their leader on his own. A mistake.

'Half choke,' he said. 'That's your problem.'

'What?'

'Half choke. Pull the choke out half ways and me and the boys'll give you a push.'

I did what he said and he joined his friends at the back of the car. I steered the car as they eased it forward until it was facing the right way. My Teddy Boy chums then picked up the pace and the Atlantic lurched as I eased off the clutch, the engine kicking into life. I drove on a few yards, leaving them behind, then stopped, revving the engine a few times.

Leaving the motor running, I got out and walked back to where they stood, wheezing and bent over. Glasgow's climate, dirty air and its passion for tobacco meant that the city was yet to produce an Olympic sprinter.

'Thanks guys,' I said and tossed an unopened packet of Players I'd taken from the glove box to the leader with the bad skin, the small eyes and the three pints of grease in his hair. Between gasps, he waved his enthusiastic thanks and I drove on.

Glasgow.

After ten years, I still didn't have it figured.

*   *   *

There was no point in me trying to find Ellis. By now he would have reached the city centre and could have taken a dozen different directions. For all I knew he could be happily on his way to Edinburgh, if it was possible for anyone to be happy about being on their way to Edinburgh. When I got back onto Maryhill Road I decided to head back to my digs. It took me on the same route Ellis had been on so I kept my eyes open for the Daimler, but it was nowhere to be seen.

It was late and I didn't want to use the shared 'phone in the hall at my digs so, as I drove back, I applied my mind to the needle/haystack conundrum of where I could find a urine-free telephone kiosk in Glasgow on a Friday night. Against my better judgement I headed into the city centre and to the Horsehead Bar. Of course, it was now far after closing time.

Which meant nothing.

When I walked into the Horsehead it was packed. This was called a 'lock-in' and all of these good citizens were, in the eyes of the licensing regulations, bona fide 'guests of the management'. It was the job of the police to make sure that this was the case and that the till, whose drawer had been left open, did not accept cash for drinks. From the number of uniformed and plainclothes coppers propping up the bar, it was a responsibility the City of Glasgow Police clearly took very seriously. And they were putting the bar staff to the test by accepting pints and shorts without paying for them. Funny thing was, something always seemed to distract their attention at those crucial moments when other 'guests of the management' handed over cash.

I was no great hand at physics, but I knew that most scientists held that air is not solid. The atmosphere inside the public bar gave a lie to that otherwise universal scientific truth. Coming in from the cold night, the air inside was dense, sweat-and-whisky humid, blue-grey with cigarette smoke, and it wrapped itself around my face like a stale barber's towel.

I ploughed a channel through the fug to the bar, its long sweep of oak, punctuated by slender brass taps for adding water to whisky, hidden from me behind a curtain of hunched shoulders and flat caps.

'Not seen you for a few weeks, Lennox.' Big Bob the barman poured me a Canadian Club from a bottle that had clearly sat untouched since my last visit. 'The Horsehead too downmarket for you these days?'

'Too many people look for me here, Bobby. The wrong kind of people.' It was my own fault: at one time I'd set up the Horsehead as an unofficial office. Somewhere those who didn't keep business hours could find me.

'Aye . . . I suppose I know what you mean. Handsome Jonny Cohen was in here a couple of nights back.'

'Oh?'

'Aye. Just for a quick pint, he said. As if he ever comes in here for a quick pint. But he came in with a couple of knuckle-draggers.'

'Looking for me?'

'Not that he said. But let's just say you *came up* in conversation. Asked me when you was last in. I said you didn't come in much any more. I thought you and Cohen were tight.'

I nodded. Of the Three Kings, Handsome Jonny was the one I trusted most, which wasn't saying much. But Jonny and I had a history and I owed him. No matter how much I owed him, he was still someone who lived in a landscape I was trying to distance myself from.

'No one else?'

'Naw.' Bob nodded towards the glass in my hand, the bottle still in his. Drinking was something done at a trot in Glasgow. I drained the whisky and he poured me another.

I noticed a knot of drinkers at the far end of the bar gathered around a younger man who was clearly holding court. His appearance struck me right away: he was small but stocky, coatless, and dressed in a white shirt and black suit. His tailoring – combined with a pale complexion made striking by the black of his hair and dark eyes – made him look colourless, monochrome. I couldn't hear what he was giving forth about, but each pronouncement was greeted with slaps on the back, cheers and encouragement from the older men. Monochrome Man was clearly basking in their admiration. However, what he was unable to see but I could, was the exchange of glances between the older men as he spoke and they encouraged him.

'Who's the bigmouth?' I asked.

'Bigmouth right enough,' answered Bob. 'He's only in here after hours because the boys enjoy taking the pish out of him. We call him Sheriff Pete – he puts on the cod Yank accent and tells everyone he's from New York.'

'And he's not?'

'Maybe he is.' Bob pursed his mouth as if considering the possibility. 'If New York is just outside fucking Motherwell.'

The small man caught me looking at him and held my gaze for a moment, his face expressionless, before turning back to his audience. They were laughing at him all right, but I had seen something in that brief look that I didn't like. Something bad. I held out a ten-shilling note to Bob. 'Do me a favour and give me change for the 'phone.'

'Chasing skirt again, Lennox?' He pushed the coins across the counter to me.

'This is business, Bob. Strictly business.'

I went out to the pay telephone that hung on the wall by the door. After confirming that Ellis had not returned home, I started by explaining to Pamela Ellis that I was having to 'phone from a public bar, lest she thought the raucous background noise indicated that I was slacking and drinking on the job. I don't think I did much to allay her fears.

'You say you lost him, Mr Lennox?'

'I'm afraid I did. Or, more correctly, *he* lost *me*.'

'I'm sorry, I don't understand . . .'

'I have to say it's not a good sign, Mrs Ellis. There's no doubt in my mind that your husband was taking measures – quite expert measures – to ensure he was not being followed. He deliberately led me all around the houses, literally.'

'So he *is* up to something . . . is that what you're saying?'

'I'm afraid it is. Quite what that something is, I promise you I'll find out. If you still want me to.'

'More than ever, Mr Lennox.'

CHAPTER FOUR

This time, the client I was meeting had made a proper appointment, although the tone on the telephone had been more that of a summons than of an invitation. I had received a call giving me the address and time I was to be there. Ten-thirty a.m.

The headquarters of the Amalgamated Union of Industrial Trades, to which I'd been summoned, was in the West End of Glasgow, housed in one of a sweeping arc of Georgian town houses. I guessed that the choice of location and architecture was in itself a statement. A statement that things were changing; that the old order was on its way out and the genteel had to get used to new neighbours.

Where once a butler would have opened the door to me, it was answered instead by a none-too-tall, lean-to-scrawny man in his late thirties, tieless and jacketless and with his shirt-sleeves rolled up past the elbows. He had a look that was common in Glasgow: a pale, pinched long face, lipless tight line of a mouth, tiny eyes and a plume of badly cut black hair. He reminded me of an older version of the Maryhill Teddy Boy who'd given the Atlantic a push. The only thing about him that was even vaguely butler-like, however, was the practised disdain with which he looked me up and down, taking in the twelve-pound Borsalino, the thirty-guinea overcoat and the thirty-five-guinea suit beneath it. I could hear the cash register ringing away in his head and it was clear he had taken an instant and profound dislike to me. I decided to save time and do the same.

'Is the master of the house at home, my good man?' I asked, stepping across the threshold without waiting to be asked. I was going to push the gag further by handing him my Borsalino, but I decided the gigantic chip on his shoulder was burden enough for him to bear.

'You Lennox?'

'I'm Mr Lennox, yes. I have an appointment to see . . .'

'Joe Connelly. Aye. We've been expecting you. You're late.'

'I'm working to rule,' I said.

My new bestest friend led me along a high-ceilinged hall with elaborate plaster cornicing stained yellow by Woodbine smoke, somehow perfectly capturing the spirit of the new age. He rushed me past several offices filled with cigarette haze and burly men who looked as at home behind a desk as a Home Counties accountant would at a mine coalface. A few hard-faced women typed industrially. I noticed I was attracting the odd look that made my skinny pal's welcome seem positively warm. I really should, I decided, make an effort to dress appropriately for the event. Unfortunately my wardrobe didn't extend to a flat cap and clogs.

We went up the stairwell and I was shown into a large office with a view out over Kelvingrove Park. A fat, florid-faced man was using a worn-down stub of a pencil to scribble into a large ledger. Looking up, he saw me, stood up and came round the desk, his face empty of expression. Like the pencil, he was a worn-down stump. Short and squat and livid and tough. He was committing several crimes against tailoring in a too-tight, dark brown suit.

'Mr Connelly?' I asked.

'Aye, I'm Joe Connelly. You Lennox?'

I nodded. 'You asked to see me. What can I do for you, Mr Connelly?'

'Did anyone see him come in?' Connelly asked the younger man.

The younger man shrugged. 'I told you we should have had the meeting somewhere private. But no one knows who he is or why he's here.'

'Sorry,' I said. 'Do I have offensive body odour or something?'

'Sit down,' said Connelly. 'I've got a job for you to do. If you'll take it.' He waited till I sat. 'It's highly confidential and it's best if no one else in the union knows about your involvement. From now on, I think our meetings should be conducted somewhere out of public view.'

'Sounds a bit cloak-and-dagger for a trade union,' I said.

'Before I go into detail, I need to establish something. Whether you accept this job or you don't, I take it anything we discuss here is considered privileged and will be treated confidentially?' Connelly's accent was broad Glasgow, but he spoke with the precise, deliberate articulation of a self-taught man.

'Of course. So long as it's all legal.'

'A crime *has* been committed, Mr Lennox. But this union is the victim of that crime. We do not, for the moment, want to involve the police. However that may change.'

'Anything you tell me will go no farther, Mr Connelly.' I looked across at the skinny guy who had shown me in. He was making no effort to leave.

'Paul Lynch here is my deputy.' Connelly had clearly read my expression. 'Brother Lynch takes care of a number of key areas of our activity, including safeguarding the good name of our union.'

'I see,' I said, and looked again at Lynch, who looked back at me with his tiny, hard eyes. There was something about those eyes that told me this was not someone on whom to turn your back. I found myself wondering what kind of 'safeguarding' Lynch did for the union.

'Why don't you tell me what this is all about? You say it involves a crime. What kind of crime?'

'Theft,' said Lynch.

'From this building,' Connelly added. 'We are having diffi-culty getting in touch with one of our union officers.'

'Let me guess. You're also having difficulty getting in touch with some union funds?'

Lynch again turned his tiny, cold eyes on me. 'A ledger has been stolen, along with thirty-five-thousand pounds in union funds.'

I blew a whistle. 'Who took it?'

'His name is Frank Lang,' said Connelly. 'He is a member of the union and was carrying out some sensitive work for us.'

'What kind of sensitive work?'

'We can only discuss that when we know you'll take the job,' said Connelly.

I took a cigarette out and lit it, blowing a blue jet into the air. 'And the *sensitivity* of this work . . . I take it that's why you're not involving the police?'

'What you have to understand,' said Connelly, 'is that a trade union is a complex body. It has many dimensions and many functions beyond the immediate one of protecting its members' rights and welfare. It is a political entity as well, and there are those who see us as a danger to the status quo. Who would wish to spy on us and do us harm.'

'The police?'

'If you could find Frank Lang within the next few days, then we can maybe persuade him to return what he took. He'll be kicked out of the union, for sure, and I will personally make sure he never finds a job again, but he won't go to prison.'

'And in return you won't have the police and the press sticking their noses into your business.'

'Believe me, Lennox,' Lynch chipped in. 'The last thing we want to do is involve someone like you in our business either. We've tried to find Lang ourselves, but he's disappeared without trace. This is something that's outside the union's expertise or resources. That's why we contacted you. This is your kind of work, isn't it?'

'Sure ...' I nodded. 'But the police have more and better resources than anyone. I know they're not your favourite people, but I still don't really understand why you are so reluctant to get them involved if a crime has been committed.'

'You don't know much about the union movement, do you, Mr Lennox?' asked Connelly.

'My usual clients tend not to be unionized.' I smiled at the thought of what union affiliation would be held by some of the people I'd rubbed shoulders with in the recent past: Singer, Twinkletoes McBride or Hammer Murphy. The Association of Armed and Allied Thuggery Trades, probably. At least it would resolve demarcation issues about who should be ramming the shotgun in the teller's ribs and who should be stuffing the cash from the safe into the duffle-bag.

Connelly stared at me with not much to read in the way of an expression. It was as if he wore the slightly livid, puffy flesh of his face as a mask to hide what was going on in the mind behind it – a skill probably honed throughout years of industrial confrontation and wage negotiation.

'I'm not what you would call a political animal,' I said, as much to fill the silence as anything. 'Maybe a touch of classical liberal. Not much Marx about me, unless you count Groucho.'

'There is a revolution going on in this country. A slow, quiet social revolution that has picked up pace since the end of the war,' continued Connelly. 'Any revolution, by its very nature, involves displacing the powers-that-be. And the powers-that-be in this nation will do their damnedest to stop that revolution in its tracks. I know what I'm talking about. I've seen the lengths the British Establishment will go to crush opposition. I stood alongside Manny Shinwell and Willie Gallacher during the Battle of George Square in Nineteen-Nineteen. I saw with my own eyes British tanks brought out onto the streets of Glasgow to crush legitimate protest.'

'Before my time, I'm afraid,' I said. But the truth was I knew all about Red Clydeside and the riots in Glasgow in 1919. The Coalition Government had thought that Glasgow was the kicking-off point for a Bolshevik revolution and had flooded the city with troops, machine-gun posts and tanks. I decided it wouldn't be helpful to point out to Connelly that, as we sat there and chatted, his communist comrades were in the process of using the same tactics, but much more ruthlessly, in the streets of Budapest. Or that, just a few months before, good socialist soldiers in Poland had gunned down unarmed strikers in Poznan.

'Well, take my word for it,' continued Connelly. 'This union is at the forefront of a social and political revolution. That means we come under the frequent and unwelcome scrutiny of the police and other government agencies. Believe me, they would just love an excuse to come in here and start poking around in our affairs. But we have to be seen to observe the law in its smallest detail, Mr Lennox, and that means eventually we will have to contact the police and report the theft – unless someone finds Lang in the meantime and we can persuade him to return the stolen items. It would save me a lot of embarrassment and Frank Lang a prison term if you could find him. Will you take the job?'

'Then I need to know what his work for the union entailed. Without that, no deal.'

Lynch looked to Connelly for guidance. The union boss gave a curt nod.

'Lang is an ex-merchant navy man,' said Lynch. 'A member of the seaman's union and active in a number of areas. I have to admit that he had some kind of shady past, but we didn't ask too many questions about that.'

'I see ...' I said, and wondered if I should apply for a full-time job with the union. 'What's he got on you?'

'What?' asked Lynch irritably.

'All of this discretion is one thing,' I said, 'but thirty-five-thousand is a lot to be discreet about. So what has he got on you? Is Lang blackmailing the union?'

'No.' Connelly sighed impatiently. 'But if Lang hands the ledger over to the wrong hands, then people are going to suffer. Mr Lennox, will you take this job on?'

'I don't know, Mr Connelly. This sounds all very political and, like I say, politics aren't my thing.'

'The politics don't concern you, Lennox,' said Lynch. 'This is a simple theft and recovery case, as far as you're concerned.'

'I have to tell you that I don't charge union rates ...'

Connelly took an envelope from his drawer and held it out to me. I left it hanging in his hand.

'There is a hundred and fifty pounds in there. In advance. This also contains all of the information you will need.'

A hundred and fifty pounds. I suddenly became filled with the warm glow of solidarity with the working man. Deciding the weight of the package was causing Connelly discomfort, I reached across the desk and relieved him of it.

CHAPTER FIVE

I spent the next couple of days getting stuff sorted out. I had taken on two jobs, both of which would need a lot of man hours. And if the Ellis job became a full-blown divorce case, it would involve a lot of paperwork. The problem I had was the Friday bank run. It was a two-man job and Archie always rode shotgun for me. Or at least he sat in the van's passenger seat with a fifteen-inch police truncheon on his lap. I decided that I would need to take on some extra casual help; someone handy enough with their fists, or a police truncheon, to sit in the van next to Archie and ensure the wages run was completed without incident.

It said a lot about my life up till then that finding someone with those skills would not present much of a problem.

Twinkletoes McBride showed up at my office on the Tuesday morning at eleven a.m. sharp, just as I had asked him to. I told him to take a seat. Twinkletoes was someone you wanted to sit, because when he stood he filled the room and made the furniture look like it belonged in a doll's house. He certainly had a primeval, backward-evolved sort of presence about him. If Charles Darwin had ever met Twinkle, he probably would have tossed the manuscript of *On the Origin of Species* into the fire.

Twinkle was a big lad – he would have made it to six-foot-six if he hadn't wanted for a forehead – and he was as bulky as he was tall. Sadly, his physical presence was not, it had to be said, matched by much of an intellectual one. More like an absence.

'I brung them letters of reference you asked for, Mr Lennox,' Twinkletoes said in a polite baritone that made the floor vibrate. He handed me two envelopes as he sat down and I half expected to hear the splintering of wood.

'Thanks, Twinkle,' I said, and read through them.

'They okay, Mr Lennox?' he asked earnestly, frowning as much as his lack of forehead would allow.

'Twinkle, you know these are for me to show the bank?'

'Yes, Mr Lennox.'

'Well, the one from Willie Sneddon is fine, but the other one is no good.'

'That's from Mr Frazer, what used to be my manager when I was in the fight game, like. He says I was a good employee with a lot of heart, he says.'

'I can see that, Twinkle. It's a glowing reference and it would be fine, if it weren't for the fact that he's written it on paper that's headed HM Prison Barlinnie.'

'Mr Frazer's had some bad luck,' said Twinkletoes dolefully.

'Yeah ... I heard,' I said, but didn't mention that the three men he'd had beaten into comas had been a tad unluckier.

'I think we'll shelve this one, Twinkle. Like I said, Mr Sneddon's should be fine.' Willie Sneddon was still one of the Three Kings, but he'd worked a public relations miracle and become a reasonably respected figure in the world of legitimate Glasgow business, if that wasn't a contradiction in terms.

'Now, you do understand that you're there to make sure nobody robs the van, don't you?'

'Oh yes, Mr L. I *app-ree-shee-ate* that,' he said with syllabic precision. Twinkletoes might not have been one of Nature's great thinkers or scholars but he had to be commended on his efforts to improve his mind – and there was immense room for improvement. McBride devoted hours each day to reading. Sometimes as many as two pages in one day. The *Reader's Digest*, *Boy's Own* and *The Hotspur* were his favoured tomes from the literary canon. He had once confided in me that he sought to learn a new word every day.

'This is a great *pre-village* for me. It being a straight job, and that. I hope them bank people know that I'll not let any bastard put a finger on their money when I'm looking after it. Nobody's gonna be better than me at spotting a robbery about to kick off . . . you know, with me knowing what it's like from the other —'

'I think we should keep details of your relevant experience to ourselves,' I said, cutting him off. He nodded gravely.

I had known Twinkletoes on and off for the last five years and, apart from one painful run-in for which he had apologized profusely, I had not been on the receiving end of his professional abilities. Especially those abilities that had earned him his nickname. 'Twinkletoes' derived from his means – his very effective means – of extracting either information or unpaid debts from the recalcitrant on behalf of Willie Sneddon. It was a method that involved bolt cutters and Twinkle's recitation of *This little Piggy* . . .

'And remember that your gaffer on this job is Archie McClelland,' I said. 'And Archie is ex-police. It would *not* be a good idea for you to share camp-fire stories.' Twinkle attempted a frown again and I could see he was trying to work out where camp fires fitted into the job. 'What I mean is don't talk about the stuff you've done for Willie Sneddon. A copper is a copper. Ex or not.'

'Got you, Mr L.'

I smiled, but somehow did not feel reassured. When Sneddon had switched to using a five-iron for its intended purpose on a golf course, rather than as a weapon, it had left Twinkletoes and Singer, his fellow thug, at something of a loose end. Sneddon kept them around and on the payroll, but more to keep them out of sight than anything, so I had had to clear it with Sneddon first before approaching Twinkletoes about the job. It would only be once a week, after all, and it would leave me free to pursue other work.

Employing a hardened thug with a criminal record as a security guard on a wages run may have been a risk, but anyone in Glasgow who ever sawed off the barrels of a shotgun or pulled a stocking over their heads would know who Twinkletoes was. And that he was connected to Willie Sneddon. My logic was that that would be enough to set toes itching before anyone thought about holding up my wages run.

At least, that was what I kept telling myself as I sent a happy and gainfully employed Twinkletoes McBride on his way.

I read through the information that Connelly and Lynch had given me on their missing comrade. Frank Lang had been a cook and union shop steward, working on cargo ships. He was a member of all the right associations and labour bodies. There wasn't a lot of background in the information, but enough for me to feel the draught of a red flag being vigorously waved.

The supplied picture of Lang was some kind of official photograph taken for records. From the picture it looked to me like Lang was in his middle thirties, with a long narrow face and a round chin. Even in the black-and-white photograph it was clear that the hair was a very light blond and the eyes were a very pale shade of grey or blue. He wasn't particularly handsome, or otherwise remarkable-looking, but there was something about his face that looked vaguely aristocratic. For no good reason, I found myself taking out the picture Pamela Ellis had given me of her errant husband and placed it next to Lang's. They were, of course, totally different in appearance and just about every other way, but it just seemed strange to me that I was involved with two men who, each in his own way, was some kind of outsider. Ellis by dint of his foreign heritage and Lang because . . . because why? What was it about the picture of this thirty-seven-year-old union official that screamed out at me that he was a misfit. A square peg.

Maybe, I thought, it takes one to know one.

It was just after ten the following day when I parked outside a row of terraced houses in Drumchapel. It was a working-class district, all right, but this particular area was the domain of the new working class. These houses were less than two years old and were part of the Corporation's initiative to replace the unsanitary conditions of the tenements with brand new, twentieth-century homes. As I stood there, the carbolic odour of The Future reaching through the damp late-autumn air, I wondered if Andrew Ellis's company had blasted away the past to clear the site on which these new dwellings stood. There were four units to a block and Lang's had a house on either side. There was no access to the back of the house that I could see without going around one of the ends, which would be less than inconspicuous. Added to which I had noticed the twitching of lace in the window next door and I spotted a woman walking her dog up the street, in my direction. A little impromptu burglary, which I had had in mind, was clearly not going to be an option.

Pausing to light a cigarette killed enough time to allow the woman walking the dog to pass me, but the ugly little pug paused himself to raise a hind leg and take a leak against the wheel arch of the Atlantic. I looked from the dog to his owner, who scowled back at me. She was a squat woman in her late forties with a headscarf-framed face to sink a thousand ships, wearing a coat of a material that could have served equally well for carpeting and whose legs were as thick at the ankles as at the knees.

Miss Scotland walked on, still scowling at the world, and I swung open the metal gate that still gleamed new, walked up the short path and rang the doorbell for appearances' sake. Stranger things had happened than for a supposedly missing shop steward to answer his own front door. But, in this case, they didn't. There was a small, fence-edged rectangle of well-kept grass to my right and I stepped onto it to peer through the window.

'Can I help you?'

I turned to see a woman of about thirty standing at the neighbouring door, leaning against the jamb with her arms crossed. I worked out that she must have been the curtain-twitcher.

'Oh . . . I didn't see you there . . .' I smiled at her disarmingly. She was worth smiling at. Dark blonde hair demi-waved and short, not too much make-up for town but too much for housework. Not knock-out but well constructed. She was wearing a pink woollen sweater that did a lot of good clinging and deep pink slacks.

'Well, I saw you. What are you up to?'

'I'm looking for Frank Lang,' I said. 'I've been sent by the union.'

'You don't look like a union type to me,' she said, looking in the direction of the car, then back to me. Her expression was full of suspicion but not fear or unease. She could look after herself.

'Can you tell me when you last saw Mr Lang?' I asked. Still smiling.

'You look more like a salesman,' she said. 'Are you a salesman?'

'No, ma'am,' I said. My cheeks were beginning to ache. 'Like I said, I've been asked by the union to find Mr Lang. Urgent business. Could you tell me when you last saw him?'

'What about those other men?' she asked. 'Weren't they from the union?'

'What other men?'

'The ones he went away with. Weren't they union people?'

I stopped smiling. 'No, I don't think they could have been. When did this happen?'

She looked me up and down then straightened up from her door jamb lean with a sigh. 'You better come in, then . . .'

I sat in the small front room – they had front rooms in Drumchapel and not lounges, like they had in Bearsden – and took in my surroundings.

Everything was new: a patterned three-piece suite that still smelled of the showroom; the same geometric patterns on the linoleum floor reversed on the hearth rug; a sideboard against one wall; a matching kidney-shaped coffee table with a chunky red glass ashtray looking like a splash of lava on the teak veneer, a chrome sunburst wall clock above the mantelpiece. It was as if they had asked for the store window display to be shipped "as is" direct into their brand-new council home.

The thing that most caught my attention was the sixty-quid

Bush television set that stood in one corner: one of the new jobs with the big seventeen-inch screens. I knew the price because I had been doing a bit of window shopping myself, playing with the idea that I could maybe get a new and bigger TV for Fiona and the girls for Christmas. I had built up a fair bit of cash over the last few years but had no one to spend it on other than myself. And except for my taste for expensive tailoring, my needs were pretty minimal. The only thing that had held me back from buying a set was my uncertainty about how it would go down with Fiona.

'Nice place you have here,' I said amiably when Lang's neighbour came back from her kitchen, tea tray in hand.

'Aye . . .' she said, almost as if bored with the thought. 'Better than our last place.'

'Do you mind if I ask how much your TV cost you? I'm thinking about getting something similar.'

She shrugged. 'Don't know. It's from RentaSet.'

'I see,' I said, and wondered how much of the Brave New World around me was on HP terms. 'My name's Lennox, by the way.'

'Sylvia . . .' she said. 'Sylvia Dewar.'

'You said Frank Lang went off with some men. When was this?' I took the duck egg blue cup and saucer she handed me. Melamine, not china.

'A week ago. No . . . nine days ago. Last Wednesday morning. About ten, ten-thirty.' There was a change of wind and the cloud of suspicion drifted back over her expression. 'What's this all about? Like I said, you're no union man.'

I laid a business card on the coffee table in front of her. 'I'm an enquiry agent, Mrs Dewar. But I *am* working on the union's behalf. Frank Lang has . . . well, he hasn't exactly gone missing.

Not yet, anyway, not officially . . . but the union have been trying to reach him and they are concerned about him.'

'Oh . . . I see.' She thought for a moment, pursing her lips. I noticed the lipstick was fresher than it had been when she went into the kitchen. 'So you think these men he went with came and took him away against his will?'

'I don't know, Mrs Dewar —'

'Sylvia. You can call me Sylvia.'

'I don't know, Sylvia. You saw them. You saw Lang go with them. Did it look to you like he was unwilling to go?'

'No. Not at all. He clearly knew them and they were chatting as they went to the car. And they certainly didn't look like union men, either. They came in a big car. Expensive-looking.'

'Do you know the make?'

She laughed. 'I don't know one car from the other. All I know is it wasn't the type you usually see around here. And that it was dark red or brown.'

'I see. Have there been any other odd comings and goings, recently?'

'Not really. Frank Lang keeps himself to himself and is hardly ever at home. No wife, no family. The only time we know he's there is when we smell his cooking.'

'His cooking?'

'I think he cooks fancy stuff. French, or something else foreign. That's what it smells like, anyway. And he keeps all of these spices and things in his cupboards. Other than that I couldn't say – my husband has more to do with him than me. He gets the impression that Frank spends most of his time attending meetings and talks, that kind of thing. Although I think he likes to dance.'

'Dance?'

'He went out every Saturday night. Always in a nice suit. A

friend of mine said she saw him at the Palais. He was very good, she said.'

'I see . . .'

'Do you like to dance, Mr Lennox? I like to dance.' The wistful expression gave way to bitterness. 'Tom – that's my husband – Tom doesn't dance.'

'Would it be worthwhile me coming back to talk to your husband? I mean if he had more to do with Mr Lang?'

Something frosted in her expression. 'No . . . I don't think that would do anyone any good. Tom does have more to do with Frank than I do, but not that much more. Anyway, there's not much point talking to my husband about anything. He gets lots of stupid ideas in his head.' Sylvia paused and eyed me. 'Tom's at work at the moment. He won't be back until six tonight.'

'The union told me that they had carried out a few enquiries of their own,' I said, ignoring the invitation in ten-foot high neon. 'Has anyone else been here to talk to you?'

'No,' she kept me held in her gaze. 'Only you.'

I stood up. 'Well, thanks for your time, Sylvia. If anything else occurs to you, please give me a ring. Obviously, I'd appreciate it if you got in touch right away if and when Mr Lang returns home next door. My number's on the card.'

'You haven't finished your tea . . .' she protested.

'It was fine, thanks, but I have to go. Thanks for your help.'

'You could stay for a while longer, couldn't you?'

She got up from the sofa, stepped around the table and stood close to me. Too close. She couldn't have signalled her meaning more clearly if she had been waving semaphore flags at me from two feet away.

'Sorry . . .' I smiled and put on my hat. 'I've got to go.'

*   *   *

As I made my way back to the car, two thoughts struck me. The first struck me like a shovel across the back of the head: I had just declined a chance of guilt-free, no-complications sex. Something I would never have turned down before. But since Fiona had come on the scene, of course, it wouldn't have been guilt-free.

The second thought was more of a nagger, like an eyelash in your eye: if Sylvia Dewar had nothing to do with Frank Lang, how come she knew what he kept in his cupboards.

CHAPTER SIX

The following night I took Fiona and the girls to Cranston's Cinema de Lux on Renfield Street to see *The Ten Commandments*. I had suggested we go to see *The Searchers*, but the girls would not have gotten in so, in the absence of a babysitter, I sat and watched an American-accented Moses argue the toss with a Russian-accented Pharaoh while a Max Factored Nefretiri smouldered. I was maybe getting paranoid, but as Chuck Heston climbed down the mountain with commandments in hand, I couldn't help wondering if it was a ploy by Fiona to remind me just how many of them I had broken.

But I had more to bother me that night. When I had come home from work and tapped on Fiona's door to remind her of the time of our date, I could tell there was something wrong. Her face was pale to the point of being ashen and there was something distracted about her manner, as if something massive and heavy was sitting in the path of her concentration. I asked her what was wrong but she dismissed the question, saying that she hadn't slept too well the night before, that was all. But I knew there was more to it. Much more. She had become increasingly distant over the last month.

When I had called again to pick up her and the kids to take them to the picture house, Fiona looked better and sounded cheery at the prospect of watching the movie. But there wasn't really a block that I hadn't been round several times and I recognized the deceit of her good cheer.

Chuck parted the Red Sea for the Chosen and I cast a glance at Fiona. It did nothing to reassure me. Whatever her thousand-yard-stare was focused on, it wasn't the screen or the peril of the Israelites. I rested my hand on her forearm and felt it tense, as if she had stifled a start. She turned to me and smiled.

'It's good, isn't it?' she said, and turned back to the screen.

After the movie, we stopped off at Giacomo's to get the girls an ice cream. I had a coffee from one of those machines that hissed like a steam train but Fiona had nothing.

'Are you sure you're okay?' I asked and rested my hand on hers. She pulled her hand away as if scalded and cast a meaningful look at the girls. I had broken the cardinal rule: no shows of affection, or any other kind of behaviour that might suggest a romantic involvement, in front of Elspeth and Margaret.

'I'm fine,' she said through her teeth, then, with the same ersatz jollity as before, started to talk to the girls about the movie.

Something was wrong. Very wrong.

I had intended to push Fiona for a truthful answer about what was going on when we got home, but she used the girls as a shield, saying that she needed to get them to bed. I got no invitation to come in for a drink or a cup of coffee and Fiona kept me on the threshold.

'That was a great night out, thanks, Lennox. If you don't mind I'm just going to turn in. Like I said, I didn't get much sleep last night.'

'Fiona, I don't know what's going —'

I was cut off by the ringing of the wall 'phone in the hall. Fiona squeezed past me to answer it.

'Yes, he's here . . .' she said and held the receiver out to me to take. It looked large and heavy in her small, slender hand.

'Hello, Mr Lennox?' I recognized the voice instantly.

'Hello, Mrs Ellis, what can I do for you?'

'You told me to telephone you if Andrew went out unexpectedly. Well he has, he's just getting into his car now.'

'At this time?' I looked at my watch. It was five after ten.

'He got a 'phone call just a minute ago,' she explained. 'Same as always, very short.'

'Did you hear the word "Tanglewood" mentioned this time?'

'I couldn't hear much of anything, I was in the lounge and the radio was on, but I don't think so. He just seemed to keep saying "yes" then he hung up. It's almost like someone's telling him what to do. As if Andrew is being given orders or instructions or something. I have to tell you, Mr Lennox, there's something about this frightens me.'

'He hasn't given you any idea where he's going?'

'Just the usual "I have to go out, something's come up with a customer".'

'And how was he? His demeanour, I mean?'

'He didn't seem anything in particular. He tried to make out he was annoyed at being disturbed . . . but whatever was going through his head, that wasn't it.'

I thanked her and said that I had better go and see if I could pick up his trail.

'I've got to go out. Sorry,' I said to Fiona, who shrugged, went into her flat and closed the door. Normally I would have expected to sense her annoyance, but all I picked up this time was relief.

I drove too fast to Maryhill Road, trying to close a distance greater than Ellis had to travel. I took the turning Ellis had taken before, just around the corner from where my Teddy Boy Scouts had helped me get the Atlantic started again, and swung the car around to face back out towards the junction where I could see passing traffic on Maryhill Road.

I switched the engine off and waited five minutes before deciding to give up, working out that Ellis must have already passed by, or had taken another route. The Atlantic conked out on me again and it took me a couple of expletive-urged turns to get her started. It was not a good night for hunting, anyway: the darkness was starting to tinge greenish as smog began to turn the air grainy. I would be lucky to see anything ten feet in front of me – which was exactly the distance I was from the glossy claret flank of Ellis's Daimler as it sleeked past the road junction.

Startled, I clunked the lever into first, offering a silent prayer that the Atlantic didn't stall again, and swung out onto Maryhill Road behind him, sticking close to his tail. The fog-turning-to-smog was getting thicker and I worked out that it was maybe drifting in from the North, which meant it had slowed Ellis's drive into town while mine had been unimpeded. I decided to leave the dentistry of this particular gift horse unexamined and focused on keeping Ellis in sight.

There was a tried and tested habit in the Glasgow smog of playing follow-my-leader, leaving the driver in front to work for you by keeping the kerb in sight, so I knew that Ellis would not suspect the lights in his rear-view were anything other than an innocent fellow traveller navigating the miasma. Fortunately, one of the many things to have failed recently on the Atlantic was the central headlamp; if Ellis *had* seen me the first evening I had tailed him, then tonight the Atlantic would not be showing its distinctive three lamps in his mirror.

Progress became painfully slow as Glasgow's night air took on the consistency of broth. Travelling little faster than walking pace, Ellis led me – and three cars behind me – through the city and out to the West End. A couple of turnings and I lost both the entourage of cars and my bearings. Mine being the only other car following Ellis's made me more conspicuous, and I eased back until the Daimler's tail lights reduced to faint red smudges in the gloom. It was practically impossible to get any kind of idea of where we were in the smog, but I reckoned we were somewhere in the Garnethill district of the city. Driving through smog demands total focus and I wasn't able to look out for some kind of landmark or street sign to become visible, but I knew I would need something if I wanted to find my way back in the daylight.

We turned into a narrow street that seemed to arc around then uphill. I wondered if Ellis was doing the same kind of elaborate stunt he had pulled in Maryhill and was taking odd turns just to check if I was following him. After about twenty yards, the Daimler stopped. We were now in a narrow street with only the odd parked car. I drove past and allowed myself to be swallowed up by the smog before pulling up after fifty yards or so at what I hoped was the kerb.

I switched the engine off and got out of the car as quickly as I could, straining to hear any sounds from the Daimler. I locked the Atlantic and found the pavement without tripping over it, then fumbled my way back to where Ellis had stopped. Smog in Glasgow is the most difficult thing to describe to someone who has never experienced it. The oily smoke that the city's industry and tenement chimneys pumped into the sky seemed to be drawn back into the ground-hugging fog that soaked it up like a sponge. The result was something dense and choking that took the lives of anyone too weak, too ill, too old or too young to resist its smothering blanket. Whatever the chemistry involved, the mix of soot, smoke and fog became something green-tinged and cloying. The simple act of walking became an experience of sensory deprivation where you existed in a tiny, arm's-length confined universe. My unease in the smog was particularly acute: I had been jumped twice before by attackers using the dense fug as cover. These were, without doubt, the worst possible conditions for surveillance and I cursed Glasgow's climate with more vehemence than usual.

The Daimler was parked and empty and I considered myself lucky to have found it. I peered through the miasma to try to estimate where exactly I was and which direction Ellis was likely to have taken. I found myself against a high, windowless wall and, running my hand along the brickwork as a guide, I tried to find a doorway.

I almost walked straight into Ellis.

He was standing at the foot of some steps that led up to an arched doorway. I realized that the masonry I had been following wasn't the wall of a building, but a soil-retaining bulwark that divided the roadway from a terrace of buildings elevated above it. As I had followed the wall around the sweep of the street, I had been climbing to the same level as the buildings.

And now I was face-to-face with the man I was supposed to be shadowing. Stealth was my middle name.

Ellis turned and looked startled for a moment when he first saw me and I was pretty sure that I must have had the same expression on my face. But I was confronted with more than Ellis: I was faced with the fact that his wife had been right all along. Next to Ellis was a young woman with unfashionably shoulder-length black hair. Like the hair, her clothes were out of fashion and looked old without being shabby. Her coat was too heavy for November in the west of Scotland, where the emphasis had to be on waterproofing rather than insulation, and the cut was something I hadn't seen in Glasgow before. Perched on her head was a small toque-type hat that did not match the coat. None of which mattered, because she had the kind of smouldering dark beauty that made you want to look through the clothes rather than at them. Set above a classical architecture of cheekbone and jaw, her eyes were large and a dark, nutty brown; her full lips had been lipsticked crimson but otherwise her face seemed naked of make-up that she would not have needed.

She was a piece of art, all right. I found myself thinking about Pamela Ellis's desperate wish to find out why her husband was acting so strangely, and her vague hope that there was something more, or less, than simple adultery behind his behaviour. But I had the answer standing right there in front of me: the kind of woman who would make Ellis, me, or any man with a pulse, act strangely.

'What a night!' I said to them both as casually as I could manage. 'Sorry . . . I nearly walked straight into you. You can't see your hand in front of your face in this muck.'

They both stared at me wordlessly, like a couple of ento-mologists studying a bug. I couldn't be sure, but I thought I detected a hint of suspicion in Ellis's eyes. He looked past me in the direction I had come, as if he could see through the smog, and I wondered if he was trying to work out if my face and the headlights that had been in his mirror since Maryhill Road were connected. I thought about claiming to have lost my way and asking exactly where we were, but I decided it would be best to move on as quickly as possible.

Ellis had seen me for only a matter of seconds, but I could almost hear the click of the camera shutter in his memory. The girl's too. There was something about the set-up I didn't like; secretive rather than furtive, conspiratorial rather than adulterous. A subtle difference.

I walked on in the opposite direction to my car and into the smog, hoping that I would be able to find my way back. I reached a corner and another doorway, in which I sheltered while lighting a cigarette. I only began to make my way back after I had finished my second smoke. This time I approached much more slowly, ready to pull back if I heard voices, but when I eventually reached the steps, Ellis, the girl and the Daimler were all gone.

I made my way up the steps to the doorway of the building. The sandstone arch, like most stonework in Glasgow, was sooty black, but I could see that this was not a tenement or any other type of residence and the building probably housed some kind of offices. Perhaps the girl had not come from inside and this had been a randomly chosen meeting point, but I guessed that she lived not far from here. I found a brass plate next to the door and noted down a couple of the company names, simply to allow me to find the exact address in the telephone directory and find my way back when the smog had lifted.

I headed back to my car.

I sat for a moment and tried to work out what it was that was nagging at me about Ellis and the girl. It was something more than the way they didn't gel as partners in extra-marital crime. I shook my head trying to loosen the thought from my brain, turned the ignition key and thumbed the starter button.

This time, I didn't even get a splutter out of the engine, just a dull, dry clunk.

CHAPTER SEVEN

It took me an hour on foot to fumble my way to a rank of stationary taxi-cabs with drivers intent on staying stationary. It was only after a twenty-minute wait and a slight easing of the smog that one of the cabbies reluctantly agreed to take my fare.

The White flat was in darkness and silence when I got back and I went straight up to my rooms. It had been a confusing day and my head buzzed with unconnected thoughts like bees trapped in a jar. It was nearly two a.m. before I fell asleep.

I dreamed that night. It was the dream that I thought I had stopped having; the dream I used to have every night, for months and years after the war had ended. But it had been a long time since I'd last dreamt it, and I woke cold and afraid with the ghost of another man's screaming echoing in the room.

A bad omen.

For some reason, I had become a member of the RAC earlier that year. Maybe because I liked watching their uniformed patrolmen wobble on their motorcycles as they passed because they were compelled, on seeing the bumper badge, to salute me. There were times I loved the British.

After I had breakfast, I checked out in the directory the address of the company names I had noted and used the hall telephone

'I don't think your husband really is having an affair,' I said with less certainty than I had intended.

'Are you telling me that my husband sneaks out to meet attractive young women because they really are demolition customers?' She gave a small, bitter laugh.

'I watch people all the time. It's my job. And after a while you start to develop an instinct about the way people behave. The way they act when they're around other people, the messages you get from a dozen little things. I don't sense a romantic involvement between your husband and this woman. And it's not just a hunch. Mr Ellis has been taking very special care not to be followed and last night, when I returned to my car, it had been hobbled so that I couldn't follow him when he left. By the way, I'm afraid I'll have to charge you for a set of jump leads.'

She shook the comment away irritatedly. 'He's hiding an affair. That's why he was trying to shake you off.' A thought seemed to take root and trouble her; she bit her lip and frowned. 'That means he knows I'm on to him. That it was me who hired you to follow him.'

'But that's my point, Mrs Ellis ... It's as if he knows I'm tailing him, but he's not sure why. Now that is confusing. Why would your husband feel he was being followed, if he's not having an affair? And if he is going to such lengths to stop me from getting evidence of infidelity, then why hobble my car *after* I've seen them together?'

'I'm confused, Mr Lennox. Did you or did you not catch Andrew with another woman?'

'I saw him *with* a young woman. And yes, you're probably right. I tend to shave situations like these with Occam's Razor.'

She frowned.

'It's a variation on *if it looks like a duck, walks like a duck, quacks like a duck, then it probably is a duck*,' I explained. 'But I just feel there's something not kosher about the whole business. And, in any case, all I saw was your husband talking with a woman. In fact, I didn't even see them talking to each other. It's not enough to confront your husband with, far less start divorce proceedings.'

'So if Andrew isn't carrying on with this woman, then what on earth is it?'

'Can you think of anything that your husband could be involved in that he would want to try to keep from you? From everybody?'

'Not a thing. Like I told you before, Andrew is a very ordinary, very honest, very reliable man. He wouldn't be involved in anything illegal or *funny*.'

'To be honest, that's also the description of a man who's unlikely to be involved in an extramarital affair, although I have seen it happen. Are you sure there isn't *something* that could explain all this subterfuge?'

She held out her arms in a helpless gesture.

'Okay . . .' I said. 'Do you want me to continue tailing your husband?'

'Yes. I need to know what's going on.'

'The way your husband is giving me the slip, it could be a costly business, not least in car parts.'

'I have enough money to pay you for another week or so. After that Andrew will know that the money's going missing. Can you find something out in that time?'

'I honestly don't know, Mrs Ellis, but I'll do my best.'

Back in the car, I examined my oil-stained tie, dabbing at the smudge with a handkerchief. It was a dark blue knitted silk tie and the stain wasn't that noticeable, but I knew it was there. Going back to my digs to change the tie was, I knew, nothing more than an excuse to talk to Fiona away from the girls and hopefully get to the bottom of what the hell was going on with her.

However, as I passed my digs I saw a car parked outside. A Jowett Javelin – and one I recognized. Instead of pulling into the kerb, I drove on.

Deafened by the sound of pennies dropping.

Like every City of Glasgow policeman, Donald Taylor was tall; about an inch and a half taller than me. He had been a Detective Constable in Central Division for four years and for three of those had been supplying me with information in return for un-receipted donations. I was not the kind of citizen that many Glasgow coppers would want to be seen hob-nobbing with – the exception being the newly promoted Detective Chief Inspector Jock Ferguson, who was above bribery and suspicion as well as being the closest thing I had to a friend. Consequently, I arranged to meet Taylor down by the river, under the shadow of a forest of shipyard cranes.

'Tanglewood, you say?' Taylor took the cigarette I offered him and frowned. 'Nope, I can't say it means anything to me.'

'I've a couple of names I'd like checked out. They're not connected but I need to know if either has been naughty at any time. Or anything else you can dig up on them.' I handed Taylor a folded slip of paper with Ellis's and Lang's names on it. It was folded around a five-pound banknote and Taylor slipped it into his coat pocket without looking at it.

'Are they likely to have form?' he asked.

'Doubt it. One's a businessman, the other's a union official.'
Taylor frowned. 'I'll have to be careful with the union bloke.'

'Why?'

'You can have more than one kind of record, Mr Lennox.
Checking out the criminal records in the Collator's Office is
straightforward enough, but a lot of these union boys are
Communist Party members and the Special Branch boys have
their own rogues' gallery. Ask the wrong questions about the
wrong people and you can end up being questioned yourself.
Shady bunch, Special Branch.'

'See what you can do, anyway, Don.' I paused for a moment,
thinking about what he had told me. 'Listen, I should maybe
warn you that the first name, Ellis, belongs to someone with a
Hungarian background. Pre-communist, but he was born there.
I guess that could be vaguely political too.'

Taylor looked worried. Purposefully worried. I took the hint
and handed him another five.

'Like I said, see what you can find out for me and it will be
much appreciated.' I smiled my gratitude, which was as genuine
as his worry had been: there was nothing more nauseating than
a bent copper, even if you were the one doing the bending. 'Any
other tidbits that might be of interest?' I asked.

'They've got a lead on that jewellery robbery in the Arcades
last month.'

'Really?' I said conversationally. 'Who's in the frame?'

'Now, Mr Lennox, you know I couldn't tell you that,' he said.
What he meant was he couldn't tell me unless I paid him for
the information. There had been a time when I would have paid
well; it was the kind of news that you could sell on at a profit.

'I don't move in those circles any more, Don, you know that.
If you can't tell me, don't. I'm just interested that's all.'

I could see that I had just pulled the rug from under him. He had valuable information that was valuable only to people he could never deal with directly. He was looking for a broker, and my days as a middle-man were behind me.

'The reason I'm mentioning it, Mr Lennox,' he said, 'is that it concerns someone that I think you know well.'

'I know a lot of people well, Don.'

'The Jew, Cohen.' The cocky look on Taylor's face told me that he really did have goods to sell. Goods I didn't want to buy but, like it or not, I did owe Handsome Jonny Cohen a favour.

'What's the information?'

'A name. A name of someone who's going to turn Queen's Evidence.'

I nodded. The police had obviously got something on one of Cohen's people and were trading his hide for Jonny's.

'Well?' he asked. I thought about old loyalties. About scrapes I'd been pulled out of. About thirteen months of trying to put distance between me and where I'd been. What I'd been.

'I'll pass, Don,' I said with a sigh. 'Like I said, I don't move in those circles any more. And if you want my advice, I wouldn't go about offering that kind of information for sale. Sell something like that to any of the Three Kings and you've sold yourself. And trust me, if they get their claws into a copper, they won't let go and you'll spend the rest of your career worrying about whether they'd trade you to get out of a tight spot.' I let it sink in before continuing. 'But get me something I can work with on the names I've given you and there'll be a bonus in it for you.'

'Okay,' he said, clearly crestfallen. I could imagine his delight when he had happened to overhear that snippet. Cash registers ringing in his head. But what I had told him was true: there are degrees of graft. What he was selling me could get him kicked out of the police; what he wanted to sell Cohen – or to get me to sell to Cohen – could get him kicked into prison.

He hadn't told me the name. But he had told me there *was* a name. What I was going to do with that information, I didn't yet know.

It wasn't the only piece of information I had that I didn't know what to do with: as I walked through drizzle back to where I'd parked, I thought about the Jowett Javelin I'd seen outside Fiona's.

CHAPTER EIGHT

I spent two days wearing out shoe leather and working up the telephone bill. The days were spent mostly on the union case, the evenings on Ellis.

Now, I considered myself to be a self-contained, independent kind of character. Maybe not a loner, but someone who tries not to give too much away about himself. I kept a lot of stuff private and a lot of the people I knew didn't know who else I knew.

Even with that, it's true that no man is an island. Each of us exists partly through others; the connections we make throughout our lives, good or bad, extending into a far-reaching web. A traceable web to one degree or another. Me included.

Frank Lang appeared to be the exception to John Donne's rule. If there was a committee or a reading group or a theatre association, then Lang's name would be on the list of members or contributors. There were lot of threads spun in Lang's web, right enough, but they just didn't stretch very far.

The calls I made and the people I visited confirmed the bare bones of Lang's existence: he *had* been a member of the merchant marine, working as a ship's cook; he *had* enrolled for evening classes through the Workers' Educational Association; he *had* been on the membership lists of several societies and committees. The only thing was that no one I spoke to could really remember ever meeting Lang.

Eventually I did manage to trace two merchant seamen who had served with Lang. I showed them the photograph and they both confirmed it was him and yes, they had seen him in the flesh. One of the sailors said that he had heard that Lang had emigrated years ago, Canada or Australia.

And that was it: all I could find on Frank Lang.

Archie had been sniffing around the Ellis case where the opposite of Lang seemed to be true. Andrew Ellis's history was eminently traceable and transparent. A well-liked and well-respected member of the Glasgow business community, he had a reputation stretching back to the end of the war. No dodgy dealings, no grey areas, no skeletons in the cupboard. His case may have been the opposite of Lang's, but it was just as baffling.

When Archie came into the office on the Tuesday morning, he balefully confirmed that he'd been unable to dig up anything of note on Ellis.

'The problem is our hands are tied,' he explained. 'I'm just nipping away at the edges here, Chief.' Archie habitually called me *Chief*, despite me asking him not to. Probably *because* I'd asked him not to. 'I can't talk to his employees or customers, because that would alert him to the fact that his missus has put a couple of professional snoopers onto him. And he hasn't answered the call of the wild for the last three nights, so there's been nowhere or no one to follow him to. If you've only got until the end of the week, then I think we're scuppered.'

'I think so too,' I said, infected by Archie's dolefulness. I ran through where I was with the union thing with him, for no other real reason than to hear myself say it out loud. It didn't sound any better.

'What's in the ledger?' Archie asked.

'That is something I am going to have to find out,' I said. 'Connelly is being unusually coy about it. My guess is that the missing money has been donated by supporters of the union who would rather keep their names out of the public eye, and the ledger details the payments. It sounds to me like blackmail, but Connelly denies that. Maybe Lang intends to sell it to the newspapers, but it is technically stolen property . . . What is it, Archie?' I noticed him purse his thin lips as he held me in his bloodhound stare.

'A list of union supporters? Joe Connelly and his union have hired us to track down a missing jotter with the names of a few Reds in it?'

'You don't think it's likely?'

'Well, *Chief*, that's relative. Compared to Twinkletoes's chances of winning Brain of Britain, it's likely. Compared to there being something in that ledger that is a lot more important or embarrassing, it's not.'

'I know what you mean,' I said. It had been troubling me since my meeting with Connelly and Lynch. Not what had been said, but what hadn't been said. 'By the way, are you happy enough to do this week's run with Twinkletoes?'

'Delighted. He gives me a warm glow of security. And it's nice to reminisce. I arrested him for breach of the peace, aggravated assault, resisting arrest and police assault back in Forty-seven, you know.'

'Really?'

'Mmm. Old times. It gives us something to chat about.'

I tried to imagine Archie and Twinkletoes chatting, but the effort made my head hurt.

*   *   *

Some people make a big show of their learning. Bookshelves dressed with the 'right' novels with unbroken spines, learned spoutings in the tap room, the dropping of the right names in conversation. The Mitchell Library was Glasgow's very public, very brash statement of erudition. It was big. Very big. The largest public reference library in Europe.

I worked my way through the Commercial Reference Library and came away with details of Ellis's company, as well as Hall Demolitions, the company he had worked for before setting up his own outfit. While I was there, I also checked out the public records on the Amalgamated Union of Industrial Trades: no mention of Frank Lang anywhere among the names of union officers.

Glasgow's air is usually too heavy and sluggish for the wind to waste effort on, but that afternoon, as autumn oozed indistinctly into winter, it had decided to make its presence felt. As I came out of the Mitchell Library and stepped into a chill, damp swirl of rain and grime, I tightened my elbow-grip on the leather document case tucked under my arm and with my other hand clamped my protesting Borsalino to my head.

It was at times like these that I reflected on how, at the end of the war, I may have been directionless and feckless, but could not work out why I hadn't chosen to be directionless and feckless in Paris or Rome or anywhere with a better climate. Which was hardly a restrictive criterion.

I pushed through the wind, the rain and the grim-faced crowds, steering a course back to my office.

Andrew Ellis wasn't the only one who was skilled at spotting when he was being tailed.

I didn't feel like going back to my digs and there was a kind of aimlessness about me when I left the office. I was still smarting about what had happened with Fiona White. I'd been all kinds of cad and swine with women, it was true, but I had been straight with Fiona White. It stung hard to be on the receiving end for a change.

I found myself in a fish restaurant in Sauchiehall Street. It was not the kind of place I usually frequented: generally, the range of Glaswegian gustatory delights was determined by whether or not they could be cooked by dropping them into a deep-fat fryer, and I generally tried to be more cosmopolitan in my dining habits. But I did call into this place from time to time on the conceit that it was slightly more sophisticated than the usual fish and chip joint. It was all high ceilings, porcelain and chequerboard floor tiles, and had huge windows that looked out onto the street; the waiters and waitresses wore waistcoats and aprons, your fish and chips were served on china, instead of being wrapped in the previous day's *Scottish Express*, and you ate with cutlery, not your fingers.

I was all class.

He didn't come into the restaurant. Instead he stood directly across the street, hiding from the rain in a bus shelter and smoking. Whoever he was, he wasn't a pro. A pro doesn't stand in plain sight of his target, especially when that target has gone into a public building with only one entrance and exit. My meal came with a pot of tea and I ate it leisurely, finishing off with an even more leisurely cigarette. The guy across the street let four buses come and go from the stop without budging.

After I'd finished and paid at the cashier's desk, I pulled my coat collar up and the brim of my hat down and shouldered my way into the rain. My 'shadow' across Sauchiehall Street turned his back to me and started to read a tattered bus timetable with sudden and profound interest.

I made my way through the crowds back in the direction of my office. The Atlantic was parked a couple of streets away but I decided to do my own little test to see how far my new chum would follow me. I turned right and crossed Blythswood Street. As I casually checked the traffic, I caught a quick glance of him bustling around the corner. He was a reasonably big guy, maybe five-ten but heavy-set. He was wearing a pale grey raincoat, a matching hat and a harassed expression.

I cut into Sauchiehall Lane, one of the intersecting alleyways that run parallel to the grid layout streets of Glasgow city centre. It was lined with the unadorned brick and steel-doored backs of the buildings that faced onto Sauchiehall Street and Bath Street, and in the rain the cobbles were greasy and treacherous underfoot. I trotted along the lane to put some distance between me and him.

He had a round, fleshy face and large eyes, and if it had not been for the smudge of trimmed moustache above the plump lips he would have looked like an overblown baby. The big eyes got bigger when he saw me waiting for him and he stood for a moment, startled.

Then he took a swing at me.

'You bastard!' he shouted, as his fist arced wide and as predictably as if he'd sent me a three-sheet telegram about his intentions. I blocked his punch easily with my left forearm and planted my own in the cushion of his belly just below the breast-bone. He doubled up and I slammed one into the side of his head. His feet slipped on the cobbles and he fell against the wall, still clutching his gut. It was quick and easy and all of the fight went out of him. The problem was – or at least always had been since the war – that the fight never seemed to go out of me. Once I had gotten started, I found it difficult to stop. But now, as I lined up another blow, I looked down at the doubled-over guy gasping for breath. He was as good at fighting as he was at tailing people, and with a sigh I hauled him up and pushed him against the wall. His hat had come off and I could see he was bald, with only a band of close-cropped hair from temple to temple. It made him look even more like some kind of overgrown infant. The fight might have gone from him, but when our eyes met, his still burned with hatred.

'You bastard . . .' he repeated breathily. 'You stay the hell away from her. Stay away from her or I'll kill you.'

I grabbed the collar of his coat with both hands and slammed him against brickwork.

'What the hell are you talking about?' I demanded. 'Why are you following me?'

'You know why, you shite.'

'Cut out the name-calling, bud, or I'll slap it out of you. Now . . . what the hell is wrong with you and why are you on my tail?'

'I know it's you. I know you've been . . . You and her. I found your card in her handbag . . .' He reached into his coat pocket and I grabbed his wrist, easing his hand slowly into view. It was my business card, all right.

'Listen, I have no idea what this is all about,' I protested. I had been chased by more than one angry husband in my time, but it had been a while since I'd given anyone cause.

'You've been carrying on with my wife, that's what it's all about, as if you didn't know.'

'Who's your wife?'

'Don't try to come on all innocent,' he blustered and straightened himself up. He was trying to regain some dignity, but it was still well beyond his reach. 'You know who she is . . . that is unless you've got a string of marriages you're wrecking, you bastard.'

I gave him a backhander, hard across the face. 'I told you to watch your mouth. What's your wife's name?'

'Sylvia Dewar. I'm Tom Dewar, her husband.' His eyes fell with the last word. The shame of a cuckold. I let him go.

'Sylvia Dewar?' The pieces began to fit. I let go of his coat and he tried to smooth the crumples out of it and his pride. 'Listen, friend, I only met your wife the other day. On business. And I'm sure as hell not playing footsie with her.'

'No?' he looked at me defiantly. A shaky sneer on his swelling face.

'No.'

'Then someone is. And I found your card hidden in her handbag.'

'Didn't you think to ask her who I was? Or do you just jump on the first mug you think your wife's spoken to?'

'She would just have lied if I'd asked her. She's a liar as well as everything else. I know all about it. There are ways of knowing. It's been going on for months.'

'Not with me, it hasn't.'

He stared at me, the bitterness and anger still burning in the large, watery eyes. But I guessed that was the way he looked at the whole world and he was clearly less sure about his accusation. I bent down, picked up his hat and handed it to him.

'Listen, Mr Dewar,' I said, 'I think we should grab a coffee. There's a place around the corner.'

We got some odd looks as we walked into the café. The harsh

neon ceiling lights threw up the oily smears on Dewar's coat and the angry swelling on his temple where I'd bopped him. We took a table in the corner and a glum, meagre, middle-aged waitress took our order for two frothy coffees as if it had been a personal insult.

'Okay, here's why your wife had my card . . .' I explained all about my work for Joe Connelly and the union and his concern for Frank Lang's welfare. I gave him all the main points of what I'd discussed with his wife, but, given that he'd recently taken a swing at me for stealing some of his apples, I missed out the part where Sylvia had offered me the whole fruit bowl. I ran through what she had told me about Lang going away with the men in the fancy car.

'She never said anything about that to me,' he said. 'And I've never seen any fancy cars outside. All I know is he's not been back to the house for a week or more.'

'Do you believe me?' I asked. 'I promise you that I haven't seen your wife before or since and our meeting was strictly business.'

Dewar stared at me. He knew I was telling the truth, but there was desperation in his eyes, almost as if that believing it had been me, that being able to put a face to his wife's secret lover, made it easier somehow.

Eventually, he shook his big, baby head glumly. 'But there is somebody. I know it. I even thought it could have been Frank next door but he's hardly ever there.'

'Quite,' I said, but thought about how his wife had known what Lang kept in his kitchen cupboards. I had recognized something in Sylvia Dewar, something I had seen in many of the women I had known. The type of women I had known. My guess was that Dewar was making a mistake in looking for one offender. Given the fact that I had nearly become one of them, there had probably been more than one notch on Sylvia Dewar's bedpost. I looked at Dewar, slumped at the table, the spirit leaving him just as the fight had. Despite the fact that he had just tried to take my head off, I felt sorry for him.

'Sylvia . . . you see, Sylvia isn't the kind of woman that goes for someone like me,' he said, desperation in his voice. 'I couldn't believe it when she went out with me and then said she would marry me. But I make a good wage and I give her a good life. I like to buy her things. She likes me buying things for her.'

'Mr Dewar . . .' I said as soothingly as I could manage. I was not good with other people's unhappiness. 'You don't have to —'

'I'm sorry about today. But I'm going out of my mind with this. I suspect everybody and when I found your card . . .'

'Forget it.' I waved a dismissive hand. 'I understand. You don't need to explain. Let's just forget about it.'

'But your card . . .' he was almost pleading. 'It says you're an Inquiry Agent. Is that like a private detective? Do you handle marriage cases?'

'It is and I do,' I said. 'But before you ask, I can't get involved. I've met your wife in another context and that rules me out of handling a divorce case involving her.' I didn't mention that the real reason I couldn't get involved was because she had invited me to test out their marital bedsprings. Which could make things complicated.

'I don't want a divorce. I just want to find out who she's messing about with. Will you take the case? I can pay . . .' He was raising his voice in desperation, attracting more glances, including from the waitress who'd clearly gone to the same charm school as Mussolini.

'I can't, Mr Dewar.' I sighed. 'Listen, give yourself a few days to calm down, then call me.' I handed him a business card. 'You best put the other card back in your wife's purse, just in case she looks for it. I asked her to get in touch if Frank Lang comes back home.'

We sat over our coffees for a while and I asked him what he knew about his missing neighbour.

'Not a lot,' he said. 'Frank keeps himself to himself. Always friendly though.'

'But?' I said, reading something in his expression.

'Nothing really. Just he seems a bit of a misfit. Not odd, exactly, but he's . . . I don't know . . . just a bit different.'

'In what way different?'

'Just not your typical union man, I suppose.' There was frustration in Dewar's shrug: we were not talking about what he wanted to talk about, all he wanted to talk about. His wife's suspected infidelity was filling his mental universe.

'I guess he's never left a key with you, in case he was away like he is now?'

'No. Like I said, he keeps his business to himself.'

'I may have to ask you and your wife more questions,' I said. 'But, under the circumstances, it would probably be best if I did that when you were both at home.'

He nodded. 'You will think about what I asked you? About maybe just keeping an eye on Sylvia to see what she's playing at?'

'I will,' I said. 'But at the moment it's a definite no-can-do. Even without the *complication* of your wife knowing who I am, I've already got two cases running at the moment.'

After a while, we ran out of things to say and we left the café. As he took his leave of me, Dewar apologized again for trying to jump me in the alley.

'We all make mistakes,' I said. 'God knows, I've made more than my share.'

'You don't know what it's like,' he said, the too-large eyes cast down. 'You don't know what it's like to think you have something special, something good, with a woman, only to find out it's all a sham.'

'Don't I?' I asked. 'I wouldn't be too sure about that ...'

CHAPTER NINE

Fiona didn't come up to my room that Thursday afternoon as we had arranged and when I knocked on her door there was no answer; no sounds from inside her flat. As I stood at her door, I became aware of the emptiness of the house. Its quiet. I could hear the traffic on Great Western Road, the playground sounds of children streets away, the shuddering clang of a mechanical digger against tarmac somewhere less distant, but these were all the wall- and window-muffled sounds from a remote universe. The house around me was still and empty, and there was something about that stillness that gave me a bad feeling that I couldn't explain.

I didn't wait. Somehow I knew she would not be back that afternoon. Instead I went back out to the car and headed back into the city centre.

Archie was out and the office was locked up, but I found Pamela Ellis waiting for me. Eagerly. It was an adverb I would never have attached to her, but it seemed to fit with her itchy impatience when we caught sight of each other as I climbed the stairs to my office.

'Ah, Mr Lennox,' she smiled. Eagerly. 'I hoped I would catch you. I thought you maybe wouldn't be back and I was about to leave you a note.'

'Normally I wouldn't be back on a Thursday afternoon, Mrs Ellis, you're lucky you caught me. My appointment was . . . cancelled.' It was one way of putting it, I suppose. 'Please . . .' I unlocked the office door and held it open for her.

She sat down in front of my desk while I hung up my coat. Her handbag sat flat on her lap, her gloved fingers interlaced on top of it. The shoulders beneath the raincoat were tense, the stare straight ahead; no relaxation in her pose. She had the demeanour of someone prepared to carry out a rehearsed task or deliver a prepared speech.

She delivered her speech.

'This is all very awkward and more than a little embarrassing for me, Mr Lennox, but I'm here to tell you that I won't be requiring your services from today. Everything has been sorted out. It was all a huge misunderstanding, just like you said it could be. I'm sorry to have wasted your time.'

'No need to apologize, Mrs Ellis. My time is your money, I'm afraid, so that's what has been wasted. I'm just happy that everything seems to have been resolved amicably.'

'Thank you Mr Lennox. I really appreciate everything you've done. I wonder if I could settle my account with you?'

'Sure, I'll send you a bill.'

'If you don't mind – I mean if it isn't putting you out – I'd rather settle up now. Could you make up your account now and I'll pay you right away.'

I shrugged. 'Suits me, Mrs Ellis.'

Now, when anybody was in a hurry to settle a bill and get me out of their lives, it tended to make me a little suspicious. But when it was a Scot forcing cash on me, it was enough to make me outright paranoid.

'If you don't mind me asking,' I said as I took my blue invoice book from the desk and slipped carbon paper between the sheets, 'what was the big mystery? Why was Mr Ellis going out in the evenings at such short notice?'

'Oh . . . It was all totally innocent. I feel such a fool, really . . .' She pulled on a fake smile. 'It really was all connected to the business. He was called to these meetings at very short notice because the client he is dealing with is a developer who has an unusual schedule and Andrew had to meet with him at all hours. What I didn't know was that most of these meetings took place during normal office hours and these other ones were . . . well, they were just when things came up that needed to be discussed urgently.'

'I see.' I tore the invoice sheet from the book and handed it to her. I had itemized my and Archie's time and, under sundries, added the replacement engine cables.

'Oh, yes. I quite understand that you have to charge for the damage to your car; after all it happened when you were working for me.' She nodded gravely. 'But you should know that that vandalism didn't have anything to do with Andrew.'

'You asked him about it?'

'Oh, gracious no. He doesn't know anything about me hiring you . . . it's just that I confronted him with all of my stupid suspicions and he explained everything. I've even met his customer. Everything is perfectly above board.'

'And what was Tanglewood? Did your husband explain that?' I asked.

'Oh, that . . .' She was too slow in clearing the frown. 'Oh, yes . . . Tanglewood is the name of the project that Andrew's client is building. That's all.'

'And the girl?'

'You were absolutely right.' Pamela Ellis nodded approvingly.

'I have to say you really know your job, Mr Lennox – you could see that there was nothing going on between them. The young lady in question works for Andrew's client.'

'Well,' I said, as she counted out my payment in uncreased five-pound notes that looked fresh from the bank, 'I'm glad that it's all been sorted out.'

I took the cash. It was exact to the last penny. No bonus. She had been told not to try to pay me extra as any hint of my being bought off would be likely to make me suspicious. I stood up and shook her hand, holding on to it for a second longer.

'Mrs Ellis,' I said, 'are you sure everything is all right?'

'Of course it is.' Another smile that was as genuine as the fairy tale she had just spun me. 'Like I said, I just feel so silly about the whole thing. Getting you involved in this. I should have talked to Andrew first.'

'Well, as I say, I'm pleased it's all sorted out, but if you need my help at any time, please don't hesitate to get in touch.'

She thanked me again and left, trying very hard, but failing, to conceal her relief.

I sat down behind my desk and looked at the neatly counted-out cash. Sometimes there were no answers, I told myself. Or at least no answers that make any sense when you looked at them. And sometimes you just had to walk away from it – none the wiser and none the worse for it.

Whatever had passed between husband and wife, whatever she believed or didn't believe, whatever story she wanted to concoct for my benefit, it was no longer my business or concern. I'd been paid, and trying to work out what the hell was going on would pay me no more.

Case closed.

*   *   *

Archie came into the office an hour later.

'Could you do me a favour?' I asked him before he could hang up his hat. 'Could you go down to the Glasgow Corporation Planning Office for me?'

'I'd be delighted.' Archie said dully. 'What for?'

'I'd like you to check out any applications over the last six to nine months that involve site demolition and clearing for a new building.'

'What? All of them?'

'No . . .' I said, looking at the crisp new fivers sitting on my desk. Next to them, where I had placed it and flattened it out, was the crumpled piece of paper with the company name and address in Garnethill I had used to direct the RAC to my disabled car. 'Just anything that involves a project called Tanglewood.'

There were no surprises for me over the next couple of days. Archie checked and re-checked, but there was no planning request lodged with the City Corporation for any project named Tanglewood. After making a few calls myself without ringing any bells, I told Archie to forget it; that we were off the case, and we could divide our time on finding the missing Frank Lang. I went from union office to union office, from shipyard to shipyard, doors opening magically for me because I carried the standard of Joe Connelly and the Amalgamated Union of Industrial Trades. Despite Connelly wanting me to be as discreet as possible, he had spread the word far and wide. Everybody was cooperative, but nobody could tell me anything to help.

I traced Lang to his home town, or at least the address the union had for where he had lived before moving to Glasgow. I drove about half an hour south into Lanarkshire and to a small village outside Wishaw.

There was a lot of mining in Scotland. Oil shale. Ironstone. Slate. But most of all, coal.

The business of digging deep into the Earth created strange landscapes. The mining village I drove to was in the middle of nowhere, surrounded by open November-bare countryside painted in a palette of greys and dull greens; mainly farmland with the odd clump of forest. But this was every bit as much an industrial landscape as the docks, shipyards and factories of Glasgow. In the case of Cleland, as with dozens of villages just like it from Ayrshire to Fife, the industry was hidden from view, deep in the earth. The only clues to what was going on under your feet were the mine head towers and gears, and the unnatural black peaks – the spoil tips of mine waste, called *bings* in Scotland – that flanked the village. And, despite the rural setting, all of the dangers of heavy industry lay as much here as anywhere else, it was just that they lurked hidden from view.

I was no Red, but there were times I could understand why Scotland had become so militantly socialist. People died here all the time, smothered or crushed or drowned in the pit galleries. Even children perished here, falling into disused shafts or through the crust of a burning bing – a spoil tip that had spontaneously combusted deep within – and burning to death. I had heard that in some places, at night, you could see some of the burning bings glow menacingly in the dark, but I was yet to see one for myself.

Scottish mining villages were designed and built as if they were meant to be in urban centres. Ranks of uniform, tiny, single-storey dwellings arranged in tight, ugly rows; exactly the same kind of housing you found in the shadow of factories in towns and cities. The difference with these communities was that the dreary urban architecture would stop suddenly and sharply and you were instantly back into a gentle, rolling rural landscape. It was almost as if someone had cut out a city neighbourhood and dropped it at random into the countryside.

The village was there. The street was there – short, straight, flanked by miners' houses and declining to a dead end – but when I looked for Lang's old place, it wasn't there. The street numbers stopped before they got anywhere close to the one I had for him. I saw an older man heading out of one of the houses further up, close to where I'd parked the Atlantic – the only car in the street. I strolled up and introduced myself and he looked at me as if I had come from another planet. He was small and stooped and had a face of wrinkled grey-white leather, the eyes sunk deep into it. The retired miner had a thick accent and I struggled to understand him, but I picked up that there had never been any houses other than the ones standing. I suspected some kind of administrative error on the part of the union and that the street was right but the number wrong, but the old guy, who had lived in the same house for forty years, assured me there had never been a Frank Lang in that or any nearby rows.

I stood and looked down the narrow, truncated street, across the fields to where, half a mile distant, the stark geometry of the mine head winding gear stood black against the grey sky.

When it came to Frank Lang, the dead ends were becoming more than metaphorical.

Time for a chat.

CHAPTER TEN

As he sat in the corner, a pint glass of flat beer on the table before him, the sound of two miners swearing at each other seeping through from the main bar, Joe Connelly's fat neck was straining another shirt collar to tolerance. He was wearing the same suit that he'd had on the last time I'd met with him and again it was stretched drum tight over his corpulence. His were not the only beady eyes that watched me as I came into the small room at the back of the working men's club: Lynch was there too, as I had expected him to be.

'This is ... *quaint* ...' I said as I sat down opposite them without being asked. I had only ever seen the inside of a working men's club when I'd been in one on business. My second impression pretty much matched my first. Living conditions for the average Scottish working man must have been dire indeed if he chose to spend his free time in a place like this.

An ugly box of smoke-darkened brick under a shallow-pitched roof, the club was for dock workers, rather than shipyard workers. It sat on the south side of the river, in Govan, at that point where the Clyde swelled into the Queen's Dock in the north shore and the Prince's Dock, with its three basins, on the south.

Rather oddly, my instructions had included an order to come

around to the back door, where no one could see me. Lynch had been waiting to usher me in unseen by the club's regulars, who, even at this time of day, were probably too drunk to notice me anyway.

'Exactly what have you got for us on Frank Lang's whereabouts?' Connelly posed the question like it was a wages demand.

'Exactly? Well, the best way of answering that would be to say I've got exactly nothing.'

'Why am I not surprised?' sneered Lynch. I really, really wanted to reach over the table and smack the sneer off his face, but instead I smiled.

'Why are you not surprised? I don't know ... because I sure am. You see, given enough time to ask the right questions, I could write a book on just about anybody's personal history. If you dig around for long enough, and deep enough, you can put together a pretty comprehensive picture of just about anyone. People exist on several levels. The first is existing in the way we all understand it:, simply being there. The second is the way we exist in the minds of others: family, friends, lovers, acquaintances, colleagues ... even people who see us regularly on the street or the bus or the tram without knowing our names or the first thing about us. The third is our bureaucratic existence: birth, marriage and death certificates, national insurance numbers, drivers' licences, rent books ...'

'What's your point?' asked Connelly.

'You have assured me that Frank Lang exists. The problem is the only footprints he leaves come to a sudden end. There is no dimension, no depth to Frank Lang. Go back two jobs or one address and there's nothing. Because he was a sailor, the people I want to speak to about him are scattered all over the world.

I've only been able to find two seamen who confirm that the face in the picture you gave me really is Frank Lang. And as for his paper trail existence, even that is minimal.'

'This all sounds like an excuse for you not being able to do the job we're paying you for,' said Lynch, his small eyes glittering in the dim, smoky light.

'Does it? It sounds more to me like I've been chasing a ghost. A ghost that, so far, only you two gentlemen, his two ex-shipmates and his nearest neighbours can confirm actually having seen in the flesh.'

'Are you telling us that you can't help us any more?' asked Connelly.

'Well, that depends.' I paused and took a cigarette from my case, tapped the tip against gold plate to get rid of the loose shards of tobacco, and lit it. 'I'll be honest. I don't think you're telling me everything I need to know about Mr Lang and his sudden disappearance.'

'We've told you all we can at this stage, Lennox.' Lynch didn't look at me when he spoke, his head lowered as he rolled loose tobacco into a cigarette paper.

'I see.' I turned to the union boss. 'What kind of car do you drive, Mr Connelly?

'I don't have a car. If I need to get about on union business, then I have an official car and driver.'

'What make is it?'

'Ford Zodiac.'

'Colour?'

'Two-tone. Grey on top and a sort of fawny-brown underneath.'

'What about you, Mr Lynch?'

'I have a Morris Minor Traveller. Green. Now what the hell has that got to do with anything?' He had finished rolling his cigarette and sealed the paper by running the edge along the tip of his tongue.

'The only thing I've been able to find out is that, two weeks ago, Frank Lang went off with a couple of men in a large, expensive car, either red or brown in colour. Whoever these men were, and wherever Lang went with them, that is the last sighting we have of him. He just dropped off the world after that.'

'Are you suggesting it was us?' said Lynch. 'If we have spirited Lang away, then why would we hire you?'

'I wasn't suggesting anything. I just need to know who picked him up that night. But I do know you're keeping something from me. Lang is turning into the man-who-never-was. So, gentlemen, why don't you cut the bull and tell me the truth about him?'

'Everything we've told you is the truth,' said Connelly, unperturbed. 'Why would we hire you and then deliberately mislead you?'

'Maybe what I'm looking for isn't important, but simply the act of looking.'

'Is this the way you sound all the time?' asked Lynch. 'Or do you, every now and again, open your mouth and make some sense?'

'Oh, I sometimes make sense all right. Even if it is only to me.' Again I turned back to Connelly. 'You see, I am a suspicious sort of cove by nature. And this suspicious streak is putting odd ideas in my head.'

'Such as?' asked Connelly.

'Such as maybe you hired me to go through the motions so you have something to show the police when whatever it is you're hiding comes to light. I don't know what that missing ledger has in it, or if that money really has gone missing. All I do know is that Frank Lang is a ghost, and I don't believe in ghosts. There's something dodgy going on here, maybe even illegal, and, like I told you, I don't get involved in anything illegal.'

'Is that a fact?' Lynch smiled in a way I didn't like. 'We know all about your past, Lennox. Your involvement with the so-called Three Kings.'

Picking up my Borsalino from the table, I stubbed out my cigarette in a cheap ashtray made of pressed tin, and stood up. 'I think we're through here, gentlemen. I'll send you my bill.'

'You just hold on a minute, Lennox . . .' Lynch protested as he stood up. It gave me no end of pleasure to plant my hand squarely on his chest and shove him back, hard, into his chair. The force of it nearly toppled him backward.

'Stand up to me again,' I said in an even, quiet tone, 'and I'll break your jaw.'

Connelly held up his hand in an appeasing gesture. 'Mr Lennox, there's no need to get fired up. Please, sit down. We really do need your help.'

I stayed standing. Lynch's small rat eyes burned up at me with resentment. But he wasn't going to do anything about it any time soon.

'You're right,' said Connelly. 'We haven't told you everything. But with good reason. Please, Mr Lennox. Sit down and listen to what I have to say. Then, if you still don't want the job, we'll settle your bill and you can forget all about us. But please, hear me out.'

I shrugged and sat down.

'When we first met, I told you that we had carried out our own limited enquiries, such as they were.'

'Yes,' I said, dropping my hat back onto the table. 'So limited you didn't even speak to Lang's neighbours.'

'Union officials are not detectives, and they would be very conspicuous carrying out any kind of public investigation. But with the enquiries we did make, we found ourselves in exactly the position you're in now. Frank Lang doesn't have much of a history, and all the history he does have seems to have been just enough to get him involved with the union.'

'Some kind of plant?'

'We don't know, and that's the truth,' said Lynch, still glowering. 'There's a history of it in the movement. MI5, Special Branch . . . we know they use informers and infiltrators to spy on the union. It's all supposed to be chummy at Number Ten these days, but the police still have their little rats burrowing away in our organization.'

'Normally they're ordinary workers who they pay for information,' said Connelly. 'Class traitors. But maybe Lang wasn't working for the police or the government and is just a skilled con man. A criminal. When we couldn't pick up any kind of trail, we thought we would involve you. Because of your *background*, we thought we could trust you not to talk to the police. And, to be brutally frank, that you may have ways of getting information out of people that we can't be seen to employ.'

I snorted. 'I see . . . you think I'm some kind of thug for hire?'

'Not that. Just someone who was more likely to get to the bottom of this matter than we are. And you know people connected to the underworld who may have a better chance of knowing who Frank Lang really is.'

'Forget it,' I said. 'From what you say, Lang is as likely to be some kind of copper as he is to be a crook. And that could buy me a whole lot of trouble.'

'Trust me, we don't like relying on outsiders, but we're out of our depth here. We don't think that Frank Lang *was* a government plant.'

'Then what?'

'Like we said, more than likely a con man who wanted to fleece the fund,' said Lynch. 'But he maybe realizes the value of the ledger. Insurance, in a way. The information in that ledger could be worth even more than the money he has stolen . . . and if it falls into the wrong hands then people may die. That's the main reason that your background qualified you for the job. You have contacts in that world. If Frank Lang is some kind of confidence man or extortionist, then you could talk to the right sort of people. Maybe even track him down.'

'So what, exactly, is in the ledger?'

'Payments made by our union to foreign workers' organizations,' Lynch answered. 'We set up a special fund for aiding groups in countries where trade unionism is actively oppressed.'

'What? Like Russia, Poland or Hungary?' I asked with a straight face.

'No, Mr Lennox . . .' Connelly rode the jibe patiently. '. . . like the United States, South American countries or Franco's Spain. Anywhere where the rights of the working man are being fought for in an environment of great adversity.'

'Why do I get the feeling this isn't exactly kosher?'

'It's a legitimate part of the union's activities,' said Lynch. 'But it has to be dealt with very discreetly. We needed a middleman. Someone with special skills.'

'Lang?'

'He proved that he had been building up contact with groups during his time at sea. Merchant sailors have access to parts of the world cut off to everyone else. And he presented himself as an active and committed trade unionist.'

'So he never actually worked in the union's headquarters?'

'No. And at his request, we conducted all of our meetings away from the offices.'

'But he took you both in?' I asked. I couldn't imagine Connelly being easy to dupe. Lynch and Connelly exchanged a look. This was going to be good.

'I never actually met him,' said Connelly. 'I spoke with him on the 'phone a few times, but all face-to-face meetings were done with Paul here, and in places where they wouldn't be seen. Lang insisted on it. And, to be honest, I thought it was a good idea not to meet with him directly.'

'And you fell for this?' I failed to keep the incredulity out of my tone.

'He had the most reliable people speak to his reputation,' said Lynch. 'And the contacts he had were confirmed as genuine.'

'Although he stole thirty-five thousand,' said Connelly, 'the fund was originally standing at fifty thousand. The first fifteen thousand made it to the groups and organizations it was targeted to help. We got confirmation of that. We were very pleased with what he achieved.'

I thought it all through for a moment.

'I'm sorry, Mr Connelly, this is all far too complicated for me. And too political. I don't want to get any more involved.'

'Then maybe this would simplify it for you . . .' He reached into the tight squeeze of his jacket and dropped an envelope on the table in front of me. Picking it up I could feel the unmistakable heft of a pleasing wad of banknotes. 'And if you locate Lang and secure the missing ledger and funds, I can promise you the same again.'

He was right. It did simplify things for me.

CHAPTER ELEVEN

I had, at one time or another, dealt with all sorts of dodgy characters – thugs, killers, torturers, bank robbers, pimps. Car salesmen, however, were in a league all of their own.

The showroom was owned by Willie Sneddon, one of the Three Kings, or at least he had a major interest in it. One of his legitimate fronts.

My experience with the Teddy Boy Samaritans in Maryhill had highlighted my need for something more reliable for work than the Atlantic. The repair bills were piling up and it seemed to be eating up fuel these days, which was a problem given that the cost of petrol had soared to over five shillings a gallon and rationing had been temporarily reintroduced because of the shenanigans in Suez. Most of all, the next time I had a breakdown in Maryhill or some other Badlands of Glasgow, it might not end so well.

I didn't tell the salesman any of that. He was the predictably eager type, about thirty and wearing a dark suit and print tie. The motor trade was trying to shed the bomb-site wideboy reputation it had built up after the war. Today, car salesmen tried to dress with less flash and more like bank managers, but the trail of slime they left in their wake as they oozed across showroom floor or car lot from one customer to the next tended to dispel the illusion.

That said, the irrepressibly cheery salesman who introduced himself to me as *Kenny* struck me as slightly less oleaginous than most of his trade, even if he was still given to grinning periodically as if to remind me of how much he really, *really* liked me.

I told Kenny I was looking for something less flash and more family and spun him the usual bull about how I really didn't want to part with my beloved Atlantic, etc. I wandered around the lot – apparently magnetized because Kenny was never more than three feet behind me – not being drawn to any particular car until I spotted a particularly nice convertible. I didn't disguise my interest quickly enough and Kenny pounced like a lion on a deer.

'Ah yes . . .' he mewed appreciatively. 'The Sunbeam-Talbot Ninety. Now that's a motor with real style . . . Three years old, a Mark Two.'

'Mmm . . .' I said. 'Bit too steep for me. And it's a convertible. Let's face it, *Kenny*, a convertible is about as much use in Glasgow as a yacht in the Sahara.'

'Ah, but just imagine summer days driving around Loch Lomond or the Trossachs, the wind in your hair,' he said wistfully. I tried hard, but all I could imagine was struggling to get the roof back up in a sudden squall.

When I asked him what kind of trade-in he would offer for the Atlantic, Kenny looked at me as if I'd asked how much he would take to sell his sister into slavery. After a minute of mental anguish, all of which played out across his face with a lack of subtlety that would have made Donald Wolfit blush, he eventually gave me a figure fifty pounds less than the car was worth. I thanked him for his time and made to leave and suddenly he found some fresh emotional and financial reserves. He was still short, so I said I would think about it and again started to leave. Kenny followed me across the lot, feeding me a line about how he couldn't offer more against the model I was considering, how he really shouldn't have offered what he had and could only keep it on the table for the one day . . . the usual bull.

He made his final offer, then another one, and by now we were on the street, Kenny trying to coax me back to discuss terms. I was trying to squeeze the last drop out of him when I was distracted. A dark green Jowett Javelin passed by on Great Western Road. I could see the passenger only briefly, but long enough to recognize her.

'What do you say, Mr Lennox . . .' Kenny oiled my ear. 'Why don't you come back in and we can discuss what I can do to let you drive this beauty away?'

'What?' I turned and stared at him as if he'd said something in Japanese. 'No. No, I'll think about it. I'll come back if I decide to buy it.'

I climbed into the Atlantic and drove off towards my digs, trying not to think about whose car it had been that I just saw Fiona White in.

She was home by the time I arrived, but the Javelin wasn't parked outside, so I guessed she had simply been dropped off at the door.

There had been no invitation to join her and her daughters for that evening's meal, and when I walked through the front entrance into the shared hall, I paused for a moment at her door. Just as earlier that afternoon, when I had sensed the complete emptiness of the house, I could now sense Fiona's presence beyond the door. And something else: her willing me to go on up to my room without disturbing her.

As was becoming a habit, I spent the evening in my room smoking, reading and staring at the ceiling. I could hear the sounds of the television from the flat below: the girls would be watching *Lenny the Lion* as they always did on a Monday at this time.

I switched on the radio. On the Third Programme, Lord Strang and some professor of Russian history discussed and debated the causes of the 'Outburst in Europe', as the programme's title described recent events in Poland and Hungary. It struck me that I wasn't the only one who didn't understand what the hell was going on.

As I lay there on my bed, leaving the radio to chatter in the background, I tried to work out what had gone wrong between me and Fiona. Since the war, there had been a lot of women. It was true that I had been less than a gentleman with most of them, although I at least had had the decency to feel bad about how I had treated them. It seemed to me that when you didn't care much for yourself, you didn't care much for other people, or their feelings. But it had been totally different with Fiona: I had worked really hard to sort myself out and make a fist of a decent life and an honest living and she had been a focus of that effort.

Fiona knew some of the bad stuff – not all of it and certainly not the worst – but enough to understand I was making a real effort to put the past behind me. We had never been explicit about the future, but I had always assumed it was taken as read that there was one.

Now something had changed. And I was sure it wasn't anything I had done.

Pouring myself a Canadian Club, I took it over to the bedside cabinet and listened to the news. After six brief days of freedom,

Hungary continued to be brutalized by Soviet invaders; more British and French bombs fell on Egyptian cities while Eisenhower flexed US muscle in the United Nations. Eleven years after war's end, the world stage seemed to be full of strutting players who didn't know any more what role they were supposed to play. Just like me.

I switched to the Light Programme and listened to Billy Cotton shouting between turns on his Bandshow, which again did nothing to lift my mood.

After a restless hour, I decided to go out.

The Horsehead Bar was a refreshing pool of pollution into which to dive: noise and smoke and the vague chemical smells of poured spirits and spilled beer. I found my usual corner of the bar and drank a couple of Canadian Clubs too quickly to get to that point where I could enjoy the third, and fourth, more leisurely. Big Bob wasn't on duty and I didn't recognize either of the barmen working the taps and optics. Which was good, because I was in the mood to do some pickled brooding, which by its nature demanded solitude.

I was ready for my fourth whisky when I became aware of a small, stocky guy in a cheap black suit at my shoulder. Resting his elbows on the bar, he ordered a pint of beer in an American accent that was so cod you could have hauled it up in a trawler net. I half expected him to turn to me and say 'Howdy Pardner'. I recognized him as 'Sheriff Pete', the loudmouth Big Bob had told me about and who had held court while simultaneously being held up to ridicule by his audience.

I made the mistake of ordering my whisky while he was still at the bar. On hearing my accent, he turned to me and beamed.

'Hey, bud . . . you from over the pond? Like me?'

'I'm Canadian, if that's what you mean,' I said wearily. 'A genuine Canadian.'

'Swell ... I'm a New Yorker myself,' he said with pride and in an accent that conjured up images of cowboys on the open prairies of Gartcosh. 'Well, I was born in New York ... Manhattan ... but my folks moved to Detroit. Tough city, Detroit.'

I turned back to my whisky and brooding.

'Say, where you from in Canada?' His persistence tapped at my elbow and I was tempted to tap at his jaw. I turned to him and was disconcerted by his eyes. Dark, intense eyes. He was small – small even for Glasgow – but thick-set, and the pallor of his complexion was emphasized by the dense swirl of oiled, jet-black hair combed back from a widow's peak on the high, broad forehead.

'New Brunswick,' I said. 'Saint John.'

'Yeah?'

'Yeah.'

'What you drinkin'?' He pulled a wad of notes from his trouser pocket and held it up enough for me, and everyone else, to see.

'I'm okay,' I said.

'Aw, come on, bud ... It ain't every day I meet a fellow American.' His accent was now drowning somewhere in the middle of the Atlantic. Or somewhere between Jimmy Cagney and Finlay Currie. I would have found him funny, but when he bored into me with those weird dark eyes of his I could sense something even darker behind them. Something really bad.

'Like I said, I'm Canadian.' I nodded to the barman and my fourth whisky arrived courtesy of Sheriff Pete.

'I heard you was a private eye. That true?'

'Private eyes only exist in movies. I'm an enquiry agent.'

'But you ain't a copper ...'

'No, I'm not a copper.'

'I hate coppers. Got good reason to.' He leaned towards me conspiratorially. 'I'm just out of the big house. Peterhead. Nine years.'

I nodded. I somehow couldn't imagine him as a Peterhead prisoner. Peterhead lay in the extreme north-east of Scotland and was home to the country's toughest jail. If you were too tough a tough-nut even for Barlinnie, you were sent to Peterhead. Its security and regime were the tightest around.

'What did you do?'

'They pinned a bum wrap on me.' Another conspiratorial lean. 'I'm a heist man. You know ... do bank jobs. Big ones. Crack safes too ... But that ain't what they got me for. Man, I'll tell you, Peterhead is a hell hole.'

'Yeah,' I said. 'And the prison isn't much better.'

He didn't get the gag and just stared at me though his coal-black eyes.

'I knew someone who did time there once,' I explained. 'He said no one tried to escape because even if they got through all of the security and over the wall, they'd just find themselves in the middle of Peterhead and would end up knocking on the prison gates to get back in.'

'No one would want back into that shit-hole,' he said moodily. Whatever it was I had seen behind the dark eyes, it wasn't a sense of humour.

I drank my fourth whisky while Sheriff Pete talked me sober. There wasn't anything this guy hadn't done, no woman he hadn't bedded, no tough guy he hadn't floored.

I got him another beer but passed on another whisky, made my excuses and stood up from the bar. He put a restraining hand on my forearm.

'It must be great,' he said, his transatlantic drawl fading to pure Lanarkshire for a moment. 'I mean, being a private eye. Spying on people. You know, the power you have over them, knowing all about their lives, looking through their stuff when they don't know you've been there . . .'

For a moment I thought he was cracking wise: mocking my way of earning a living, but I saw the earnestness glitter in the coal of his eyes.

'I'd like that,' he said. 'I'd like that a lot.'

'Don't believe all you see in the movies. My job offers very little power, no glamour and less pay. Anyway, it was nice talking to you,' I lied, and made my way out into the street.

I had a lot on my mind as I drove home: the going-nowhere-fast Lang job, the went-South-even-faster Ellis case, and whatever it was that was going on between Fiona and me.

But, despite these large and pressing problems, something odd kept intruding into my thoughts. Something disturbing. Sheriff Pete was a pathetic, loudmouth failure who could bore for Britain. A small man with big ideas about himself, like a thousand losers just like him.

So why was it that, every time I thought of those intense, penetrating dark eyes, I got a chill down my spine and a feeling in my gut that I had just encountered something completely evil?

CHAPTER TWELVE

Before going into my office the next morning, I telephoned Handsome Jonny Cohen from a Central Station call box. I was probably being too cloak-and-dagger about the whole thing but, at the end of the day, what I was going to tell him could probably end up with someone's murder. Jonny was an okay guy in many ways but he was still a gangster, one of the Three Kings, and someone of a biblical disposition when it came to rewarding betrayal.

I knew I should have been walking away from the whole business, but I owed Jonny. Whoever was trying to save their neck by ratting out Jonny to the police was a traitor, and one thing I couldn't stand was a traitor. I tried to keep that thought foremost as I dialled, and not the thought that I was about to condemn a man to death.

Jonny and I did the pals' act, haven't-seen-you-in-a-long-time thing, before I got down to business. I told him to meet me down by the Queen's Dock at two-thirty that afternoon. When he protested that he was too busy I told him he wasn't going to be busy for the next twenty-five to thirty if he didn't meet me and hear what I had to say. I also told him to make sure he wasn't tailed.

'And come alone, Jonny,' I said before hanging up.

*   *   *

I didn't stop to take my hat and coat off when I called into the office. Archie was there and didn't seem to be doing much other than chain-smoking the air blue-grey.

'Can I borrow your car Archie?' I asked after we had briefly run through where we were with finding Lang, which wasn't far. 'I've got something to attend to and the Atlantic is acting up.' I didn't tell Archie about my meeting with Handsome Jonny Cohen. Archie, the ex-cop, was as straight as Donald Taylor, the serving officer, had ambitions to be crooked.

Archie shrugged, muttered some kind of gloomy assent and tossed me his car key. I grabbed my coat and hat and headed out.

It was true that my car hadn't been reliable over the last month or so, but the real reason I wanted to borrow Archie's ancient Morris Eight was that it was a lot less conspicuous than the Atlantic. I had something to do before I met with Cohen. The something I had to do was the thing I always did, what I did best: I was going to spy on someone else's life and I needed a car that would not be noticed.

Because the person I was about to spy on would be able to identify the Atlantic.

Even though I was in an unknown car, I parked as far along the street as I could while still being able to watch the house. There is nothing more unpleasant than when what you suspected was going to happen happens, and something lurched in my gut when I saw the Jowett Javelin pull up and a man get out. He was about the same age as me but shorter, with blond hair. He trotted up to the front door and rang the bell, and I saw he was dressed in a sports jacket and cavalry twills with the collar of his checked shirt open and a cravat at his throat. I recognized the uniform of the British middle-class male and I recognized the British middle-class male wearing it.

I recognized the little bastard all right.

When he came back out to the car he had Fiona with him. He held open the door and she climbed in. I watched the Javelin drive off, but didn't follow. There was no point. It wasn't their destination that mattered, it was the fact that they were making the journey together.

And, anyway, I had an appointment to keep with Jonny Cohen.

From where I stood and smoked, I could see that there was a huge hulk in the dry-dock: either the hull of a cargo ship or Twinkletoes McBride's bath tub. Whatever it was, it was rust-brown and grey-black in the November afternoon. The cold air rang with the clanging of metal on metal, and every five yards or so along the hull's flank there was the bright sodium fizz and shower of sparks from either welding or cutting gear. From this distance I couldn't tell if the object of the labour was construction or dismantling.

A dark green Bentley fastback purred to a stop behind me and a tall, hatless man in a camel military-style coat stepped out. He had thick, dark hair perfectly barbered and was absurdly good looking. In a world where your nickname usually derived from the weapon you used or whatever scars or disabilities you'd picked up in the course of your criminal career, in Cohen's case it was his movie-star looks that had earned him his epithet: Handsome Jonny.

We shook hands and walked along the quayside a little without speaking until eventually we came to some iron railings. Hunching his camel-coated shoulders against the cold damp, Cohen leaned his forearms on the railings, interlocked his pigskin-gloved fingers and looked out across to the dry dock.

'Okay, what is this all about?'

'That's quite some beast you've got there.' I nodded to where he had parked the Bentley. 'A pretty conspicuous set of wheels. Are you sure you weren't followed?'

'Why would I be followed?' he asked.

'Were you?'

'No,' he said emphatically. 'Now tell me what the hell this is all about.'

'You know I've been trying to go one hundred percent legit, don't you, Jonny?'

'Yeah . . . I guessed that from the way I've been dropped from your Christmas list.'

'Nothing personal,' I said. 'It's just that I've been trying to keep a low-profile and turn an honest buck. But I owe you big time and that's the only reason I'm here. I need your word that you'll never let on to anyone that this came from me . . .'

'Okay, Lennox, you've got my word. Now what's this all about?'

'I needed you to make sure you weren't followed because the police are probably keeping a close watch on you.'

'And why would they do that?' His tone darkened.

'Let's put it this way, they're maybe looking to pick up some bargains for Christmas. Jewellery for the wife, that kind of thing.'

Cohen said nothing, his expression opaque. It was the same empty face I guessed he would show the coppers when they came knocking on his door. The silence was broken by more ringing echoes of metal clanging over in the dry dock.

'They maybe think you could offer them bargain-basement prices and undercut, say, the jewellery stores in the Argyle Arcade.'

'Now where,' said Cohen, with deliberate slowness, 'would they have got an idea like that?'

'I get the impression it came from someone close to you. Maybe someone who's visited a jeweller's with you. Recently. Maybe last month, say.'

'You don't have a name?'

'My police contact is looking for payment for that information, but he needs someone in the middle and I've told him I'm not that kind of girl any more.'

'I need a name, Lennox. I'll pay for the name. Tell your copper that.'

'No can do, Jonny. And it's best for you if you have no dealings with him. If this ends the way I think it will, then he's the kind to get scared and blab. Anyway, you don't need the name, Jonny. All you need to know is that a link in your chain is about to break. I'm guessing that, in this case, it's a pretty short chain. And like the proverb says, it's always the weakest link. I reckon you can work it out from there.'

He nodded without taking his eyes off the hulk across the dock. 'Maybe you're right at that. Thanks, Lennox. Thanks a lot.'

'Jonny?'

'Yes . . .' He turned to face me, still leaning one elbow on the railings.

'Do me a favour. I really don't want anyone to come to . . . *permanent* . . . grief because of what I've just told you.'

'I can't promise you that. You know that. It's best you don't ask any more.'

It was my turn to be quiet. I'd spent more than a year house-cleaning my life, sweeping out the shadows and cobwebs of dodgy dealings, and I had just condemned a faceless man to a few hours in a darkened room with a torturer. Once they were convinced he'd told them exactly how much he'd passed to the police, they would give him something to ease the pain. Permanently.

'You know I appreciate this, Lennox. If there's anything I can do . . .'

'I didn't do this for a quid-pro-quo, Jonny,' I said. 'I would much rather have had nothing to do with it. It was information I wish I never had. But I did, and I had to tell you.'

'Well, if there's anything . . .'

A thought struck me. 'There is maybe something. If I gave you a photograph, could you have it copied and passed around your people? It's a missing person I'm looking for. I've been given the idea that he enjoys a dance and he's maybe been a face at one of the dance halls you own. His name is Frank Lang.'

'Sure. It's the least I can do.'

'There's a chance, maybe a good chance, that Lang isn't his real name. I don't know for sure what his game is, but he *could* be into blackmail and extortion. So maybe someone will recognize him in a professional capacity.'

'Get me the picture and I'll ask around. Personally. That means I'll get answers.'

'I should warn you that there is a chance that there's a political element to this. Lang's a Lefty. Or purports to be. Like I say, he might just be a con man and the politico crap is just part of his cover, but it's best to keep it discreet.'

Jonny nodded. I could have asked him for anything and he would have given it me. I had just saved him from spending most of the rest of his life behind bars.

And it had come at a small price: a man's life.

It was my day for clandestine meetings. Taylor, the semi-crooked copper on the cusp of becoming fully bent, had made a 'phone call to my office and told me he had something on the names I'd given him. I thanked him without mentioning that I had passed on for nothing everything he had told me about there being a snitch in Cohen's organization; I guessed he wouldn't appreciate my charitable nature. And when their informer turned out to be the deadest of dead-ends, it would be best that there was no trail to follow. Jonny had his weak link; Taylor was mine.

I could tell from Taylor's tone on the 'phone that he felt he had something worthwhile for me and we arranged to meet at McAskill's boxing gym in Dennistoun. The gym was a huge barn of a building of bolted-together corrugated iron that flaked dark green paint, and looked more like a shipyard shed than a centre of sporting excellence. Taylor and I used it a lot to meet; old man McAskill was glad of the fiver he got each time for his discretion and it was the last place on earth you would expect to come across a private and public detective exchanging notes – of one kind or the other. For that matter, it was also the last place on earth you would expect to come across any kind of boxing talent; but Dennistoun was the kind of place where, if you grew up there, you had an understandable urge to punch someone's face and there was a steady stream of Dempsey wannabes, from the brawlers and sluggers to those with genuine talent, and McAskill had a reputation for sorting the wheat from the chaff – even if he never made a penny out of it.

When we met, Taylor and I sat in McAskill's office-cum-locker-room at the back of the gym. I lit a cigarette to fend off the stale-sweat odours of jock-straps and singlets, and offered one to Taylor.

'You've got something worthwhile for me?' I asked.

'I have that, Mr Lennox,' he said. 'On those names you gave me . . . Andrew Ellis and Frank Lang . . . But I've drawn a blank with Tanglewood. Means nothing to me, means nothing to anyone I've talked to. But Ellis and Lang are much more interesting. You say these two people aren't connected?'

'They're not,' I replied. 'In fact I'm not interested in Ellis any more. Just Lang.'

'Oh . . .' Taylor looked like I'd stolen his fire. Or some of it, at least.

'Why? Are they connected?' I asked.

'You said Andrew Ellis was Hungarian by birth, so I decided to check out his immigration record and his proper name is, or was, András Elés. He was a kid when he came over. A baby.'

'I know most of that already. Anyway, like I told you, Ellis is a closed case now.'

'But you're still interested in this Frank Lang character?'

'Yes . . .' I failed to keep the impatience out of my tone.

'Well, seeing as I was in immigration records and the bird behind reception was being very cooperative, I thought I'd check to see if there were any records for Frank Lang.'

I leaned forward. 'And there was?'

Taylor nodded. 'Now, it's maybe not the Frank Lang you're looking for . . . in fact it would be a hell of a coincidence if it was . . . but there is one in the system. Also Hungarian by birth. It's not the same as Ellis who's been British most of his life. Until a couple of years ago this Frank Lang had to report regularly to his local police station as a resident alien.'

'Do you have any more on him?' I asked. 'Has he served as a merchant sailor?'

'That I don't know.'

'What was his original name?' I asked. 'I mean the Hungarian one?'

'You're not going to believe this,' said Taylor, 'but *Lang* is a very common Hungarian surname. Or so the lass in the records office told me. Just as common as it is in Scotland, but from a completely different origin. Anyway, I got details on this fella Lang . . .' Taylor reached into the inside pocket of his raincoat and handed me a handwritten sheet of paper. 'Again naturalized British, but, like I said, he's a much newer mintage.'

'How new?'

'Came over after the war. Been in Scotland for just shy of ten years. Goes by the name of Frank Lang but the real first name is Ferenc. I just thought that it was quite a coincidence . . . that you gave me two names to check out and it turns out that they're both Hungarian.'

I thought about what Taylor had told me. I took a couple of leisurely draws on my cigarette before answering.

'It is, isn't it?'

When I 'phoned the union's headquarters, Connelly wasn't there, so I had to settle for Lynch.

'You know how I asked for all and any information on Frank Lang that might help me find him?'

'I remember.' Lynch's tone was dull and flat on the line, as if I was boring him.

'Well, I know it's a small point, really, but mentioning the fact that he has an accent like Bela Lugosi would have been helpful.'

'What are you talking about, Lennox?' The tone still flat.

'Is or isn't Frank Lang a naturalized Briton and Hungarian by birth?'

'Well my guess would be that he isn't . . . Isn't Hungarian, isn't Romanian or Transylvanian or from the fucking Shetland Islands. He isn't even some Canadian smart arse.'

'You're saying he isn't foreign by birth?'

'How the hell should I know? But if Frank Lang is anything other than Scottish, then he disguises it well. No foreign accent, unless you count Wishaw as foreign. Anyway, it's not something we would have missed. It would have come up somewhere in his records.'

'Such as they are,' I said.

'Is that it?' asked Lynch. 'Is that the only reason you're 'phoning?'

I thought for a moment. It didn't make sense that no one else I had spoken to had mentioned Lang being foreign or having any kind of accent. And, of course, Andrew Ellis and his wife's involving me in their marital concerns had nothing to do with the union case whatsoever.

'It's something I needed to check out, Lynch. The leads you've given so far have been less than useful. And there is a Frank Lang in Glasgow who was born a Hungarian national. It's just a coincidence.'

'Is this how you approach your investigations? You pick whatever nationality happens to be in the news and see if you can tie the missing person into it? Before you ask, he isn't Egyptian either.'

An idea struck me. 'Does the word Tanglewood mean anything to you?' I asked.

'No,' he said and I could tell it didn't. 'Is that it? I hope you get yourself sorted out soon, Lennox, because all I'm hearing at the moment is a dog barking up the wrong tree.' He hung up.

So much for coincidences. The Ferenc Lang Taylor had tripped over was obviously someone different from the Frank Lang I was looking for.

I started to feel the pain of separation every time I thought about the cash I'd greased Taylor's palm with.

CHAPTER THIRTEEN

To say the least, my experience of the opposite sex in Glasgow had been very *eclectic*. Sex is perhaps one of the most unlikely but nevertheless effective ways of building a network of contacts; of expanding your experience of different walks of life. I am the first to confess that there had been a disproportionate number of barmaids, waitresses and actresses in the mix, but I had, nonetheless, met some interesting women from all walks of life during my time in Scotland.

One such contact had been a pretty, slim redhead who worked in a photographic studio close to the *Glasgow Herald* offices. She was a sweet girl who had married the boss when she had been too young and he had seemed mature and worldly wise. Worldly wise soon became plain old and I had held her hand for a while, at a time when the odd adultery had been one of the lesser of my moral infractions. I guessed she still had a thing for me and she was pleased to see me when I called, and agreed to run off a dozen prints of the picture of Frank Lang.

I had arranged with Jonny to mail him the photographs, keeping our visible contact to a minimum until the Arcade jewellery business cooled off, which we both knew would be many moons. In the meantime, he would get in touch one way or another to let me know if he had any news. It was a long shot, but Jonny owned the hottest dance halls in Glasgow; which was appropriate, because nothing came hotter than the cash he had used to buy them. If Frank Lang was a regular at any of the halls, then there was just a chance that one of Jonny's people would recognize him.

On the Friday morning, I dropped Archie and Twinkletoes off at the hire place in Charing Cross where, as usual, they picked up the van for the wages run. They were the oddest looking pair, that was for sure: Archie with his usual hangdog look and dry wit, Twinkletoes stretching the stitching on his best Burton off-the-peg and exuding earnest eagerness from a face that looked like he'd used it to beat someone to death.

Seeing them together was a disconcerting experience, which reassured me, hoping that they would have the same effect on any would-be robbers. Hiring the van each week meant we got preferential rates, but it still cut into the profit of the job and was, potentially, a security risk. Another reason for me to lose the Atlantic for something more reliable and substantial that could be used for the wages run.

I left them to it and headed back into town.

When you scratched the surface – and you really had to scratch – Glasgow was surprisingly cosmopolitan. Probably because it was such a major world port and a gateway between Europe and the Americas. There were significant populations of Jews, Irish, Poles and Italians, and the city's map was dotted with various clubs and societies representing expatriate, émigré and immigrant groups. As I already knew, there was the aptly-named Canadian Club in Woodlands Terrace, not far from Connelly's union headquarters; the *Cercle de Français de Glasgow* and the *Casa d'Italia* were to be found at separate addresses in Park Circus;

'You know?' There was genuine surprise, and worry, in her eyes. I noticed again how pale she had become. And tired looking. I consoled myself with the fact that her betrayal must have been costing her sleep.

'Yes, Fiona. I know. I've seen him.'

'Seen who?' Confusion swept away the surprise and worry.

'You know who. James White.'

'Oh . . .' she said. 'Jim . . .'

'Yes, Jim,' I said bitterly. 'Brother of the dear departed Peter White. I've seen him around. I saw you in his car. I thought he had given up sniffing around but it would appear that there was something worth sniffing about for.'

Fiona's face hardened. There was no hint of guilt or remorse in her expression, just anger. Resentment.

'Who the hell do you think you are to tell me who I can or cannot see? Jim is Elspeth and Margaret's uncle and he is entitled to come and visit the girls . . . to visit *me* . . . whenever he wants. He's all the family the girls have.'

'Don't be naïve, Fiona . . . you know he's been after you for years. He's not hanging around because he has some sense of avuncular duty. But this isn't just about him. It's about *us*. Things haven't been right between us for over a month and you expect me to believe that his reappearance on the scene has got nothing to do with it?'

'I don't give a damn what you think, Lennox. Nothing I do has got anything to do with you.' Her voice was raised now. Shrill. She composed herself and dropped it down a tone. 'This is a family. My family. There are things about holding a family together that someone like you could never, ever understand.'

'Really? And what is "someone like me"?'

'I'm too tired for this,' she said, but the fire still burned in her eyes. 'I told you I couldn't be the kind of woman you want me to be. I can't give you what you want.'

'I would have thought that I'm the best judge of what I want. And I do want you, Fiona. You know that. I've made that clear to you, haven't I? But I'm not competing for you. And especially not with that little cretin. You say you can't be the woman I want . . . isn't it more the truth that I'm not the man *you* want?'

It was then that Fiona did something that took me by surprise. She reached up and placed her hand on my cheek and looked at me for a moment, wordlessly, the fire gone from her eyes. It was a gesture that should have reassured me, put my mind at rest, but the tide of sadness that washed across her expression did exactly the opposite.

'I can't talk about this just now, Lennox. There are more important things, bigger things than you and me to be thought about. To be sorted out. I'm sorry if I've hurt you, I really am, but there's nothing I can do about it.'

'Fiona, I don't understand . . .'

'Nor do I. I don't understand either. But sometimes things are the way they are and there's nothing we can do about it.'

'Things? What things?'

She let her hand drop and stepped back from me. 'I want you to know that this has nothing to do with Jim. You're wrong to think that.'

I shook my head. No matter how she dressed it up, I knew what was going on.

'I've got to get back to the girls . . .' she said. I made to stop her but checked myself. She turned and went back down the stairs, and I stood, arms hanging at my sides, watching her go.

CHAPTER FOURTEEN

While Jonny Cohen was checking out his places, I did a tour of the remainder of Glasgow's dance halls. For a century, Glasgow had been the workshop of the British Empire. As the Empire had grown, so had Glasgow to become the second most populous city in Britain and by far the most densely inhabited. It had been a city that, for most of its history, had rung with the sound of iron and steel being hammered, bent, moulded and fused. An expanding Empire had meant the shipyards and the factories had belched ever more smoke into the air as they swallowed ever greater numbers of workers. And to feed the factories and yards, the city had piled people on top of each other – literally – in rows of soot-black tenements. Glasgow had been a city of hard, grimy toil. And on a Saturday night, it liked to wash the grime off for a few hours and pretend it was somewhere more glamorous. On a Saturday night, Glaswegians danced.

They also drank, vomited and fought, but at least they cleaned up nice first.

It was a ritual in Glasgow to dress as much like a movie star as you could and head off to one of the various dance halls. All of which meant knowing Frank Lang liked to dance was as much use as knowing fish liked water. But, in the absence of news from Jonny and with no other lead to follow, other than the long shot that Lang was the Hungarian Donald Taylor had found in the records, I decided to do the rounds of the halls. If nothing else, it would take my mind off all of the other crap that was going on in my life at that moment.

I did the Grand Tour, starting with the city centre ballrooms: the Playhouse in Renfield Street, the Berkley and St Andrew's Hall in Berkley Street, the Locarno and the Astoria in Sauchiehall Street, the Albert in Bath Street. Nothing. I knew a few of the doormen and swapped the odd lewd remark and off-colour joke, as you do, and, if nothing else, my rounds helped maintain a network of contacts I'd built up over the years. The dance hall staff had been useful in many of the cases I'd worked on of wandering husbands or wives. It never failed to amaze me how some men – and women for that matter – believed that for infidelity to go unnoticed, all you had to do was conduct your illicit courting in a different dance hall less than a mile and a half away from your home and in view of a couple of thousand fellow Glaswegians.

But no luck tonight. Lang's photograph didn't spark any flames of recognition.

The Locarno was probably the most popular of the dance halls and I asked the doormen if it was okay for me to take a five-minute walk around the place, just to see if my luck would change. They agreed, and I weaved my way between tables and around the dance floor. The place was packed and fumed with cheap perfume and pomade while the big band on stage did violence to *Love is a Many Splendored Thing*. The Locarno was like an alien planet, its atmosphere thick and blue-grey with smoke under the sparkle of a glitterball sun. Adrift in an ocean of cheap suits and imitation Perry Como and Liz Taylor hairstyles,

I realized that I was on a fool's errand: even if Lang was in here, I stood no chance of spotting him.

I was making my way out when I spotted someone whom I did recognize, however: Sylvia Dewar was sitting at a table near the wall. She didn't see me as she was engaged in intimate conversation with a man who was definitely not her husband. They must have been discussing the price of their next drink because, from the angle of her arm as it disappeared beneath the table and from the expression on her friend's face, I got the impression she was checking his trouser pocket for small change. I decided not to go over and introduce myself, just in case she felt like shaking my hand.

I thought of Dewar, driven to the brink of reason by suspicions he chased like ghosts, and felt sick. Then I thought of myself and felt sicker.

The Atlantic began acting up and it took me a few turns to get it started before driving south, across the river, and down to the Plaza in Eglinton Toll. Same story: no one knew Lang.

Back across the Clyde I checked out the Palais de Dance in Dennistoun and finished up at the Barrowland.

And it was outside the Barrowland that the Atlantic decided to give up the ghost. The Gallowgate is not the kind of place you want to be stranded at night, or any other time of day for that matter, and when my repeated oaths did nothing to get the car started, I got out and opened the hood so I could swear at the engine more directly. When that didn't work, realizing I'd exhausted my mechanical expertise, I locked up the car. I looked up and down the Gallowgate. It was nine-fifteen, and the street was empty. I decided to head back across to the Barrowland to ask if I could use the 'phone.

I was still on the other side of the street when I saw them.

The couple had spilled out from the ballroom and even from that distance I could see – and hear – that whatever the guy's intentions were, the girl wanted no part of it. There again, Glaswegian courting rituals had an elegance and charm to make the average mate-clubbing Neanderthal seem like Charles Boyer; but I could see that this was all wrong and the girl was desperately trying to free herself from the man's grip on her elbow.

A solitary car slowed down as it passed, but the guy yelled obscenities at it and it drove on. Other than me, there was no one else in the street. It was too late for people to be arriving at the dance hall and too early for the crowds to be spilling out onto the street. From what I could see, the guy was trying to drag the girl around the side of the dance hall. It was a distraction I could have done without, but the Canadian in me exerted himself and I walked purposefully across the road towards them.

The man had his back to me and I had just reached them when he slashed her across the face with the back of his hand. I grabbed him by the shoulder and spun him around.

'Take it easy, friend,' I said, but I was taken aback for a second. 'Oh . . .' I said. 'It's you . . .'

'Aye . . . it's me,' said Sheriff Pete, without a trace of his cod-American accent. Snakes of oiled black hair hung across the pale brow and as his eyes locked with mine, they burned with a cold, dark fire. 'Stay the fuck out of this. It's not your business.'

I looked at the girl, still desperately trying to wriggle free from his grasp.

'Help me, mister . . .' she pleaded. 'Please help me.'

'Let her go.' I crushed the cheap gabardine of his coat and

pulled him away from her. Then, I said to the girl, 'On you go, love. I'm going to have a little chat with Pete here.'

I watched her run all the way to the junction of Bain Street, where she disappeared around the corner. She had run as if her life had depended on it and I knew she had seen in Pete's black eyes the same thing I had seen that night in the Horsehead. I let him go.

'I think you need to calm down, fella,' I said as soothingly as I could. But the dark fire still burned in his eyes.

'Who the fuck do you think you are?' he said, and I knew then how this was going to have to end. 'Sticking your nose into my fucking business. You think you're so fucking great, don't you? Big man, are you?'

'Well, truth be told I'm more of a man than you are,' I said, still calmly. 'I don't feel the need to knock women about. And anyone who does is less than a man.'

'What? Her?' He jerked his head mockingly in the direction the fleeing girl had taken. 'That hoor? She was in there, in the dance hall. That place is no more than a shagging shed and tarts like her go there for one thing and one thing only. They're all sluts. They only want one fucking thing, then they make out they're virgins.' He stepped forward and looked up at me, doing his best to push his face into mine. I was tempted to ask if he wanted me to find a crate for him to stand on, but I decided it wouldn't do much to defuse the situation.

'You think you're so fucking big, don't you?' he hissed at me. 'A big fucking man. Let me tell you, you're a nothing. A fucking nobody. But I'm somebody. No one is ever going to remember you. Nobody's going to give a shit about you.'

'But I suppose *your* name is going to be carved into immortality, is that it?'

'Aye. That's right. No one is *ever* going to forget my name. I'm going to have a big name all right. I already have, it's just that nobody knows about it . . . yet. But they will. They'll remember all right. People are going to remember my name and my face long after I'm dead. You can bet on it.'

'Okay, fine. I get it: in my old age I'll tell my grandkids I knew you. Now why don't you go home and cool off, that's a good boy. But take the opposite direction from your girlfriend.'

He sighed, took a step back from me and let the tension ease from his shoulders.

'Okay . . .' he said dejectedly, as if defeated. It was this sudden and complete change of demeanour, intended to put me off my guard, that alerted me to his real intention. But even with me being ready for it, when he made his move it was so fast and expert that he managed to catch me on the side of the head. Not just a fist, and I felt a trickle of blood from my temple. He swung again and I saw something metal flash in the streetlight.

I slammed a kick into the middle of his abdomen, just the way they'd taught me in the army, and he didn't have enough weight to stay on his feet. I followed through on his fall and dropped down on top of him, squeezing the air out of him with my knee on his chest and pinning the hand with the weapon in it to the asphalt. I was relieved to see that it was a short length of steel tube and not a razor. I smashed the heel of my right hand into his nose and gouts of blood spurted from the nostrils. Then I started to punch him. Over and over and over. This wasn't like the episode with Dewar in Sauchiehall Lane: I was dealing with a bad bastard here who walked around with a weapon in his pocket. So I kept hitting him.

I was still hitting him when the two uniformed coppers hauled me off.

CHAPTER FIFTEEN

They threw me into a cell on my own, although the previous occupant was still there in spirit if not in substance. I sat on the edge of the bed contemplating how long someone would have to go without bathing and how much cheap hooch you would have to have in your system to stink a place out like that.

I was pretty pissed with the way things had turned out. Sure, they had chucked Sheriff Pete into a cell further down the block, and I could hear him giving forth in his fake American accent to the custody sergeant as if they were long lost buddies, but I knew things didn't look too good for me. I'd banged Pete up bad enough for them to call out the police surgeon and, after all, it had been me they'd had to haul off of him, and I had no witnesses to back up my side of events. Even the girl Pete had terrified had disappeared into the night.

In all of my time in Glasgow, despite several brushes with the police and having gotten involved in all kinds of dodgy goings-on, I had managed to keep my dance card unmarked. And now, all because of a psychotic little loudmouth, I was going to chalk up an aggravated assault charge and probably thirty days in chokey.

But things never turn out the way you expect.

I had only been in the cell for an hour when the custody

sergeant opened up and told me to follow him. That was confusing enough, but he had tied it up in ribbons: he had said *please*.

There were two other uniformed coppers waiting at the custody desk, one with inspector's pips on his shoulders. Again, I got the polite treatment, and I formed the distinct feeling that the custody sergeant would have liked to shake my hand.

'Have you found the girl he was harassing?' I asked.

'No, Mr Lennox,' said the inspector. *Mr.* 'Unfortunately we haven't. But let's just say your story is consistent with what we know about your chum. Unfortunately we can't charge him with anything either, but we'll keep the little shite overnight, anyway.'

'He's no chum of mine. Am I free to go?'

'Aye . . . you are, Mr Lennox. But we have a favour to ask . . . would you mind coming across to St Andrew's Square?'

'You want me to go to police headquarters? At this time of night?'

The beefy custody sergeant leaned his stripes on the desk. 'CID would like to talk to you. About chummy in there, if you don't mind.'

'It really is important . . .' the inspector added. 'I can't tell you why, but it is.'

I shrugged. 'Sure,' I said. 'Always happy to help . . .'

The streets were empty and shades of slate and black, sleek in the early morning rain, as we drove through them. I was dog tired, but nevertheless enjoyed the unusual experience of travelling in the back of a police Wolseley without the encumbrance of handcuffs.

When we arrived at St Andrew's Square, I was conducted into

a normal room, not a cell, with a table and four chairs. They left me in it for five minutes until a policewoman came in with a large china mug of tea for me. The five-star treatment was beginning to make me itch.

As I sipped the too-sweet tea, the door opened to reveal Jock Ferguson. I was genuinely surprised to see Jock. He was a nondescript sort of man, tall and lean and with a hooded look and tired eyes.

'I hear you've been administering justice on our behalf, Lennox.'

'What can I say? There was a maiden in distress and my armour was shining. You seem to be taking the chivalry thing a bit far yourself, Jock. You really turn out of bed at this time of night because I got myself lifted?'

'Your celebrity isn't that great,' he said, offering me a cigarette. 'It's the fellow you roughed up that we're interested in. Or to be more truthful, *I'm* interested in. I think he's a killer. One of the kind that do it because they enjoy it. But my colleagues think I'm off down the wrong track because we've already got somebody else lined up for the murder.'

'Well, that must be it,' I said ingenuously. 'I know that the City of Glasgow Police never make mistakes.'

Ferguson gave me a look.

'I don't know what I can tell you about him, Jock,' I said. 'I don't really know him.'

'I know, I've read your statement. You say you've only met him once before?'

'Met, once; but I saw him in the Horsehead once or twice before that.'

'And you say he bought you a drink? Why would he do that?'

'Because I have ears, Jock. Sheriff Pete's the kind of loser who'll make friends with anyone who'll listen to that fake accent. He claims he's American. American my ass.'

'Actually, he is. He was called up for National Service and he got out of it because the US Army have prior claim. So he ended up dodging both.'

'You're kidding me?'

'No kidding. He was born in New York then lived in Detroit till he was seven. Then his parents moved back to Britain. Coventry. Then he moved up to Motherwell. So the cod Yank accent is only half cod. Apparently he had a lot of it beaten out of him at school. What did he talk to you about?'

'Just that he was a big shot. That he's just done nine years in Peterhead. That he was a real tough guy and a bank robber but that's not what he'd been in for, that he's been framed for something else.'

Jock Ferguson snorted, his expression the kind you had if you'd eaten a bad clam. 'Our friend likes to sneak into women's bedrooms, wake them up and beat them over the head with a metal pipe . . .' He nodded to the weal on my temple. 'Like the one he clobbered you with. Then he pulls their pants down. He's a sick, sick bastard. He did the time in Peterhead for the beatings and indecent assaults and he's been done for rape in the past. I tell you, Lennox, you intervening when you did saved that girl from Christ knows what.'

I took it all in. I remembered the custody sergeant's approving look. Sheriff Pete was the kind of creep that everyone wanted to see get a hiding. Cops, citizens and crooks alike.

'So what is it you have him in the frame for?' I asked.

Ferguson leaned forward, resting his elbows on the table and locking me with an earnest stare. 'You and I have known each other a few years now and we've been reasonably straight with each other. Well, I'm asking for a favour, and if it sounds like I'm trying to warn you off, then I'm not. I'm asking you, as a personal obligement, to walk away from this and forget it ever happened. Don't talk to anyone about it and, most of all, don't have anything more to do with that piece of shit we've got locked up over there. I need to ask you a couple of questions that aren't going to sound important but, believe me, they are. I need to get straight answers from you and afterwards I need you to keep your nose out of this whole business.'

'Sounds big,' I said.

'You have no idea. Do I have your word?'

I had been warned off a dozen times by coppers to keep my nose out of cases, but my natural curiosity – and resentment of anybody telling me what not to do – had always gotten the better of me. This was different, I could tell.

'You've got it, Jock. Now what is it you want to know?'

'He told you he was a bank robber and safe-cracker?'

'That's right.'

'Any details?'

'No. None. It would all have been crap anyway.'

'And he bought you this drink?'

'Yeah. A whisky. I couldn't get out of it.'

'And you say he paid for it out of a wad of cash?'

'Only after he waved it around for half an hour for all to see.'

'What kind of cash? I mean the age and denomination of the notes?'

I gave Ferguson a look.

'Seriously, Lennox, try to remember. It's important.'

I thought for a moment, trying to rebuild the picture in my head. 'Now you come to mention it, they were all brand new notes. Crisp new fivers.'

Ferguson's expression changed to something that I felt in the back of my neck. Whatever it was he wanted, I'd just given him it.

Coming home at two-thirty in the morning was something I hadn't done for a while. As I knew it would be, Fiona's apartment was in darkness. No point in me tapping on her door for a wee small hours heart-to-heart. Even if that was exactly what I felt like doing.

I felt even more like a heart-to-heart when I reached my rooms and found an envelope addressed to me in Fiona's handwriting pushed under the door.

I took it through to my small living-room and, switching on the table light, sat down and opened the letter. Here, at last, I thought, was the explanation I had been waiting for.

Except the envelope didn't contain any explanations. Instead it held a glowing reference for me as a tenant. And a one month notice to quit my flat.

I had intended to march down first thing the following morning, dismissal notice in hand, and challenge Fiona to give me a good reason – any reason – for her asking me to leave. But when she answered the door, she looked so pale and drawn and tired that the fight went out of me. Her pretty eyes above the high cheekbones were shadowed, as if she hadn't slept at all the night before. There was something about her frailty, about the obvious pain I was somehow causing her, that struck me harder than anything she could have said. I told her I was sad she felt the way she did but I would, of course, honour her wishes. The only thing I asked for was that we had a chance to talk; to meet somewhere away from the house to talk the whole thing through. She was too important to me for me to just walk away from, I told her. Whatever it was that had gone wrong, I wanted a chance to discuss it.

'Okay,' she said softly. 'But not for a while. I need to get some things sorted out first. It may be quite some time, Lennox, but I will explain. I promise you I'll tell you everything, when the time's right.'

CHAPTER SIXTEEN

Looking for another place to stay was a distraction I could have done without, but I followed the logic that a new flat might just be something I might actually manage to find. I certainly wasn't having any success in locating Frank Lang.

I took the morning off to look at places I'd circled in the local classified ads. Circled, then crossed out. The ones that weren't cold and grubby were run like borstals by middle-aged landladies who were probably on some Israeli wanted list. I knew I had time to look around, but staying on longer than necessary at Fiona's would be unpleasant for both of us.

The last place of the morning – a basement flat in a West End tenement – started me seriously considering a boat ticket back to Canada.

At least there would be no danger of romantic involvement with the landlady there: she lived in the street-level apartment above the flat for rent and was a short, stocky woman in brogues, with pitch-black hair coiled in a bomb-proof permanent and whose too-pink make-up powder had gathered in tiny clumps on her incipient moustache. Zapata in drag showed me the flat while quizzing me about my religious allegiances with what she clearly thought was undetectable subtlety. The basement flat was clean, but dark in the November morning and smelled dank;

at the front it had bars on windows that looked out on nothing but a sooty brick wall and the steps leading up to street level.

Life in Glasgow above street level was grim enough and the idea of a subterranean existence there plunged me into near-pathological depression.

I was pretty dejected and took my circled classifieds to a coffee bar with steamed up windows in Byres Road, where I sat over a cup of bitter froth, desperately trying to seek out alternatives. There was one. But it was so absurd I laughed out loud. I circled it anyway.

'It is an awful day, isn't it?'

A man in his thirties, still hatted, sat down at my table. I noticed he hadn't brought a coffee over from the bar.

'Terrible,' I said. I drained my coffee. 'At least it's not snowing. Excuse me . . .'

The guy at the table placed his hand on my forearm as I stood.

'Please, Mr Lennox. I'd appreciate a moment of your time.'

I looked at him but didn't sit. I also took in the two other men sitting at the table behind my new friend. They sat with untouched coffees, watching me. I sat back down. A busy Glasgow café wasn't somewhere they could pull a stunt and I was safer here than out on the street.

'You have been asking around about one of our friends, Ferenc Lang, I believe.' He took his hat off and laid it on the table, revealing a wedge of thick, blond hair. He had a long, thin face with a long nose that had a kink in it where it had been broken at some time or another. Strangely, it didn't make him look tough, but seemed to add to his faintly aristocratic look. When he spoke, there was something foreign flowing through it. I guessed it was the Danube.

'Or Frank Lang, as he seems to prefer these days,' I said. 'Yes, I would like to speak to him.'

'I'm afraid that won't be at all possible, Mr Lennox. Mr Lang is a very private person and he does not appreciate your intrusion into his affairs. For good reason, I have to say.'

'So you and your chums here have come along to warn me off . . . is that it?'

'No. Not warn. Ask. We would be obliged if you forgot all about Mr Lang.'

'I'm afraid that's not possible. You see, naturally inquisitive as I am, my interest in Frank Lang is professional, not personal. I'm being paid to find him. But I guess you already knew that.'

He nodded the long head slowly, as if considering my words carefully. 'By whom, may I ask?'

'You may not. Confidentiality is everything in my business, but I'm sure Mr Lang could have a pretty good guess about who's looking for him and why.'

'Perhaps he could,' said the blond man. His English was near perfect: near, but not quite.

'You are Hungarian?' I asked.

'I am Hungarian. As is Mr Lang, as you already know. He is also a great patriot. You know what is going on in our country at the moment?'

'Of course I do. Exactly what kind of patriot are you? I'm trying to work out how much red there is in the flag of your particular brand of patriotism. Do you work for the Hungarian government?'

'Now what makes you ask that?'

'Just that this little encounter . . . please, don't get me wrong, charming as it is . . .' I held up my hands and smiled appeasingly. 'But this little encounter seems to coincide with me talking to Mr Tabori, the Hungarian consul in Edinburgh. Now what was it that I said to him that has provoked your interest? My asking about Ferenc Lang, or Frank Lang, or whatever he wants to call himself – or was it because I mentioned Tanglewood?'

'Mr Lennox, I understand that in your particular line of business, you have to have a suspicious mind, but let me assure you that I am not here to issue ultimatums or threats.'

'Just appeal to my better nature? Then why do you have two goons with you? And why didn't you call into my office?'

'People are dying in Hungary. Others are being thrown into prison or driven from their homes. The Soviets are sending a message to the whole of Communist Europe that any move towards liberalization will be crushed mercilessly. And that message, Mr Lennox, is being written in Hungarian blood. If we seem *cautious* in how we approach you, it is simply because we have to be. We are watched. The communists would give anything to find Ferenc Lang. And they would use any means to do so. And anybody.'

'You're telling me that I'm being used as an instrument of the great socialist revolution?' I laughed.

'Ask yourself who you are working for. And what they are paying you. Your enquiries could end badly for a truly good man.'

'And what do I get out of it if I do drop this enquiry?'

The blond man laughed bitterly. 'I see ... it's like that. We don't have much, but I suppose we could reimburse you for your trouble.'

I held up my hand. 'I wasn't canvassing for a bribe. I'll think about what you've said. What's your name?'

'Mátyás will do. It's Hungarian for Matthew.'

'Well, Mátyás, I understand that there is a lot of stuff going on with your people at the moment, but we're on the shores of the Black Clyde, not the Blue Danube, and what I've been asked to investigate is a simple case of theft. I have been engaged to avoid the embarrassment, principally to your friend Frank Lang, of having to get the police involved. Now, I'm sure you would much rather that the police did not start sticking their noses into you and your friends' goulash club.'

'Theft?' Mátyás looked genuinely confused. 'Ferenc Lang is accused of having stolen something?'

'That's a surprise to you? He is. And there's a definite time limit on how long I have to return the property and *resolve* differences between the parties concerned.'

'This is nonsense. Absurd. Do you not see that this accusation is trumped up? A pretence to get you to pursue Ferenc and find him for them?'

'I admit it could just be a possibility,' I said. I didn't want to tell him that the chances were his Lang wasn't really the one I was after. 'So here's the deal . . .' I pushed my card across the table to him. 'Telephone me at my office to arrange a time and a place for me to meet with Frank Lang. I'll show him mine if he shows me his. And you have my word I won't discuss any of this with my client until after Lang and I have met. But one thing: let's make the meeting in a public place.'

'How do we know that you won't inform your client, or the police, if it's supposed to be a criminal matter?'

'You don't. But I've given you my word and I'm a Canadian. We make Boy Scouts and Quakers look like ne'er-do-wells.'

He looked puzzled. I had clearly stretched his English or Middle European sense of irony to its limit.

'You just have to trust me,' I said.

He looked at me for a minute, then pocketed the card before standing up. His two escorts did the same.

'All right, Mr Lennox. We will be in touch. I doubt if Mr Lang will agree to this, but I will put it to him nevertheless.'

'What I want most of all is to have the stolen item returned to me, so that I can give it back to the party concerned.'

'I don't know to what you are referring, Mr Lennox, but I shall put everything you have said to Mr Lang. In the meantime, I would be obliged if you could desist from your enquiries. I want you to understand that it is not you or your interest we fear, but that you may draw the attention of others who do pose a significant danger.'

'Let me guess . . . I would be advised to drop it for my own sake too?'

'You have nothing to concern yourself about from us. But yes, there are forces at work here that you too would be advised to avoid.' He gave a valedictory nod of the head that was so formal I missed the sound of clicking heels. Maybe he was wearing crepe soles.

I watched them go. And they watched me watching them. They were obviously itchy about being followed. Like someone else in my recent past.

I ordered another cup of bitter froth and tried to remember what I had done with a page I had torn out of my notebook, the page on which I'd written the address of where I had seen Andrew Ellis and the girl.

CHAPTER SEVENTEEN

I wasn't sure what kind of welcome deposed Hungarian premier Imre Nagy was going to get when he arrived in Moscow, but I guessed it would be marginally warmer and less awkward than the encounter I had with Fiona White in the hallway.

It was obvious that she had been avoiding me, and given the effort she made for our eyes not to meet, I guessed that she wouldn't be making contact with any other part of my anatomy for the foreseeable future. To be honest, I was less than grown-up about it myself and the few words I had exchanged with her had been brusque and ill-mannered. I told her not to worry, I would be out of the flat as soon as I possibly could, and that I had already viewed some alternative accommodations. To be fair, I had caught her off-guard, having come home in the middle of the day. I excused myself with the charm of an adolescent and went up to my rooms.

An odd thing about me, something that many would find unexpected, was that I was pretty fastidious when it came to neatness. Not just in dress, but in every aspect of my life. I had always been a little like that, but it had become something of an obsession during the war. My military career in itself could have been described as untidy, and – after I had been *encouraged* to resign my commission – there were certainly more than a few loose ends left in Hamburg that the military police had taken an unhealthy interest in. Nevertheless, I had developed this habit of keeping myself and my immediate surroundings in order. I put it down to the experience of war, or more particularly the type of experience of war that I and most of the First Canadian Army had had. People talk about the harsh reality of war, but when you got right up close to it – and I had gotten as close to it as it was possible to get – war is so brutal and chaotic that it seems unreal. Maybe my orderliness had been all about locking out the chaos and misery by keeping one part of my life controlled and ordered.

Whatever the reason, while I might have come close to being cashiered for black market activities and other peccadillos of one sort or another, I would never have been brought up on a charge of having my tunic unbuttoned.

So, when I went into my rooms, I had to negotiate around the crates and chest into which I had already started to pack my books and other stuff, in preparation for quitting my flat. I was yet to empty the wastepaper basket and I found the Garnethill address I had torn out of my notebook.

Even though the day was yet to reach the pivot between morning and afternoon, the November day outside was gloomy and I switched on the table lamp. I took the crumpled note over into the pool of yellow light and smoothed it flat on the occasional table.

The Staedtler-Moran International Company Limited.

The name certainly did not sound Hungarian, but it certainly wasn't typically Scottish either. There was no clue to what particular trade the Staedtler-Moran International Company Limited plied and there had been no signs of life when I had passed Ellis and his dishy foreign friend that night.

But it would still be worth a look.

*　　*　　*

I knew of a solicitor whose offices were not far from Garnethill and I went in with the name of his firm scribbled down on a piece of paper. My plan was to claim to be lost and looking for the solicitor, clearly having gotten the address wrong. The genuine office was far enough away for no one at Staedtler-Moran to recognize the name, but if someone did get suspicious, or decided to be extra helpful by looking it up in the 'phone book for me, they would find a nearby solicitor of the name I claimed to be looking for.

In the event, the elaborate subterfuge was unnecessary.

There was no smog or dark to cloak my surroundings this time. In fact the clouds had parted but, if anything, the cold, hard sunlight seemed to etch the dark buildings with a harsher and more uncompromising hand. It took me a while to pinpoint the exact doorway again: Glasgow's smog created a palette and a landscape all of its own and things always looked disorientingly different in the clear light of day. Eventually a dulled bronze plaque informed me that I had again found Staedtler-Moran International.

I stepped into a fluorescent-tube-lit entry hallway of shiny green and white porcelain-tiled walls and a dull linoleum floor. In front of me, a flagged stone staircase arced up and into darkness. The offices of Staedtler-Moran were to my right and when I entered, I found a reception desk blanked off with opaque glass, with a kiosk type window at the far end. It was a common form of reception in Scottish commercial premises and it always made me feel I should be buying a railway ticket. A sign above a button instructed me to *Press for Attention*. I did.

The receptionist pulled open the small sliding section of window that allowed us to hear each other, but her face was framed in a circle of clear glass in the frosted pane. I could hear the clatter of typewriters behind her.

'May I help you?' She was a girl of about twenty-two or three and had clearly taken an instant shine to me, which always made things easier. I ran through my demi-fiction of looking for the solicitor's office and it became obvious she was not going to be the suspicious or inquisitive type. She was, bless her, as dim as she was homely and blinked at me through horn-rimmed bottle-bottom glasses that were so heavy that she had to continually push them back up her nose with mouse-like twitches while her mouth gaped slightly.

She did not, of course, recognize the solicitor's firm I claimed to be seeking and she explained that the Staedtler-Moran International Company supplied bakery equipment to 'bakeries throughout the Scottish Central Belt and beyond'.

'And what about the *International* in the name?' I asked. 'Do you have offices abroad.'

'Not really,' she said dully, as if worried that it might disappoint me.

'Do you sell equipment to bakeries in other countries?'

'No.'

'I see.'

'We have an office in Motherwell . . .' she chirped hopefully.

I thanked her and took my leave. She watched me balefully through the small clear circle in the frosted glass. I opened the door that led into the hall just as someone who must have come down the stairwell was leaving through the main door to the street.

My little goldfish was delighted when I reappeared at her window.

'Are there other offices upstairs?' I asked.

'Oh yes, but not the name you was looking for,' she said, again eager to please.

'I didn't notice a plaque outside for any businesses except yours,' I said.

'There's only one,' she said. 'It's some kind of small concern and I don't know its name. It's something to do with foreign languages, I think. Translations or something like that.'

'Okay . . .' I said as I headed back in haste to the main door, waving my thanks and leaving my homely little goldfish in her circle of glass.

I just made the street in time to catch a glimpse of the figure that had passed as I had opened the office door into the hallway. She was just disappearing around the corner at the top of the rise. I sprinted up the street to the corner, closing just enough space for me to keep her in sight when I rounded the bend without drawing attention to the fact that I was following her. I could have been wrong, of course, but it had been the odd mismatch of hat and coat that I had recognized more than anything else.

And her shape. I had not had a chance to see her face, but her figure looked right to me. As right as it was possible to be right.

There were, I had been told, whisky connoisseurs whose taste-buds were so attuned, they could identify each and every distillery; and wine buffs who could pin down a wine's source almost to the specific vine. When it came to appreciation of the female form, I displayed pretty much the same set of skills. Once a set of curves had registered with me, it wasn't just imprinted in my memory, it was card-indexed, cross-referenced, categorized and star-rated. Even though I had only ever seen it through the weight of her unfashionable coat, hers was one chassis that had been given its own reference section.

She walked with a steady pace, determined but not rushed, and it was no ordeal to follow her from behind, but I was concerned that there was no one else around on the street. Maybe I was flattering myself, but I felt pretty sure that if she got a good look at my face, she would recognize it as the one who had disturbed her and Ellis in the smog.

She crossed Sauchiehall Street and I trotted along behind her. There were more people about and I relaxed a little, feeling I could take better cover in the foliage of other pedestrians. When we reached Charing Cross, she walked directly to the taxi rank and I picked up the pace. I was on foot, having abandoned the Atlantic at almost exactly the same place as I had that night in the smog, and there was a real danger I was going to lose her if she jumped into a cab.

Which was exactly what she did. I sprinted to the next taxi in the rank and jumped into the back.

'Follow that car . . .' I said breathlessly.

The cabbie turned in his seat and presented me with the kind of leathery face that you could only cultivate in a boxing ring.

'Are you trying to be funny?'

'Right now, no . . . but I do have my lighter moments. Hurry up, or we'll lose them.'

'That taxi that that young lady just got into?'

'That's the one. What's the problem here?' I looked past him and through his windshield. Her cab had turned west along Sauchiehall Street and was about to disappear from view.

'Listen pal, this is the way it works: if you have a destination, then give it to me and I'll take you there. If not, get out of the cab.'

'I really need you to follow that taxi before we lose it, it's important.'

'I don't know what your game is, *sir*,' he said, his tone heavy with menace. 'But I'll repeat the way this all works: you give me a legitimate destination and I'll take you there. Then I charge you in accordance with the City of Glasgow Corporation's Hackney Fare Regulations: anywhere in the city for two shillings for the first mile, plus fourpence for each additional quarter of a mile, first five minutes of waiting free, thereafter fourpence for each completed period of five minutes. Luggage not exceeding fifty-six pounds in weight is free, excluding bicycles, perambulators and-or children's mail-carts. Maximum quantity of luggage one hundred and twelve pounds weight. Have you got it? If you've any complaints, please address them, quoting my driver number, to the Chief Constable, Traffic Department, twenty-one Saint Andrew's Street, Glasgow, C-one. Alternatively, you can shove them up your arse.'

I sighed and handed him a business card. 'I'm an enquiry agent and I'm on a case. Now would you *please* try to catch up with that taxi.'

'I don't care if you're Dick-Fucking-Barton . . . I'm not taking you to follow some lassie without her knowing. Try reading the Sunday papers, pal. With these murders going on, you're lucky I don't just take you straight to the polis.'

I sank back into the seat, the fight gone from me. A couple of months before, three woman had been shot to death in their beds, the kind of murder never committed in Scotland, and now all of Glasgow was looking over its shoulder for a crazed killer in the shadows.

'You sure are a by-the-book kind of guy, aren't you?' I said dully.

He replied by getting out of his cab and coming round to hold the door open for me.

'If you don't have a destination, *sir*, then I suggest, with the greatest respect, that you fuck off.'

'Is that the wording from the Regulations too?' I asked as I got out of the taxi.

'I'm paraphrasing.'

I looked along Sauchiehall Street. The cab was gone.

'Thanks a bunch, friend,' I said. I thought about getting him to drive me back to Garnethill, but the idea of paying him two bob stuck in my throat. I walked across Charing Cross and back towards where I'd left the car. At least this time, I thought hopefully, it wouldn't have been sabotaged.

I was half way up Garnett Street when I stopped to take in the view. The sun was still bright but now hung lower in the winter sky and the dark glass of Glasgow's smoke-hazed air split it into a spectrum of golds and reds. Standing there watching the sky above the city, I lit a cigarette and took a long, slow pull on it.

I should have known better than to indulge in reflective moments.

I was so busy meditating on how industrial pollution makes for great sunsets and savouring my slow smoke that I didn't notice until the last minute the brand new Rover as it gleamed to a halt beside me. I found myself flanked by a couple of brushed and polished burly types.

There are two types of heavy one was wont to encounter in my line of work: the professional criminal thug whose weight is all muscle and fist; then there are those who carry the weight of authority invested by the state. Policemen, mainly. I knew I was looking at the latter kind.

A third man slid out from the front passenger seat. He was taller but less built than the other two. His tailoring, unlike theirs, was the kind that was priced in guineas, not pounds. He was wearing a country set type herringbone-tweed overcoat and a matching flat cap. He wasn't wearing plus-fours – I checked, the thought having run through my head that this could have been a press gang for shooting party ghillies. From the outfit and the casually authoritative demeanour, I guessed that his education had involved dreamy spires and his school, like his tailoring, had been paid for in guineas.

He had also been enjoying a smoke and I didn't like the business-like way he dropped the cigarette onto the kerb and crushed it under the heel of a burnished Oxford brogue.

'Would you be so kind as to get into the car, Mr Lennox,' he said in an accent so cut-glass it made Waterford Crystal look slapdash. The heavy to my left showed me a warrant card. He was a policeman all right, but one of the secret denomination. But I guessed the public-school boy was slumming it. He was no Special Branch copper; he was something other.

'What's this all about? Are you arresting me?'

'Arresting you? Do we have to?' The public-school boy affected a look of confusion. 'I rather hope not, Mr Lennox. We simply require your help to clarify a couple of matters. I hoped you would be willing to help us and we would be able to do this without any fuss. Now, if you would be so kind . . .'

He opened the back door of the Rover for me. He did it very well; he must have watched his batman do it for him countless times before. It was nice to have been given the illusion that I had some choice in the matter and, shrugging, I got in and we drove off. As we did so, we passed my parked Atlantic and I turned to look back at it. A bit of me left in full view in the street.

As I sat in the back of the Rover, squeezed between the heavy shoulders of two pillars of the law, the thought struck me that it might end up being all of me that would be left visible.

CHAPTER EIGHTEEN

I wasn't surprised when we didn't head into police headquarters. Instead we drove into the city centre and pulled up outside a four-storey sandstone building in Ingram Street: one of those large, impressive, Art Deco-type edifices you found scattered through Glasgow. Alternating between the huge windows were large embossed copper panels set into the walls and I could imagine it had been some place before the caustic Glasgow climate had grimed the sandstone and turned the panels' rich copper to verdigris. Now it was just another city block you would walk by without noticing. Which was probably why it had been chosen by my new friends.

My escort had to ring to gain entry into a large, marble-flagged entrance hall of the type that seemed designed to announce your arrival by resonating and magnifying every footstep. After my public-school chum signed us in at a desk manned by two uniformed commissionaires, we echoed all the way to the cage elevator at the far end of the hall. We went up two floors and the corridor we came out into bustled with staff moving from office to office, but there was no indication of the business conducted here, other than a few of the offices seemed to be locked and unlocked by the staff as they came and went. There were no uniforms, police or otherwise.

'Excuse me for a few moments please, Mr Lennox, Roberts and Lindsay will get you comfortable . . .' He nodded to the two Special Branch heavies who eased me along the corridor. As he showed me into a room, one of them actually managed a smile; I appreciated the effort, because he looked seriously out of practice.

I was left alone in the locked room. A huge window looked out over the street and I guessed it was one of the expanses of glass I had noticed from the outside, between the huge wall panels. The room was empty except for a large table with a foolscap notebook sitting on it and four chairs. One of the walls had two vast maps on it: one of the Glasgow metropolitan area and the other of Scotland.

The door was unlocked and a young woman came in, setting a tray with a coffee percolator, two cups and saucers and a plate of Rich Tea biscuits on the table. I smiled; she ignored me and left, the door locking again behind her.

I walked over to the window. As I looked out over the city, the street lamps came on. In November in Scotland, latitude and climate conspired to squeeze afternoon into a mere sliver wedged between morning and night. I watched shoppers and office workers mill around on the street below and tried not to think of the careless freedom they enjoyed while I was locked in a room by a man without a name, in a building without a name.

Ten minutes later he came back in, on his own. Laying a buff file on the table, he asked me to sit and he did the same. He was one of those types who were practically impossible to age, having adopted at twenty a look that would stay with him till sixty. He was unremarkable but pleasant enough looking, and his lightly-oiled blond hair was immaculately combed back from a broad, high forehead and pale blue eyes.

'I know that your chums are policemen,' I said, 'but I'm guessing you're not.'

'Then your guess would be right, Mr Lennox. I am a humble civil servant and as such I have no powers of arrest or detention, but our colleagues in Special Branch supply us with the support, should we need it.'

'Am I detained?'

'Not at all . . . You're free to go whenever you choose, but it would most definitely be in your best interest to cooperate. Let me put it that way.'

I looked around the room. 'I didn't know you people had a place in Glasgow,' I said.

'We people?'

'Humble civil servants who may beg favours from Special Branch.'

'Quite . . .' He smiled. I got a better look at the by-the-guinea tailoring: an expensive houndstooth-check sports jacket over a mustard waistcoat, Tattersall shirt and camel-coloured corduroy trousers. The kind of country-wear worn by those whose idea of the country was Kensington Gardens. I noticed his tie: a pattern of alternating diagonal bands, broad black broken by a narrow white edged with a red pinstripe.

'We have only moved in here temporarily,' he explained. 'Needs must basis, you understand.'

'Your old regiment?' I asked, nodding towards his tie.

'Oh . . . this? Something like that,' he said airily. I never understood why his type always pretended to be dismissive of their school or military backgrounds, when they wore them around their necks. I had never felt the need to wear either my Rothesay Collegiate School for Boys tie or a regimental badge-emblazoned blazer. Both my old school and regiment probably appreciated my discretion.

'I was in the First Canadian, myself,' I said conversationally.

'Yes, Captain Lennox. I'm fully aware of what is in your service record. And what isn't.'

'I see. It's like that, is it? Why don't you tell me what this cloak and dagger malarkey is all about? And if we're going to get all chummy, I should at least know what to call you.'

'Oh . . . didn't I introduce myself?' He placed his hand on the breast pocket of his jacket, as if that was where he kept his name, like a bus ticket. 'I'm dreadfully sorry. My name is Hopkins.'

'Does that come with a prefix . . . Colonel . . . Major . . . Captain . . . ?'

'As I told you, I'm a civil servant. Civilian. Or at least I am these days.' He took a silver case from his pocket and offered me a cigarette, which I took.

'What can I do for you, *Mr* Hopkins?'

'These are troubling times. Take this unfortunate situation in Suez, or the current tumult in Hungary. Events in Hungary are coming to a regrettable close. Unfortunately for the Hungarians, Suez has taken everyone's eye off the ball.'

'But not your eye, that it?'

'I'm a Middle Europe, not a Middle East expert. I was never looking anywhere else. The Hungarians, like the Poles, misinterpreted Khrushchev's so-called *secret speech* and judged the Soviets would give them their freedom. The Poles played their hand much better and got their man Gomulka back in the premiership. But Gomulka didn't talk about breaking free of Moscow, Nagy did. This will all end very badly for the Hungarians.'

Hopkins stood up and poured coffee from the percolator into each of the cups. He held up the cream jug and I shook my head.

'But my interest is in what that can mean for us,' he continued. 'Our experts estimate that as many as a quarter of a million Hungarians will flee their native land over the next few months. That's more than two hundred thousand threats and opportunities.'

He handed me the black coffee.

'We picked you up because you were following a young lady we have an interest in. Her and her friends. Why were you following her?'

'I heard she has a good goulash recipe.'

'I believe you operate as some kind of private detective here in Glasgow, Mr Lennox.' Hopkins adopted a tone of measured impatience. 'I am assuming your interest in the young woman was professional? I do hope you don't mind me asking, it's just that we're aware of your significant *recreational* interest in the fair sex, shall we say.'

'You seem to be very well informed about me.'

Hopkins laid a proprietorial hand on top of the buff file. Whether it signified he felt owned the file or the subject of the file was hard to say.

'Why were you following the young lady?'

'Business, Mr Hopkins. Mine and not yours. You deal in secrets, I deal in confidences. I'm not prepared to betray a professional one on account of a cup of lousy coffee and a Rich Tea.'

'I see,' he said. 'I deal in facts, in information. One of the facts is that the Hamburg police – and our own Redcaps, for that matter – still have an open file going back to Nineteen Forty-five. A young man called Dietrich Holzmann was found floating face down in the Alster Lake with a broken neck. Holzmann was the front man in a major black-market opera-tion, but he had a partner. Not so much a silent partner, as an invisible one who was suspected to be an Allied officer stationed in Hamburg. British . . . or Canadian. The German police would really like to talk to that officer.'

'So this is how you win friends and influence people? By threatening them with the bent arm of the law?' I asked without ire. 'May I ask you a question?'

'Please feel free . . .'

'You spirited me off the street . . .' I looked at my watch, '. . . thirty-five minutes ago. You and I have been together for all but fifteen of those thirty-five minutes. You haven't once asked my name or to see some I.D., yet you are impressively well versed in every particular of my military service, both on- and off-the-record, and you seem to know all my personal details right down to my inside leg measurement.'

'We picked you up because you were going to compromise our surveillance of the girl. I didn't say that we were unaware of your involvement until today.'

'So, because I innocently stumble onto your cricket pitch, you threaten me with a free ticket back to Hamburg.' I stood up. 'If you have anything to pass on to the German police, the Redcaps, the Mounties or my tailor, then I suggest you do it. In the meantime I'm leaving . . .'

'You're free to leave if you wish,' he said. 'But, I would strongly recommend you stay and answer my questions. We both know we don't have to look as far as Germany to find something inconvenient in your past. There are answers to questions the City of Glasgow Police would be grateful to receive.' He paused, watching my face while his remained unreadable. 'You are a very special kind of man, Mr Lennox. Not unique, however . . . I have met you many times before. Different faces, different cities, different languages, but the same type of man.'

'And what type of man is that?'

'A man who leaves behind him a trail of dead men and broken hearts.'

'Dead men and broken hearts?' I smiled appreciatively. 'Very lyrical.'

'As a matter of fact, I did read it in a book. But that is exactly what you have left behind you. Here in Glasgow too. If you want, I can be very specific about the dead men part.'

I said nothing.

'Listen, this doesn't have to be about threats,' he cradled his coffee cup as if sitting in a vicarage parlour, 'There are also opportunities for us both.'

'What kind of opportunities?'

'We could use someone like you. On occasion. You have . . . *skills* . . . we could use. But, for the moment, I really do need to know why you were following our surveillance suspect. Then, hopefully, we can discuss opportunities for future cooperation – or at the very least get out of each other's hair.'

I weighed him up; Hopkins was as in control of the situation as it was possible to be. But, there again, he had had a lot of experience. The pattern on his tie told me he would be expert at getting more out of someone in five minutes with a cup of tea and a digestive biscuit than the average Glasgow copper could beat out of a suspect after a month of swinging a rubber hosepipe. I sat back down.

'So why *were* you following that particular young lady?' he asked again.

'The truth? No politics, no cloaks and no daggers. A marital fidelity case, plain and simple. I saw her with the husband in question. I was just following it up.'

'I see,' said Hopkins. 'We seem both to be in the business of assessing fidelity, of one kind or another. And you are working on this case at the moment?'

'I am ... I mean, I *was* ... It's complicated.'

'You are either being paid to follow this woman around Glasgow or you're not. I don't see anything complicated in that.'

'The wife paid me off. She said she was happy with her husband's explanation.'

'So why are you still following the girl? Why not the errant husband? If you are going to do some *pro bono* tailing, that would make more sense.'

I had the answer, of course: a simple coincidence involving two men called Frank Lang. But Connelly's union wouldn't appreciate being brought to the attention of someone like Hopkins.

'Look,' I said, trying to sound appeasing, 'I understand I've trodden on toes – but all that's happened is I've innocently stumbled into a much bigger deal than anything I'm interested in.'

Hopkins sat with his hand still resting on the file, his expression unreadable beneath the cloak of his polite smile.

'Okay,' I nodded again to his neckwear. 'Unless I'm mistaken, that's an Intelligence Corps tie. I'm guessing you're now with the Security Service or MI5 or whatever it is they call themselves these days and your job is to keep tabs on Johnny Foreigner on British soil. Am I right?'

'In spirit if not in substance. Who was your client?'

'You know I can't tell you that. But I promise you that whatever your interest in this girl or her chums, it has nothing to do with why I was following her.'

'My department does indeed deal with monitoring the activities of foreign nationals. Specifically émigré, refugee and other expatriate groups active within the UK.' He opened the file and slid a large head-and-shoulders photograph across the table to me. The woman I had seen with Ellis. In this official picture, however, her hair was scraped and tied back and her face was naked of make-up under the harsh, uncompromising light of a flashbulb. She still looked a knock-out.

'This is the woman you were following?'

I nodded. Hopkins slid a second photograph across to me.

'Do you recognize this man?' he asked, his eyes locked on my face.

I made a big deal of studying the photograph before shaking my head. Too big a deal, from the weary expression on Hopkins's face.

'You were seen talking to this gentleman in a café in the West End of Glasgow just two days ago. Listen, old boy, I really would rather avoid any unpleasantness so I would ask you not to insult my intelligence.'

'Okay,' I said. 'So I've seen him. But it wasn't an arranged meeting. He pulled the same stunt as you and introduced himself and made it clear he was pretty up-to-date with my social calendar too. So he followed me to the café and you followed him. You know something? I must wander about Glasgow blissfully unaware that I have an entourage bigger than the Queen's.'

'What did he discuss with you?'

'He asked me to keep my nose out of his business. I guess he knew that I'd seen my client's husband with her ...' I stabbed a finger at the photograph of the woman. It was a lie, of course, and I didn't mention that my call to Tabori the Hungarian consul was really what had spiked Mátyás's interest. I had to keep Hopkins away from my looking for Frank Lang for Connelly. But for all I knew, Hopkins knew all about that as well.

'And he told you his name?' Hopkins asked as he topped up his coffee cup.

'Just his first name. Mátyás. Matthew.'

'Yes . . . Mátyás Pasztor. He was a founding member of Petofi Circle . . .'

I shrugged.

'A group of writers and intellectuals who started off the protests against the Rakosi government in Hungary. Pasztor is a poet. He has organized his own émigré group here in Glasgow. The young lady you followed belongs to his group.'

'He doesn't sound like a dangerous alien,' I said.

'Probably not. But he is helping others escape from Hungary – and it would appear some chaff is getting through with the wheat.'

'What kind of *chaff*?'

'Let's just say undesirable elements. Undesirable on both sides of the Curtain.'

'Would one of those elements go by the name of Ferenc Lang?' I asked.

For a moment, Hopkins looked at me long and hard.

'I think, Mr Lennox, you had better tell me absolutely everything you know about Ferenc Lang.'

And I did.

CHAPTER NINETEEN

Two Frank Langs. There had been two of them all along.

I had lectured Pamela Ellis on how it was always best to apply Occam's Razor, or the Duck Rule, to every situation, and that the simplest explanation was usually the right one – but I had failed to do the same thing myself. There had been two Frank Langs from the beginning, completely unconnected other than for the fact that the name had cropped up when Taylor had been sniffing about and his Frank Lang had been Hungarian-born like Ellis.

There was, of course, every chance that Hopkins had been playing me. Deception was his stock-in-trade, after all, but there was no reason for him to throw up a smokescreen: I already was as lost as it was possible to be. And the truth was I didn't care. Sometimes you just had to learn to take a warning and the warning I had been given had done the trick. Hopkins had rattled the right skeletons in the right closets for me to get the message loud and clear. I resolved to drop the whole Ellis thing and go back to looking for *my* Frank Lang, the Frank Lang whose Lanarkshire origins were less than exotic.

My resolve didn't prevent me becoming increasingly para-noid over the next three days. It was the right place at the right time for paranoia: the world had dimmed a little more as the

Scottish winter days shortened and the weather took a turn for the worse. I spent much of my time looking over my shoulder for shadowy Hungarians, even shadowier government agents, or even the odd ghost from Hamburg lurking somewhere in the gloom. I also grew cagey about whom I spoke to and what I said on the 'phone.

Hopkins had kept me for four hours, with a break for sandwiches and more crap coffee, all the time telling me how free I was to leave whenever I wished. In my time, I'd been put through the mill by all kinds of cops, both civilian and military. No one had ever gotten a word out of me that I didn't want them to have. Hopkins, I had decided, would be no different. Putting up a stonewall defence, I had been absolutely determined to stop him getting anything from me.

By the time his beefy chums from Special Branch had dropped me back at my car, Hopkins had wheedled every last bit of information he had wanted to get out of me. There wasn't a bean that I left unspilled. The one thing I had been determined to keep out of his view was my involvement with Connelly and the union and the truth of why I'd been looking for a Frank Lang.

I told him all about that too.

The information you get from people by pulling out their fingernails is never reliable. Any sane person tells their torturer whatever the hell they think he wants to hear, whether it is the truth or not, just so they can hang on to their ability to scratch their backsides. Hopkins was the most skilled interrogator I had ever experienced, and he hadn't even resorted to being brusque – which caused me to reflect on how different history would have been if the Spanish Inquisition had relied on the use of muffins and sherry.

Every time I had lied or bent the truth to send Hopkins in the wrong direction, it seemed to expose another truth elsewhere. It was like plugging holes in a dyke only to see the water break through somewhere out of reach. And all the time, whenever I had managed to hold something back, he would bring the conversation back to my dubious history and I would tell him the truth to keep him away from my personal demons and secrets.

The only thing he didn't get out of me was the word Tanglewood. It wasn't that I made a huge effort to keep it from my scrupulously polite, Savile Row-tailored inquisitor; it was simply that it didn't come up. That meant it was either of no significance or, if it was, Hopkins did not know about it. Of course, there was always the chance that *he* was keeping it from *me*.

By the time we were through, I guessed he knew that he had gotten the truth out of me. It was an odd feeling: both relief and self-disgust. He had somehow managed to make me feel unburdened, as if he had done me a great favour by getting me to betray every professional confidence I had made over the last four weeks.

Afterwards, Hopkins had escorted me himself to the front door of the building where the Rover was waiting for me, and I hoped to hell it was the last I'd ever see or hear from him again. But as he shook my hand, he again alluded to future cooperation that might benefit me and promised he would be in touch. I had smiled and said 'sure' and tried to resist the temptation to run for my life.

After my encounter with the forces of official darkness, I made a real effort not to dwell on everything that had happened. I wanted to put it all behind me; far behind me. I didn't know why, but I didn't even tell Archie about my encounter with Hopkins. As it turned out, that was a mistake. A big one.

In the meantime, thinking back to the way Andrew Ellis had been so careful to make sure he wasn't followed, I started taking elaborate routes from A to B that took in the rest of the alphabet on the way. And did a lot of looking over my shoulder. Whatever Ellis, the girl, Mátyás or Ferenc Lang were involved in, it was big and, despite my best efforts, I found myself puzzling over what it could be. But every time it came to mind, I made a huge effort to shut it out. I had enough on my plate as it was.

We got another store-pilfering job in and I put Archie onto that, leaving me free to do the rounds again of all the contacts I had for the Frank Lang I'd been hired to find at the start of it all. This time round was proving no better than the first, and I could see that I was heading into another dead end.

In between my enquiries, I made more rounds of dismal boarding-houses, bed-sitting rooms and tenement flats. I even circled an ad for a barge for rent down near Renfrew Ferry.

Of course, there was the other ad I had circled. But that would be a big step to take, and I left it for the moment.

In the meantime, I looked at the barge.

It surprised me. After tenement flats where the running water had been mostly on the walls, I had fully expected the barge for rent to be a rotting, stinking hulk – boyish optimism was a weakness from which I didn't suffer. The bargee himself showed me around. He was a wiry, youthful man of sixty in a city where sixty was old and usually decrepit. He explained that he had worked the Forth-Clyde canal for more than forty years but had recently injured his back badly and, although he was largely recovered and short of retirement age, he wasn't fit to operate the barge. He now helped out on his son's, he told me. It was clear that the old bargee took enormous pride in his boat, and he explained that he was looking to rent it out to anyone who would look after it, whether they worked it or kept it moored.

'There's no' as many contracts as there used to be,' he confided. ''Specially for my kind o' barge. No coal, you see. I would'nae ever take coal, which is what most o' the barges take, you see.' He leaned in conspiratorially. 'Coal's a bastard. That coal dust gets everywhere when you're loadin' it. You end up caked in the bastard. You and your boat. So I only ever took clean cargo.'

I nodded. The old bargee clearly loved this inanimate lump of floating wood and steel. Everyone had to have their focus, I thought, something in which they could invest pride. As I surveyed the boat, I could understand the bargee's passion: it was a real piece of craftsmanship and smelled of polished wood and burnished brass, with paintwork that looked like it had been done that morning.

Somewhere along the line I had gotten the idea that I would be turning up to see a narrowboat. The fact was that there was no spidering network of canals in Scotland: barges operated mainly on the Forth-Clyde canal that guillotined Scotland at the neck and connected its two major cities, Glasgow and Edinburgh, or the Monklands Canal, which brought cargo from the coal mines in Lanarkshire to feed the ever-hungry industry of Glasgow. These were wider waterways than many of the canals south of the border and the craft were, correspondingly, broader.

'She's a widebeam,' the bargee informed me with pride. 'Fifty-two foot long and fourteen foot beam. Three foot six draught.'

I nodded sagely, as if any of it meant something to me.

At the back of the boat there was a balustrade-ringed deck

where the helm was located: a varnished wooden wheel exposed to the elements but which allowed the bargee the clearest view in every direction. A short staircase led down from the deck to the sliding door that offered access to the living quarters, basically the back third of the boat.

It was the living quarters that surprised me the most. Obviously, it was cramped, but there was an amazing economy in the use of space. I found myself surrounded by burnished, gleaming wood.

There were a lot of things I could be accused of. Being a cynical bastard was one of them. I had sneered and laughed at the deprivations in Glasgow; at the low expectations and short stature, at the limited imagination and even more limited ambition of the city's people. But there was one thing I had seen and seen often: what Connelly and his kind would brand as the 'nobility of the working man'.

Sure, there were lazy bastards about, and a lot of larcenous Govan shipyard workers' tenements that looked like they had been fitted out by the designers of the Titanic's first class lounge, but standing in the living quarters of that barge, I saw the Scottish work ethic at its purest. Everything gleamed. Everything was in its place. Everything spoke of a man who had focused those limited ambitions and aspirations into a single, solid form.

I was tempted by the idea of renting the barge, at least for a little while, but I told the old guy that I'd other places to see and I'd get back to him about it.

The truth was that, while the barge itself had held some kind of gypsy-caravan appeal for me, its mooring had been less than romantic. It was tethered to a quay under a canopy of cranes and sat in water as black as liquid obsidian, the oil-sleeked surface shimmering with dark rainbows. The stone quay, the cranes, the water, all were black against the slate winter sky and standing there I felt sketched in charcoal.

I got the Renfrew Ferry back across the Clyde, again checking out my fellow passengers for types foreign or secretive. Driving back into town through Clydebank did little to lift my mood. The traffic, such as it was, came to a halt before I reached the city centre. A delivery cart had shed part of its load through a loose tailgate and the coal-dust-ingrained driver was piling sacks of coal back onto the cart between bad-temperedly directing cars past him, all the time being watched uninterestedly over its shoulder by the carthorse: a Clydesdale who looked of a vintage to have pulled cannon at Waterloo.

I wasn't delayed for long, but just long enough to take in my surroundings. A wall of grey-black tenements flanked the roadway, tight against it and separated by the narrow ribbon of pavement. To my right was a gap: a bomb-site breach in the wall of tenement buildings, no more than a square of rough ground, which, like the tenements, was soot-dark and broken by piles of bricks, other debris, and the occasional pool of greasy rainwater.

There was a child playing on the site, a boy of no more than eight or nine who should have been at school. He wore rubber boots and a black coat that looked too thin to protect him from the damp Glasgow winter and his head was bare, a shock of ruffled red-blond the only colour in the monochrome. He was oblivious to what was going on in the street and poked at a smear of oily water with a stick, completely lost in a world of his own imagining.

I had seen so many things, so many sad or bleak or terrible things, while I'd been in Glasgow, but for some reason the sight of that small boy depressed me more than anything else. I wondered, as I watched him lost in play, if he was contemplating his future – because I sure was. And it wasn't good. For an instant, I understood why there were so many people like Connelly and Lynch in Glasgow. Why there were so many chips on so many shoulders and why so many wanted to turn the system on its head.

The car behind sounded its horn and I looked ahead to see the toothless mouth of the carter shape something obscene as he furiously waved his arm about to indicate I could pass his cart. I drove on, but something sat heavy in my chest whenever I thought about that small boy and his lack of future.

It was then that I made a decision about my own future. A long overdue one.

CHAPTER TWENTY

As if to reinforce my decision, I drove past my digs and, sure enough, the Jowett Javelin was parked outside. White's visits were obviously becoming more frequent and less discreet. I drove on. Decision made and confirmed.

Back in the office I sat at my desk and did a few calculations. Or re-calculations. The classified ad I had circled in the evening paper had been for a largish top floor apartment in Kelvin Court, a six-storey complex on Great Western Road. The apartment was considerably more up-scale than the places I'd looked at so far; Kelvin Court was an elegant Art Deco building that had been put up in the late Thirties. But it wasn't the style or the size of the flat that set it apart: what had made it an unusual choice for me was that it wasn't for rent, it was for sale. And that would mean, for the first time in ten years, putting real roots down in Glasgow.

When I had considered buying the flat, I had sat at my desk and totalled up all of the accounts and stashes I had put together since Germany, including my *Nibelungengold* – the little super-annuation plan I'd arranged for myself in Hamburg and to which Hopkins had alluded. All together it was a tidy sum: enough to place me in the property-owning classes.

But that had been before my epiphany.

As I had sat watching that small boy play in the waste ground's oily muck, a revelation had come to me. A revelation so clear and bright and shining, it made any received by Abraham, Moses or Mohammed look equivocal and woolly. And what had been burned into my particular stone tablet had been simple: *Lennox, what the FUCK are you doing here?*

Naturally, it wasn't just the little roadside tableau that had convinced me, there was the nagging sting every time I thought about how Fiona White had rejected me for some insignificant little pen-pusher. And, of course, Canada was a long way for Hopkins to reach, although I guessed he could, if he put his mind to it.

So now, instead of calculating down-payments and mortgages for a property that would anchor me in Glasgow, or how much I could afford on a new car to drive at walking pace through the smog, I was working out how much I could mail and wire to an account in Canada, and how much it would be safe to carry on me.

I made several 'phone calls that afternoon. By the time I was finished I had the dates and prices of passage to Halifax, Nova Scotia and quotes per crate for shipping my stuff back. After the last call, I swung my captain's chair around so I could look out of my office window at the dark graphite sky above the darker hulk of Central Station. Lighting a cigarette, despite the gloom I felt bathed in a warm light and resisted the urge to yell 'So long, suckers!' at the commuters bustling in and out under the ornate wrought iron of the station's entrance canopy.

Glasgow was bad for me. And I was none too good for it. There had been a time, right after the war, when we had suited each other, but the way things had been going, and despite all of my efforts to clean up my act, the truth was I knew too many of the wrong people here and had gotten involved in too many of the wrong kind of goings-on. I had pinned too much on Fiona White without knowing what it was I was pinning on her. The truth was, just like me and Glasgow, Fiona and I would probably be better off without each other.

Somewhere along the line, I had gotten it into my head that I wasn't ready, wasn't *clean* enough to go home to Canada, as if I had been loitering in Glasgow in some kind of quarantine, afraid of taking my contamination back home with me. Everything Hopkins had said to me about my past, about the dead men and broken hearts in my wake, had been true, and I guessed I'd always been afraid to drag the ghost of my recent past, like Jacob Marley's chains, back to Canada.

Growing up in Saint John had been a different time, a different place – and I had been a different person. The Kennebecasis Kid, all big ideals and big ambitions. Or maybe I hadn't, and it just took the war to unlock whatever it was that lay waiting to turn me into a wartime killer and a post-war asshole.

Maybe it was possible to become the Kennebecasis Kid again. Or something like him. My folks were still back there and, even though he had officially retired, my father was a big enough figure in the community to pull a few strings for his prodigal. Maybe I couldn't put it all behind me, but I could have a damn good try. At the very least, it would save me the depressing prospect of looking for new digs in Glasgow.

I took a few runs at the wording of a cable to my folks, but decided it would be best to wait till I had everything sorted. There was always the chance that I might wake up the following morning full of forgiveness for Fiona's rejection and a new-found love of squashed-flat square sausage, Scotch and smog.

But I wasn't counting on it.

*   *   *

I left the office before five.

It was late night closing and I headed to R.W. Forsyth's, on the corner of Renfield Street and Jamaica Street – a stone's throw from my office. It was a convenience that had cost me dear over the years: Forsyth's was a six-floor, top-end tailor and gentleman's outfitter and I had had a habit there of spending out of proportion to my income. The salesmen in Forsyth's styled themselves as 'gentlemen's gentlemen' and it always disconcerted me how pleased they were to see me. There was such a thing as being too good a customer.

I was welcomed by 'Robert' who had served me before. The Ronald Coleman-type moustache on his upper lip looked like the product of pencil and ruler, and he was immaculately turned out and barbered in a way that was more prissy than well-groomed. I had guessed long ago that Robert was a gentleman's gentleman in more ways than one. He had an effeminate way of speaking, which was emphasized by his attempts to sound cultured and approximate what he thought a gentleman should sound like, despite his grammar having shadows of Govan in it.

I explained to Robert that all I needed was four shirts, four pairs of socks and some underwear: I had decided not to go back to my digs that night and needed the change of clothes. Robert looked disappointed, but I wasn't sure if it was because I had bought too little or that what I had bought didn't call for him measuring my inside leg. If he was disappointed with that, he was devastated when I answered his question about if I wanted everything I had bought put on my account.

'No thanks, I'll pay cash. In fact, while I'm at the cash desk I'll settle my outstanding balance. I'm closing my account.'

Robert looked shocked; crestfallen in the unique manner of the salesman on commission.

'Oh *jings* no, Mr Lennox. I am very sorry to hear that. After all of these years? I do so hope you're no' dissatisfied with the service with what we've endeavoured to provide you with.'

'No, no . . . it's not that at all, Robert. It's just that I'm probably going to be . . . *out of town* . . . for a while.'

'Well, Mr Lennox, we are always here at your disposal, so we are.'

I told him I appreciated it and left with my packages tucked under my arm. I dumped them in the boot of the Atlantic before heading up to Sauchiehall Street. I went into Copland and Lye and, after picking up a new shaving kit and some toiletries, bought two suitcases and a trunk and arranged for them to be delivered to my office the next morning.

Finding a hotel room in Glasgow in November was never going to be difficult.

The Paragon Hotel was in the West End and across the narrow street it faced the Glasgow School of Art, an ornate Art Deco Mackintosh-designed building of which Glaswegians were almost religiously proud. Maybe it was just my contrary and cussed turn of mind, but the Art School building always struck me as out of proportion with the street it was on and reminded me of some overly ornate Viennese bus station.

What the Paragon Hotel was a paragon of remained a mystery to me, unless it was mediocrity. It was neither good nor bad, and its blandness somehow fitted with my need for the nondescript and anonymous. The cute copper-redhead behind the reception desk certainly wasn't mediocre. She was about twenty-two or -three with pale green eyes and an exemplary set of curves and looked very pleased to see me. I didn't know if it was my boyish charm that won her over or if she was just relieved to get a booking at that time of year. She asked how long I would be staying in the hotel and I paid for three nights in advance, telling her that it could be longer, but I would let them know over the next couple of days.

For some reason I did not fully understand, I checked in under a phoney name, telling the redhead I was a Mr Kelvin. This small act of deception surprised even me, and I told myself that I had done it as a precaution, given the interest that Hopkins had taken in me of late and his fondness for attaching invisible tails to anyone he thought might be worth the scrutiny. The truth was probably more that I needed a rest from being me; or maybe it was part of my transition back to an earlier definition of me. Whatever the reason, my pseudonym gave me a strange comfort.

The redhead gave me the key to number twelve and I told her I could find my own way up, despite my instinct to follow her up a staircase. She informed me that there was a shared bathroom at the end of the hall and announced, with great pride, that the hotel now boasted, on the second floor, that most up-to-date of conveniences: a Television Lounge. I thanked her and went up to my room, a square functional box with no view to speak of. The bathroom, common to all rooms on the floor, was reasonably clean and I washed, shaved and patted my jaw fresh with cologne before changing into one of my new shirts. The dining room was on the ground floor and my table was set into the bay window, looking out across the street. Only two other tables were occupied, one by an older couple with a gangly, bookish-looking daughter. Cherishing my quiet anonymity, I took no interest in the other diners, who returned my indifference. The meal was perfect: bland and forgettable.

Then I went up to my room and turned in early.

I slept like a baby.

CHAPTER TWENTY-ONE

The cute redhead was on duty the next morning at breakfast and I spun her a few lines and she smiled while she served me bacon, eggs, fried oatcake, black pudding and square sausage on what I first thought was a wet plate, but then realized was glossed with the fat that had leeched out onto it from the food. I tried not to think about how much more fat would be leeching out into my arteries and consumed my 'Full Scottish Breakfast Medley' with as much gusto as I could manage. The truth was it was less of a medley and more of a cardiac funeral march, but I tucked in anyway.

I had half expected that I would wake up in my hotel bedroom with that disconcerting feeling of not knowing where I was for a moment, but I hadn't. The instant I had woken, I had known where I was and what I was going to do that day. It was going to be a big day and I determined to meet it with enthusiasm, an emotion I had become especially unaccustomed to over the last few years. And if I was going to embrace the day with gusto and resilience, then my digestive system was just going to have to do the same.

A month, I thought to myself. Or maybe six weeks. It would take me that long to arrange everything about the business and, in any case, I still had the Frank Lang case to finish for

Connelly's Union – if there was any end to the case. In the meantime, I decided it would be best to keep my decision from everyone, including Archie. Just until I got it all sorted out. I'd see Archie all right before I went. I might even hand the business over to him; but maybe that would just be handing him a poisoned chalice.

Getting to the office early, I was at my desk when Archie arrived. Before he headed off for a morning's spying on Sauchiehall Street store assistants, I asked him if he could round up Twinkletoes for that afternoon; I had a job for him.

I joined the small queue waiting for the bank doors to open at nine-thirty. When I eventually got to the desk, I struggled to get the teller to understand that I wanted to withdraw everything from my cash account and wire the balance from my savings account to a bank in New Brunswick. It took ten minutes of explaining and the intervention of an under-manager before the penny eventually dropped, as if the removal of funds from their bank was an act of incomprehensible folly, and all the time I was given the impression that I was taking away their money, not mine. It made me more appreciative of Jonny Cohen's instant withdrawal methods, but I lacked his stocking mask and sawed-off.

'I'm afraid that will take some time to arrange,' said the under-manager with a shake of his head, referring to the wire transfer. 'Quite some time. But we should have it transferred by the beginning of next week. Are you sure you want to close your accounts, Mr Lennox?'

'I'm moving back to Canada,' I explained. 'I would have thought that a transfer like that could be done much quicker.' I felt like asking if they'd considered a faster method, like passenger pigeon or pony express, but I didn't. The cash would see me through all I had to do and there was still a lot to be organized.

When I got back to the office, I used the 'phone number from the newspaper advertisement and left a message for the old bargee. I guessed it was his son who was 'on the telephone' and I explained that I wasn't in the market for a long-term let any more but, if the bargee was interested, I'd like to rent the barge for a month on a static basis. The son agreed to pass on the message and we arranged that I would 'phone back early that evening.

Again I tried to contain my shock as I stepped out from my office building onto Gordon Street to feel the prickle of an all-pervading chill drizzle whisked into my face by a swirling wind. Glaswegians perpetually maintained that this type of rain – *smirr*, as they called it – always got you more wet, soaked you more thoroughly, than normal rain. The logic behind this remarkable piece of Glaswegian physics was beyond me. Having an office directly opposite Central Station had its advantages and, instead of walking around the corner to where I'd parked the car, I took a cab from the station rank and told the cabbie to drop me off at the Charing Cross garage where I hired the bank run van each Friday. I had telephoned ahead and the van was ready for me, despite it not being the usual day or time, and I drove it back and parked it close to the office.

I'd locked up the office when I'd left to pick up the van and I was aware of the stairwell being darker than usual as I made my way back up it on my return. The human eclipse blocking out what light came in through the landing window was waiting patiently for me outside my office.

'You got a job for me, Mr Lennox?' Twinkletoes McBride asked amiably, but resonated menacingly in the echo chamber of the stairwell. 'Archie said you was wanting me this afternoon.' He pronounced Archie 'Erchie' and afternoon, 'effternoon'. I knew that when I left the city, I would miss the majesty of the Glaswegian vowel, flatter and broader than the Saskatchewan prairie.

'Nothing grand, Twinkle,' I said. 'I just need to borrow your muscles.'

'Oh aye? Nae problem, Mr L. Do I need to get any tools?'

'No, no, nothing like that . . .' I said emphatically, seeing he'd gotten the wrong idea. 'I just need you to help me load and unload some stuff onto a van. But give me a minute . . . I have a quick 'phone call to make.'

He waited in the hallway while I 'phoned the bargee's number again. This time I got to speak to him directly and he agreed to the short-term let.

'Okay, Twinkle, we're on,' I said, as I came back out onto the landing, locking the office door behind me.

'Where's we goin', Mr L?' he asked.

'I'm moving address . . .'

I parked the van where I'd positioned Archie's car to watch the house before. We arrived at one-thirty and I decided to give it until two or quarter after. If I could avoid Fiona, I would; if I couldn't, I wouldn't.

I cursed the predictability of it all: the Jowett Javelin pulled up outside at two and James White trotted up to the house. After five minutes he re-emerged with Fiona in tow and they drove off.

'Okay, Twinkle,' I said, 'let's go.'

I drove up to the space vacated by the Javelin and parked, leaving enough tailgate space for us to load the van.

'We're just going to get my stuff. There's not much but I've got a couple of heavy crates with books in them.'

'Sure thing. You doing a midnight flit? You know, with us waiting for the place to be empty?'

'No. I'm paying up for the month,' I said. A 'midnight flit' was what the Scots called a sneaking your stuff out of property to avoid paying overdue rent.

It took less than twenty minutes for us to clear out my rooms. Most of the time was spent carefully packing my suits and other personal stuff into the trunk and two suitcases I'd bought from Copland and Lye, while Twinkle lugged my crated library down and into the van with disturbing ease and speed.

I felt strangely numb leaving the rooms I had occupied for more than three years. Everything going through my head came together from opposite directions, continually clashing. Standing there, I knew I had had real feelings for Fiona White. Strong feelings that I'd felt only once before. Yet I had this overpowering urge to get as far away from her, from Glasgow, from everything I'd known there.

'You all right, Mr Lennox?'

I turned to see McBride standing there, his demi-brow furrowed with concern.

'I'm fine. That us?'

He nodded.

'Then let's go.'

On the way out, I pushed an envelope under Fiona's door. More than two months' rent in cash. I hoped that would cover things until she found a new lodger. Nothing else: no note, no explanation, no forwarding address.

I pushed my key through the letterbox as I stepped out onto the street, pulling the main door closed behind me.

'I want you to understand something,' I said to Twinkle as we drove out of town along Great Western Road. 'Where we're going . . . no one knows about this place. No one. We'll dump most of my stuff there but only you and I are to know about it. Got that?'

'I got it, Mr L. You know I am the soul of *description*.'

I decided against correcting him. 'Good. And once we've done this, I want you to drop me back in town, near the Art School, then take the van back to the garage.'

'Okey-doke.'

The old bargee was standing on deck when we arrived.

'With the greatest respect, and I dinnae mean no *diss-parrage-ment*, Mr L.,' said Twinkletoes, enunciating yet another recently learned word syllable by tortured syllable, as we pulled up on the quayside. 'But you've got to be fucking joking. You're gonnae live on a boat?'

'Don't worry about it,' I said. 'You just forget all about the barge and where it is. Like I said, this is between us.'

'Aye . . . but a fucking *boat*?'

I left McBride to deal with his disappointment and spoke to the bargee. The barge was his baby and his tone continually shifted from pride to distrust and back again as he ran through the essentials of barge maintenance. I could understand him being like that: his barge had been his livelihood, his transport, his work tool and his home all rolled up in one.

'I promise you that I will look after it,' I assured him. One thing about a Scotsman's gloom is that it is as easy to dispel as it is deep, and I handed him twenty pounds extra on top of the advance rent I had paid him. 'Consider ten pounds of that as a deposit,' I said as his eyes lit up. 'Against damages. But I assure you there will be none and you can refund it.'

'And the other tenner?' he asked, a flint gleam in the grey eyes.

'A goodwill gesture.'

He seemed to be satisfied with my cash-backed assurances and he volunteered to help Twinkle and me with loading my stuff into the barge.

'We'll be fine,' I said. 'I'd worry about your bad back.'

'Aye,' said Twinkle helpfully. 'Lifting heavy stuff could *exasperate* a bad back.'

'The word's exacerbate, Twinkle,' I said and he scowled.

The bargee shrugged, but hung around while we loaded the stuff. I got the impression that he had only volunteered to help because he wanted to make sure none of his precious paintwork got scratched.

It took even less time to unload my earthlies into the barge than it had to empty my flat. Not much for the sum total of a man's life, even if it was just the ten post-war years of it.

'Do you ever have any problems with break-ins?' I asked, casting my gaze around the quayside, the cranes and the Nissen huts beyond.

'No one comes down here unless they have river business,' he said.

I nodded. But some of the people I'd dealt with over the last few years had a different idea of 'river business' – usually involving a midnight rowboat ride, a weighted body and an unofficial burial at sea.

I locked up the barge anyway.

I hung onto a single case with a change of suit, and McBride dropped me at the hotel on his way to return the van. It wasn't my redhead on duty, but a skinny runt of a man in his late fifties who acknowledged me with a forced smile. His thick-framed National Health Service spectacles looked so heavy they must have given him neck strain. His thinning hair was the same copper colour as the girl's, if peppered with grey, and I had worked out that the hotel was owned and run by a family: he was the father and she the daughter.

'Will you be dining with us this evening, Mr Kelvin?' he asked.

'Yes, I will.'

'Dinner is at six-thirty,' he said, over the top of his dense spectacles frames. 'Sharp.'

I nodded, went up to my room and changed before heading back out and taking a cab to my office.

After all the focused activity of sorting out personal business, I sat at my desk slightly at a loss about what to do next. Now I was faced with the task of continuing the Frank Lang case and I had even less to go on than when I had started.

My old man had always lectured me about how you can't sit around and wait for something to happen, you had to get out there and make it happen: a philosophy that had led him out of Glasgow and over the Atlantic; then into a business that put us pretty much at the top of the New Brunswick tree and me in the private Collegiate School. But sometimes you just didn't have the raw materials to make something spark. And that was where I was with the Lang case.

Dad had been wrong. Sometimes things do happen without you making them happen or even expecting them.

And something was about to happen that would make me wish I'd planned my return to Canada a lot earlier.

CHAPTER TWENTY-TWO

Connelly agreed on the 'phone to meet me, but again asked that we convene at the working men's club. It confirmed my suspicion that he didn't much want to be seen talking to me. Apart from our first meeting at the union headquarters, whenever I had talked with him or Lynch, it had been either on the telephone or somewhere else. Whatever it was that Lang had on Connelly, his union, or both, then the union boss wanted it dealt with as off-stage as possible.

It also strengthened my conviction that when it came to the goods on Lang, I still hadn't been handed the full basket. I more or less accused him of that, for the second time, and again I didn't get as vigorous a defence as I had expected.

The receiver had just hit the cradle when the telephone rang. It took me a while to recognize the voice, which launched into a garble as soon as I answered. I swam upstream a torrent of words for a while before I got him to pause for breath.

'I can't take it any more. It's driving me mad. I need you to help me, Mr Lennox. I need to know who it is. Who she's seeing behind my back.'

'Calm down, Mr Dewar,' I said as the penny dropped. 'What's happened?'

'He's been here. They've been at it. In my bed. I know they

have. I know she has him round whenever I'm not here.'

'Who?'

'I don't know. That's what's driving me mad. I don't know who he is. For all I know she's at it with more than one of them. I need your help. I can't go on like this. Please . . .'

'I'm sorry, Mr Dewar,' I said as soothingly as I could, 'but I just can't get involved when there's a crossover with another case.' It was all bull, of course. I felt genuinely sorry for the guy and, when the Ellis job had stopped being a job, I had considered taking on Dewar's case. I certainly had a head start, having seen his wife get handy under the table with the dance hall Romeo. But it was all too complicated and I was trying to tie up loose ends, not unravel new ones.

A thought struck me. I had only gotten involved with the Dewars because they lived next door to the missing Frank Lang, and I had my suspicions that Lang had tested Mrs Dewar's bedsprings at one time or another. Maybe I could pin down Lang if he had been pinning down Sylvia Dewar. But there was a lot of hot emotion that would make Dewar's marital problems too hot a potato to handle.

'I need your help,' Dewar's tone was beseeching. Desperate. 'I don't know what I'll do if you don't. She's driving me mad.'

'Okay . . .' I said eventually. 'I can't promise anything. The truth is I'm probably going to be leaving Glasgow for good in a few weeks. But we can talk about it and maybe I can help. Where can we meet?'

'Tonight. My house at eight.'

'What about your wife?'

'She going out. Again. She says she's meeting her sister, but I know it's all lies. Her sister's as bad as she is. A couple of hoors.'

I calculated my timetable for the evening, centred on the immovable feast of bland dinner at the Paragon Hotel at six-thirty, on the dot.

'All right,' I said. 'I'll see you there at eight. Just don't do or say anything until then.' I was going to ask him if there had been any sign next door of Frank Lang, but decided he wasn't in a place where I'd get a coherent answer out of him. I'd slip it in tonight, when I got a chance to calm him down.

I had never understood how something as vague and woolly as 'instinct' could ever have been an accepted scientific principal. Personally I split instinct into two types: the first was memories we must have inherited from our long-lost tree-climbing ancestors – fears of spiders or the dark, that kind of stuff; the second was the stuff we know without knowing we know it, deep-stored somewhere out of sight of our day-to-day thinking, only surfacing as some impulse or urge that pushes you to act in a certain way.

I had relied a lot on instinct over the years. Which probably explained why I so often ended up in the shit.

Whatever it was, and wherever it came from, the same instinct that had made me give a phoney name at the hotel made me uneasy about using the Atlantic. The fact that I was having increasing trouble getting it started was probably a big part of it, but I also was aware that it was less than inconspicuous, and – after my ambush tête-à-têtes with Mátyás and Hopkins – I still got that itch between the shoulder blades that someone was tailing me.

Willie Sneddon, one of the Three Kings and the most powerful, owed me a few favours and I called one in. Not that Sneddon would have wasted the time to actually do anything on my behalf, but a 'tell them I said it's okay' carried a ton of weight. He owned the car showroom on Great Western Road I'd visited before and Kenny the salesman looked perturbed when I returned. One of Sneddon's people had 'phoned ahead and the car was waiting for me when I arrived. Not the Sunbeam, of course, but a black Ford Anglia 100E, one of the new-shape models. Small, characterless and anonymous, it was, like the hotel, perfect for my purposes.

I told Kenny that the Anglia was exactly what I needed and I settled up for the hire costs, discounted as per Sneddon's instructions. The Atlantic was to be parked around the back and out of sight.

'I'll only need it for a few days,' I explained as he handed me the keys. 'Maybe a week.'

'Have you thought any more about the Sunbeam-Talbot Ninety?' Kenny asked hopefully.

'It's never far from my mind,' I lied. 'Tell you what,' I said, 'why don't you have a good look at the Atlantic while it's here and tell me what you'd give me for it.'

'Against the Sunbeam-Talbot?' The hopefulness in Kenny's tone was less forced.

'Why don't you give me a price to buy it from me. Then we can talk about what I might replace it with,' I said, omitting that my intention was to replace it with a ticket to the other side of the Atlantic. If Kenny offered enough, I might join the Jet-Set instead of taking a boat.

Whatever my theories about instincts, they were going wild when I pulled up in the Ford Anglia outside the Dewar house in Drumchapel. Pretty much as I expected it to be, unless my luck was going to change radically, Frank Lang's place was in darkness; but so was the Dewars'. I checked my watch. Exactly eight p.m., just as I'd agreed with Dewar on the 'phone. I sat in the car for fifteen minutes but there were still no signs of life. The only soul I was aware of was a woman walking a dog through the drizzle. I recognized her as the same woman whose ugly little dog had taken a leak against the Atlantic's wheel-arch the first time I'd been at Lang's house and I wondered how much walking the pug's stumpy legs could take each day. As she passed, the woman scowled in at me through the wind-shield. On balance, it was fair to say that the dog was prettier.

When the ten minutes was up, I got out and walked up to the door. The house sat dark and silent and I didn't get an answer to my ringing of the doorbell. I was about to turn on my heel and put it down to Dewar getting confused about the time, given his agitated state of mind, but, on the 'phone, he had been so desperate for this meeting. It didn't make sense that he wouldn't turn up for it. I rapped on the door instead of ringing again. Still no answer.

There was no handle on the door; it was one of the new kind with a small Chubb cylinder lock with only a small brass lip curled below the keyhole with which to pull the door shut. I laid my gloved hand flat against the door and it opened with only a light push.

'Mr Dewar?' I called into the darkened hall. 'Tom?'

Nothing. I roughly remembered the layout of the place from my visit with the potentially obliging Sylvia, but it took a few fumbling seconds before I found the wall switch and illumi-nated the hall. I closed the front door behind me, went into the living room and switched on the ceiling light.

Everything was just as it had been the last time – the only time – I'd been there. The three-piece suite still filled the room with a showroom smell, the Bush television rented from RentaSet still watched from the corner with the glossy graphite-grey eye of its huge seventeen-inch screen; every item still coordinated shop-window perfect. But something was amiss in Hire Purchase Heaven: something I had noticed before wasn't there, but I couldn't work out what it was.

I went through to the *kitchenette*, again switching on the lights. It was then I realized what had been missing from the front room. It was there, on the floor: the chunky glass ashtray that had sat on the kidney-shaped coffee table and which I had thought looked like a lump of lava. It had been dropped on the linoleum-covered concrete but hadn't smashed, instead snapping clean into two halves, white ripples of shockwaves from the impact running through the deep red glass like tree rings.

I leaned against the doorframe while I had one of my more inspired detective moments. In an instant I worked out, Sherlock Holmes style, exactly what chain of events had led to the ashtray falling and breaking. I did it by piecing together small clues: like the body of Sylvia Dewar lying sprawled on the kitchen floor, or the dark red, viscous puddle that bloomed on the linoleum around her now misshapen skull. And, of course, there was the hair, blood and other matter stuck to the cleaved glass ashtray.

Yep. I had it all worked out, all right.

CHAPTER TWENTY-THREE

While I was waiting for the City of Glasgow Police to turn up, I checked the rest of the house and found Tom Dewar upstairs in the dark of the front bedroom. He was staring out through the window with nothing much of an expression on his face, other than whatever it was he was staring at was making his eyes bulge. Which wasn't surprising, as he had clearly decided to improve his point of view by stringing himself up from the ceiling light fitting, an extra length of electrical flex around his neck. Given that his bloated face and swollen hands were purple-black with post-mortem lividity, I didn't bother checking for a pulse. He wasn't going to share his troubles with me after all. And whatever those troubles had been, they were now most definitely behind him.

I remembered what Hopkins had said about dead men and broken hearts. Now I was finding them together in the same place.

I went back downstairs when I heard the trilling bells of approaching police cars and was at the front door to greet the uniforms as they arrived. The first copper was one of the many Highlanders who made up the force and he actually did ask me, 'Are you the one who 'phoned us?'

I was about to point out that, of the three occupants of the house, the other two were currently indisposed to using the telephone, but I couldn't be bothered and simply nodded instead.

Jock Ferguson was on the scene within fifteen minutes of the first car arriving. I was glad to see him, as the uniformed Gaelic geniuses first on the scene had treated me with undisguised suspicion. I was, it had to be said, well used to coppers treating me with suspicion, but I had had a long day and I was bone weary and felt more than a little sick. I'd seen a lot of death – too much for one lifetime – but there was a difference when women were involved.

Towards the end of the war, just outside Bremen where we had encountered particularly fierce resistance, I had happened on the body of a woman defender. She had been one of the hundreds of women and kids that the SS had equipped with old rifles and too little ammunition and forced to fight the advancing Allies. The heroes of the SS had ensured the compliance of the women and kids by hanging behind and forcing them to advance, shooting anyone who tried to retreat. It was difficult to tell how old the woman was, anywhere between late teens and early thirties, but her muddied body had lain in a ditch, her rifle beside her, shot in the face and head. Her skirt was up around her waist and her underthings ripped. Indignity and humiliation before death. I had no idea which side had done it, and I didn't care. It had been one of the many things I had seen that had convinced me that any ideas of fighting a noble war was a crock of shit; and that all of the systems and rules and codes by which we were supposed to live our lives came from the same crock. Seeing what happened to women and kids was the one thing I couldn't take during the war.

And seeing a murdered woman in her kitchen had turned my gut.

Again I thought of how right Hopkins had been about the trail left behind me. In a day of big decisions, I made another, that the bodies of the dead woman in Germany and the dead woman in Drumchapel would mark the beginning and end of that trail.

I now knew that I didn't just want to get back to Canada; I had to.

It hadn't just been the sight of Sylvia Dewar sprawled on the kitchen floor, spilling brains and blood onto the linoleum, that had turned my gut: it was the knowledge that I could perhaps have stopped it happening. I couldn't have stopped her fooling around with other men, but if I had said yes to Dewar's request, if I hadn't been blind to the desperation and mental anguish of a man who had attacked me in a back alley because he thought I was someone his wife was messing around with, then maybe I could have prevented this from happening. I tried to tell myself that I wasn't a social worker or a marriage coun-sellor, but none of that helped when I thought of the broken ashtray and broken skull on the kitchen floor.

Jock Ferguson had me go through the whole story there and then. Well, when I say the whole story, I told Ferguson that Dewar had 'phoned me at my office and arranged to meet me at his home that evening. The reason for his call, I told Ferguson, was that he wanted me to investigate his wife's alleged infi-delity. I explained that I'd arranged to meet Dewar at short notice because he had seemed agitated and desperate on the 'phone.

Everything I told Ferguson was the truth. But not the whole and nothing but. I missed out the part about me having been at the Dewar home before and that my real professional interest had been in their neighbour, Frank Lang. It wasn't that I was trying to protect Connelly and his union as my client – after all, I'd spilled the beans to Hopkins who would be a greater concern to Connelly – I was aware that simply finding a body, or bodies, is a lot less complicated an involvement in a murder case than having any kind of entanglement or history with the deceased.

And I had a boat to catch in a month's time.

By my reckoning, this was a straightforward case of murder-suicide and I should be able to walk away from it free and clear by giving a signed deposition for the inquest. I certainly wasn't going to tell Ferguson about my plan to skip town in a month or so. That I would do nearer the time in a less professional and more boozy context.

As it turned out, it took two hours to satisfy Ferguson, and even then there was a hint of suspicion in his manner. After he was done, I had to give the whole spiel again to a plain-clothes constable who took it all down in longhand in his note-book, getting me to sign it when we were done.

I was just glad that Hopkins hadn't been there to beat the truth out of me with doughnuts and a cup of Earl Grey.

'Just stay in touch, Lennox,' said Ferguson, and I braced myself for him telling me, like they always did in the movies, not to leave town. But he didn't.

Before I climbed into the unfamiliar Ford Anglia, I had to ask the cops to move a couple of black police Wolseleys that were blocking me in. All the lights were on in the street now, dressing-gowned neighbours standing urgently cross-armed at doors, others peeking out through curtains at the police inactivity in the street.

As I turned the corner out of the street, I passed the last

ghoul hanging over her gate, scowling eagerly down the street at the knot of police cars. As I passed she scowled in at me. I nearly didn't recognize her without her dog.

Bad dreams again. To be expected I told myself.

It wasn't my pneumatic little redhead on duty at breakfast the next morning but her parsimonious little father instead, who tottered about bad-temperedly between the only two occupied tables and the kitchen. I was yet to see the mother working in the hotel. Leaving as much of my breakfast as I could without provoking the ire of the hotelier, I decided I would pick up something less fatty, like a half-pound of lard, on my way, and headed into the office early.

After the usual morning catch-up on cases with Archie, who had already built up quite a case on the pilfering store staff, I told him about what had happened the night before and my discovery of Dewar and his wife.

'You don't think there is any link between what happened and Frank Lang?' Archie asked when I was finished.

'No. Or at least not directly. I suspect that Lang may have been one of the troop of bedroom jockeys Sylvia Dewar went over the jumps with, but I doubt if he was the only one. Well, I know that for sure, having seen her manipulative skills with that guy in the Locarno.'

'Race . . .' said Archie flatly.

'What?'

'Race,' he repeated. 'A race of bedroom jockeys. Race is the collective noun for jockeys, not troop. Apes, mushrooms and kangaroos come in troops. Sometimes lions. But not jockeys.'

'I'm indebted, Archie.'

'I do a lot of crosswords,' he explained.

'What about enquiry agents?' I asked. 'Is there a collective noun for them?'

'Private detectives? That's one I don't know. Probably a *snoop*. Do you have anything else on Frank Lang or has that line of enquiry gone completely dead?'

'It was never alive,' I said. 'Frank Lang has no history to speak of. And Connelly is still holding something back. Lang was no government or police spy, but I do believe that he's not who or what he said he was and he has infiltrated the union for some other reason.'

'Then I can see only two possible reasons for someone going to so much trouble,' said Archie. 'Maybe Lang is spying on the union for some political party or group, or even for some foreign government, although that's all too James Bond.'

'James who?' I asked.

'A book the wife's reading. About some super spy. Gives her something to do while I'm doing the crossword. Anyway, I don't think your Frank Lang is a Russian spy, and I think it highly unlikely that the Milngavie Conservative Association use secret agents to infiltrate unions, so that leaves the second option, which is that Frank Lang is a common-or-garden fraud merchant.'

'That's where I'd put my money,' I said. Archie had mirrored my own thought processes. 'But maybe not so common-or-garden. Two years of building a back-story is a big investment of time and effort just to steal an address book with a few embarrassing names in it. This has echoes of long firm to it. Who do you know in the long firm racket?'

Archie paused to roll and light a cigarette. Like everything with Archie, it was done slowly and deliberately and as a diversion while he was thinking. As I waited, I thought about him taking over the business. Archie was smart and persistent, but lacked drive and ambition. But he'd do well taking over the enquiry agent business; he'd probably be better at it than me.

'I was in uniform, not CID,' he said eventually, blowing a thin jet of blue smoke into the air and picking a shard of tobacco from pursed lips. 'The City of Glasgow seemed to feel my talents were better employed dodging pish-filled beer bottles at Parkhead football stadium. More Old Firm than Long Firm. But I would have thought you had people in CID you could get the information from.' Archie said it without looking at me, instead examining the shard of tobacco he now held up in the air between finger and thumb. I didn't know if he was hinting that he knew all about Taylor, my bent copper, or if he simply meant Jock Ferguson.

'Come on, Archie, you must know someone,' I protested. It was a question Jonny Cohen would have been better placed to answer, but asking would be difficult, given the attention he was getting from coppers investigating the Arcades robbery.

'Give me a minute . . .' Archie picked up the receiver and dialled a number he clearly knew by heart. After a few minutes talking and scribbling in a notepad, he hung up.

'It would appear I am better connected than I thought,' he said, handing me the note. 'Three names. The last two have done time for dishonesty offences and they've all been linked to long firm frauds. The name at the top . . . he's never been done. No record.'

I read the name: Dennis Annan. 'So how come he's known?'

'He's never been caught, but he's been questioned about several big frauds. He's too clever . . . all of his scams are blind and double-blind stuff and he runs rings around the average flatfoot. Christ knows how you'll find him though.'

'But he's in Glasgow?'

'Glasgow, Edinburgh ... anywhere he can run a scam. My contact says that he thinks Annan is originally from somewhere in the Borders.'

'The Borders?'

'Aye ...' Archie raised the two huge beetles of his eyebrows. 'Not the usual starting point for a career con man. Maybe when he left Galashiels his head was turned by our fancy city ways, like wearing shoes and using cutlery.'

'And your guy has no idea where I could find Annan?'

'Not a hope. And half the time he won't be going by the name of Annan. Your best bet, according to my contact, is to work on the other two lesser mortals. As you can see, I got addresses for them. Annan's not going to be Frank Lang ... from what I gather about him the union would be too small time and labour-intensive, if you'll pardon the pun. But Annan knows everyone in the business. He'd be the best way to Lang, if you could get him to tell you anything, that is.'

'And you can't tell me anything more about him?'

Archie shrugged. 'No, not really. He was in the merchant marine during the war. Ship's cook. There was some talk of him training as a chef, but he gave up the *petit pois* for petty larceny.'

'Ship's cook?' I asked.

'Aye ... why?'

'That's what Frank Lang was supposed to have been. For a time, anyway.' I looked at the names. I still had the sense that I wasn't getting anywhere, but at least it was a new direction in which not to get anywhere.

The second name on the list was Edward Leggat, or Eddy McCausland, or Ted Cuthbert, depending on which way the wind was blowing and which old ladies he was tricking out of their life savings. The address I had for him, in a tenement block in Raeberry Street turned out to be a dud, and I considered moving on to the third name on Archie's list, but first I called St Andrew's Square from a pay telephone. I was told Donald Taylor wasn't on duty until the backshift and I hung up when asked for my name.

Leaving the Ford Anglia parked outside the hotel, I decided to take the trolleybus. Introduced seven years before and nicknamed 'the Whispering Death' by Glaswegians, the near silent, double-decker electric buses had frequently conspired with Glasgow's dense smog to take a life.

I got off at the Broomielaw, a flank of ornate Victorian buildings that lined the Clyde, housing shipping companies and other dock-related businesses. The place I was looking for was in a totally different type of business, however.

The Pacific Club was a private cocktail bar tucked into the basement of a soot-blackened Broomielaw five-storey. It was one of those members-only joints where you had to sign in, meaning it was exempt from the licensing laws that applied to ordinary bars. Jonny Cohen had told me that he had gotten the idea from 'business associates' in Soho, London. I had never been there in the evening, only ever having graced it with my presence when meeting up with Cohen. The truth was that Handsome Jonny was very rarely to be seen in the place, unless by prior arrangement. Given Jonny's current predicament, I knew he wouldn't be there.

I was let in by a dinner-jacketed heavy who could have been Twinkletoes long-lost, and who defined exactly why some people called evening wear a 'monkey suit'. His tailoring certainly wasn't off-the-peg, given that the jacket's arms had to be long enough to allow his knuckles to reach the ground.

The Pacific was a drearily South-Seas-cum-nautical-themed

place dressed in coconuts, crab-shells, anchors and ships' life rings. In the corner was a palm-fringed bar with the words 'HAWAIIAN HULA BAR' above it.

I had done a lot of bad things in my life and, whenever I visited the Pacific Club, I found myself in fear for my mortal soul: if hell really was waiting for me, I knew this would take the form of an eternity's membership to the Pacific.

There was a small, dark-haired guy behind the bar. He was jacketless but didn't have his shirtsleeves rolled up and was lost in calculation of some figures in a ledger. He looked up when he realized I was across the bar from him and his face broke into a broad grin.

'Lennox . . . how are you?'

'I'm fine, Larry, you?'

'What can I tell you? Business could be better, as Jonny keeps reminding me.' Larry Franks was a good-looking Jew in his forties. He had an accent that most people in Glasgow would have taken for London but, if you listened closely, you would hear the traces of something much more distant. I liked Franks. Despite his employer's other business activities and the company he kept, Franks wasn't really a crook. He ran the Pacific as legitimately as he could, even if he knew the hostesses were running their own enterprises and allowed them the use of the private 'Luau' rooms. He seemed to be perpetually cheerful, one of nature's optimists, which I greatly admired. Mainly because I knew why he kept his shirt sleeves rolled down.

'Can I get you a drink, Lennox?' he asked. 'I've still got some of that Bourbon that Jonny got in for special.'

It was too early in the day for me, but the bourbon was something special, all the way from Bardstown, Kentucky. For a rye drinker in Scotland, it was like finding an oasis in the Sahara.

'I'm sure the sun is over the yardarm somewhere,' I said and smiled.

He poured me the bourbon and it went down smooth and easy.

'What can I do for you, Lennox?' asked Franks.

'I need to get a message to Jonny and, seeing as things are *awkward* at the moment, I thought we could use you as . . .'

'A messenger boy?'

'Well, you know what I mean. I hope you don't mind.'

Franks smiled. 'Sure . . . What is it you want me to tell Jonny?'

'I gave him a picture a week or so ago. A guy I'm trying to find.'

'Yeah . . . I've seen it,' said Franks. 'Jonny's been doing the rounds personally with it. Not anybody I've seen before, but Jonny said he was maybe more a dance hall type.'

'That's the one. There's a slim chance that he's maybe some kind of con-merchant and I'm trying to talk to other faces in the game to see if they can point me in the right direction. There's a well-known long firm fixer called Eddy Leggat, and he could maybe help. Actually the feller I'm really after goes by the name of Dennis Annan, but he's the invisible man, apparently, so Leggat's a better bet to find. I've got another name too, so any pointer I can get on any or all of them would be good, but I'm concentrating on Leggat first. I thought there was a chance that Jonny might know of him or where I might find him.'

Franks took the stub of pencil from behind his ear and scribbled down the three names I gave him.

'I'll ask Jonny.'

'Larry . . . do me a favour and wait until you see Jonny face-to-face. The way things are, I wouldn't want you to discuss it on the 'phone. That's why I'm going through all of these hoops.'

''Course, leave it with me.'

I sipped at my Bardstown and we chatted about nothing in particular. Somehow we got onto current affairs. That November, almost any conversation with anyone anywhere in Britain had a tendency to turn to current affairs. Like everyone else we talked about the mess in Suez, how the Americans had reacted and everything that it was going to mean for Britain. The conversation naturally turned to the other crisis that was rapidly being side-lined: the revolt in Hungary. Or at least I turned it in that direction; Franks didn't seem to have much to say and I detected, like a subtle shift of wind direction, a faint change in his mood.

'It's their problem,' he said eventually, the smile gone. 'They brought it on themselves.'

'What?' I laughed. 'Don't tell me you're a closet commie. You think they should lie down for the Ruskies?'

'I was born in Hungary,' he explained.

'You're Hungarian?' I asked.

'That's not what I said. I said I was born in Hungary. I used to think I was Hungarian, but it was made very, very clear to me that I was mistaken.'

'Ah . . .' I said, and looked down into my glass, as if in it I'd find my way out of the corner I'd talked myself into.

Franks rolled up his left sleeve and held his forearm toward me. I had known there was a tattoo there, but had never seen it. The letter B followed by four numbers.

'They gave me this, just to remind me of my error.' There was irony but little bitterness in Franks's tone. 'June Nineteen-Forty-four. A present for my twenty-first birthday. I'm a *B* because I came in the second shipment, after they'd already done twenty thousand As. The Germans started rounding us up as soon as they moved in in March 'Forty-four. But their pals in the Arrow Cross and other Hungarian Nazis had made sure we were all ready for them.'

I realized I was staring too hard at Franks, searching his face for a lost youth. I had always taken him as being somewhere in his forties, a few years older than me. If he had been twenty-one in Nineteen Forty-four, he could only be thirty-three now. Along with a lot else, ten years had been stolen from him in a place I could name but could never understand.

'Shit, Larry . . .'

'Sorry, Lennox.' Franks's habitual good-natured grin returned. 'I didn't mean to make you feel awkward.'

I shook my head in disbelief that he was apologizing to me.

'The only reason I'm going on about it,' he said with a shrug, 'is that I know the Hungarians are going through a tough time at the moment, but, frankly, I don't give a shit – just like they didn't give a shit when I was rounded up along with my family. What people forget is that the Hungarians started to pass anti-Jewish laws long before the Germans even got the idea. My father wasn't allowed to study at university because of Horthy's laws restricting Jewish places way back in Nineteen-Twenty.' He paused and shrugged. 'Sorry . . . I get a bit heated when people get all sympathetic about the Magyars. Just because the Germans took over in March Forty-four, and then the Russians in Forty-five, they're treated as victims.'

As quick as we could, we moved on to more general chat about the weather and how we both wished we were sitting in the Melbourne sun watching lithe-limbed female athletes, and anything else inconsequential we could think to talk about.

I arranged with Franks to call back in the next couple of days and left after a second Bourbon, which warmed me against the chill damp of the day. I took the trolley bus back into town and had lunch in Rosselli's, keeping my Bourbon glow burning with a couple of glasses of rough Italian wine. I needed it, and not just because of the Glaswegian winter that glowered at me through the restaurant window. There were ghosts there too, the most vivid being the flashbulb image of Sylvia Dewar from the night before, her head caved in, and her husband's plump baby face swollen and dark as he hung from the bedroom ceiling. And the blue-black numbers on Larry Franks's forearm kept intruding. I thought that I had long ago been beyond the emotional reach of man's-inhumanity-to-man-and-all-that-jazz, but maybe I wasn't as immune to suffering as I had thought. Or maybe the immunity was wearing off.

Finishing my spaghetti and red wine, I skipped coffee and picked up the Anglia at the hotel. I had an appointment to keep.

CHAPTER TWENTY-FOUR

That itch was still there between my shoulder blades. I was pretty sure I hadn't been followed and I had avoided using the rental car anywhere I would be expected to be seen. I even took circuitous routes back to the hotel from my office, often taking me far out of my way. My meeting with Hopkins had shaken me, added to which was the odd feeling I had that I was trying to shake off my old life before starting a new one. The fact remained, however, that I still got an uneasy feeling that I was being watched. Stalked.

Jock Ferguson didn't need to go to such extremes to find me. He called into my office the following morning, just before ten and just after I'd finished talking through the caseload with Archie. I had an old hunting knife that I'd had since I was a kid in Canada, and when Ferguson walked in, I was opening the mail with it.

'I hope you never walk around with that on your person,' said Ferguson, nodding to the hunting knife.

'This? No, Inspector . . . that would be against the law. It was a gift from my Dad for weekend hunting trips, but I've given up the outdoor lifestyle since I moved to Glasgow. I only use it as a letter opener these days. '

Ferguson and Archie spent a few minutes chatting while I

boiled up the electric kettle I kept on top of the filing cabinet. It had been Ferguson who had put me in touch with Archie in the first place and I knew that, somewhere along the line and before Ferguson had begun his ascent of the ranks, the two had served together as beat coppers.

After Archie left I sat drinking black tea with Ferguson and chatting casually; which was a ploy, because Ferguson wasn't the type of friend, or copper, just to drop in on you while passing. Or chat casually.

'What happened with my buddy, Sheriff Pete?' I asked, as much to divert him as anything: I didn't give a damn about the bad little bastard.

'He's locked up nice and tight, for the moment,' said Ferguson. 'We've got him for a theft from a colliery in Lanarkshire. Small-time stuff but enough to keep him under lock and key. While we're on that subject, the night you got into a tussle with him, who was the woman involved?'

'The girl he was manhandling?' I asked, confused. 'I haven't a clue. I don't even know if he actually knew her or if they'd just bumped into each other in the ballroom or on the way out. Why?'

'Oh, nothing. I just wondered if you knew who she was.'

'I'm aware I have a certain reputation in Glasgow, Jock,' I said, 'but, believe it or not, I don't actually know every beddable woman in the city.'

'Sure . . .' he said and we danced about a little more. It took him five minutes of carefully aimless chat to get to the punch-line, which he went out of his way to make sound as casual as possible.

'We're just putting the initial report to bed on the Dewar murder-suicide,' he explained. 'Tying up any loose ends.'

'Oh?' I said with equally forced casualness. I couldn't think what ends I had left in my statement, loose or otherwise.

'Yes . . .' He stretched the word. 'Remind me . . . you got the call from Dewar just after lunchtime, and he was distraught . . . agitated . . . is that right?'

'Like I told you before, Jock. Several times, if I remember. He told me he didn't know what to do or where to turn. I said I would come up and discuss his case with him that night.'

'How did he get your name and number?'

'That I don't know. I didn't ask.'

'But you didn't know him previously?'

'Nope.'

'What about his wife? You never met her before?'

'No. Why? What's this all about?'

'Like I said . . .' Ferguson stood up, leaving the tea I'd poured him half-drunk, '. . . just checking up on all of the details, that's all. See you . . .'

And that was it.

The 'phone rang shortly after Ferguson left.

'This is Mátyás,' said the Mittel-European-tinged voice. 'I have discussed your suggestion with Ferenc Lang and he has agreed to meet you. With certain conditions.'

'Oh he has, has he?' I said, leaning back in my chair and putting my feet up on the desk. 'A little birdie told me that I should have nothing to do with you or Ferenc Lang.'

'A little birdie?' The voice at the other end of the line sounded confused, but maybe more at my choice of expression than what I was saying. 'I don't know what you mean. Do you want to meet Ferenc or not?'

'Not. It turns out that your Frank, or Ferenc, Lang is not the

Frank Lang I'm looking for and, anyway, I'm no longer working on the Ellis case. So thanks for getting back to me as we arranged, but I no longer have a professional interest in meeting you or Ferenc Lang.'

'I see . . .' There was a pause while he processed the information. 'That is unfortunate. It was you who pressured me to arrange this meeting for you and I have done so at no small inconvenience.'

'Then I apologize for your trouble, but I am no longer employed by that client and, like I said, I therefore have no professional need to meet with Mr Lang. To be honest, this has all been a matter of mistaken identity. Like I said, Mr Lang is not the Frank Lang I was after.'

'Well, that is of course up to you, but I think it may have profited you to talk to Mr Lang. It is a great pity that you have become involved in our business and Ferenc wanted the opportunity to set you straight on a few things.'

'Well, like I said, I'm not involved anymore, so I don't need *setting straight*.'

'If you change your mind, Mr Lang will meet you at the coffee bar in Central Station, across from your office, in exactly one hour. He will give you ten minutes. If you don't turn up, that's up to you. But I really think you should hear what he has to say.'

'I'm sorry, but don't you understand what I've explained? This is no longer any of my business.'

'One hour, Mr Lennox. Mr Lang will make himself known to you.' He hung up.

I held the receiver out for a moment and examined it, shaking my head in disbelief. Maybe Mátyás's English wasn't as perfect as I had thought.

I sat with my feet still up on my desk and smoked a couple of cigarettes while I thought through where I was with everything. The three issues most prominent in my mind were finding Frank Lang for the union, my preparations for getting back home, and distancing myself from the events at the Dewar home in Drumchapel and all of the red tape that could go along with them. Getting tangled up in that was the one thing that could delay my escape from the Second City of the British Empire.

Smoking and idly looking out of the window across Gordon Street to the frontage of Central Station, I thought back to my 'phone call with Mátyás and how he simply would not take the hint that I was no longer interested in whatever his little group was up to. By the time I had finished my second cigarette, I really felt like a cup of coffee. I took my hat and coat from the stand, locked the office behind me and headed down the stairwell and across the street to the station.

CHAPTER TWENTY-FIVE

If she had been wearing a red cape and I had been on my way to her Grandma's house, my smile would probably have been less wolfish.

'If you are Ferenc Lang,' I said, 'then I would seriously consider changing my affiliation.'

She frowned in puzzlement. 'I do not understand,' she said. Her voice was deep, rich, rolled and foreign in a way that weakened your knee joints. Walking across the concourse of the station, I had recognized her instantly as the woman I had seen Ellis with that night in the fog and whose curves I had followed unsuccessfully to the taxi stand.

She was dressed in exactly the same mismatched coat and toque-type hat I had seen her wearing on both previous occasions. Her black hair wasn't loose as it had been the last time, but was swept up and fastened with a clip, and again her face was naked of make-up other than the crimson that emphasized her full lips. In the smogless, illuminated environment of the station, her nut-brown eyes were even more captivating than they had been that night in the fog.

Up close, her beauty was intoxicating. I sobered up from it pretty quickly, however, when I remembered how following her curves had led me directly into the clutches of Hopkins and his

Rich Tea biscuit interrogation techniques. I scanned the station for anywhere a tail might be lurking, which was of course everywhere.

'I can assure you I haff not been vollowed . . .' she said huskily. If I hadn't been right next to her when she spoke, I would have looked around to see where Marlene Dietrich had concealed herself.

'Where's Lang?' I asked.

'Something has come up and it is not safe for him to come here. He asked me to meet you and explain.'

We were standing on the main concourse and, taking her by the elbow, I steered her towards the coffee bar where there would be fewer eyes on us. Whatever Mátyás's little émigré group was up to, and despite all of their attempts at subterfuge, it seemed mad to use a woman like this as a courier. She was less than inconspicuous: no matter how dowdy her outfit, there would not be a man with a pulse and within visual range who would not have given anything to get inside it.

It was maybe something she was aware of, because she insisted that she went into the coffee bar first. She would find a quiet table and when I came in I could buy two coffees and bring them over. I went along with her little dance and ordered the coffees at the counter from a cute little blonde in a waitress uniform.

It took me a moment to find my Hungarian beauty; she had chosen a table right at the back, tucked into a corner and out of sight of the counter, and was sitting with her back to the rest of the patrons. She knew her business all right.

'So is Lang coming or not?' I asked as I placed her coffee before her.

'You have to understand,' she purred Continentally, 'that we have to be very careful. Ferenc particularly. He fully intended to be here, but we realized he was being followed. I was nearest so they 'phoned me and told me to meet you and explain, if you turned up.'

'And what's your name?' I asked.

'Magda.'

'Okay, Magda, perhaps you can tell me what Lang had to tell me.'

'That I cannot,' she said. 'I do not know what he was going to tell you.'

'Well, maybe you can tell me a little bit about your little sewing club.'

'Sewing club?'

'Sorry,' I said, realizing I was going to have to park the metaphors, and the humour. 'Your group. What can you tell me about your group?'

'Nothing. I'm afraid that I am not authorized to discuss anything about our *group*, as you describe it. Please understand that this is difficult times for us.'

'But Ferenc Lang is your leader?'

'No. Not really. Ferenc has lived here many years, and offered to help us when we escaped from Hungary. We don't have a leader, as you put it. But I suppose Mátyás would be the closest thing to that.'

'Well, as I told Mátyás on the telephone, I no longer have a professional interest in your group. But maybe you can tell me something specific – just for my personal curiosity, you understand – are you involved with Andrew Ellis? I mean, romantically involved?'

'Again, please excuse . . . I do not understand . . .' She frowned. Beautifully.

'I mean you, personally, Magda. Were you having a romantic affair with Andrew Ellis?'

The clouds began to gather in her expression and the nut-brown eyes darkened.

'No, Mr Lennox, I have had no such involvement with Mr Ellis.'

'Well, I don't know if you remember me, but I was the mug lost in the smog in Garnethill that night. I saw you both together.'

'I remember.'

'So what were you to up to if you have no personal relationship with Mr Ellis?'

'That is not anything of your business,' she said, the dark fire still in her eyes.

'Fair enough,' I said. I smiled as disarmingly as I could. 'May I ask if you are involved with anyone else? At the moment, I mean.'

Again it took a while for the significance of my question to sink in.

'Again, this is not anything of your business,' she said defiantly. 'And no, I am not interested in any such . . . *entanglements*.'

'I see,' I said philosophically. 'Then I think we are pretty much done here, Magda. Nice as it was to meet you, I don't think either of us has benefited much from the experience.' I stood up. 'Now, if you'll excuse me.'

'I have something for you . . .' she said conspiratorially. She sure did have something for me, but our little exchange had revealed I wasn't going to get it. Nor had Andrew Ellis, apparently. 'I've been asked to give you this.' She reached into her handbag and laid a package on the table. It was a slab about four inches by six and an inch or so thick, wrapped in brown parcel paper and bound with string.

'What is it?' I asked.

'I honestly do not know,' she said. 'It is from Ferenc, and I was told to tell you that he will be in touch to discuss its significance.'

I picked it up. It was light and had a little give in it, like it contained paper. I made to untie it when she laid a hand on mine. A warm, firm hand that sent an electric current through me.

'Do not open it now. Ferenc tell me that you must open it only in private. It explains everything . . .'

'Okay . . .' I slipped the package into my coat pocket. 'But my mother always told me never to accept presents from pretty girls . . .'

She looked at me blankly. Magda was one of the sexiest women I had ever clapped my eyes on – and my eyes really were clapped on her – but she had absolutely no sense of humour. For some reason I could never understand, a sense of humour in a woman was important to me. Maybe because she'd needed it to go to bed with me.

I shrugged. 'Well, Magda, we seem to have run out of things to say. It's a pity Ferenc couldn't have showed up in person, and I will have a look at what he sent me, but I don't see that we have any more business together.'

'You stay here,' she said, rising from her chair. 'Drink another coffee. It is best that we are not seen leaving together. I will go first but I suggest you wait at least ten minutes before you follow.'

'Okay . . .' I resisted the temptation to smirk. It was all too Orson Welles for me. This was Glasgow, not Vienna or Budapest.

I watched her go. She had the kind of figure you watched go.

As soon as she was out of sight, I looked at my watch and decided I had better things to do than play secret agent. Without waiting, I drained my cup, got up and headed out of the station and darted through the chill rain and across the street to my office.

The stairwell that led up to my office was narrow; wide enough to allow two people to pass each other if they angled shoulders appropriately. The two large figures who came charging down the stairs did so so fast that I had to flatten myself against the wall. Even with that, the shoulder of the second one slammed painfully into me. I expressed myself loudly and in eloquent Anglo-Saxon and grabbed his raincoat as he passed. I am pretty quick on my feet and I was ready to get chummy but he moved with professional speed, arcing his arm up and around mine and locking it, the heel of his other hand hammering home into the side of my jaw. His buddy joined in and within a second I was down on the steps with blows raining down fast. I was stunned but not out and it gave them the time they needed to get down the stairs and out of the door. I pulled myself up into a sitting position and put a shaking hand up to my face. My nose was bleeding but not broken.

There was no point in chasing after them. They could have headed in any direction when they hit the street and, anyway, there was always the danger I might catch up with them.

And, looking up the stairwell towards my office landing, I decided it might be more beneficial to find out where they had come from, rather than where they were headed.

The last person I expected to find waiting for me when I returned to my office was Andrew Ellis. After all, it had been his wife who'd been my client, not him.

But, on balance, that wasn't the most discomfiting thing about Ellis's presence in my business premises.

Alarm bells had begun to ring as soon as I found my office door unlocked. Not jemmied or forced, unlocked. Archie had a set of keys, of course, but I wasn't expecting him back until later that afternoon. As I had suspected, this was where my stairwell dance partners had come from.

I stepped into my office and found it trashed. Not as if someone had been rifling through it, more as if Rocky Marciano and Jersey Joe Walcott had decided to hold a rematch there.

And then there was Ellis.

I heard him before I saw him: short, shallow urgent breathing. I found him behind my desk, next to where my captain's chair had been tipped over and paper and the shattered glass shade of my desk light lay scattered on the bare boards of the floor. He was staring up at the ceiling, the expression on his face one of intense concentration, like a track athlete focusing on the race. But Ellis wasn't going to win a Melbourne gold. This was a race he was going to lose.

There was blood everywhere, welling up from the wound on his chest, a vast bloom of crimson on the white of his shirt-front. The weapon lay next to him: a broad-bladed hunting-style knife. The sight of the knife did nothing to cheer me up; not just because the size and type of blade would have done the maximum damage.

It was my knife.

The one I kept in my office drawer and never used for anything more violent than rendering open my rent bill.

I knelt down beside Ellis and applied some pressure to the wound with a handkerchief that I folded into a pad. I looked around for the 'phone; it lay thrown across the room, the lead ripped from its connection box on the skirting board. Not that that mattered much. I probably wouldn't have made the call to summon an ambulance then anyway. In the war, and on one occasion after, I had stayed with a man to ease his way out; and that was my job here. But I needed to know something first.

'Who did this to you, Andrew?' I asked.

He turned his intense gaze from the ceiling to my face, moving his eyes only and keeping his head still, as if held in place by a vice. His breathing came even faster, as if he was summoning up the energy to speak. He moved his pale lips but nothing came out. Ellis had started to shiver, a sign that he had passed that point where there was enough blood left in him to maintain body temperature. He tried again, and this time when it came out, it was short and hissed and I couldn't make out what he said.

'Who?' I repeated. 'I couldn't hear you.' I could feel the handkerchief warm and wet under my hand. I felt damp seep into the fabric of my suit trousers, at the knee, and realized I was kneeling in a pool of Ellis's blood. Not long.

'Tanglewood.'

'Who is Tanglewood? What is Tanglewood?' I asked. He shook his head. Small, sharp, urgent movements.

'Tanglewood. You've got . . . to get . . . to Tanglewood . . .' He reached up with his right hand and grabbed the collar of my coat, pulling me close to him. His breath spilled in my face and I could feel there was no warmth in it. His eyes were locked on mine, urgent, pleading, desperate. Then, in a second, like I had seen so many times before, the light went from them.

And it was in that pose, his hand slipping from its grasp on my collar, his face still close to mine, which itself was bruised and bloodied from my encounter on the stairs, and looking for all the world like Ellis and I were in the last stages of a fight to the death, that the coppers burst in through my office door.

CHAPTER TWENTY-SIX

I was given the third degree by Stan Laurel and Oliver Hardy.

The balding, fat Detective Inspector, who did most of the talking, didn't introduce himself or the skinny, vacant-looking Detective Sergeant next to him who did none of it. Throughout the questions about when I was *supposed* to have gotten back to my office and found Ellis, and what my *supposed* connection with him was, and where and when I was *supposed* to have been when Ellis was being filleted with my knife, I half expected the Detective Sergeant to unfold a handkerchief, tap a hard-boiled egg on the desktop and start peeling it, only to have the fat senior copper slap it out of his hands. I knew I was being too glib, too flippant about the position I was in, but there were too many people to back up my story for them to seriously believe I had murdered Andrew Ellis.

And the duo across the desk really did remind me of Stan and Ollie.

I had already given a full written statement, in detail, but they made me go through everything over and over again. I accounted for my time down to the last minute, including toilet breaks.

It was the usual police procedure. A big lie is easy: saying you didn't commit a crime you had committed is a granite block of a lie that no amount of chipping away at will break. But get the tiniest detail wrong – change the brand of the cigarettes you say you bought at a certain place at a certain time, or who was standing in front of you in the bus queue – and that tiny crack in your carefully constructed story will bring the whole thing down on you. Coppers were never particularly bright, but you didn't have to be; all you needed to be was methodical, patient and take notes.

The fat copper may not have introduced himself or his partner, but I knew who he was. Inspector Shuggie Dunlop.

Shuggie was one of those strange Scottish diminutive forms that was actually longer and infinitely uglier than the original name, Hugh. And Shuggie Dunlop was infinitely uglier than his name. A big man in all three dimensions, he was clearly a keen collector of chins and, in keeping with his surname, spare tyres. Jacketless, the roll of blubber that spilled over his belt and strained his cheap white shirt seemed completely to encircle him, like a built-in life-ring.

It had become clear from the outset that I was not being treated as a witness, but a suspect. This time, no one had called me *Mr* Lennox when I had arrived at St Andrew's Square, and Dunlop was engaging me in a battle of wits. Which, to be honest, was kind of like being challenged to an arm-wrestling contest by Shirley Temple.

The first thing I had asked when I'd been taken into custody was that I be allowed to get a change of clothes. The fine worsted of my suit trousers had absorbed Ellis's blood like blotting paper. What hadn't soaked into the material as a red-black stain had dried and crusted on the surface of the cloth and I doubted if any cleaner could restore the suit to wearable. Which was annoying, because it was one of my bespokes and cost me far more than I should ever have paid for tailoring.

But it wasn't my sartorial sensibilities that had been my main reason for wanting to get out of the suit: it was a skin I needed to shed to lose the taint of death. Maybe then, the image of Ellis's face as he stared up at me, letting go of my collar and his life, would stop pushing its way to the front of my mind, jostling with the image of Sylvia Dewar's broken skull.

Once more, I felt Canada beckoning. But this time it seemed to beckon from much further away.

As it turned out, the police were only too happy to assist me get out of my stained suit. In fact they insisted on it. I was put in a custody cell and ordered to strip down to my underwear and they took everything – coat, jacket, trousers, hat, shirt, tie, shoes – and placed each item in a separate canvas bag, labelled it and took everything away.

They refused my request that I be allowed to pick up fresh stuff from my hotel and instead I was given a neatly folded stack of clothes to change into. It was an interesting get-up: a collarless grey-white shirt and a prison uniform of battledress type jacket and formless trousers. It was scratchy, uncomfortable and smelled as if it could have done with another couple of runs through the laundry. The ensemble was rounded off with a pair of laceless, army-style boots, the leather of which was dull and scuffed.

The prison uniform instantly gave the interrogator an advantage: dressed in that outfit, even I started to believe I might be guilty.

'You realize you could hang for this Lennox, don't you?' Dunlop leaned forward, resting his fat elbows on the wooden desk between us.

'Really?' I asked amiably. 'I would have thought that there was a tiny obstacle in the way of that – and I know it's a technical point, really – but I didn't kill Andrew Ellis.'

I was smart-mouthing to push for a reaction, even if it was to come in the form of a fat fist. I was a little disconcerted when I didn't get one. Dunlop gave a quiet, contemptuous laugh that quivered his fleshy face.

'Well, I say you did. And it's not just Andrew Ellis you'll hang for . . .'

'What are you talking about?'

'You're here for more than the one killing, Lennox. You thought you were going to get away free and –'

Dunlop was interrupted by the door behind me swinging open. When I turned, I was relieved to see Jock Ferguson framed in the doorway, although the timing of his appearance troubled me. Dunlop had just been about to give away more than he had gotten out of me and the unpleasant suspicion crossed my mind that Ferguson had perhaps been listening to Dunlop's questioning from a neighbouring room and had judged it was time to intervene.

'Jock . . .' I said. 'Am I glad to see you.'

'I'm afraid I can't say the same, Lennox.'

I didn't like the look on Ferguson's face one little bit. He nodded to Laurel and Hardy and they stood up wordlessly and left the room. Taking the chair vacated by Dunlop's bulk, Ferguson took a packet of cigarettes out, lit one and slid the pack and lighter across the table to me.

The room was lit by a couple of neon strips, suspended by wires and thin, painted chains from the ceiling. The walls were distempered in two tones: dark green to waist-height, then a buttery cream above. It was a bleak, stark room and, somehow,

Jock Ferguson, with his ill-fitting, dull grey gabardine suit, his long, pale face and hooded eyes, seemed to fit right in.

He leaned forwards, elbows on the desk, his gaze empty and focused on the desktop.

'You're in trouble, Lennox,' he said when he looked up to face me. 'You're in an awful lot of trouble, and I don't think there's much I can do to help you.'

'What?' I twisted my face in disbelief and it hurt like hell from where my chums on the stairs had given me the beating. 'Just because I found Ellis dying? That makes me a witness, Jock, not a suspect. I had nothing to do with his death.'

'Whoever killed him just happened to choose your office as the place to do it, wrecking the joint in the process, is that it?'

'How the hell do I know, Jock? Maybe Ellis found out that his wife had hired me because she had suspicions about his fidelity and he wanted to set me straight. Or maybe he had something to tell me about Tanglewood, whatever or whoever it is, or this Hungarian crowd he's involved with and they followed him to my office and killed him there.'

'Your locked office?'

'Oh, I don't know, Jock . . .' I said exasperatedly. 'Maybe I forgot to lock it when I left to meet Magda at Central Station. Maybe whoever broke in knows how to pick locks. Or had a key, somehow.'

'Oh yes, this mysterious Hungarian brunette you say you met at Central Station?'

'Yes, Magda the mysterious Hungarian brunette. Are you telling me that you don't believe me, Jock?'

'Now, there's the thing . . . you seem to automatically expect me to believe you. Why is that, Lennox? Is that because you never lie to me?'

'You think I've been lying to you?' I said defensively, but there had been a touch of bitterness in Ferguson's voice. Perhaps I should not have been so relieved to see him walk into the interrogation room; what I thought was the cavalry was maybe just more Apaches.

'I don't know, Lennox. Have you been lying to me?' The bitterness was still there. I could tell Ferguson had caught me out on something, or thought he had, but I had no idea what.

'Do you think I've been lying about Magda? Magda is real enough, believe me. And she played her part pretty damned well, keeping me occupied while her pals did in Ellis in my office. In fact, she was pretty insistent that I wait ten minutes after she left before going back to my office. If I had done that, then I wouldn't even have bumped into the two heavies on the stairs. *They're* the guys you should be looking for. Anyway, I've already told Dunlop all of this. Magda was involved with Ellis in one way or another and it's a hell of a coincidence that she keeps me busy while Ellis meets his end, don't you think?'

'That's if she exists. And I wouldn't push the importance of coincidences too much, if I were you. There are too many coincidences revolving around you over the last week or so. And when you get enough coincidences, you get a circumstantial case. You know what a circumstantial case is, don't you?'

'Something you put a picture in before you hang it on the wall, in the case of most coppers.' It was my turn to be bitter. I had expected support, not suspicion, from Ferguson.

'No one is trying to frame you, Lennox. You've done a pretty good job of doing that yourself.'

'What the hell is that supposed to mean? Listen Jock, I understand that being found with a dying man in my office is likely to raise a few eyebrows, but it doesn't take a genius to work out that a killer doesn't use his handkerchief to try to halt the bleeding of his victim.'

'We found your handkerchief stained with Ellis's blood, all right. But we also found the knife that had been used to kill him wiped clean of fingerprints. A knife you admit is yours.'

'Oh yes ... I'm a master criminal covering up my tracks. I wipe my fingerprints off *my* knife so you'll never be able to link me with a dead man stabbed to death in *my* office. That would throw you off the trail all right, wouldn't it?' If my sarcasm was making an impression on Ferguson, then it didn't show.

'Yes, *your* knife. But there again you had to admit it was yours, because I saw you opening mail with it that day I came to your office.'

'Aw come on, Jock, you know this is all crap. You know I didn't kill Ellis. And what's this crap that Dunlop is throwing in about me being in the frame for more than one killing?'

Ferguson stubbed his cigarette out on the pressed tin ashtray and stood up. 'We'll talk about this tomorrow. We're still carrying out some enquiries and you and I are going to have a lot to talk about. In the meantime, I'm afraid you're going to be our guest for the night.'

'This is bull, Jock. All bull.' It was all I could think to say.

'We'll talk tomorrow.' Ferguson said as he went to the door and called in a uniform to see me back to my cell.

CHAPTER TWENTY-SEVEN

The rough blankets they gave me had presumably been laundered but still oozed a fusty odour into the tiny cell and I lay, fully clothed in the uniform they had given me, on top of the bedding. If I could have summoned the power of my will and hovered, Indian guru-like, above them, I would have. But levitation was only one of the many abilities I seemed not to possess. Like common sense. Or the ability to sleep.

The facilities of the City of Glasgow Police headquarters did not run to a resident chef and I was passed a body-warmth package wrapped in grease-transparent newspaper through the fold-down flap in the heavy steel cell door. The fish and chips were caked in salt, and despite being ravenously hungry I could only eat half of them. The same went for the tea: the enamelled tin mug handed through the door was skin-peelingly hot and filled with tea turned to syrup by a ladleful of sugar. They obviously had focused their menu to meet the demands of their regular clientele.

The custody sergeant turned out the lights at nine-thirty and I did my best to sleep. I would need my wits about me the next day, and I felt bone-achingly tired, but my face hurt like hell and my brain was burning with images and thoughts and memories as it tried to make sense of what was happening. Lying in the dark, I found myself thinking of Fiona White, sleeping alone in her flat, my rooms empty above her. That was if she was sleeping alone.

I wondered how long it would take for all this crap to hit the headlines. I hoped I'd be out of this jam before the papers got a hold of my name. In the meantime, I found myself thankful that I had quit my digs when I had instead of waiting the full month. At least I wouldn't have to see that look of weary disappointment on her face when she found out I was in deep trouble again.

I must have dozed off eventually, but was woken again at three by voices from a cell further down the block: one voice loud, strident and shrill, crying out in pain; two others deep, quiet and controlled, occasionally grunting as if engaged in physical labour. Obviously a couple of Glasgow's guardians of law and order had dropped in on a miscreant – at the dead of nightshift – to discuss the error of his ways. Maybe the grunting was them rearranging the furniture for their guest.

I wondered if I would get a visit, but guessed I wouldn't. Paradoxically, that troubled me. The coppers were doing everything by the book with me, and that smacked of keeping their act clean for a date in the High Court, where the judge was allowed to wear a black cap when passing sentence.

The only window in the basement cell was high up and out of reach, but still barred and meshed. When they came round with a breakfast of the same scalding brown sugary sludge and butterless toast, the small square of window was still dark and they switched on the cell block lights again.

It was mid-day when they again parked me in the interrogation room, having left me to stew in my cell until then.

Ferguson and his dumb stooge Dunlop were waiting for me at the cheap oak table and a homely, uniformed WPC sat in the corner with a notepad, ready to take down in shorthand everything that was said. Everything by the book for the judge with the black cap.

Dunlop kicked off by mumbling through my caution that my answers could be used as evidence in court. Then they went through the questions. Had I killed Andrew Ellis in my Gordon Street offices? How did I get the bloody nose and the marks on my face? Could I identify the two men I *claimed* to see running away from my office?

'And while Ellis was being murdered in your place of business,' asked Dunlop, 'you were meeting a Hungarian woman you say called herself *Magda*, attached to some refugee group?'

'That's right. You can ask at the station coffee bar.'

'We have. You were there, all right, the girl at the cash counter recognized your photograph right away, but she didn't see you with anyone else – mysterious foreign woman or otherwise.'

'We sat over at the back. You couldn't see us from the counter and Magda kept her back to everyone. At least it proves *I* was there, doesn't it?'

'It proves you were in the coffee bar, but not when. I get the feeling that the girl behind the counter took a shine to you, which is why she remembered you. But she's hazy about the times. In fact, she guessed you were in a half hour before you said you were. And that doesn't put you in the clear at all.'

'She's just muddled about the timing. Come on . . . if I went to the coffee bar deliberately to rig up an alibi, I'd have asked her the time, or if the station clock was right or some crap like that.'

'Maybe you did,' said Dunlop, his smug smile straining under the weight of his fleshy cheeks. 'Maybe she just forgot that you asked . . .'

I didn't answer but made a face to suggest the question was just too dumb to warrant a reply. Jock Ferguson gave him a similar look and Dunlop's fat neck and cheeks reddened.

'Let's talk about something else,' said Ferguson. 'I came into your office a couple of days ago and asked about the deaths of Thomas and Sylvia Dewar in their home in Drumchapel. Do you remember that?'

'Of course . . .'

'And you told me, when I specifically asked, that you had never met either of the Dewars before that date.'

'That's right. What's this got to do with Ellis?'

Ferguson ignored me. 'So you just went to the Dewars' home in response to his telephone call earlier that day?'

'That's what I said.'

'I know that's what you said . . .' Ferguson held me in a hooded gaze. He rested his hand on a thick buff folder that sat on the desk. I had déjà-vu of Hopkins doing exactly the same thing during his interrogation. 'Tell me, Lennox, has business been good? Of late, I mean?'

I shrugged. 'Okay, I guess.'

'I thought things might be a bit tight for you. You know, making you feel like you need to drum up a bit of business.' Ferguson was trying to be sarcastic and he did so with the grace of a rhinoceros on ice-skates.

'Your point?'

'The Dewars' door was open, right?'

'Yes.'

'Just like you found the door to your office open?'

'Just like I find a door open when a door is open anywhere.'

'You found Mrs Dewar dead on the floor of the kitchen?'

'Yes.'

'And found Thomas Dewar hanging dead upstairs?'

'That's right. What are —'

'You touched nothing in the Dewar home?'

'Other than the 'phone to call the police, no.'

'Okay.' Ferguson paused, looking down at the desk and pursing his lips for a moment. 'Do you know Mrs Maisie McCardle?'

'Who?

'Maisie McCardle. Do you know her?'

'No. I've never heard the name before.'

'No reason that you should have. She lives along the street from the Dewar home. A widow. Her husband died eight years ago and she has no family, so she devotes herself to her dog. She walks it regularly, three times a day, rain or shine.'

I hadn't heard the name before, but an ugly, scowling woman and her ugly dog came immediately to mind. I was in trouble.

'Listen, Jock —'

'Mrs McCardle doesn't have a lot in her life, so she tends to remember people. She remembers you, for example. She remembers seeing you drive away the night the Dewars' bodies were discovered, but — and here's the odd thing — she also remembers having seen you outside the Dewar home a week before, during the day. She's very clear on that. The funny thing is you had a different car the first time. Now that would make me believe you've not been entirely straight with me. Of course, there's always the possibility that old Maisie is mistaken, so let's not get ahead of ourselves. Back to my question about your techniques for canvassing for business. You have just confirmed that you didn't touch anything at the Dewar house . . .'

He paused to reach into the folder. He laid a small white

rectangle of card on the desk for me to see. I recognized it, of course: my business card. He repeated the process and placed a second next to it.

'I have this very strange image of you entering the Dewar house, finding both spouses dead, then taking the time to take the wallet out of a dead man's hip pocket while he's dangling from the lightshade, slipping your business card in and putting the wallet back. Then, on your way out, you tuck a second business card into Sylvia Dewar's address book next to the hall telephone. You see, that *must* be what happened . . .' Ferguson leaned forward, dropping his tone a bar or two. 'Because if it isn't, then you have been telling me lies. You lied to me in your office when I asked you if you had previous contact with Dewar and you just repeated that lie to me just now.'

'Okay, Jock, I can explain . . .'

'I'm not finished.'

I waited for him to say his piece. Maybe that would give me enough time to put together how I was going to tell him the truth without it sounding like a cobbled together collection of hastily improvised lies.

'We've been talking to a lot of people and tracing a lot of your steps,' continued Ferguson. 'I must say, I wish I had whatever it is that you've got going for you as far as the ladies are concerned. They all seem to remember you, even the more unlikely candidates. For example, a waitress in a tearoom in Blythswood Street. She recognized your picture too. She would swear in court that it was you who came into her tearoom and ordered coffees for you and your friend – your friend who looked more than a little shaken up. More than a little roughed up too. She remembers his face wasn't so much swollen, but in the process of swelling up, as if he was fresh from a fight or a beating.'

I stayed silent.

'Do you know the *really* odd thing?' he continued. 'We showed her a photograph of Thomas Dewar and guess what? She positively identified him as your chum with the face like a slapped arse.'

'Like I said, I can explain all of that.'

'I'll look forward to your explanation . . . but first, I'd like to explain something myself. A couple of the finer points about evidence. We talked about a circumstantial case; well, for a circumstantial case to have any value, it has to comprise a number of mutually supportive, court-admissible proofs. One of the main proofs is flight or intended flight. If a prosecutor can demonstrate that the accused was in the process of running away, or preparing to run away, then it is an admissible possible indicator of guilt. For example, if – immediately prior to the commission of a crime or crimes – the accused empties his bank account, quits his lodgings and cancels all of his charge accounts.'

I sighed. 'I know you're not going to believe this, Jock, but I decided to go back to Canada. I was going to tell you, but I've only just made up my mind to go.'

'And you intend to go back when?'

'Three, four weeks . . .'

'That's odd, because I called round to your digs and Fiona White – and correct me if I'm wrong, but you and Mrs White have more than a contractual relationship – Fiona White told me you've quit your digs and she has no idea where you've moved to. Then there's the under manager at the bank, who actually used the phrase "indecent haste" when describing you badgering him to speed up the transfer of money out of your savings account, as well as emptying your cash account there and then.'

'Christ Jock, he's a Scottish bank clerk. The Earth's crust moves at "indecent haste" in comparison. I was just getting everything sorted out in advance, that's all. I had to chase the bank or it would take forever.'

'On its own, that might sound almost reasonable. But let's go back to circumstantial proofs. Another is proof of concealment – if the accused had taken steps to hide himself. Where are you staying for the three or four weeks until you leave Bonnie Scotland?'

'I already told Dunlop. The Paragon Hotel. In Garnethill.'

'Yes,' said Ferguson contemplatively. 'We sent a couple of CID boys round to check it out. The rather attractive redhead there is another female under your spell it would seem. But there seems to be some confusion about your name – she swears blind that you are Mr Kelvin. Can you explain that?'

I felt my shoulders slump. 'As a matter of fact, Jock, I can't. Least not in a way that would make any sense.'

'And then there's the question as to why you have changed cars, less than a month before you return to Canada.'

'I haven't changed cars,' I protested. 'The Atlantic has been acting up and I've rented a car for a while. The garage that has the Atlantic is coming up with a price to buy it from me.' It should have sounded more convincing, but it didn't. 'Are you seriously telling me that you think the Dewar deaths had anything to do with me? Everything I told you about him 'phoning me that day and the reason for his call ... all that was absolutely true. I didn't tell you about my previous visit because it had nothing to do with whatever was going on between the Dewars. All I was doing was trying to keep things *uncomplicated*.'

'Thing is,' said Ferguson, 'there's a possible anomaly in the times of death of Sylvia and Thomas Dewar. Added to which there are no fingerprints on the ashtray. Now why would Thomas Dewar, knowing he was going to kill himself immediately after, wear gloves to murder his wife? And the pathologist's guesses at timing suggest that she died sometime in the early afternoon, when Dewar was at work. So instead of a murder-suicide, what we could be looking at is Dewar, whose state of mind was pretty fragile because of his suspicions about his wife, coming home to find her murdered, decides he wants to join her and goes up to his room and strings himself up.'

'But that puts me in the clear . . . I was there *after* Dewar hanged himself. Anyway, why would I then 'phone the police?'

'Because you were there in the evening doesn't mean you weren't there earlier in the day. Maybe you forgot something, or maybe you were puzzled as to why there hadn't been word of a murder in Drumchapel, and you went back to check it out. You get there and find a grief-stricken Dewar dangling from the ceiling and instantly you've got a patsy for his wife's murder. It's a godsend for you so you call it into the police.'

'Or maybe it's just the way I told it. Dewar is driven mad by his wife's repeated infidelity, finally cracks and kills her, then himself.'

'What about the delay between her death and his?'

'I don't know . . . maybe he's in shock. Maybe he sits with her for a while or can't make his mind up to do himself in too.'

'And let me guess,' chipped in Dunlop. 'The day in the tearoom in Blythswood Street . . . he had the smacked-looking face because you had been slapping the idea of murder-suicide out of him, is that it?'

I ran through what had happened that day and how Dewar had tried to jump me in Sauchiehall Street Lane, and how it was all a huge misunderstanding because he thought I was one of his wife's wrestling partners. Maybe it was the prison uniform I was wearing, but when I heard myself say it all out loud, even I didn't believe it. Ferguson sat impassively, as did his fat friend, and made no comment when I was finished.

'Let's move on,' he said. 'Ellis's murder. You say that you were originally hired by Andrew Ellis's wife to investigate the possibility that he was having an affair?'

'That's right.'

'So you followed Ellis about, and got Archie McClelland to do the same, because you were being paid to by Pamela Ellis?'

'Yes'

Ferguson frowned. 'Well, that gives us a bit of a problem. You see, Mrs Ellis told us not only that she never hired you, or any other private detective, but that she never had any suspicions whatsoever about her husband's fidelity. She's never heard of you, Lennox.'

'And you believe her?

'I have no reason not to believe her.'

'She was in my office, Jock. And we spoke on the 'phone. How does she explain that?'

'Archie confirmed that you had him follow Ellis's car.'

'Well then? I told you . . .'

'All that proves is you told Archie to keep tabs on Ellis. And that you, for some reason, were following Ellis yourself. Archie would do anything for you, Lennox, except lie. He couldn't tell me that he had been there when you were supposed to have met with Pamela Ellis. In fact, he's never met or even seen Pamela Ellis.'

'*Supposed* to have met?' I looked at Ferguson beseechingly. 'For Christ's sake, Jock, just tell me straight if you don't believe me.'

'This isn't about what I believe or don't believe. This is about what can be proved or disproved in court.' He sighed. 'And, call me picky, but my belief in you tends to get shaky when you tell me outright lies.'

'I'm sorry I didn't front up about having had prior knowledge of the Dewars. It was just that the Dewar thing looked like a straightforward murder-suicide. I thought if I kept it simple all you would need would be a deposition and the inquest and paperwork wouldn't get in the way of me getting back to Canada. And, if you must know, I felt pretty shitty about the whole thing. Dewar was in a hell of a state that day he jumped me and after that he badgered me to take on his case. The fact remains that I turned my back on a desperate man. And that is the extent of my responsibility for the Dewar deaths. And the extent of my lying. Everything else I've told you is true. Can I have another cigarette?' I stubbed out what was left of the one I'd been smoking. Ferguson pushed the pack and lighter to me and I lit another.

'Listen,' I went on, blowing a jet of smoke towards the ceiling strip lights. 'I'm not saying that I haven't bent the truth on occasion – but if I were lying to you to cover up that I'd killed either of the Dewars or Andrew Ellis, I'd make it a hell of a lot more convincing and a hell of a lot less elaborate than this crap. Shit, Jock, it even sounds made up to me.'

'But the fact remains that there is no evidence of you ever having met Pamela Ellis.'

'Like I said, she was in my office and I 'phoned her. You can check her 'phone records.'

'That'll take both a warrant and an age.'

'But it will at least prove we had a conversation.'

'Okay. I'll look into it. Can you give me a date and a rough time?'

My heart sank and the sinking must have shown on my face.

'What is it?' asked Ferguson.

'I 'phoned her from the pub. The Horsehead. I don't think I 'phoned from the office at all.'

'A call from a pub doesn't prove anything.'

'Yes, Jock,' I said forcefully, 'I'm well aware of that.' Another thought struck me. 'Wait . . . she made a call to my digs. She 'phoned to tell me her husband had just gone out. Fiona White took the call before passing it on to me.'

'Did she tell Mrs White who was calling?'

'No. But at least it's proof of contact.'

'If we can track the call down with the GPO. Even then it doesn't prove much other than a woman 'phoned you from Andrew Ellis's home. The fact is his wife flatly denies hiring you and that leaves you following her husband around for reasons of your own. A husband who ends up dead in your office.'

'She's lying. This Hungarian group killed her husband and have probably threatened to do the same to her if she talks. You convict me and they're free and clear. I've been set up very professionally and they're not about to let Pamela Ellis unhitch it all.'

'Listen, Lennox, this all smacks of you holding back on me. Like you held back on me about your involvement with the Dewars. I have to tell you that we also have witnesses – the doormen – who say you and Sylvia Dewar left the Locarno at almost the same time. Separately, but within a couple of minutes of each other. The same night you get into a tussle in the street with Sheriff Pete outside the Barrowlands over an unnamed woman.'

'Jesus, Jock . . . now you're really clutching at straws.'

'The truth is I've got a lot to clutch at.'

'Well,' I said with as much confidence as I could muster, 'the one thing you don't seem to have been able to come up with is the most important thing of all: a motive. Say one or both of the Dewars was murdered by a hand other than Tom Dewar's own; say the Ellis killing, which is completely unconnected in any way to the Dewar deaths, went down the way you're suggesting it did, the question remains, *why*? What possible motive would I have for either killing?'

'On the night before he was murdered, Andrew Ellis's business premises were broken into. As you know, he was in the demolition business but the target of the raid wasn't the secure explosives locker. The night watchman was held at gunpoint, tied up and had his public spiritedness pistol-whipped out of him. The one thing he could tell us about the raiders was that they carried the whole job out with military precision. And they communicated by hand signals, not speaking once.'

'What's this got to do with me?'

'The raiders stole fifteen thousand pounds in wages cash from the office safe. Everything this team did was highly professional and showed they had really done their homework. They knew the money would be there that night and the night watchman said they seemed to know their way around perfectly. Almost as if they had had someone on the inside.'

'Well, don't you see?' I said, suddenly energized. 'All of that with the hand signals ... that's exactly what you would do if your team had voices that would be remembered, either because they would have to talk in Hungarian or Bela Lugosi English. Maybe Ellis himself was their man on the inside, either because he sympathized with them or because he was coerced. I'm telling you, Jock, you find who carried out that robbery and you'll find who murdered Ellis.'

'So, let me get this straight,' Ferguson spoke slowly and deliberately, as if laying down one thought after the other like paving slabs, 'Whoever took the cash that night murdered Ellis? That's what you're saying?'

'Exactly!' I held my hands out then let them fall onto my thighs with a slap.

Ferguson reached into the folder again. This time he laid a package on the table next to where he'd left both my business cards lying. The package had been wrapped in brown parcel paper and tied with string, but the police had obviously opened then loosely re-wrapped it. Ferguson eased back the paper to reveal an inch-and-a-half thick brick of banknotes. Fivers.

I hadn't known what had been inside it, but I recognized the wrapping paper, the string and the size of the package. With everything that had happened with Ellis and subsequently, I had forgotten the package Magda had passed on to me from Ferenc Lang.

'We found this in your coat pocket. The serial numbers match the stolen cash.' Ferguson leaned back and folded his arms. 'Like I said, Lennox, you've been holding back on me and now, most definitely, is not the time to be holding back. So let's have it. Everything.'

And that was exactly what I gave him.

CHAPTER TWENTY-EIGHT

I talked solidly for an hour or more. I didn't think about what I was saying or pause to consider how believable or ludicrous it sounded. I just talked. And, just as I had with Hopkins and as I had promised Ferguson, I gave them everything. Including Hopkins.

I could see from their faces, especially Dunlop's fat one, that the Hopkins story was a big fish for them to swallow, but I gave them the names of the two Special Branch men who had kept Hopkins company. If there's only one thing a copper will take at face value, it's another copper's word. As I spoke, Ferguson wrote the odd note into his notebook and the WPC scribbled everything in shorthand onto her pad.

Like I say, I gave them everything. Almost.

I left one small detail locked up safe and sound. They knew I had moved out of my digs and into the Paragon Hotel, and that would be enough for them. At least for now. I hoped to hell that Ferguson – because it certainly wouldn't be Dunlop – wouldn't catch on to the fact that I couldn't have all of my stuff at the hotel. They had bigger and more pressing issues they wanted to deal with so, for the meantime, I decided to keep quiet about the barge I had rented to stow my stuff. After all, it could come in handy.

'So you were working on these two cases simultaneously?' Ferguson asked when I eventually paused to draw breath. 'The job Connelly and his union took you on to do and the potential infidelity case you say Pamela Ellis hired you for.'

'That's right. For a while I thought there was a connection between them: that, by coincidence, the same Frank Lang the union was looking for was the same Frank or Ferenc Lang who is behind this Hungarian émigré group.'

'And they're not?'

'No. I was looking for a coincidence where none existed. And it led me straight into all this crap. Pamela Ellis became very keen to drop me from the case, feeding me this all-a-big misunderstanding and how-could-she-have-been-so-stupid bull. Whatever it was that made her want me to drop the case is the same reason she's now claiming she never hired me in the first place. I don't know how or why, but Andrew Ellis was playing cloak-and-dagger games with this Hungarian outfit and they have something – everything – to do with his death. I just stumbled into their little game because of a simple case of mistaken identity – but my guess is that they thought I was investigating them and whatever they're up to specifically. Dangerous people, Jock.'

'Well, if the link between the cases and the two Frank Langs is coincidental, then you are the unluckiest man I know when it comes to coincidences. It just so happens that, completely independent of each other, both end up with people dead. Murdered.'

He had a point.

'Could someone get me a change of clothes from my hotel?' I asked when it was time to go back to my cell.

'No can do, Lennox,' said Ferguson. 'We've already cleared

out your closets and the science boys are examining them for evidence.'

'I see,' I said. Ferguson knew my taste for fancy tailoring and would realize they were looking at only a travelling wardrobe, when he got the report back listing the stuff examined.

'Well,' I said, 'can I at least have a pair of laces for these boots? I can hardly keep them on my feet.'

'No laces.' Dunlop made his first and only contribution to the interrogation. 'Suicide risk. We don't want to find you strung up like Dewar, do we?'

'No?' I sneered back at Dunlop. 'I thought that was exactly the point of this exercise.'

They put me back in my cell and I was given a bread roll with some kind of gelatinous luncheon meat in it and another cup of near-boiling, sugary tea. Practically no one in Glasgow over the age of twenty had a full set of teeth, and I could have sworn I felt a fizzing in my mouth as my dental enamel started to dissolve.

I ran a hand over my jaw and it rasped on the stubble. Unshaven, bruised from my encounter with the two guys on the stairwell, without a comb for my hair and in my fetching prisoner's ensemble, I must have really looked the part of a guilty and desperate felon. I tried not to think of the stakes I was playing for and did my best not to imagine the kiss of three-quarter inch, white Italian hemp around my neck.

It wouldn't come to that. It *couldn't* come to that. They may have had circumstantial evidence, but surely not enough to prove a case beyond reasonable doubt. But, there again, I certainly wouldn't be the first innocent man to drop through a trapdoor in Barlinnie Prison.

I found myself reflecting on the irony that there had been more than one thing for which I could have hanged. And about how much I hated the idea of dying here, in Glasgow.

It was already dark outside and my cell was bathed in the sickly yellow light of the caged ceiling bulb when Jock Ferguson came to my cell, around four-thirty in the afternoon. He came alone and waited till the custody man's footsteps had faded before sitting on the edge of my bunk and offering me a cigarette.

'You don't really believe all of this crap, do you, Jock?'

'The truth? No. Everything I know about you tells me that you didn't kill Ellis. But as a police officer I'm having a really hard time finding anything to put you in the clear. Listen, Lennox, there's only the two of us here and it's off the record. Is there anything you're not telling us? Have you been doing your usual and got into bother because you've been shagging other men's wives?'

'You're not really being serious . . . ?'

'It's the only possible link and it's the one that Dunlop is putting forward.'

'I wondered why he was so quiet in the interview room . . . he was obviously plum tuckered out from doing all that thinking.'

'I wouldn't be so glib about it, if I were you. Dunlop's theory is the only thing at the moment that makes any sense. More sense than anything you've told us so far. You do realize I shouldn't be giving you any kind of inside dope on this, don't you?'

I nodded. 'I appreciate it, Jock.'

'The way Dunlop has this playing is this: Sylvia Dewar was

well known for enjoying the company of men other than her husband. You have a reputation for chasing any piece of skirt. So Dunlop has it that you and Sylvia Dewar were carrying on together. And he has a witness who places you at the Dewar house a week before the deaths and at a time when Thomas Dewar would be at work and you and Sylvia would be alone. Then Dewar jumps you in Sauchiehall Street Lane, exactly as you said, because he suspects you've been sleeping with his wife. Except, in Dunlop's version, Dewar's jealous rage is entirely justified and that, I have to say, does sound more credible than him ambushing an innocent man just because he found a business card in his wife's purse.'

'Okay . . . go on . . .'

'Dunlop has you painted as this manipulative Don Juan who moves in on Pamela Ellis too. Now, even Shuggie Dunlop admits Pamela Ellis is a little too old and too plain for you to take an interest in her for her own sake. Instead, he has you moving in on her so that she becomes your accomplice in knocking off her husband for his business, money and insurance payout. But you get caught and Mrs Ellis gets scared and denies all knowledge of you. The clever part in Dunlop's theory is that it explains any telephone or other contact between you and Pamela Ellis as two accomplices planning a murder. In fact, the more difficult it is to find evidence of contact, the more it points to you going out of your way not to be seen talking to each other.'

'So why did I kill Sylvia Dewar?'

'Sylvia Dewar finds out about your affair with Pamela Ellis, gets jealous and blackmails you for a cut of the proceeds. She already has a previous conviction for dishonesty. You have to keep Sylvia quiet and prevent her from spilling the beans to

Ellis about you and his wife, so you cave in her head with the ashtray, making sure you don't leave prints. Then Dewar comes home and, distraught, kills himself. You come back in the evening to find out why no one is talking about Sylvia's murder, or maybe because you're worried you've left something incriminating behind. Probably the business cards, but you can't find them.'

'Because they're cunningly hidden in a wallet and an address book?' I snorted.

'I didn't say it was my theory. And remember you'll be playing to a Glasgow audience. Murder juries here are not used to the accused being sophisticated in his thinking. I have to tell you, I think Dunlop's line could run . . .'

'You really think this will end up in front of a jury? What about everything I told you today?'

'We're checking into all of that,' he said. 'But I have to tell you it's not piecing together very well.'

'Did you speak to the union?'

'We talked to Paul Lynch. He had a pretty good stab at trying to disavow you, but Joe Connelly confirmed that they had hired you to look for Frank Lang and some missing items. What is it?' Ferguson read the expression on my face.

'Nothing . . . just I'm relieved. Connelly and Lynch were almost obsessive about meeting me in secret and I thought they would deny knowing me.'

'Like I said, that little shit Lynch was thinking about it, but I reminded him of the penalties of obstruction, false information, that kind of stuff. Connelly is just pissed off that we were there at all.'

'And the rest?'

'The rest still isn't too good. Pamela Ellis still denies having hired you, even though I told her we were getting her 'phone records. And the Hopkins thing . . . well, I'll talk to you about that later. We're going to go out for some fresh air.'

'So we're travelling out of Glasgow . . .' I said with dull malice.

CHAPTER TWENTY-NINE

A uniform came for me half-an-hour after Ferguson left. He was capped, coated and gloved and he handed me an army surplus greatcoat, one of those things with fabric so dense it could probably have stood up by itself. He led me down the cell passage to where Ferguson and Dunlop, also both in their outdoor wear, were waiting for me. Dunlop's tent-sized raincoat emphasized his bulk.

'We off camping boys?' I asked gleefully and Ferguson shot me a warning look.

It was only just before six, but it was night outside. Despite the heavy army coat I felt the bite of the chilled air. I still didn't have laces for the one-size-too-big boots and I struggled to keep them on my feet as I walked to the black police Wolseley. I felt something more than the chill in the air: a tightening in my chest warned me, as it always did, of a coming fog, and there was no sparkle to the streetlights or car headlights as they were dulled by something gathering in the dark air.

Sitting in the back of the police car between Dunlop and the burly uniformed constable would be tolerable providing our journey was short enough that I didn't need to breathe till we arrived. Ferguson sat in the front. I was surprised that they hadn't handcuffed me and wondered just what, exactly, my legal status was. I hadn't been charged yet, but I had been cautioned before giving my statement, and it was clear that Dunlop was trying to build a case against me that would stand up in court.

Maybe, I thought, I should ask for a lawyer.

'Where are we off to?'

Ferguson twisted around in his seat. 'The address you gave us in Ingram Street. It's past office hours but, if the people you say operate out of that building really are who you say they are, then I wouldn't think that they keep banker's hours.'

As we made our way through the city, the fog that had dimmed the sparkle of the streetlights became thick and viscous, on the tipping point to becoming smog. By the time we pulled up in Ingram Street and got out of the car, across the street from the Art Nouveau frontage of the building in which I had met Hopkins, I could only see the street for one block in either direction, and approaching headlights only a block beyond that. I don't know why, but I took a strange, sad comfort in seeing the smog close in, closing in my perception of the world with it. Sometimes, in the smog, you could imagine that the entire universe, the whole of reality, only extended as far as you could see, and that anything else beyond it, and any time before or after that moment, did not exist. It was a form of solipsism that, given my current situation, I found very comforting.

'Another bad one,' Dunlop muttered to Ferguson as we all decanted from the car, with me struggling not to lose an oversized, unlaced boot in the process.

'Soon be a thing of the past,' said Ferguson, 'with this Clean Air Act coming into force. Won't you miss that back in Canada?' he asked, turning to me.

'Me and my lungs both,' I said, cheered by the thought that Ferguson could see a future for me that did not involve Italian hemp or a twelve-by-eight prison cell.

My cheer did not last long.

The uniformed copper grabbed a fistful of my coat sleeve at the wrist and led me across the road. A short, skinny man in his thirties waited for us outside the building, huddled against the gathering damp. He looked like some kind of mid-range clerk and Ferguson addressed him as Mr Collins, thanking him for coming along outside office hours. Collins had a heavy set of keys and let us in through the main door.

'Isn't there a buzzer too?' I asked. 'A sort of security system?'

Collins looked me up and down and it was clear he didn't like what he saw. Despite there being three coppers to protect him, the sight of a dishevelled, unshaven and bruised desperado in a prison uniform clearly shook him. Before answering he looked at Ferguson, who nodded.

'No,' he said in a thin, wheedling kind of voice. 'There is not.'

And there wasn't. Nor were there any commissionaires on the empty desk, nor any sign of occupancy of the building on any level. I led everyone across marble to the cage elevator and pressed the button for Hopkins's floor. When we came out there was no bustle of office types, no office furniture, no locked doors to rooms full of secrets.

'Where did Hopkins question you?' asked Ferguson. I appreciated his omission of the word *supposed*.

I led them into the room and put on the lights. No Hopkins. No table, no chairs, no foolscap notebooks, no maps on the walls.

'Jock . . .' I turned to Ferguson.

'I checked this afternoon, Lennox. This building has been

empty for two months. It's about to be refurbished for a new commercial tenant. And before you ask: no, the new occupants have nothing to do with national security. I don't have many contacts in that area, but those that I do have say they've never heard of anyone called Hopkins operating North of the border.'

'That doesn't mean he doesn't exist,' I said and failed to keep the pleading out of my tone. 'The very nature of that type of work means there'll be lots of outfits and people operating independently of each other.'

'True . . . but where I don't have a lot of contacts in the security and intelligence services, I do have contacts in every police force in Scotland. And I can't find any officers with the names Roberts or Lindsey in any Special Branch division. I'm sorry Lennox, but I don't see where we go from here. Without Hopkins to support your story, there's nothing to prove that this elusive Hungarian émigré group exists.' He held his arms out and looked around the empty room. 'No Hopkins.'

I looked around the room too. I had exactly the same sense of unreality I had had outside in the smog: a feeling that the empty building around me was all that was real, and my memory of Hopkins was some kind of illusion. I felt suddenly dizzy and wobbled slightly on my feet.

'Are you okay, Lennox,' asked Ferguson. I nodded impatiently.

'When I was here Hopkins said something about them only using this building on a temporary basis. Maybe they've moved on to somewhere else.'

It sounded lame even to me and I could see a sad weariness settle into Ferguson's expression.

'If you didn't believe that I met Hopkins here,' I said, 'then what was the point of going through this charade?'

'Because I wanted to see if *you* believed it. Come on, Lennox, let's go.'

I found my focus again and my mind raced as we made our way back down to the ground floor in the cage elevator. None of this made any sense to me, so God alone knew what it must have sounded like to a couple of professional coppers who had heard every hare-brained and half-assed story under the sun.

The elevator bounced to a halt and we stepped out onto the marble of the grand entrance hall.

I turned to Ferguson. 'I need to get to the bottom of this, Jock. It's all an elaborate set-up and I need to find out why and who's behind it. Let me loose.'

Ferguson gave as small laugh. 'No way, Lennox. If anyone's going to get to the bottom of this case, it'll be us.'

'Listen, Jock . . .' I jerked my head in the direction of Dunlop. 'Your fat friend here has already made up his mind about me, and that means he's not even going to start looking for an answer anywhere else. If you want answers, real answers, then let me go so that I can ask my own questions in my own way. Only then will we really get to the bottom of all of this.'

Dunlop grunted, which was appropriate for his physique. 'Do you honestly think that we're going to let you wander about free as a bird?'

'If you want some proper answers, then yes. Let me go on police bail or whatever you have to. You can put a tail on me. I'll give you hourly reports. Whatever you need. But a bunch of coppers flat-footing it all over the place isn't going to clear this up.'

'Maybe we think we already have got it cleared up,' said Dunlop.

'And that's exactly what this Hungarian mob want you to

think, don't you see that? I'm not a moron, Dunlop. Do you think that if I had killed Ellis, especially if it was premeditated, I wouldn't have come up with something a lot less cockamamie than what I've told you?'

Dunlop smirked and shook his head.

'Sorry, Dunlop. That was maybe too difficult for you to take in, the question having a double-negative in it and all.'

The fat detective took a step towards me but Ferguson checked him.

'You have a point,' said Ferguson. 'But there's absolutely no way we can release you until we've carried out more enquiries.'

I sighed, the fight out of me.

'Let's get back to the Square,' said Ferguson. 'There's nothing more to be gained by hanging around here.'

Collins, who I now guessed to be some kind of letting or estate agent, let us out of the building, switching off the lights and shutting the door behind us. There was an urgent exchange between the policemen on the pavement, I guessed about the smog that had grown denser while we had been inside. Getting back to St Andrew's Square was going to be quite an undertaking. Ferguson said something to the uniformed cop, who renewed his tight grip on my coat sleeve.

In that kind of smog, crossing the road becomes a job for all your senses. When taxis or buses have a habit of looming suddenly out of the murk, only feet away from you, you learn to listen out for the sound of approaching motor engines, hearing them long before you see a glimmer of headlights.

I was given my chance by the Whispering Death.

To be more precise, I was given my chance by the Number Thirteen Whispering Death to Clarkston. I acted on instinct

more than anything else. My police escort was leading me across
the street when the trolleybus, its electric motor silent, surged
out of a wall of grey-green smog. On seeing us, the driver sounded
his claxon and the police constable pulled me back towards the
pavement.

It was more an instinctive reaction – the fly's impulse to pull
against the spider's web – than a conscious decision to escape.
I yanked my arm hard, pulling the copper with me into the
path of the trolleybus. He shouted something obscene and let
go of my sleeve and I threw myself in the other direction, placing
the trolleybus between me and the uniform, Dunlop and
Ferguson.

I could hear Ferguson shouting behind me but I lunged
forward. I tripped up over my own feet, made larger and more
cumbersome by the unlaced army boots, and came down hard
onto the cobbles of the street. I picked myself up instantly and
ran headlong toward the other side of the road.

And right into the path of a taxi.

Fortunately, the cab was travelling slowly because of the poor
visibility and I suffered no injury other than the slurs on my
mother's virtue bawled out through the window by the driver.
One of my boots had come off and I kicked the other one free
and ran on in my sock soles. It made my feet slip on the cobbles,
but when I made it to the opposite pavement, dodging in front
of the parked police car, I got full purchase and was able to
sprint. There were shouts and the sound of running behind me
and the blast of a horn told me that one of my pursuers had
also run out in front of a vehicle.

Running full pelt in the smog had a certain edge to it, like
playing Russian roulette. With only a three- or four-yard visibility, there was the constant risk of a bone crunching collision

with another pedestrian, a lamppost or an unpredicted wall. It also had its advantages: there could only be two of them after me, Jock Ferguson and the burly uniformed constable. I reckoned Shuggie Dunlop's running range was even more limited than the visibility. They couldn't see me now; I had become hidden behind a curtain of smog within a few yards, but unfortunately not before seeing the direction I took. That meant they wouldn't have had to split up and each take a direction, and both Ferguson and the uniform would be heading this way. I thought about re-crossing the road and heading back the way I had come, but that was too obvious and there was always the chance that they were each taking one side of the street.

I took a random right into an alley and sprinted full pace, again hoping I didn't tumble over an obstacle. I came to another alley, cutting across the first, so I took another right. Eventually I reached the gloomy, indistinct mouth of the alley and found myself in what I guessed was a bigger street, although it was difficult to tell in the smog-tightened pool of visibility. I took off again at random, eventually slowing to a trot, my stocking-soled feet silent on the pavement.

Peering into the smog around me, I occasionally picked out the sounds of footsteps and the indistinct bloom of hand-held flashlights. No one was looking for me here – the torches were those of pedestrians equipped for the smog, following a wall or a pavement edge to find their way. Ferguson, Dunlop and the uniformed policeman had no chance of finding me now and, if they had split up, I guessed they'd struggle to find each other, blind in the smog. But they weren't the only ones who were lost. I had no idea where I was.

I found another alley way and dodged into it, moving the few feet back from the street necessary to be concealed from view. My feet were beginning to hurt, not so much because I'd been running on stone and asphalt without shoes but because of the cold that was beginning to penetrate deep into the bone. That was something I needed to sort out sooner rather than later. I leaned my back against some stonework and made a conscious effort to calm myself and think through my situation. Apart from the small inconvenience of being a wanted man on the run, dressed in a prison outfit, hunted by the police and without any kind of footwear, it was all going swimmingly.

CHAPTER THIRTY

Think, Lennox.

I kept repeating it to myself, trying to push back the panic. After all, I'd been in worse situations.

There had been some kind of cockeyed logic behind my escape. I wasn't kidding myself that I could live the rest of my life as a fugitive, even if I did somehow get back to Canada, but I knew that my prospects were no more sunny if I had stayed put with the police. I had to find the answers myself, and I couldn't do that from a cell. I even toyed with the idea that Ferguson had taken me to the Hopkins building, even though he already knew there was no one there, just to give me a chance to make a break for it. I dismissed the thought: no matter how sympathetic he was to my plight, Jock Ferguson was a straight-down-the-line copper. Creative thinking or expedient dodges were not in his makeup.

And I tried not to think about the little lecture Ferguson had given me about flight being an indicator of guilt.

I tried to look on the bright side: I may have looked grubby, dishevelled, black-eyed, unshaven, shoeless and probably half-mad, but I comforted myself with the thought that this was Glasgow, so there was no problem with me looking out of place.

There really were genuine advantages to my situation. The

smog was a godsend: Ferguson wouldn't call out search parties, knowing it would be a fool's errand. I could bet, however, that every patrolling beat bobby would have my description the next time he made the routine call from his police box to check in with his station. It all meant that I had time, but not much. And, of course, the smog was as much an encumbrance to my escape as it was to their manhunt.

I had to get my bearings.

Glasgow's artery was the Clyde. And, like all arteries, it had a pulse. There was always loud activity on the river or along its shores. If I could get to it, I could get some kind of bearing.

I strained the smog for the sounds of the river. Nothing. Just the bleating of car and bus horns as drivers warned each other of their snail's pace approach in the smog. Guessing that the sounds of traffic would indicate the city centre, I took it as a bearing and headed in the opposite direction, again dodging the sounds of footsteps in the fog. I still managed to scare an older couple when I nearly bumped into them. The old man drew his wife to him as they both took in my appearance with startled, terrified eyes. I mumbled an apology and stumbled on, leaving them shocked and puzzling as to whether I would turn back into Dr Jekyll before midnight.

I reckoned I must have been heading toward the Trongate, but when I found myself following the flank of a massive, ornate building, and could hear the rhythmic sounds of chugging loco-motives, I realized that I must have staggered across the street without recognizing any landmarks and was now at the back side of the St Enoch Station. Again I paused, resting against the wall and massaging my feet, one by one. This was good and bad: I was nearer the river but also closer to Buchanan Street. More people. And more coppers.

I pushed off again, heading into the maze of streets and alleys behind the station. A sign told me I was in Dunlop Street. Now I could clearly hear the horns and claxons of barges and tugs navigating the smog-bound water. If I handled this right, I might even find the suspension footbridge near Custom Quay and get over to the south side of the Clyde, where I could either get lost in the warren of the Gorbals or trace my way along the river.

I paused at the end of the street, which opened out onto Clyde Street and the riverfront. I checked both ways as much as I could: the smog had gotten no denser but nor had it lifted; I guessed it had settled in for the night and that gave me some added comfort.

Down here, next to the river, the streets would be empty at this time of night, particularly on a night like this. All the sounds of activity came from the Clyde. I turned right and, after a few yards, ran across the street to the riverside, following it until I could make out the stone arch of the suspension foot-bridge. The suspension bridge across the Clyde was like a scaled down version of the Clifton Suspension Bridge, with two stone-built arches, one at either end, supporting the steel cables that held the bridge in place. Again I paused to listen out for the sounds of anyone about before passing through the arch and walking quickly across the bridge.

I saw the uniformed copper at the same time he saw me, when I was halfway across the river. It was the black silhouette of his high-crowned peaked cap in the grey-green smog that identified the approaching figure as a policeman. To him, I would have just been a shape in the gloom. But, as soon as he got close, even with my prisoner jacket hidden beneath the army coat, he would see my shoeless feet and generally disreputable mien. In Glasgow, 'don't like the look of you' was grounds enough for a copper to feel your collar until something more substantial could be trumped up. In my case, no trumping-up would be needed. I turned on my heel so fast it was practically a pirouette; my thinking was that, in this miasma, the copper wouldn't be sure if I had been heading towards him at all, or if he had simply caught up with someone walking in the same direction as him.

'Hey ... you ...' he called out and I picked up the pace, hunching my shoulders and pulling my coat collar up. My balletic skills had clearly not been up to scratch.

'Hey you ... I'm talking to you! Wait there a minute!' I heard his hobnails match my pace. I didn't look over my shoulder, instead breaking into a sprint, back the way I had come. More shouts and I could hear him running after me. I had to open enough distance for the smog to cloak me again, but the heavy greatcoat was holding me back.

I had to risk it: when I broke through the stone archway I turned sharp right, then jumped the railings on the riverside, hoping there was enough bank to stop me careering straight into the Clyde. There was, and I dropped flat into some foul-smelling, oily muck. It was all over my hands and, in a moment of desperate inspiration, I smeared my face with it. My hair was black and the mud on my face should make me less easy to spot. I lay low and listened as the copper ran past on the other side of the railings.

I was just about to congratulate myself on my quick thinking when I heard the metal segments in the soles of his boots grate as he came to a sudden halt.

CHAPTER THIRTY-ONE

The policeman was only feet away from me and, even in the smog, if he turned and looked down, he would see me. At that range, I doubted very much if my improvised camouflage would do much to conceal me. I tried to ease back and down the slope, but I was afraid that doing so would cause a sound, any sound, to attract the beat copper's attention.

I watched him. He was a big lad, right enough, youngish, probably in his early twenties. He used a bicycle-type lamp to shine around him as he searched for me. He was too green to know that the only use a flashlight has in the smog is when it's pointing at the ground; pointing it into the mist only served to make the smog more impenetrable. For some reason that only a physicist could explain, it reflected any light directed at it.

I could tell he was listening intently. But, as I had hoped, he was searching in the wrong direction, thinking I'd run off along Clyde Street. The big question was this: had he challenged me because he had been alerted to look out for me, or was it simply because he had seen a suspicious-looking character who clearly had tried to avoid him? If it was the first, then I had trouble; if it was the second, he would probably give up and go back to patrolling. The one thing that made me hopeful was that he hadn't blown his police whistle to attract other coppers.

After what seemed an interminable time of peering into the smog and listening, he shook his head irritatedly and headed back towards the footbridge. I watched him until he was swallowed up again by the smog.

There was no point in trying to cross by the bridge, so I turned around and slid down the embankment on my backside, again trying to make sure I didn't end up in the Clyde. As it turned out, there was a towpath running along close to the river. I guessed that it had been used at one time for horsedrawn barges, although it was elevated and separated from the waterline by a high, brick-reinforced embankment. I offered up a small prayer to whatever gods were looking after me: the towpath meant I could move without being spotted. Hopefully.

My feet didn't hurt any more, something that caused me concern not relief. They didn't hurt because they were numb. Sitting down on the towpath, I eased off my mud-caked sock and felt my right foot. Like the left, it had the body temperature of an iceberg and was insensitive to my massaging.

I needed to get sorted out. And quick.

I hobbled along the towpath, not encountering anyone or anything other than the occasional scuttling sound of rats scattering as I approached. As I approached the Jamaica Bridge, I was aware that I was right in the heart of Glasgow, but passing through below street level. I kept going along the path, trying to ignore the strange experience of walking on feet that couldn't feel the ground beneath them; but the combination of physical numbness with the enclosure of my senses by the smog, the quiet fluid sounds of the river and the distant noises of the city above me all conspired to add to the feeling of unreality.

For some reason, the song *You Take the High Road* started running through my head. The song was about the ancient Celtic belief that while the living travel on the surface of the earth, the dead take the 'Low Road', passing underground; and only occasionally do the two paths meet, when the 'Low Road' travellers reappear as ghosts. As I walked smog-blinded and cold-numbed along the towpath, I started to wonder if this was what it was like to take the Low Road.

In a time of crisis, I sure knew how to cheer myself up.

As it happened, I had to come up to street level when the towpath ended, not passing under the bridge but leading back up to the main road. I crossed the road and tramway at Jamaica Bridge, but as soon as I was on the other side, I found my way back to the waterfront on the Broomielaw. I paused, questioning the logic of sticking to the river. This was no forgotten towpath anymore, but the point at which the Clyde became the factory floor of the city, and I found myself with quays to my left and grimy warehouses and store-yards to my right.

I had a decision to make: whether to take to the city streets and try to cross to the west side in as plain view as the smog afforded, or stick to the waterfront and risk running into night-shift workers on the Clyde. Of course, there was a limit to what I had to fear from Glaswegian dockside workers swinging hammers or swinging the lead on the backshift, and the smog was still a cloak I could hide behind, but there was another concern: the River Police.

The Clyde was as important a thoroughfare as any road – more so – and the City of Glasgow's River Police regulated it with vigour. Patrol boats scoured the river constantly with nothing more to do than fish out of the water the odd corpse that the Glasgow Humane Society had missed, or check the lighting on the *Clutha* tugs, barges and other boats that plied their trade on the waterway. And if there was anything to watch out for more than a keen-as-mustard copper, then it was a bored one looking for something, anything, to break the monotony of their shift.

I heard voices.

I stopped in my path and listened, straining to pinpoint who was talking, where they were, and what they were talking about.

I eased forward, careful not to break into view. From what I could make out, I had stumbled into a nightshift of river workers. There was a faint amber glow in the fog and I guessed they had a brazier burning, as if the smog needed any more thickening. On my left, I could just about perceive the outline of a quay jutting out into the river. I was faced with a stark choice: either walk on past the workers, as close to the quayside as I dared, or double back and lose a lot of the advantage I had gained by using the towpath. I worked out that walking past them would normally not have presented a real problem: they would assume I was another worker making my way to my shift further along the river and my grubby appearance would not be deemed anything unusual, but going to work a nightshift in November in your sock-soles would raise an eyebrow even here in Glasgow. I decided not to risk it and retraced my steps twenty yards or so. I headed away from the water, across a patch of greasy grass and mud, weaved my way through stacks of empty wooden barrels and between two brick warehouses, all the time seeing these objects loom in and out of my tiny pool of smog-edged awareness.

Back on the Broomielaw, I would have been in full view of any cars passing along the riverfront, if it hadn't been for the dense smog remaining my ally. I made a mental note to write to my MP and ask him to oppose the implementation of the Clean Air Act.

Foggy or not, it still wasn't safe for me to be back on the streets. The murk could hide coppers just as well as it concealed me. I had to get across town as fast as possible, ideally dropping back down to the waterfront as soon as I passed the clutch of bridges that connected the north and south sides in the city centre, each bridge a broad and normally busy roadway to be crossed. Moving as quickly as I could on my numb feet and in the smog, I only came into view of one passing tram and a couple of cars, but at a distance where I would have been just another shadowy figure in the gloom. My only big error was when I walked directly past a police box, burgundy-red in Glasgow when they were blue everywhere else. The roof-mounted light was flashing red, forlornly trying to summon the beat policeman in the gloom and indicating he had to 'phone into his station from the box. Unless the copper was within ten yards of the box, there was little hope of him seeing the beacon; but worrying that the call he had to make would be about me, I quickened my pace anyway and crossed the road. I passed through Anderston, back down to the riverfront. And right into a crowd of people.

For a moment, I thought I was hallucinating. There was a line of sixty or seventy people snaking across the quayside in the fog – men, women, even several children. What caused me greater concern was the uniformed men in peaked caps and holding flashlights, who seemed to be shepherding the others into a queue. It took me a moment to realize the uniforms were not those of policemen, and that the others in the queue were carrying luggage.

Think it through, Lennox, I told myself. I looked around me.

All I could make out of the steamer anchored to my left was its stern, with the lettering *The Royal Ulsterman*. No hallucination; I cursed my stupidity: I had walked straight into the passenger boarding of the Burns and Laird night-time service from Glasgow to Belfast. For a split second, I considered sneaking into the back of the queue and stowing away on the steamer. A crazy thought with no logic and born of desperation.

I had a plan and had to stick with it.

Another detour.

Common sense told me that not everyone in the Second City of the British Empire was on the lookout for me, but my lack of footwear made me noticeable; being noticeable made me memorable, and I didn't want the police to be able to use eye-witnesses to retrace my sock-soled steps.

But I couldn't go on like this. The smog usually kept the worst cold at bay, like a turbid blanket pulled over the city, but the temperature seemed to me to have plummeted, or at least my tolerance of the cold had. If I wasn't careful, the sole result of my great escape would be that, when they caught me, I'd be confined to a hospital room rather than a cell.

I skipped around the terminus building and back onto Anderston Quay on the other side of the passenger queue. I got as far as the Finnieston Ferry, which ran all night, before I had to make any more evasive manoeuvres. By now, my desperation had intensified to something close to panic. I felt cold, lost and increasingly without a firm plan. I had started out with a destination in mind, but it now seemed as achievable as making it to the top of Mount Everest. In my socks.

I was approaching the Queen's Dock, which was still ringing with the sounds of metal being worked. The most risky part of my westbound journey: I would have to loop around the Dock, which would take me right past the police station on Pointhouse Road. And if I was spotted, I doubted if I could outrun another copper.

Then Fate decided to deal me a better hand. It was tethered to the bottom of a steel ladder on the dock's Centre Pier: a rowboat. I had nearly walked on past it, hardly seeing its outline in the murk, but something instinctive took hold of my actions and before I knew it I had clambered down the ladder, untied the tether and was rowing out past the vast hulk of the hull I had watched being assembled or dismantled when I had met Jonny Cohen. I knew there would be workers and night-watchmen all around the dock, but being on the water in a small rowboat in the fog made me practically invisible. I paused when I was a safe distance out from the pier before fumbling around in the dark to feel for anything useful in the boat. I found some rags that I couldn't see but which felt thick and oily. Nevertheless, I wrapped them around my numb feet and set to rowing my way through the dock's ship-width bottleneck and out onto the Clyde. I knew that what I was doing made me almost impossible to find, but I didn't try to kid myself that rowing an unlit small boat in the main navigation channels of the Clyde at night, in these conditions, wasn't a highly dangerous business. At one point something large and dark, its navigation and cabin lights glowing dully in the fog, passed dangerously close and its wake nearly tipped me overboard. I guessed it was the Kelvinhaugh Ferry. At least I was heading in the right direction.

I tried to get a bearing on the north shore so that I could stick close to it, but again the smog closed everything in to a tight circle of viscous-looking water. I could have been ten feet from the riverbank or in the middle of the Atlantic.

I kept rowing.

CHAPTER THIRTY-TWO

By the time I approached the quays beside the Renfrew Ferry, the fog had thinned to a river-hugging shroud. Rowing all night, probably not always in the right direction, I had had to traverse the river north to south as well as the city from east to west. The sky was still night-black but my watch told me it was five in the morning. Not long until the ferry started to throng with early-shift workers making the crossing to the shipyards, offices and factories on the other side of the Clyde.

Approaching from the water instead of the land shifted my perspective and I had some difficulty in finding the barge, making sure that there was no one to see me approach. With shaking fingers I unwrapped my feet from the oil-black rags and rubbed them as clean as I could with the fringe of my army greatcoat, clambered up onto the barge and stumbled my way to the helm deck at the stern.

The cabin door was locked, and my key – thankfully unmarked and unidentifiable other than as the type used for most padlocks – was with my other stuff back at police headquarters in St Andrew's Square. But I remembered what the old bargee had said about keeping a spare key hidden.

My shivering had become almost convulsive and my fingers shook uncontrollably as I slid back the wooden panel, retrieved the key and unlocked the padlock. Maybe it was the exhausted state I was in and the prison outfit I was wearing, combined with my fugitive crossing of the city, but every movement I made seemed to be desperate and furtive, including the look I cast around the dark quay before I slid open the door and slipped into the cabin.

There was a cooking range with a vertical pipe set into one corner of the cabin and I decided that warming up was worth the tiny risk of someone seeing smoke from the stack in the dark. The bargee had left a pile of chopped wood in a wire basket next to the stove and it took me a couple of drawer-rifling minutes to find matches and paper. Once the fire was lit, I left the door of the range open and was amazed at how quickly it heated up the small cabin. Feeling the tiredness sweep over me, I knew I wouldn't be able to stay awake for much longer; but I had things to do before I slept and before daylight; last traces to be wiped off.

I donned the waders that were hanging in a curtained closet and, fighting the sleep that welled up and tried to claim me, I took a grappling pole and climbed back out onto deck. Once I checked there was no one within hearing, I stabbed down repeatedly at the bottom of the rowboat moored at the barge's side. I couldn't risk anyone identifying it as the boat stolen from the Queen's Dock, bringing the River Police to my barge door. It took longer and more effort than I could spare, but eventually the clinker splintered and I unhooked the tether as the rowboat began to fill with oily water. I helped it to the bottom by leaning hard on the grappling pole.

Back in the cabin, I filled a kettle with water and let it boil. I stripped out of the greatcoat and prison outfit before filling a basin with hot water and rinsing my face and body as much as I could. Dumping the filthy water in the sink, I refilled the basin with more clean, warm water and, gently peeling off the soiled and shredded silk socks, I carefully washed my feet, the darkening water blooming black-red with blood and dirt. I let my feet soak until the water began to cool, relieved when they started to hurt.

I would get my stuff from the hold and clean up properly later. But now I would sleep. I crawled into the cabin's bed space, pulled the blankets over me, and fell asleep. Instantly, deeply.

I slept most of the next day, but woke with a start every time I heard footsteps on the quay close to the barge.

I had let the fire die, not wanting to risk making smoke in daylight despite the fact that no one would notice it, far less think it unusual; but I had it in my head that I should make the barge look as unoccupied as possible. The wood panelling, and the fact that I hadn't once opened the door, seemed to keep captive in the cabin the heat I had built with the stove. When I wasn't asleep I sat on the edge of the bunk, naked except for my shorts, the scratchy blanket wrapped around my shoulders. My body ached and my feet now throbbed from the abuse they had suffered the night before but at least I was warm and, for the first time since I'd been arrested, I felt reasonably safe. For now, at least. And as the day passed, and I became accustomed to the comings and goings around the barge, my paranoia eased a little.

To get my stuff from the barge's hold would mean going back out on deck and I decided it would be best to stay put until late afternoon, when it became dark again. While I waited, I scoured the cabin to see if I could find any morsel of food the bargee had maybe left behind, but there was none. All I could manage to find were the scrapings of a tea barrel with just enough leaves to brew up a tinful. But my self-imposed injunction against making smoke meant I wouldn't be able to boil the kettle until after dark. I had water to quench my thirst, but I was ravenously hungry.

About three times during the afternoon I heard voices and footsteps directly beside the boat, causing me to tense, then relax as they faded into the distance.

Then came the fourth set of footsteps. The ones that didn't fade.

I heard them approach. Heavy, deliberate. When they reached the boat, they stopped. I went to the side of the cabin that flanked the quay and stood on the low bunk-type couch so that I could peer through the narrow ribbon of window that ran along the wall, just below ceiling height. From this vantage point, I could just about see the top of the quayside and no more. Whoever it was who had stopped and was standing there, surveying the boat or considering their next move, I couldn't see them. From the footsteps, I was pretty sure there was only one of them; maybe a single beat policeman checking the moorings. The worst it could be, I reckoned, was a routine and random check. If the police had known for sure I was here there would be more of them and, in any case, I couldn't see any way they would have found me here so fast.

I listened intently, holding my breath: for a moment there was nothing, then I heard the footsteps again; but this time not on the stone quay. The cabin resonated as my visitor made his way along the side of the barge. Then I saw him: just a flash of trouser cuffs and shoes as he passed the window. Not a uniform, not work boots. A suit and Oxfords.

I dropped down into the cabin and looked around for something to use as a weapon. Grabbing the range poker, I got as far to the side of the door as the cramped cabin would allow and gripped the poker tight, ready to bring it down on the first head that appeared.

I desperately tried to think the situation through. I was in enough trouble as it was without coshing a copper, whether he was in plainclothes or not. The City of Glasgow's constabulary took a dim view of such assaults on one of their number and were wont to demonstrate their disappointment physically. But I couldn't let them take me back in now; I remained the only one who could come up with the evidence to prove my innocence.

But if I misjudged the blow and killed a copper . . .

I tensed as I heard the cabin door slide open, raising the poker in a double grip above my head, and the cabin filled with light before whoever was on deck blocked it with his frame as he came down the steps.

I readied to swing.

'Mr Lennox?' asked a baritone voice so deep it resonated through the cabin's wood panelling, and probably down into the Clyde water the boat sat in. I imagined a whale somewhere in the mid-Atlantic pausing in its tracks to consider replying.

'Twinkletoes?'

McBride lurched into the cabin, head bowed, massive shoulders hunched and probably doubling the barge's displacement. His arms were full with a couple of large brown paper bags and when he turned to see me, he looked up disapprovingly at the raised poker.

'Sorry about that, Twinkle,' I said, lowering the poker. 'I didn't know it was you. Could you shut the hatch?'

Before he went up and drew the cabin door closed, he set the two large brown paper bags on the cabin table.

'I brung you some *comm-est-ables*,' he explained when he came back, nodding to the grocery bags.

I dived into the bags. Tea, a bottle of chicory coffee, powdered milk, bacon, bread, sausages, eggs, three packets of cigarettes, matches and even a half-bottle of Scotch. In the other bag, a safety razor, brush, shaving soap, a comb and some pomade sat on top of a folded jacket, trousers and shirt. There was even a smaller bag inside with bandages, antiseptic cream, sticking plasters, a brand new toothbrush and a tin of tooth powder.

'I heard you was *app-re-hended* by the police, but managed to scarper.'

'Is it in the papers already?'

'Naw ...' He frowned, obviously wondering if he was being too sweeping with his answer, given that the only papers he read were the *News of the World* and the *Beano*. 'Naw ... you know how word gets around.'

I did.

'I remembered that you said we was the only people to know about this boat. How I wasnae to tell nobody. So I reckoned you was likely to head straight here, so I thought I'd come to help.'

'I can't tell you how much I appreciate it. But how did you know what to bring with you?' I said, holding up his improvised first aid kit.

'The clothes and that? Well, you know, I have been in the same *pree-dick-ament*, in the past like. I remembered the kind of things you need.'

'I see. All I can say is thanks, Twinkle ... you've restored my faith in people.'

'You've always been decent to me, Mr L. Not like Mr Sneddon

always making jokes about me being stupid. Snide remarks, nasty like, about me being not all there. And some of them I didn't understand. And he didn't *app-ree-ciate* my effort to improve my mind and my *voh-cabbie-larry*, so he didn't. You've been very considerate with giving me work an' that.'

I smiled. In a way, Twinkletoes McBride was a child, viewing the world with childish simplicity. A six-foot-six, twenty-stone, occasionally psychopathic child, admittedly, but still a child.

'You're welcome,' I said. 'And let me tell you, you've more than paid me back for anything I've done for you. I don't know what I'd have done without your help. You're a good man.'

McBride shook his massive head dolefully. 'No, I'm not, Mr Lennox. I've done some really bad things. I've hurt a lot of people.'

'So have I, Twinkle, so have I . . .'

'Aye . . . but no' with a pair of bolt cutters . . .'

I found myself at a loss for an answer and we sat in gloomy silence for a while, each contemplating his own dark history. Or more truthfully, we were both contemplating Twinkletoes's dark history. Whatever his past sins, I was delighted to see him. I owed him big time.

'I'd make you a cup of tea,' I said, 'but I don't want anyone to see the smoke from the stack.'

McBride shook his massive head dismissively. 'There's no one around. I checked to make sure before I came over to the boat. Even the ferry is quieter at this time of day. I'll make it, and I'll heat enough water for you to shave.'

Twinkle filled the stove and lit it with an expertise that told me he had probably been brought up in a slum tenement, where a living room range was the usual, and only, form of heating.

'Thanks for the clothes,' I said to him. 'But, if you remember,

I have all of mine stashed here. I don't need those.'

'I hadn't forgotten,' he said. 'You're a very smart dresser, Mr L. I always think how much I'd like to have suits like yours.'

'When I get out of this, I'm going to take you to my tailor and have a bespoke suit made up for you. My treat. Least I can do.' I smiled, dispelling the concern that they maybe didn't have looms that spun cloth wide enough.

'That would be great,' Twinkle beamed a childlike grin. 'That would be really great ... But that's no' my point. Everybody knows you're a smart dresser. The polis too.'

The penny dropped. Maybe McBride wasn't so dumb after all, or maybe it was just that I had wandered into an area where his experience was much greater than mine. I took the clothes out of the bag. The trousers were a dull camel colour and of that dense kind of material that is resistant to holding a crease when pressed. The jacket was the usual Scottish job, a box of scratchy tweed that seemed to have been spun from steel wool and bracken. There was a flat cap in the same material and everything seemed to be roughly my size.

'I'll change once I get cleaned up,' I said. Despite my once-over with hot water, I was still filthy, especially my feet. 'Could you go up top and get me some stuff? You know, where we put it in the forward hold.' I ran through a list of some of the things I needed. As he struggled back up and out of the cabin and onto deck, I hoped he was right about there being no one about. Six-foot-six of muscle in a Burton off-the-peg was less than inconspicuous down here.

When he got back, I set about the business of having a serious clean-up while McBride made tea and fried the sausages on the stove top. The smell of hot lard and sizzling sausages fumed in the tiny cabin and would normally have turned my gut, but today it smelled nothing short of divine. Next to the barge's head was a tub – more of an oversized Belfast sink set on the floor, with a flexible rubber hose attached to its one tap. This, I had worked out, was the ablutions: the latest dab with cold-and-cold running water. I guessed that the Martinez in Cannes or the Savoy in London had similar arrangements.

Once I had shiveringly lathered and rinsed, re-lathered and re-rinsed, I let the cold water run over my feet. When I came out of the tub, I was chilled to the bone but felt clean and refreshed. The soles of both feet felt excoriated, and hurt whenever I put any weight on them, and my right foot looked swollen. I patted them dry and rubbed them both with the antiseptic cream that Twinkle had brought with him, then wrapped each in a bandage, more for support than as wound dressings.

I used some of the water Twinkletoes had boiled to shave. By now I had about three days growth and because my hair was so dark, leaving my upper lip unshaved meant the band of black stubble gave the appearance of a moustache. Another couple of days and it would be even more convincing. I dressed in the shirt, cardigan, trousers, tweed jacket and cap McBride had brought with him and used the shaving mirror to examine myself. I hated the outfit, but nowhere near as much as I had hated the prisoner one, and McBride had been right: this was as anonymous a get-up as I could imagine and was so different from my usual wardrobe that, along with my incipient moustache, I was pretty sure even those who knew me well wouldn't have recognized me at any kind of distance. Even the swelling on my face had gone down, but there were signs of the skin discolouring into a dark arc on my temple and around my eye.

'Great job, Twinkle,' I said, as I examined myself with the mirror held at arm's length. 'Really great job.'

He beamed joyously at me and I decided that if I ever did manage to get out of this jam I was going to see Twinkle all right.

We sat and drank the tea and I tried not to bolt down the sausages. As it was, I had to mop the grease from my chin as I ate. I had dined in some fancy places over the years, admittedly none of them in Scotland, but, at that moment, that meal of tea, buttered bread and sausages tasted better than anything I had ever eaten. Afterwards I smoked a Capstan untipped as if it had been the finest Havana cigar hand-rolled against the dusky maiden thigh of a Cuban *torcedora*.

When we were finished, Twinkletoes handed me a key and a red booklet with a crown-topped coat-of-arms on the cover.

'What's this?' I asked.

'My car key. And my driving licence, in case you're stopped by the polis. There's a petrol ration book there and all.'

I looked at the stuff he'd handed me. Petrol had been off the wartime ration for some time, but the government had temporarily reintroduced rationing because of shortages caused by the crisis in Suez.

'This is really very good of you, but I can't take these . . .'

'It's all right. I don't use the car much anyways. I keep it locked up in the garage most of the time.'

'It's not that, Twinkle. If I get caught by the police in your car with your licence and ration book, then they'll arrest you for aiding and abetting. With your record, you'll be sent to prison. I can't have that.'

'No, no . . .' he waved his vast hands emphatically. 'I've got it all worked out, you see. Like I said, I keep the car locked up in the garage almost all of the time and there are people what know that. Neighbours, like. So if you get caught, all you've got to say is that you stole it and I'm in the clear. You're not, like, but I am. If someone stole my car for real it could be days before I'd find out. But you won't get caught, Mr Lennox. I know that. You're too clever for them bastards.'

'Really?' I said gloomily. 'I've been doing a good job of hiding it lately. But thanks for the car. I can't tell you how big a help you've been.'

'How long do you think you can hide out here?' he asked. His bulk seemed to fill the cabin, making it feel more like a closet than living quarters.

'I reckon I'm okay for a while,' I said. 'We'll need to keep checking the papers to see if there's anything in them. Like you said, only you and the bargee know I've rented this place, and unless he sees my name in the paper and connects it to the one on the lease, then there's no reason he'd contact the cops. I have no record, so the police don't have any photographs of me.'

We sat and talked. I tried to explain what had happened – about my encounter with Hopkins and how all trace of him and his people had vanished into thin air, about how I had stumbled into something big and dangerous just because two people had the same or similar names – but talking it through made even my head hurt and I decided to stop before Twinkle frowned himself to death or a blood vessel burst in his brain.

He sat for a minute, the frown still creasing his almost-brow. He was silent and completely still, even his eyes focused but not focused on the stove. In McBride's case, cogitation clearly necessitated the shutting down of all other functions.

Then, suddenly, he reached out and snatched up the car key I had left on the table.

'What's up, Twinkle?'

'Listen, Mr L. You're a nice man. Maybes too nice. You need answers, right?'

'Right.'

'Well, getting answers is my business. I'm sticking with you.'

I didn't argue. A resolved Twinkletoes McBride wasn't something you argued with, like you wouldn't argue with a steam hammer.

The thought of him riding shotgun while I got to the bottom of what the hell was going on troubled me greatly. But, oddly enough, it also comforted me.

CHAPTER THIRTY-THREE

We waited until it was beginning to get dark before heading off the barge, across the quay and out onto the street where Twinkletoes's car sat, gleaming, in a pool of light, as if it had been placed there by the gods themselves.

'I always park under a lamppost,' Twinkle explained, 'in case I don't get back to it before dark.' He glowered disapprovingly from under his eyebrows. 'There are some *thoroughly dis-rep-uh-table* people around in Glasgow, you know, Mr L.'

'So I believe,' I said, ignoring the irony of an ex-gangland torturer commenting on the moral decline of his home city.

'Aye ...' he shook his head mournfully. 'Steal the ground from under you. Wee fuckers.'

And there it was. What I was presented with was, exactly like the barge we had just left, one man's pride and joy.

'She's a beaut ...' I said appreciatively, and Twinkle beamed back.

It was a one-year-old burgundy red Vauxhall Cresta, polished and burnished until it shimmered in the lamplight. It clearly seldom made it out of its garage and I thought back to how McBride had handed over his key and driver's licence. Seeing the car, I appreciated the gesture even more. The truth was I could have done with a downpour of sooty rain to dull the car's conspicuous lustre. But it was good to be mobile and to have the feeling that there was at least one person on my side.

The interior of the Cresta was filled with the smell of unguent polishes and was as luxurious as Connelly's Zephyr: piped two-tone claret and white leather, white leather panels on the doors and a white steering wheel and column. Twinkletoes slid in behind the steering wheel and suddenly the proportions of the car shrank. Looking at him, he was the most unlikely person to imagine spending evenings and weekends polishing and tinkering at a motor car, but it strangely fitted with my experience of him.

'There's a raincoat in the back,' he said. 'To go with what you's got on.'

I reached over and picked up the raincoat, laying it folded on my lap. The usual grey-green job, shapeless, style-less and totally anonymous. It was perfect and I told McBride so.

'Where to then?' he asked me.

'Bearsden . . .' I said. 'I'll give you directions.'

We drove by the house several times before parking far enough around the corner not to be seen getting in or out of the car. Mind you, this was Bearsden, the most twitchy-curtained part of Glasgow, and if being noticeable had been an event at the Melbourne Olympics then McBride would have cleaned up the golds. There were no signs of police or any other unusual cars outside the house, so I reckoned it was safe enough for us to make our approach.

We reached the gate of the house and I was about to lead the way in when I became aware of a car slowing to walking pace beside us.

'Keep walking,' the driver leaned across and spoke through

the open window. 'Police . . . in the Ellis house . . . waiting for you inside. Keep walking and I'll park around the corner.' He drove off along the road and turned into the next adjoining street.

'Let's do as the man says and keep walking, Twinkle, and try to look casual,' I mouthed sideways and, without looking towards the Ellis residence, walked on with a sense of purpose in the direction taken by Archie McClelland's ancient Morris Eight.

Archie had parked even further up his side street than we had ours, and no sooner had Twinkle heaved, wriggled and squeezed into the back seat and I had slid into the front than he took off.

'You two need to rethink your double-act,' said Archie, his tone even more doleful than usual. 'If I could count the number of times you drove past the house, then I'm sure the uniforms inside will have too.'

'You saw us check the street out?'

Archie turned his spaniel eyes to me as if I had said something profoundly stupid. 'I was dazzled by the gleam on your car. What's the story? Did you steal it straight from the showroom?'

'Naw . . .' There was a gratified rumble from McBride in the back. 'It's a year old. I keep it clean, but.'

'Point taken,' I said to Archie. 'How do you know there are coppers in there?'

'Because they gave me the third degree when I went calling a couple of hours ago. I take it your current state of liberty is self-instigated?'

'Naw . . .' rumbled Twinkle again. 'He ran away . . .'

'What were you doing at the Ellis house?' I asked Archie.

'Seeing as you've got yourself up to your ears in shite, I thought I'd try to get to the bottom of what is going on. Wait a minute . . . how did you and Twinkletoes get together?'

'He found me,' I said. 'He worked out where I'd be hiding. I owe him, Archie. Whatever happens to me, remember that. I owe Twinkle big time.'

'Thanks Mr L. . . .' Another rumble.

'Well, wherever it is you're hiding,' said Archie, 'don't tell me. If I don't know, I can't tell. Just having you in the car could land me a stretch inside.'

'I know. It's appreciated, Archie. It sounds like I owe you too for trying to get me out of this. Did they let you speak to Pamela Ellis?'

'No. I get the feeling she's scared witless. And, of course, instead of looking to see who's putting the screws on her, the police are putting her terrified state down to you being at liberty . . . that her husband's murderer is going to come after her for not backing up his insane story, that kind of thing.'

'Yeah,' I said. 'Thanks for putting it that way. Makes me feel all warm inside. So that's why the police are there?'

'They obviously think that you would be stupid enough to make straight for her as soon as you escaped . . . Oh, but hold on a minute, that's exactly what you did . . .' Another wryly doleful look.

'But if they think that's what I'd do, then they must realize it would be to try to get the truth out of her?'

'Or to silence your partner in crime, in case she turns Queen's against you to save her own neck. If you have a clarty mind like Detective Inspector Shuggie Dunlop.'

I sighed. I had hoped to have gotten the truth out of Pamela Ellis and have her believe that between us, the police and I could guarantee her safety. But that just wasn't going to happen any time soon.

'Cheer up, boss,' said Archie, cheerlessly. 'You've got me and Twinkle here on the case. And I suspect we aren't your only friends.'

'What do you mean?'

'As soon as you did a runner, I was hauled in by Jock Ferguson. He knew I didn't know where you were, but he went through all the motions. But, while I was in there, he made a point of telling me all of Shuggie Dunlop's *Double Indemnity* theories about you and Pamela Ellis. I mean, he really went into detail, like he was laying the whole case out for me. He also gave me the usual warnings about what to do and not to do if you got in touch.'

'Sounds pretty much what you'd expect,' I said.

'Except he then starts to tell me all of this stuff that I really shouldn't know and if he ever found out that *you* found out about it, he'd know it was me who told him. So *I* was to make sure I never told *you* what he'd found out, if you catch his drift.'

'Bastard . . .' growled Twinkle.

'No, no . . .' I explained over my shoulder. 'It's his way of getting information to me.' I turned back to Archie. 'What did he tell you?'

'Shuggie Dunlop may be the one-line-of-enquiry type but Jock isn't. He's obviously been following up a few leads on his own. You were right that Andrew Ellis was born in Hungary, but his family were no penniless peasants; more like political refugees. It's all confusing, you know, the history over there: there were all types of revolutions and counter-revolutions and a hell of a lot of bloodshed. There was a Red Terror, as they called it, then a White Terror – or maybe the other way around – anyway, there were left-wing extremists and right-wing extremists and each took turns at seizing control and murdering the others.'

We were now several blocks away from the Ellis house and Archie pulled into the kerb.

'Anyway, Ellis's family were involved with one side or the other and ended up having to skip the country. Ellis grew up in poverty in Glasgow knowing he should have been living the high life in Hungary.'

'Where did Ferguson get all of this from?'

'There's a sister. Didn't have much to do with Ellis, lives in Edinburgh. He got it all from her. You know how Ellis's wife told you he had to volunteer for bomb disposal because the army was sniffy about him being born in what became an Axis country?'

'Yeah . . .'

'Well, they were sniffy about more than that. Ellis tried to get in as an officer, but the army wouldn't have it. All his young adult life, he was a member of this Scottish-Hungarian friendship society. It even paid for him to travel to Hungary on at least one occasion. Turns out he got himself involved with some kind of youth movement when he was over there. Jock doesn't know the colour of the movement's political complexion, but whatever it was, it didn't ring the right bells with the army enlistment people here.'

'I see . . .' I thought through what Archie had said. 'Did he say anything about Hopkins, the government man who seemed to know all about Ferenc Lang and his outfit. And all about me, for that matter.'

'Mmm . . . To be honest, Jock thinks you've been played for a mug. He thinks that *Hopkins* as he called himself was just trying to find out what you knew about the Hungarian outfit. The

office was just some kind of short-con set-up. The clincher for
Jock was you saying that Hopkins was wearing an Intelligence
Corps tie, which there was every chance of you recognizing. Or,
as Jock put it, nothing short of wearing a big collar badge that
said "I am a spy, but keep that secret."'

'Yeah ... That makes sense,' I said sarcastically. 'Hopkins is
really a Hungarian who just happens to speak perfect, cut-glass
English. And because I've been spotted following their girl –
instead of simply bundling me into the back of a van and taking
me to a quiet back alley or abandoned cellar somewhere where
they could simply beat the truth out of me – they decide to
pick me up with fake-but-perfect police IDs, move into a phoney
office with dozens of extras to make it look more convincing,
and then get more facts on my background than even I know
– all in the time it takes to drive me there? Sure, that sounds
credible.'

'I take it you and Jock aren't as one on this then?'

'You take it right. I'm telling you, Archie, Hopkins was the
real deal. Maybe not in the way he put himself forward, but he
was a professional interrogator and had access to official files.
I don't know what the hell is going on with them doing a
midnight flit, but it was no elaborate short-con. Why go to all
that trouble?'

Archie sat and stared out through the windshield for a
moment. 'Well,' he said turning to me at last, 'if Jock and the
City of Glasgow Police can't nail down Hopkins or his louche
pals ...'

'Louche?' asked Twinkle from the back.

'Louche,' Archie repeated. 'It means sinister or shadowy.'

'Loooosh ...' McBride stretched the word out, relishing it.
'Shadowy or sinister. Aye ... I like that. How do you spell it?'

I spelled it for him while, with a stub of pencil that looked preposterously small in his huge hand, he scribbled the word into a small notebook he took from his coat pocket.

'Loooosh . . .' he savoured the word again, then said, 'Sorry . . . ', when he saw Archie's impatient face.

'If Jock can't track them down,' continued Archie, 'then I don't think you have much chance while doing your Richard Hannay act.'

'There was a clerk from the solicitor's or estate agent's . . . the other night when we went to the office. He is obviously responsible for the let or sale of the building. Collins was his name. Is there any chance you could have a word, Archie? He must know something about the set-up. They couldn't have just broken in in broad daylight and put together that phoney set-up. Collins must know something.'

'Sure,' said Archie. 'I'll track him down and see what I can squeeze out of him.'

'Excuse me for *inter-jetting* . . .' Twinkle leaned forward, resting his forearms on the seat backs and shifting the car's centre of balance. 'But if you don't mind me saying, I think I'd be better *squeezing* information out of this wee shite Collins. It's what I do, like.'

'I know, Twinkle,' I said. 'But the last thing we need is to put some office worker in traction. Or remove his toes with bolt cutters.'

'Oh no,' said McBride, almost offended. 'I wouldn't do that. I would use the *piss-eye-cho-logical* approach.'

'And what does that involve?'

'Showing him the bolt cutters and tellin' him what I'm going to do, without actually doin' it.'

'You know something,' said Archie. 'Maybe if Twinkletoes was with me I'd get farther, quicker than if I was on my own. And we don't have a lot of time.'

'Aye . . . Erchie could go with me. Make sure I don't lose the rag and that.'

'Okay . . .' I said reluctantly. 'But remember Twinkle, no rough stuff. And no bolt cutters . . . even the psychological kind. Just stand beside Archie and look menacing.'

'And what are your plans?' Archie asked me. 'A fugitive life in one of the darkest and most inhospitable regions of the world where the law has no reach? Venezuela? The Congo? Dundee?'

'The first thing I have to do is to catch up with Larry Franks at the Paradise Club. He was checking out some names for me.'

'This to do with the Hungarians?'

'Actually, no. I'm still trying to track down the original Frank Lang. The one the union hired me to find.'

'If you don't mind me saying,' said Archie, 'your current predicament may make carrying on as usual with work a mite tricky.'

'I'm doing it for me, not Connelly or his union. Shuggie Dunlop is determined to pin a murder on me. If he can't make Ellis's stick, then he'll try to nail me for Sylvia Dewar's. But that's not the real reason I want to find Frank Lang. Something stinks about the whole union thing.'

'But I thought you said the two Frank Langs are unconnected?'

'They are. I stumbled into one while looking for the other. But there are two people dead who were connected, if not very closely connected, to Frank Lang.'

'And the Hungarians?'

'I need to get into the Ellis house or his office or both. His wife told me when I first spoke to her that he had to write everything down. Sometimes it was just a one-word scribble or a doodle, but he couldn't function without notes to himself. There must be something, somewhere, that might give me a hook on where to find our Magyar chums, or even what the significance of the word Tanglewood is.'

'So you're just going to ask the policemen nicely to let you in to the Ellis home and poke around – the policemen who are only there to make sure your feet don't touch until you're in a cell?'

'That's a wrinkle all right. I'll have to think of something.'

'And I don't see you faring any better at Ellis's company. Remember, it's just been turned over by a gang of mime artists. Security is even tighter than it was before.'

'Yes, Archie . . . I know that too. Listen, shouldn't you be somewhere else offering words of comfort . . . to someone called Job?'

'Just trying to keep you out of the cells, boss. You get caught in the Ellis house, then it's not exactly going to do your case much good, is it?'

'Then I'll make sure I don't. Talking about getting caught, we should split up. Twinkle, I'll take you up on two of your offers. If you don't mind, I will borrow your car and Archie can get you home. But I'll also call on your *moral support* when it comes to getting some answers. In the meantime, I don't want either of you to be caught giving succour to a fugitive.'

I saw Twinkle reach for his notebook again and I spelled out 'succour' for him. When I asked, he confirmed with deep pride that he was indeed *on the telephone*, and I got a note of his number. I told Archie I would keep in touch too.

'I'll leave Collins the estate agent to your tender mercies,' I said. 'Twinkle, you know where to find me. Let me know what you get out of him.'

'What are you going to do in the meantime?' asked Archie.

'In the meantime? I've got to see a woman about a dog.'

CHAPTER THIRTY-FOUR

Old Charlie Darwin would probably have some naturally selective reason for the way we instinctively hate the ugly. Me, I always thought that ugliness tended to come in two types: the pitiable kind, where you sympathized with the person in much the same way you would a three-legged dog, and where you consoled yourself that they were most probably 'lovely on the inside'; and then there was the loathsome ugly, where you sensed that the homeliness on the outside was merely the reflection of their inner obnoxiousness.

Maisie McCardle's ugliness was definitely of the latter kind. Her too-long face was all points and angles. If she had painted it green, she could easily have had a career chasing Dorothy and Toto around Oz.

When she opened the door to scowl at me, the odious little pug who had taken a leak against my car appeared at her ankles, yapping shrilly. It screwed up its ugly little face too, and I wondered if they spent the long winter evenings together in front of the fire, scowling at each other.

This was going to be fun.

Her scowl soon evaporated and was replaced by an expression of alarm when she recognized me as the suspicious-looking character she had ratted on to the police. I had taken certain precautions before coming up: going back to the barge and changing out of the gear McBride had brought me and back into one of my more usual suits, hat and coat from my water-borne store-room. I had also, reluctantly, shaved off my incipient moustache. Maisie McCardle was clearly observant in a way that made the average eagle seem myopic and I didn't want her to pass on to the police any changes in my appearance. I would start again on the moustache the next day. In fact, it would be good for the police to hear that I had made no attempt to change my look. I had also made sure that I parked Twinkle's car out of sight. I was aided in my mission by the fact that, as far as I could see, there had still been no mention in the papers of the police looking for me.

'Mrs McCardle?' I said. 'Please don't be alarmed. My name is Lennox and I am an enquiry agent.' I handed her my card. 'I am working on the same case as the police. I'm afraid I was the person who found poor Mr and Mrs Dewar's suicide.' I knew that the police would not have offered an opinion on the nature of the deaths and chucking in the word 'suicide' probably took the gleam off my axe-murderer's axe for her. She hadn't slammed shut the door, so I kept talking. 'I know you mentioned my being here before to Inspector Dunlop and Chief Inspector Ferguson, but I can assure you I am working *with* the police on this.'

Maisie eyed suspiciously first my card and then me. She was either weighing up my authenticity or checking to see if I was wearing ruby slippers.

'Although I am helping the police in trying to get to the bottom of why Mr Dewar did what he did,' I said, pressing on, 'there really was no connection between the tragedy at the Dewars and the case I was investigating originally, which concerned your other neighbour, Mr Lang.'

I let it hang there. My experience had been that the naturally observant were usually the pathologically inquisitive, and I could see that her interest had been piqued.

'Mr Lang?'

'Yes. Mr Frank Lang. I was engaged by his employers to make sure nothing untoward has befallen him. You see, Mr Lang has been missing for some weeks now.' I fidgeted theatrically on the doorstep, as if performing on too small a stage. 'I'm sorry to disturb you, Mrs McCardle, but Chief Inspector Ferguson told me what a wonderful eye witness you were – that nothing gets by you – so I thought you would be able to help. I wonder if I may . . . ?' I nodded in the direction of the hall behind her. Her eyes narrowed for a moment, but the flattery and her curiosity got the better of her caution.

'You'd better come in then.'

'Nice place you've got here,' I said appreciatively as she led me into the house, not adding that I was surprised it wasn't made out of gingerbread and the window glass out of sugar.

The layout of the nearly-new house appeared to be identical to that of the Dewars' place, but, where Sylvia Dewar had embraced the Atomic Age in all of its synthetic modernity, Maisie McCardle had sought to hide it, wherever possible behind lace doilies. The clock on the mantelpiece, the sofa and two-chair suite, the heavy, dull brown curtains all had that hard, uncompromising solidity of pre-war furniture. I guessed that anything in the house newer than that bore a Utility Mark. There was no television, but a pre-war Pye radio, the wooden box type with a suitcase handle on the top, sat in the corner.

The one thing that surprised me was the mirror above the mantelpiece; not that it was of a different style or vintage of any of the other pieces, just that it was there at all. Uncracked.

'The police seemed awfully interested in you . . .' she said, still eyeing me suspiciously.

'Oh yes . . . I understand that. You see, I was able to give them exact times I was here and that helped them establish the sequence of events from your statements. Chief Inspector Ferguson *really* thought the information you gave was invaluable . . .'

Suddenly Maisie became uglier, her features contorting. Then I realized she was smiling.

'Will you be wanting a cup of tea, then?' she asked dully, as if I'd forced her into the offer.

'I wouldn't want to put you to any trouble . . .' I said.

It was obvious that she wasn't about to let me put her to any trouble; she didn't push her offer of tea and instead sat down in the armchair by the radio.

'What do you want to know?' she asked.

'May I sit down?' I asked and she nodded sharply. 'Like I said, I'm trying to locate Frank Lang. I spoke to poor Mrs Dewar before her death and she told me that she hardly ever saw him and had practically nothing to do with him.'

'Did she now . . . ?' Maisie wriggled in her seat maliciously.

'Are you saying that wasn't the case?'

'It's true that he was hardly ever here. I hardly ever saw him and I see everything and everyone, especially when I'm walking Prince.'

'Prince?'

'My dog.'

I looked down at the little pug. It looked back at me, all bug eyes and a face wrinkled like a brain, its turned-up bottom lip almost wrapped over its snotty nose.

'Of course,' I said.

'It isn't right,' she said scowling, which was beginning to lose its expressive effect. 'I told the police that. There's something fishy when someone pays rent for a Corporation flat and they're never there. Very fishy.'

'But you're saying that Mrs Dewar's statement wasn't accurate?'

'Aye . . . if she said she didn't have anything to do with Lang, then it's a lie. And I told the police that too. They wanted to know everything about Lang too.'

'That doesn't surprise me, Mrs McCardle. What did you tell them?'

'That she was a slut and a whore.' Another malicious wriggle. 'Interested in anything in trousers.'

'Including Lang?'

'Like I said, he was hardly ever there, but she seemed to know when he was going to arrive. She thought she was being *so* clever, sneaking in through his back door, but I saw her. I heard them.'

'So you believe that Frank Lang and Sylvia Dewar were carrying on an affair together? Have you told the police that?'

'Yes.'

I sat and thought it through for a moment. Shuggie Dunlop was all bluff on the Dewar deaths. Good old Maisie, God bless the ugliness that reached from her face deep into her soul, would relish standing in a witness box, smearing Lang's and Sylvia's reputations. And, if it hadn't been Dewar who killed his wife, then that placed Lang in the queue for the execution cell well before me. It was all beginning to form a picture.

'The day she claimed to have seen him leave with two other men in a big car . . . ?' I looked through my notebook and gave her the day and date. 'Did you see him leave?'

'No. And I would have been in and normally I see everybody. I watch, you see. There are a lot of dodgy characters around,' she said, her tiny eyes fixed on me for long enough to make her point. 'I didn't see anyone around his house ever, except for her. And no car. He hardly ever brought his own car here. I don't know where he kept it. Maybe a garage, but not one near here.'

'He had a car?'

'That's what I just said.'

'What kind of car?'

'It was one of these cars with the wood on them. A shooting-brake or station-wagon or whatever you call them. It was pale green. He only brought it here once or twice.'

'A Morris Traveller?'

'I don't know. I don't know anything about cars.'

Again I thought it all through. Sylvia Dewar's previous convictions for dishonesty. The kind of company she probably at one time kept. Her manipulation of her husband. Yes, I was beginning to see it all now, but I needed to confirm it.

'Do you know this man?' I said, reaching into my pocket and handing a photograph to her.

'No.'

'Are you sure?'

'I wouldn't say if I wasn't.'

'And you definitely haven't seen this man around here, visiting Frank Lang's house?'

Her scowl deepened, broadened, intensified and her ugliness followed suit. 'Do I have to keep repeating myself?'

'No, Mrs McCardle, you don't. I'm sorry,' I said. Putting the photograph – the photograph of Frank Lang given to me by Lynch and Connelly – back into my jacket pocket, I took out my notebook.

'I wonder if you could give me a description of Frank Lang.' I smiled at her. 'And from what Chief Inspector Ferguson has told me about you, it will be a good one ...'

CHAPTER THIRTY-FIVE

This was not the time to be juggling two unconnected cases, but that was exactly what I found myself doing. Mainly because my continued liberty, and maybe my neck, depended on my finding a solution to each of them.

After I left the Wicked Witch of the West, I headed back to the barge and changed once more into the outfit of flannel shirt, scratchy tweed jacket and shapeless trousers that Twinkletoes had brought me. I dressed it up a bit with a knitted silk tie; not because my sartorial sensibilities had been stretched to breaking, but because I felt the outfit was just that little bit too blue-collar for me to be seen wearing it while driving a car like Twinkletoes's sparkling Vauxhall Cresta.

There was a Navy-issue dark blue duffle coat in the same barge closet where I'd found the wellington boots. It was in reasonably good condition and I decided I would wear it over the tweed jacket rather than the cheap, thin raincoat McBride had provided. Duffle coats were a kind of classless attire in Britain, where ex-navy captains were as likely to wear one as an ex-navvy. Again I dressed up the proletarian look with a pair of pigskin gloves that probably cost me three times what the bargee had paid for the coat. If stopped by the police, I might play the part of the eccentric dressed-down ex-naval officer.

Pulling on the duffle coat, I wondered bitterly if the ensemble would have done anything to improve my chances with Fiona White.

The other advantage of the coat was, of course, its dark colour: ideal night attire for the professional prowler and loiterer. And, of course, I wasn't just taking the gloves for their look. I would have a practical need of them too.

It was after seven when I headed back to where I had parked the Cresta, got into it, and started it up without casting guilty looks around me. It was strange to be at liberty – albeit a surreptitious liberty – in the city I had had to flee across just the night before with numb feet and in a prison uniform. But I was still a fugitive, and I knew that couldn't last.

I stopped at a public telephone and, jamming the door open with my foot to allow the fume of urine odour to escape, I jammed my pennies in, dialled the number of the Paradise Club, jabbed the A button, and asked to speak to Larry Franks.

'Hi, Mr Franks, this is Mr Bardstown, from Kentucky,' I said.

'Oh yes,' said Franks after a short confused silence. 'The bourbon drinker.' He paused for a second. 'I'm glad you 'phoned, but we've been having problems with the telephone recently. Like you mentioned.'

'That's what I thought . . .' Even this coded contact was dodgy. Coppers were dim, but if there was one listening in on the line, trying to catch out something relating to Jonny Cohen's involvement with the Arcade robbery, this stilted conversation was clearly fake.

'Is everything all right with you?' asked Franks. 'You've been missed . . . a couple of friends have been looking for you two nights in a row. They were really keen to talk to you.'

'Oh?' I asked. 'I'm surprised that they looked for me there.'

'You left a wallet behind at their place. My card was in it. Your friends are really keen to reunite you with your wallet. Maybe if you were to call by the Club, they would catch up with you.'

'That's what I thought. I won't be able to make it to the Club.'

'I thought as much. That's a pity,' said Franks. 'Because I found out some stuff about the names of those Bourbon brands you gave me and I was looking forward to chatting to you.'

'That is a pity,' I said.

'I'm afraid I'm so busy I don't get a chance to chat with anyone. Tonight, for example, I'm working until ten-thirty – then I have to cadge a lift home.'

'Well, I'm sure we might bump into each other some time soon. Goodbye, Mr Franks,' I said and hung up.

I headed up to Bearsden. On the way, feeling reasonably secure in a strange car and change of clothes, I drove past my old digs. I kidded myself that I was doing it to see if the police were watching the place but the truth, I knew, was that I just wanted to drive past Fiona's. The curtains were drawn but I could see the light from the living-room leaching through them. I wondered what she and the girls would be doing, what they would be watching on television or talking about. What an ordinary, safe life would be like.

I drove on.

In Bearsden, I found a public-house car park and left the Cresta there. It was a busy pub, and up-market for Glasgow. Normally in the West of Scotland, if a bar wanted to show itself a cut above, it would have a special rack for you to hang up your bicycle clips next to your flat cap, so I reckoned that, having a car park, this place would be the local bees-knees, no-Catholics-no-Jews watering hole for the local golf-club-swinging crowd – lawyers, accountants and surveyors.

The car park was busy for a Wednesday night and I reckoned the Cresta would be less likely to arouse suspicion left there than parked for a second time in a side street around the corner from my goal.

It was a fog-free night, but not cloudless, and damp-cold without raining. Walking the mile or so to my destination, I pulled the hood of the duffle coat up over my head and cap. The streets of Bearsden were hardly bustling at the best of times and were empty as I walked through them in the chill early evening.

When I reached the road junction, I walked briskly and purposefully across to the other side and out of sight of the black Austin Cambridge sitting outside Pamela Ellis's home. If the occupants of the unmarked police car had noticed me, then they would simply have seen someone look in their direction to check the road was clear before crossing. The secret was never to look tentative. Maybe, when this was all over, I could write a book: *The Fugitive's Handbook and Guide to Barge Maintenance*.

I looped around one block and then another, bringing me to where Ellis's house and its neighbours backed onto a narrow street that was more an up-market alley. The high brick wall surprised me, as most of the gardens in Bearsden were hedge- or tree-fringed, but I put it down to the fact that the backs of the gardens on one side of the narrow street looked onto the backs of those on the other side, and the walls were probably there to boost security. Even though I would not be over-looked as I scaled the wall, it would be a struggle to get over it and I knew that the locals had the habit of having broken glass cemented into the tops of walls to discourage riff-raff like me.

But it was a problem I would have to wait to deal with. Until eight-ten or eight-fifteen, if my calculations were right.

I walked the length of the narrow street and took a right turn, which meant I was now walking parallel to the one I had originally come down. My orienteering was right and I came back onto the street the Ellis house was on, but a block farther away on the other side, now looking at the back of the unmarked police Cambridge.

I checked my watch. Eight-fifteen. Maybe I was out of luck.

With a lot of time on my hands, I had lain in the barge and thought over every detail and every moment of the last three weeks. I remembered the only time I had visited the Ellis house, catching Pamela Ellis on her way out to her religiously-observed bridge night. And that was when I had gotten the idea.

But, as I stood cooling my heels on the street corner, she was yet to leave the house. There was always the chance that her current state of grief and fear had curtailed Pamela Ellis's bridge-playing activities. But, even at a time like this, a rubber or two of bridge would be the one distraction I would put my money on Pamela Ellis indulging in.

I waited another five minutes, then ten, and decided I was not going to get the opportunity I had hoped for. My other concern was that hanging around on a dark street corner in Bearsden was a whole lot more conspicuous than in other parts of the city – like neighbouring Maryhill, where it was positively encouraged – and I had already been there for ten minutes.

I was just about to give up when I saw the maroon gleam of Ellis's Daimler Conquest glide out of the drive. The big question now was whether the coppers in the Cambridge had been told to keep eyes on the house or on its occupant.

'Come on, boys ...' I urged them near silently and through tight teeth. After what seemed an age, they started up and peeled off from the kerb, following the Conquest along the street and out of sight.

I decided against the high rear wall, instead striding confidently along the street, not slowing my pace as I reached the open drive gate of the Ellis house, where I wheeled breezily into and up the drive. Nothing tentative.

Without breaking pace I walked along the path at the side of the house and into the back garden. The high wall that I had checked out at the end of the garden shielded me from being seen from the large house across the way, but the neighbouring house to my left had a much better view of the rear garden. Fortunately, there were no exterior lights left on which, while encumbering my progress and colouring my language as I tripped over a plant pot, offered me added concealment.

A largish lean-to shed was doing its leaning-to against the boundary wall between the Ellis home and its immediate neighbour. I remembered what Pamela Ellis had said about the shed being her husband's refuge and his constant complaining about her leaving it unlocked. I tried the handle. Without her husband to reproach her, she had left the door unlocked and I slipped into the shed, using my penlight to check its contents. Even if I found nothing to help me break into the house, the way every screw, nail and tool in the shed was boxed, jarred, arranged by size and labelled gave me hope for my ultimate mission. It was the rigorous, all-or-nothing organization of someone afraid of their own internal chaos, just as Pamela Ellis had described her husband.

Ellis had been an ordnance handler and bomb-disposal NCO in the army, and had then worked his way up the commercial ranks of the demolition business. Exactitude wasn't just a quirk that gave you an advantage; absolute precision was essential and Ellis had obviously applied it to every aspect of his life.

An old, heavy, double-pedestal desk was used as a workbench with the shelves above it. To one side was a massive-looking chest, made of the same dark wood as the desk. I rummaged through tools in the desk drawer until I found a long, narrow chisel.

Before I headed back out, I cast my torch around the shed once more. I was about to break into a house, a home, yet I felt a greater sense of having intruded here, in this lean-to garden shed. This confined environment was the extension of one man's personality, of his mind, of his particular way of seeing the world. Right at the start of all of this nonsense, I had quizzed Pamela Ellis to try to get a handle on her husband's character; I would have been better rummaging through these drawers and shelves.

Then I thought of Ellis's eyes searching mine, just before the light went out of them. About his final moment being shared with me.

I stepped out of the shed just as a figure walked past the mouth of the drive. I ducked around the side of the shed and into the shadows just as a dog began to bark in my direction. For a split second I wondered if the ever-vigilant Maisie McCardle and her ugly pug had a city-wide beat, before a male voice ill-temperedly told his dog to shut up and come on. I waited a moment to make sure the dog-walker was well along the street before crossing the path to the back of the house.

I found two doors into the rear of the building, both locked.

The first looked like it led into some kind of pantry or boot room, so I gave up on that one, fearing that it may lead to a second time-consuming locked door. The other door led directly into the kitchen. It too was locked, so I eased the chisel in between the door and its jamb, slowly and steadily leaning my weight against the chisel until I was rewarded with a splintering crack and the door flew inwards. I shot an arm out and caught it before it crashed into something and made more even noise than I had already made. I paused for a moment, listening so hard I thought my ears would bleed, watching the house next door for lights coming on.

No lights, no dogs barking, no footsteps on the drive. Once I was convinced that no one had heard me, I slipped into the kitchen and drew the door closed behind me. Laying the chisel down on the kitchen table, I made a mental note to pick it up on the way out and return it to the garden shed. The damage to the back door would make it obvious that the house had been broken into, or at least someone had attempted to break in, but I wanted to leave as few traces of my presence as possible. After all, the police would be able to hazard a pretty good guess at who the burglar had been.

I started with a quick survey of the whole house, just so I would know what I was dealing with. Downstairs there was a large kitchen, a cloakroom and WC, a laundry room attached to a small vestibule – which had its own separate door to the back garden, the one I had discounted as a way into the house – the large flock-wallpapered lounge I had been in before, a dining room, the hallway leading to the front entrance vestibule and Ellis's study. I marked the study for special attention later, once I had checked out the upstairs. The upper floor had a bathroom, two double bedrooms and a single bedroom that was little more than a large closet with a window. From what I could see in the small pool of light cast by the penlight, everywhere was furnished with the same predictable conservatism as the lounge.

The study was definitely my best bet. But there was nothing to say that Ellis hadn't secreted information about Tanglewood somewhere less obvious; somewhere his wife wouldn't think of looking. But I didn't have time to turn over mattresses, dip into toilet cisterns or rifle through sock drawers. I had been accused of all kinds of crap over the last few days, none of which I had done, but this time I really had committed a crime by deliberately breaking into the Ellis home. If I were caught, it would give Dunlop all the excuse he needed to keep me locked up while he took his own sweet time to pin on me anything else he could dream up.

I was jumpy. This wasn't the first time I had broken and entered, and the last time I had very nearly been caught in the act. Speed was of the essence and I would have to concentrate on the study. Then, if I didn't find anything worthwhile, and I had time to spare, I would maybe look elsewhere in the house.

I came down the stairs as quickly as I could. It was a detached house, and empty, so I didn't have to worry too much about sound, but I had to make sure the light from my penlight didn't scan across the drawn curtains.

At least that's what I thought.

I heard the key in the front door.

I was half way down the stairs and froze. The stairway led into the hallway that fed from the entrance vestibule; there was no way I could get down into the hall and through to the kitchen before whoever was unlocking the front door came into the hall. I had to go back up. Which meant I would be trapped.

I had closed the door from the kitchen to the garden behind me and only close examination would reveal that it had been forced, all the damage being on the outside, but if anyone tried the door handle, then it would be obvious that an unwanted guest had gained entry. And could be still in the house.

Killing the penlight, I backed up the stairs, keeping my eyes fixed on the glass panel door that led into the hall. Just as the hall light was switched on, I reached the small stair landing, where the staircase turned on itself and couldn't be seen from the hall. I let out a long, slow, quiet breath, realizing I had held it since hearing the key in the door.

I heard footsteps in the hall, one set, high heels sounding on the parquet. I looked around the angle of the stairs and saw Pamela Ellis drop her keys onto the hall table. I braced myself for her heading towards the stairs and readied myself to make a quiet dash for the single bedroom, which looked as if it hadn't been used for anything in some time. I'd be very unlucky if she looked in there. Another sigh of relief as she headed along the hall, away from the foot of the stairs. I congratulated myself on leaving Ellis's study till last. She made her way into the kitchen, where, unless she had some reason for going out through the back door, she would see no evidence of my presence.

Shit. I closed my eyes and gritted my teeth in a silent curse. Shit. Shit. Shit.

The chisel.

I had left the chisel in plain view on the kitchen table.

CHAPTER THIRTY-SIX

Once more I measured the distance to the front door. If I made a dash for it while Pamela Ellis was still in the kitchen, there was a chance I could make it out through the front door without her seeing. But the odds were against it and, anyway, her police escort was probably sitting patiently outside and I would run into the welcoming long arms of the law.

I heard her switch on the kitchen light, the sounds of her moving around.

Making sure I didn't cause a single floorboard to creak, I went up the rest of the stairs two at a time, along the upper hall and into the front bedroom. Easing back the heavy drapes I checked the street. Right enough, the Austin Cambridge was back on sentinel duty. I cursed again. I tried to remember any details of the rear wall of the house, such as any drainpipes that might offer an escape route from the single bedroom; but, skulking around outside in the near pitch dark, I had been too focussed on breaking into the house to check out any ways of getting out of it from upstairs.

I made my way back to the stairs landing. I could hear Mrs Ellis was still in the kitchen. Only a matter of time before a shrill scream or shout brought the two coppers in from the street.

Then, suddenly, she switched off the kitchen light and marched back down the hall, something tucked under her arm, snapping up her keys as she passed the hall stand and walked out through the front door, slamming it behind her. She had forgotten something. That was all. I couldn't guess how she had missed the chisel on the kitchen table, but she had.

A horrible thought seized me and I rushed back up the stairs and into the front bedroom, again checking through the carefully parted drapes. What if she *had* seen the chisel and was acting cool until she was out of the house and safe. Now, she could be telling the coppers what she'd found and her belief that the burglar was still in the building.

Instead, she climbed back into the Daimler and drove off. When the Cambridge took off after her, I realized that they had had their engine running all the time she'd been in the house.

I watched for a while longer, ready to sprint down the stairs and out the back door, down the dark garden and over the high wall, broken glass or not, if I saw either car return. After five minutes that passed like five hours, I went back downstairs. I was aware that my heart was still pounding away and I felt sick. I was a pretty cool customer at the best of times, and I had talked, fought or run my way out of a lot of sticky situations, but now the stakes were higher than they had ever been.

I went into the downstairs WC and washed my face, patting it dry with the towel hanging on the back of the door. Easy, Lennox. Take it easy. I went through to the study and decided it was worth the risk of switching on the desk lamp.

The desk was a square, solid job and in no way unusual. Other than the desk lamp, all that was on the desk was an ivory Bakelite telephone, one of the GPO 200 series dating from the Thirties, a clock, address book, a pen and ink set, and a leather-trimmed rectangular desk-blotter. No Tanglewood in the address book. The blotter drew my attention. The otherwise pathologically fastidious Ellis had clearly had a habit of doodling on the blotting paper. Most of the doodles were on the right hand side of the blotter, while the telephone sat to its left. My guess was that the bizarre geometric shapes and curlicued letters had been done absentmindedly while Ellis had taken phone calls. It's funny the route the unconscious mind takes to express itself independently of the conscious, and I examined the doodles closely. Again, if there was anything significant in amongst the scribbles and doodles, it escaped me.

Then I noticed something unusual. Everything on the blotter had been harmlessly doodled and left; sometimes over-drawn with something else, but never deliberately obscured. Except in one corner, the top right. There, Ellis had scored out something he had written. I peered at it but couldn't make much sense of it. Something beginning with a T in it, but too short to be Tanglewood. More like initials. I thought about taking my glove off, licking my thumb and trying to rub off some of the obscuring ink, but inking my own fingers to leave prints would probably offend the coppers' union. Instead I tore the corner off the blotting paper and reshuffled the sheet within its leather holder to conceal my vandalism as much as possible.

There was a bookcase along one wall; from what I could see, most of the books were technical manuals and textbooks, mainly concerning all things related to demolition, but also a few novels – the usual stuff: Hammond Innes, Dennis Wheatley, Nevil Shute. But what caught my attention most was a huge, single-volume English-Hungarian dictionary. I slipped it out from the shelf and took it over to the table. Pamela Ellis had been right about her husband's obsessive note-writing. The dictionary had several sheets of paper jammed into its pages. Some were small notes with one or two words scratchily scribbled onto them, some with the English translations, some not. Others were full sheets, folded neatly in two, containing hundreds of immaculately copied out grammatical rules, or perfectly declined verbs. Ellis had certainly been serious about learning his original native language. As I looked through the dictionary, I found his dedication admirable. I could speak fluent French, reasonably good Italian and some German, but in each of these languages there was some identifiable commonality, some shared rudiments, that allowed you to build a bridge from one to the other. Hungarian, as far as I could see, was somewhere out there on its own.

I looked through the notes he had made. If there was a significance to be read in any of them, it was beyond my reading. I put the dictionary back.

I spent half an hour going through Ellis's desk drawers. I did it carefully, methodically. Fruitlessly. There was nothing. I pulled drawers out, upended his desk chair to check beneath the seat, ran my fingers over every surface to find somewhere something significant could be hidden. Nothing. There were plenty of notes, that was for sure, a diary full of appointments, the address book full of contacts, but not a single reference to anything that could not be linked to his business or social activities. The only thing that leapt out at me was how unbelievably dull his day-to-day routine had been. Again the image of the dying man in my office came to mind and I couldn't bridge the gap between the mundane life before me on the desk and the horror and drama of its end.

I checked my watch. I had spent three-quarters of an hour going through Ellis's stuff and, although I had made an effort to do so methodically, it would take me another fifteen minutes to get everything back the way it had been. When I left, I wanted to leave no trace of where I'd been, nothing disturbed or out-of-place. The only evidence of a break-in would be the back door.

When I finished up, I felt frustrated. It had been a hell of a lot of effort and twice as much stress – and for absolutely nothing other than a torn-out doodle from a dead man's desk blotter.

I made my way back through the kitchen, picking up the chisel on the way, and out into the garden. I closed the back door carefully, pushing some of the splintered wood back into place with my pigskin-gloved fingers. Depending on how often Pamela Ellis used her back door, it might be a day or two before the damage was noticed.

A waste of time.

I replaced the chisel in the drawer of the old desk in the garden shed. It was an odd-looking job: dense, dark wood. It had that sort of mittel-European solidity and I guessed it was Hungarian in origin, along with the heavy chest that looked like it had been hewn from the same forest. I wondered if it was some kind of heirloom passed down from Ellis's Hungarian parents, but that didn't make sense. From what Archie had passed on from Ferguson, the *Elès* family, like so many European refugees over the last hundred years, had left all their belongings and half their family behind them.

Then it struck me.

I had spent an hour in Ellis's study scrabbling through paperwork that had told me nothing about the man. Yet the moment I had first stepped into this shed, I had had a real feeling that *this* was the space inhabited by his personality. It was here I should be looking. I thought again how Pamela Ellis had told me that her husband insisted that the shed was always kept locked, and how angry he got when she forgot.

I had a practical problem. In the house, with the curtains drawn closed, and in a back-facing study, it had been easy to search with the desk lamp switched on. But every second I spent in the shed, with its shadeless square windows and using my penlight to illuminate my searching, exposed me to a real risk of being seen. I got down on my knees, the penlight between my teeth, and pulled the drawers out one by one. They were heavy with tools and I eased each to the ground before emptying its contents, tool by tool. It was going to take an age.

Nothing in the first drawer. Or the second. Ellis had lined the bottom of each drawer with newspaper and when I emptied the third drawer, I eased up the newspaper to find a square, flat package wrapped in waxed paper. When I opened it, I found an Ordnance Survey map and nothing else. But there was no doubt that a real effort had been made to conceal the package, so I slipped it into the pocket of my duffle coat. At last, I was maybe getting somewhere.

The chest was locked with a heavy padlock. Retrieving the chisel from the desk drawer, I jammed it as a lever into the loop of the padlock and twisted, using all my strength, but it wouldn't give. I was running out of time, but there was a differ-ence in being stuck in the shed if Pamela Ellis and her escort returned and being caught in the house itself. Nevertheless, it was still a risk I didn't want to take. I opened the shed door and leaned my head out, checking down the drive and the street as far as I could see it, and listening for any sounds nearby. Everything was quiet. I went back into the shed and took a large steel-headed mallet from where it hung on the shed wall. I swung. The padlock clashed and rattled but didn't break. Hitting the padlock made too much noise and I was going to have to be quick. I hit it another three times, taking full swings at it and was rewarded with a deformed, but still clamped shut padlock. I tried the chisel again and this time the weakened padlock gave way.

It was a huge effort for nothing. The chest, as far as I could see, was filled with more tools; larger or heavier ones that would not have fitted into the desk drawers. Ellis's fastidiousness made my job easier; other than the largest tools such as the heavy bolt cutters with two foot long handles which were left loose, everything was sorted and kept in wooden boxes, which I was able to lift out and examine one by one, laying them on the shed floor. But it was another fruitless search. The only discovery I had made was that Ellis had a staggering array of tools even for the most dedicated do-it-yourselfer. I picked up the bolt cutters, trying not to think how Twinkletoes had used such implements in his colourful past, and placed them back in the chest.

I noticed the carved chest was thick-walled and heavy-lidded, so I assumed the base would be similarly thick. But, putting the bolt cutters back, I was aware that the chest was far shallower than it should be. Using the handles of the cutters as a guide to measure the well of the chest compared to its outer wall, I reckoned there was a good six-inch disparity, over and above the thickness I would have expected from the walls and lid.

A false bottom.

I ran my fingers around the inside edges of the chest's base, looking for a trigger or catch to release the bottom, but all I could find was a natural looking notch in the wood, a few inches from the edge. I went back to the shelves and ripped the lid off a jar of nails, took one and leaned on it with the head of the steel mallet to bend it into a hook. My bet was that Ellis already had a hook hidden somewhere in the shed, but I didn't have time to look for it. Going back to the chest, I twisted and wiggled the bent nail into the notch. I got purchase on the base and it lifted clear. I had been right.

This hulking, ugly hunk of wood in the corner of a garden shed turned out to be a treasure chest. There were four packages, all wrapped in the same waxed paper as the map I had found. But these had been hidden away more carefully. And with good reason.

The first contained a heavy cardboard box, just big enough for the automatic pistol and spare magazine it held. The Bearsden Rotary Club, I guessed, hadn't known about this. The other three packages contained cash. Banknotes. One contained US dollars, the second Bank of England ten-pound notes, the third German marks. Even without counting it, I could tell it was a small fortune. It was the kind of pot-of-gold that gave you ideas and made you jump to conclusions. My first idea was where I could stash the cash to add to my repatriation fund, should the local constabulary decide to be difficult about me liquidating my other assets. And my first conclusion was that this was dirty money. Maybe not from a dirty source, but for a dirty use. Whatever his little Hungarian cycling club were up to, I guessed that Ellis had been the treasurer. The banker. Something he had found out had made him hold back funds, which was why his playmates had hit his business safe.

That, as far as I was concerned, made this money up for grabs. But I came down with a bout of that ailment that had been plaguing me increasingly of late: a bad attack of morality.

I thought of all that Pamela Ellis had been through – the

confusion, the grief, the fear. She wouldn't know about this stash. Nobody except Ellis did, I guessed.

Dirty or not, this money belonged to Pamela Ellis and I was going to make sure she got it. I didn't want the coppers to get their hands on it and would do everything I could to avoid that happening, but, at the end of the day, I had probably just worked out the motive for Ellis's murder – someone else's motive – and it might end up being the only card I had to play.

Stuffing the three packets into the duffle coat's pockets, I turned my attention to the pistol. It was a Browning-type nine-millimetre automatic, and when I examined it, I saw the name *Femaru-Frommer* tooled into the barrel flank: a gun I'd neither seen or heard of before. Despite being a pretty standard Browning configuration, it had one highly unusual feature: a curved finger rest that hooked out from the base of the magazine.

I released the box magazine from the well and slipped it and the spare into my inside coat pocket. Then I tucked the pistol into the waistband of my trousers. Given my current predicament, it was probably on the insanely reckless side of inadvisable to wander around Glasgow heavy with an illegal gun, but I suspected that the police were the least of my worries.

There was no way I was going to end up like Ellis without putting up a fight.

CHAPTER THIRTY-SEVEN

It was still a bright, cold night and I found myself wishing for a wisp or two of the smog that had cloaked my city-crossing skulk the night of my escape. I guessed, however, that my get-up and set of wheels were as good a disguise as I could have.

Stopping the Cresta out of sight, I tugged my cap's peak down over my eyes, walked back to where I'd seen a late-night street vendor and bought an evening paper. Still nothing about me. I was beginning to find my lack of mention, however welcome, rather strange.

I took a slow drive along Broomielaw without stopping, checking out for any watching coppers or cars with their engines running, before doing a city block loop and coming back.

Larry Franks was doing his best to look casual, hanging on the corner across from the Paradise Club and smoking. I was on time, so I guessed he couldn't have been waiting too long. He snapped a cigarette away into the street as he saw my second approach; I pulled up to the kerb.

'The coppers give you that?' he asked when he got in, nodding to the bruise on my face. I had hoped it would have faded, but it had simply changed tones: an identifying mark that would be with me for a week or so.

'No, not the coppers,' I said, looking in my rear-view mirror before driving off.

'Nobody's watching the club,' he said. 'And I really don't think anyone's tapped the telephone. The coppers aren't taking the subtle approach. Jonny's been hauled in three times and they've leaned on him pretty hard. But they're doing the leaning because they've got nothing else now. He told me he owes you for that and wanted me to tell you he won't forget it.'

I didn't say anything. Having sentenced a man to death was not something I wanted gratitude for.

'Jonny also knows all about your problem with the police. Like I said on the 'phone, a couple of coppers came in twice, asking for you. Turn here, over the bridge,' said Franks. 'I live in Newton Mearns. But you'd have guessed that already.'

I smiled. Newton Mearns was known locally as Tel Aviv on the Clyde. Jonny Cohen lived there as well.

'These two coppers . . .' I said, as we crossed the Jamaica Bridge and into the South Side. 'Anyone you know?'

'Never seen either of them before. One had an Englishy-type accent, which you don't often hear in a Glasgow copper.'

'But they showed you their warrant cards?'

'Yeah . . . or more that they flashed them at me. But these boys couldn't be anything other than coppers. You know the type.'

And I did. More specifically, I knew two in particular who were exactly the type. With Special Branch warrant cards.

'So what did you find out on those names?' I asked.

'I've got more than the names for you,' said Franks. 'I'll go over it all when we get back to my place. I've fixed up a bed in the spare room. I guess you're looking for a place to lie low.'

'The bed for tonight's great, Larry, I appreciate it. But after that, I've got plans.' I trusted Franks and I trusted Cohen more, but the barge was going to stay a secret between me and Twinkle. Who, bizarrely, I found myself trusting the most.

We spent the rest of the drive chatting, but I kept checking the rear-view mirror as we did so and was aware of Franks doing the same with the wing mirror.

Franks's flat was in a newly built, boxy concrete horseshoe of apartments. It was right on the edge of Newton Mearns and, even in the dark, I could see the black clouds of silhouetted trees rolling across the landscape and into the distance. It was, for me, a uniquely Scottish thing: the way hard-edged, asphalt urbanism could come to a sudden stop and open landscape began, without any graduation between. It was the same phenomenon I'd experienced in the Lanarkshire mining village when I'd gone hunting for Frank Lang's supposed birthplace.

Larry Franks's flat was on the top floor of three and it was a nice place. Cool and calm, and somehow nothing like I had expected. Everything was clean and modern, including the Danish-style furniture; but it wasn't the strident, clumsy modernity of the Dewars' Dennistoun terrace. It was tasteful. And expensive: I guessed that Franks made more than a bob or two running the Paradise Club, and much of that income would not have been allowed to add to the taxman's workload.

'You hungry? I'm hungry,' he said, and headed towards the kitchen. 'Sit down and I'll fix you a sandwich.'

I did what he said. I was hungry. Before he went into the kitchen, Franks poured two Scotches and handed me one. As I sipped it, I took in more of my surroundings. Everything new. This was what it was like, I guessed, not to have a history. To have to start everything again anew.

The only things that were of any kind of vintage were the photographs on the mantelpiece. Even they were in modern frames, but the photographs themselves were creased and one had a corner torn and missing. I guessed they were of family, but when Franks came back in from the kitchen, I didn't ask. There were a lot of questions you didn't ask of a man with a number tattooed on his forearm. Asking about his family was one of them.

He placed a plate on the G-Plan coffee table in front of me and I started to eat.

'Cheese and ham?' I asked disbelievingly.

'Don't you like cheese?' he asked, grinning.

'Cheese and ham's fine by me. Now, what did you find out about those names?'

'Well, all three are scam-merchants, like you say. But that's like saying the guy who does the toilet signs for the Corporation and Michelangelo are both painters.'

'So who's the signpainter and who's Michelangelo?'

'Well, let's put it this way, you were right to say Eddy Leggat was your best bet to find. Dennis Annan, or whatever name he uses now, is definitely the Michelangelo of long-firm fraud. He can spend years setting up a fraud and then makes a big hit. Eddy Leggat is the middleweight. The third guy on the list is small fry, and anyway he's in prison.'

'Does anyone know what Annan looks like?'

'I don't. I think Jonny's maybe met him, but a long time ago. He isn't your Frank Lang, or whoever the guy in the photograph was. Jonny would have recognized him.'

'Have you got me anything on Leggat?'

Franks got up and went over to a low level oak bureau. When he came back he had a heavy envelope and a slip of paper in his hand. He handed me the note and I saw it had an address in Anniesland on it.

'Anniesland?' I asked incredulously. 'The profits of long-firm fraud only get you as far as Anniesland?'

'That's where he is now. Recuperating.'

'Recuperating?'

'Recuperating . . . His last scam was a phoney travel agency business, taking cash directly from punters for bus tour holidays of the Lake District, Blackpool, that sort of crap. But his big score was selling tickets for a bogus trip to Lourdes for the genuflection set. Turns out one of the punters he ripped off was some old biddy with a bad back she wanted *Our Lady* to fix for her. An old biddy by the name of Murphy . . . as in her nephew, Hammer Murphy.'

'Ouch . . .'

'Yeah . . . ouch. I believe Leggat said that when Murphy and his boys came to visit. Over and over again.'

'He doesn't sound like he's the mastermind of deception I'm looking for.'

'It's not what he knows, it's who he knows,' said Franks.

'You said you had more than the names for me?'

'That I have . . .' He handed me the envelope and I opened it.

'Shit . . .' I said, bemused, when I saw the contents.

'Travelling funds, Jonny said. Enough to get you out of the country and back to Canada. Enough to take the less conventional or obvious route.'

I looked at the swollen envelope. There was a couple of thousand in it, enough to buy all of the flats in the block.

'Tell Jonny that I'll return this, when everything is over.'

'I got the impression it was non-returnable. Whatever happens.'

I took a deep breath. 'Okay,' I said, and slipped the envelope into the pocket of the tweed jacket.

We finished our sandwiches and then another whisky. We sat and smoked and drank and Franks even made me laugh with some bad jokes. For the first time in days I felt like a normal guy with no worries.

He asked me if I wanted a coffee and I said yes, following him into the kitchen with my plate. The kitchen was like the rest of the flat: clean, tidy, efficient, all built-in and modern lines. Even the jumble of notes, calendar and photographs pinned to the cork notice board on the wall by the door seemed to have a kind of organization to it. He had a small espresso pot on the hob and I knew that I was going to taste real coffee for the first time in a long time.

'Do you miss Hungary?' I asked. He turned to me, as if surprised by the question.

'Do you miss Canada?'

'Every day.'

'Well then. The difference is you rejected Canada instead of the other way around. That's the difference between an emigrant and a refugee, I suppose. Hungary didn't so much reject me as spit me out.'

He handed me my coffee and I turned to head back into the living room when I noticed one particular photograph, actually a press cutting, pinned to the cork board.

'Larry . . .' I said, the confusion obvious in my tone. 'Why would you have a photograph of a Nazi pinned up in your kitchen?'

'Oh . . . old Werner there?' Franks laughed. 'Werner's my hero.'

I examined the picture again: a black and white head-and-shoulders image of a steel-helmed German infantryman. His eyes were bright and he had movie-star looks.

'I'll tell you something, Lennox,' said Franks, 'and I'm not crying for sympathy or any shit like that – but I saw some things, I'll tell you. In the camps. Before the camps, and after. You either spend the rest of your life hating everyone because you know what they're capable of, or you try to make sense of it and see some good in people.' He took another sip of whisky and screwed up his eyes, lifting a finger from the glass to point it at me. 'But if there's one thing I learned, it's this: no one is who he seems. Ever.'

He tapped the picture on the cork board with his free hand. 'Take Werner here . . . good old blue-eyed, square-jawed, blond-haired, handsome-as-fuck Werner. This picture was taken for a Berlin newspaper and was titled "The Ideal German Soldier". Goebbels or one of his monkeys cottoned on to it and Werner was plastered all over recruiting posters for the German army. This . . .' he tapped the picture again, 'was what all good Nazi Aryan soldiers should look like.'

'I don't —'

Franks cut me off by wagging the finger extended from his glass. 'The thing is, Werner was kicked out of the army in Nineteen-Forty. You know why? Because this particular Ideal German Soldier's surname was Goldberg.'

'Jewish?' I looked at the photograph again.

'Half. A *Mischling*, as the Nazis called them. So you see, no one is ever who they seem in this life. Good or bad. But I think you're someone who already knows that. Jonny says you've been through a wringer or two yourself.'

I smiled, contemplating my Scotch. 'I guess I have at that. The First Canadian had a shitty war – from Sicily all the way to Hamburg. And I've got mixed up in a lot of things since. Things I shouldn't have gotten mixed up in. I've seen a lot of crap all right. I even once had to spend a weekend in Aberdeen.'

'Shit ...' Franks affected mock shock and sympathy. 'Aberdeen?' He laughed. Franks was all right. We had another couple of snifters and I began to feel the world's rotation on its axis so we called it a night and I crashed out in his spare room. I felt relaxed and tired and grateful.

But I tucked the automatic under my pillow, all the same.

CHAPTER THIRTY-EIGHT

'Lennox. *LENNOX* . . .' It was hissed into my ear. I woke to see Franks leaning over the bed, his hair mussed up and dressed in just his trousers, braces hastily pulled up over naked shoulders. I reached for the lamp but Franks grabbed my wrist. 'No lights!'

'What the hell is wrong?' I said, easing up on my elbows, trying to push back the waves of sleep that tried to regain me. My mouth was thick with sleep and whisky.

'We've got company . . .' He stood back to give me room to get up. I reached under my pillow and pulled out the gun.

'Jesus . . .' said Franks. 'What the hell have you got that for?'

'It's my comforter, I can't sleep without it. What's going on? What company?'

'Outside.'

He led me to the window and eased the curtain back only just enough for me to see out without being seen. A car, a big one, parked outside in front of the main entrance to the block of flats and right behind the Cresta. I saw a dull red-orange glow as someone took a pull on a cigarette; too dull and too far away for me to see a face.

'And he has a pal . . .' Franks led me through the apartment to his bedroom, which looked out onto the street behind the building and towards the apartment blocks beyond. Again he eased the curtain back gingerly and I caught sight of a tall figure across the street, trying to stay in the shadows by standing midway between the street lamps.

'They haven't put him out there to stand all night,' I said. 'There's going to be at least two others and my guess is that they'll be on their way up to pay us a visit any time soon. How long have they been there, do you think?'

'Out front? No more than ten minutes. But my guess is that they followed us here and have been watching from a distance and waiting for the time to be right. Unfortunately for them, I learnt long ago to sleep with one eye open, if you know what I mean. Anyway, I heard the car pull up outside, really quiet like.'

I nodded, watching the man in the shadows. He was wearing a camel coat and a narrow-brimmed hat. What light there was on him from the lamps on either side was shaded by the hat's brim, keeping his face in shadow. And he was a fair distance away.

'What do we do?' asked Franks, no signs of fear or panic in his voice or expression. I guessed that the fear had been burned out of him a long time ago. He was a good man to have at your side at a time like this.

'We wait. If they try to break in, we let them.'

'And you're going to use that?' He nodded to the gun in my hand. 'Listen Lennox, I don't want to swing or spend the rest of my life dodging dicks in the prison showers.'

'I'm not going to kill anyone, Larry. But waving this around has a habit of evening the odds a little.'

'Unless they wave back. It's a no-go, Lennox.' Franks's eyes were locked on the gun, a strange expression on his face. Then he looked up at me decisively. 'Listen, gather all your stuff up, I've got an idea ...'

I did what I was told. I put the gun down, pulled on my shirt and jacket, stuffing the tie in my pocket, then put on the duffle coat. I picked up the automatic again. Once more, I caught Franks's expression as he looked at it. As if it was some object of great evil.

'What's wrong Larry? You got a thing about guns?'

'About that particular kind of gun, yes.'

'You know it?'

'Intimately. That's a Femeru-Frommer. Hungarian-made but manufactured for the German army. Very popular with members of the Arrow Cross. The last time I saw one of those a Hungarian *Hunyadi* SS *Oberscharführer* had it jammed into my cheek, threatening to blow my eye out with it because I hadn't spotted a piece of litter I was supposed to be clearing up. Never thought I'd see one again ... Never wanted to see one again, I tell you that.'

'I'm sorry, Larry,' I said, tucking it into the waistband of my trousers and pulling my jacket over it. 'That other case I was talking to you about ... the Hungarian one. I think I've gotten mixed up with some bad bastards. And I have a horrible feeling that's who we're dealing with here.'

'Then it's time you took a powder. Listen carefully: just outside the front door there's a hatch in the ceiling. It gives maintenance people access to the roof void and the skylight. If our chums aren't already outside the door, you could get up onto the roof and cross over not just to the other side of this block, but right across the next two. There's a skylight for each block. You can come down in the farthest away block. They're not watching that.'

'And what about you? You better come along too.'

'I'll be fine. I can keep them occupied.'

'I don't know about that, Larry. If it's the Hungarians, they play for keeps, as I've found out to my cost.'

'Yeah? Then I think I'd better contact the constabulary. Get ready . . .'

He went back into the living room and picked up the telephone. I heard him dial three numbers, then ask for the police.

'This is Mr Franks, over in Dugdale Avenue. Listen, there are four men who have just turned up in a large green car . . . I think they're trying to break into my downstairs neighbours, the Ashers . . . Yes, yes, please come quick . . .'

He turned to me when he replaced the receiver in its cradle. 'You've got a couple of minutes, no more . . .'

Keeping the lights off in the flat, Franks carefully opened the front door without making a sound. He leaned his head through the gap and peered out. Once he was satisfied that the coast was clear, he stepped into the hall and beckoned for me to follow. The landing and stairwell were illuminated by wall globes and there was no sight nor sound of anyone coming up the stairs. Yet.

Franks pointed silently to the square hatch above his head; crouching, he made a cradle with his hands and I put my foot in it. He boosted me until I could reach the hatch which I pushed up and clear. Franks heaved again as I pulled myself up into the roof void. I turned round, looked back down at him and we exchanged silent thumbs-up signals. He disappeared back into his apartment and I put the hatch back into place, becoming immersed in the pitch darkness of the roof void. It took several seconds for my eyes to adjust and I lay motionless, listening for sounds of activity in the stairwell below.

The only light that leached into the void was coming through the skylight Franks had told me about: the dim, blue-grey luminosity of the night sky, lightened from below by the diffuse glow of streetlights. The skylight was about ten yards to my left, which meant it was directly above the block's central stairwell. One false move in the dark, one crossbeam missed, and I would fall through the plaster ceiling with nothing to stop my plunge straight to the bottom of the stairwell.

I fumbled in my duffle coat pocket and found the penlight. Shining it around me, I could see that this was no attic but simply an access crawlspace too low for me to stand up in. It was obviously intended for use by maintenance workers, electricians, plumbers and the like, just as Franks had said, and although the roof void wasn't floored, there was a crawl-way, like a gangplank, leading from the hatch to the skylight.

I moved as quickly as I could towards the skylight, crouched over and trying to make as little sound as possible. There was a screw catch holding it in place, but only finger-tight, so I was able to release it and slowly push the skylight up and over, allowing me to squeeze through onto the flat roof of the apartment block. Franks was a smart cookie, all right.

I eased the skylight shut behind me. The temperature had taken an even deeper dip and I felt the raw night bite through my clothes. I crossed to the edge of the roof, staying on my hands and knees. The car was still there, parked behind the Cresta. I went over to the other side of the roof, still keeping low, and confirmed for myself that the camel-coated watcher between the streetlamps was also still in position.

There was no sound of police cars approaching with bells ringing and I was beginning to worry about having left Franks alone in his apartment, so I hung off starting my journey across all three blocks and coming down the other side.

I went back to the front edge and again looked down to where the cars were parked. Right enough, two heavy-set men slipped out of the back seat of the car behind the Cresta and, after exchanging a few words with the driver through his window, started to make their way towards the apartment block's main entrance.

This was it. No coppers yet and Franks was on his own, so I pushed away from the edge and prepared to cross back to the skylight. I was halted by the sound of a car pulling up. Then a second.

I scrambled to the roof's edge once more and was enormously relieved to see two police Wolseleys pulled up at angles to block in the goons' car. Unfortunately, one of the patrol cars had blocked the Cresta as well. Four big coppers got out, two from each patrol car, and they closed in on the two heavies, who didn't put up any resistance.

Time for me to go. Satisfied that Franks would be okay, and already chilled by the night, I ran crouching across the connected flat roofs of the horseshoe of apartment blocks. The roofs were covered in some kind of pitch that muffled my footsteps, but all the same I tried not to think what they must have sounded like in the apartment bedrooms beneath me.

I made it to the third block and tried to ease up the skylight. When it didn't budge, I cursed inwardly at my stupidity. Of course it wouldn't open. The skylights were engineered to be unlatched only from below. In my haste to get up onto the roof, I hadn't thought through the fact that I'd had to unscrew the fastening from inside the void to release the first skylight. Muttering obscenities at myself, I indulged in a moment of panic, lost as to what to do next. I threw a forced calm over the panic like a fire-blanket and made myself think through options. There were only two.

The first was that I take off my duffle coat and drape it over the skylight to muffle the sound as I broke the glass with the muzzle of the automatic. Yeah, Lennox, I thought, brilliant thinking – smashing my way into an apartment block in the dead quiet of night, with a deadly weapon, while there were already four coppers on the scene looking for burglars.

The alternative was to go back the way I came and drop down into the stairwell of the first building. It was my only option, but blocked for the foreseeable by the presence of the police, who would no doubt pay Franks a visit to reassure his good citizenly concerns.

In the meantime, I had to stay put. I tugged the duffle coat collar tighter around my throat and pulled the hood over my head, trying not to think about the cold that was penetrating my flesh like an x-ray. It made sense to stay on the roof: no one was going to look for me up here and I decided to remain exactly where I was, not yet crossing back to my original escape hatch on the first roof for fear of alerting residents to my presence.

I crawled to the edge and looked over. The coppers were still talking to the two heavies. Then the driver stepped out. He was a tall man in a dark coat and hat, and he moved with a quiet, unhurried authority. As he unfolded from the car, he reached into his pocket and held something up for the coppers to see. And with that, the whole dynamic of the conversation below changed. The uniformed policemen moved back from the heavies and the driver of the car did all of the talking. He pointed up to Franks's apartment. By this time it was obvious he was exerting some kind of authority over the constables.

'Don't believe him . . .' I muttered, trying to will some intelligence into the coppers' thick Highlander skulls. 'Don't believe him . . . the warrant card's a fake . . .'

My telepathic skills were clearly not up to scratch. There was a little more chat, then the driver of the car headed towards the entrance to the flats, flanked by one of his own heavies and a uniformed copper.

Again my mind raced through options. Even if I could do the hundred-yards dash faster than Lindy Remigino, I wouldn't be able to get across the roof, through the crawlspace and down to Franks before they got to him. And, even if I did, they had gotten a copper to tag along; and coppers were decidedly sniffy about people waving ordnance in their direction.

Undecided what to do, I simply froze, in all senses of the word. All I could do was wait to see what happened.

They came back out after a couple of minutes. They had Larry Franks with them, hatless but with an overcoat pulled over his tieless shirt. He was steered out by the boss man-driver and his heavy, each of whom had a proprietorial hold of one of his elbows; the uniformed cop just tagged along. When they got to where they were parked, the uniforms began to get back into their cars, leaving their fake colleagues in charge of Franks. And that was something I couldn't allow. If they took him away, the least that would happen to Franks is that he would be tortured to tell them where I was. And I had seen what these bastards had done to Andrew Ellis.

I pulled the Hungarian automatic from my pocket and snapped back the carriage, putting a round in the chamber. I didn't have much of a plan, other than to get their attention and try to convince the uniformed coppers that their new chums were phoneys. It was desperate and dangerous and more than likely stupid, but it was all I had.

Then Franks solved the problem for me. He'd obviously been thinking the same and began to remonstrate loudly with the uniforms, clearly trying to persuade them to take him in. The driver of the other car said something to them and the policemen again started for their patrol cars, leaving Franks to the mercies of the heavies and their boss.

It was perfectly done. Little Franks's right arm arced hard and so fast that the big uniformed policeman took the punch square on the side of his jaw. The copper didn't even twitch or stagger: Franks had switched his lights off and he was felled like a big, dumb Hebridean tree. I grinned. It was a very impressive punch. The other three uniforms laid into Franks, but nothing he couldn't handle, then they handcuffed his hands behind his back and bundled him into the back of a police Wolseley, which was exactly what Franks had wanted them to do when he hit the copper. Again the driver of the other car protested and tried to exert authority over the uniforms, but one of their own had been clobbered and they were having none of it.

Franks was in for a rough time, all right, but he'd survived worse, much worse, and avoiding being taken by the bogus detectives had probably saved his life. Yep, Larry Franks was a smart cookie, all right. And I owed him a drink or two.

The cop Franks had sent to sleep came round and his partner eased him up and into the second police Wolseley. Then they were gone.

Once they were left alone, the three men had a discussion. One of them disappeared around the back of the building, coming back with the guy in the camel coat. He was obviously being quizzed about the chances of me having dodged out the back and past him and there was some vehement shaking of his head. Then they all seemed to be talking about the Cresta. I guessed that they were trying to work out why – if I'd managed to slip out before they closed their trap – I hadn't taken the car.

There was a lot of pointing to the open fields and trees beyond the parking area and then the tall boss man turned and scanned the flats, as if to check they weren't being watched. I ducked back. When I inched forward to see again, he was trying the handle of the door of the Cresta, only to find it locked.

I was desperately cold but I knew it was maybe going to be a long, chilly wait. At least I could be reasonably confident that the only person I was likely to encounter up here on the roof would be Captain Oates out for a stroll.

I watched them. The tall man who had been driving the car took a few steps towards the building. He looked up at Franks's top-floor apartment, then back at the Cresta parked behind him. I felt a chill that ran deeper than the cold night. He was trying to work it out. Put it together.

Once more he looked back to Franks's apartment, then again at the car, tracing steps I hadn't taken. Still trying to work it out.

Then he looked up at the roof.

CHAPTER THIRTY-NINE

Or at least, from this distance, it seemed to me as if he was looking up at the roof. Of course, I was at the far side of the three blocks, and he was looking up at where I had been, rather than where I was now. But if he made the connection, worked it out, then there was nowhere for me to go.

I held my breath, not wanting to give my position away by it fuming into the cold air. If they came up for me, was I ready to use the gun? I was pretty certain they were the Hungarians, but what threw me was the man in charge being able to pass himself off as a senior copper. And I couldn't see a Bela Lugosi type pulling that off.

The tall man continued to stare at the roof, then down to the entrance, then back to the Cresta. He turned his back to the flats and looked out over the fields. That's it . . . I willed the thought into his head . . . out there, that's the way I went.

Another discussion. They were clearly debating the value of splitting up and searching the fields and woods for me. If they did that, my guess is they would leave one guy by the Cresta, just in case I came back for it. I now had no doubt that they weren't genuine coppers. No one disappeared to make a 'phone call to organize a search party; but there again, they'd maybe given me up as a lost cause.

Then they went.

The tall man slammed the flat of his hand down on the wing of the Cresta and barked some orders at the others. They all simply piled into the car and were gone. Up here, elevated above the streets in the chill, clear night, I could hear the engine, the only car on the road, as it faded into the distance.

I waited a while before crossing the roof back to the first block of flats, this time taking more care to make my footsteps light and quiet. One of the reasons I believed the party wagon had rolled out of town was because they were in full view of the apartments, and the little show put on by Franks and the uniforms would probably have woken several of the occupants. I didn't want to attract any more attention.

I retraced my steps, crawled back through the roof void and eased back the hatch. Convinced the coast was clear, I lowered myself gingerly and dropped as quietly as I could onto the landing outside Franks's apartment. I had to leave the hatch open behind me.

My breathing hard but controlled, I stood for a moment on the landing, gathering myself. I tried Franks's door, in case it had been left unlocked in the haste of arresting him. Not that there was anything inside I needed; I had gotten all of my stuff together before leaving. It was locked up tight and I headed down the stairwell to the entrance hallway.

I dashed to the Cresta, started her up and drove off into the night.

My route was, to say the least, circuitous. Instead of taking the main road back to town, I drove south, only staying on the A77 until I was out of Newton Mearns and could cut across country on back roads. I dodged Eaglesham and then East Kilbride,

Scotland's first New Town, another Brave New World of soul-
less concrete and unshared bathrooms for Glasgow's displaced
working classes.

My plan was to take a long, slow loop to the east, then back
north. It meant I would end up driving into Rutherglen and
right through the middle of the city in the middle of the
night, not something that was advisable given my current
fugitive status. In fact, driving around anywhere at this time
of night increased my chances of being stopped by some bored
nightshift copper. Lying low could be as risky an option:
sleeping in the car in some secluded spot was just as likely to
arouse police suspicions, were I unlucky enough to be stumbled upon.

I decided to risk the second option and turned into what
looked like a farm track. After a few yards I came to a large
barn-type thing, wall-less but with an arched corrugated iron
roof supported on wooden shafts – some kind of empty dry
store. I bumped the Cresta over chilled-hard mud, lights off,
and parked under the shelter, killing the engine.

And waited.

I hadn't planned to fall asleep, but I found myself in one of
those dreams where you know you're dreaming but can't get
out of it.

In my dream, steel-helmed Werner Goldberg, the 'Ideal
German Soldier', sat at a baize-covered card table playing
Canasta with Frank Lang – or at least the Frank Lang of the
photograph supplied by Lynch and Connelly – as well as Mátyás,
who insisted on being called Ferenc. I sat at the table too, but
hadn't been dealt a hand and was there mainly to settle a dispute
about whose turn it was to play. Except I kept getting confused

about how many people were really at the table. Then, when I next looked, there was only one.

'I thought you needed a partner to play Canasta,' I said.

'You do,' he said. 'I am my own partner. But you've known that for some time now.'

'Yes,' I said. 'I've known for some time now.'

When I opened my eyes it was beginning to get light, which, at this time of year, meant it was already getting on in the morning. I checked my watch. Eight-thirty. I got out of the car, took a shivering leak against the barn post, then drove back into town.

The roads were reasonably busy and, by the time I reached Rutherglen, the Cresta was camouflaged by lorries, buses and cars heading into the city. I stopped at a call box and 'phoned McBride, asking him to meet me at the barge, but to make doubly sure he wasn't followed.

I exerted even more caution than usual when I got back to the barge. The team who had followed Franks and me into Newton Mearns had been good, and my head ached from the drive back, constantly aware of every vehicle around me, every turn that I did not take alone.

I heated up some water in the kettle and washed and shaved, again sparing my upper-lip the razor to allow the moustache to start back. I desperately wanted to get changed out of the tweed jacket and flannels. Normally, I would never have worn the same suit of clothes two days running, but I decided sartorial offences were the least of my concerns at the moment. I did pull a clean set of underwear and a shirt from my stores in the forward cargo compartment, stuffing my worn clothes into a canvas bag. Laundry was one of the challenges of a fugitive life that most people don't consider. Launderettes were becoming all the rage and maybe, if I got out of all of this crap, I could open up a specialist service for today's man-on-the-run. I brewed some tea and drank it, considering the business opportunity that offered itself. *Laundry on the Lam* struck me as a good name for my enterprise.

First taking out the items I'd stuffed into it, I hung the duffle coat back in the closet. I laid out on the galley table the spare magazine clip, the wax-paper-wrapped bundles of cash, the Ordnance Survey map and the torn-off corner from Ellis's desk blotter.

I turned my attention to the scrap of blotting paper first.

I took some stale bread left over from Twinkletoes's Red Cross parcel and moistened it under the tap, squeezing out the excess water. I held the blotting paper in place with the fingertips of one hand, while rocking the damp bread over its surface with the other. To start with, all I succeeded in doing was making a bigger mess, the ink now wet again and spreading, but I used a piece of dried bread to soak it up.

It still wasn't clear, but it was clearer. I repeated the process with the damp bread, working away steadily but gently.

Three initials had been doodled in ballpoint pen, while the scoring out had been done with a fountain pen, making it more delible. I was also helped by the way Ellis had leaned hard as he had written the initials. NTS. Gone over and over again. NTS. Three initials significant enough that he felt he had to obscure his absent-minded doodling of them.

Three letters that had meant something to him. And meant absolutely nothing to me.

I turned my attention to the Ordnance Survey map. It covered a huge area: from the north shores of the River Clyde in the south to Breadalbane and Loch Tay in the north, and from Argyll in the west to the Ochil Hills in the east.

As far as I could see, that was it. No annotations, no circles drawn around any features, nothing. The only thing that struck me was that this was the 'other' Scotland. The Scotland that was neither Glasgow nor Edinburgh: vast, open and often wild spaces of moorland, highland, loch and bog. Where true Scotsmen roamed and sheep had learned to look over their shoulders.

I was folding the map up again when I saw a small, raised line on the unprinted reverse side. I flipped the map open again, my finger resting on the almost imperceptible bump on the back. I had missed it because it had been done so carefully, so precisely, and in a red ballpoint pen that almost matched the colour of the printed road it traced. This, I realized, had not been done for future reference, but had been the tracing out of a route to burn it into the memory.

The line followed the A82 out of the north side of Glasgow towards Dumbarton, then up north to run along the west shore-line of Loch Lomond. I traced its progress north along the shore, through Arden, Aldochlay, Luss ... I followed the thread Ellis had so faintly spun past the north end of the Loch and up to where the road swung towards Crianlarich. Then, again barely perceptible, I found it. A small, indistinct cross, as much a faint indentation on the paper as a marking.

Whatever was there, it had been Ellis's destination.

I picked the map up from the table, took it over to the narrow ribbon of cabin window, and examined the mark again, more closely and in the daylight.

And then I saw that the mark wasn't a cross at all.

* * *

I heard Twinkletoes as he lumbered his way up the boat deck.

'Hello, Mr. L.' He beamed brightly at me as he descended into the cabin, his arms again full.

I forced some cash on him for the groceries he'd brought with him.

'But you'll need all the money you can get . . .' he protested.

'I'm fine. Honestly,' I said, not wanting to elaborate by telling him that I probably had access to more ready cash than I'd had in my entire life.

We breakfasted on sausages again, this time with eggs, and china mugs full of tea fortified from McBride's hip flask.

'I need your help, Twinkle,' I explained.

'Sure thing, Mr. L.'

'No . . . I need you to understand something. I need your help in the old way. I need to frighten a couple of people into telling the truth. Do you understand me?'

He frowned what brow was available. 'If you says it's necessary, then it is necessary.'

'Okay,' I said. 'Let's finish up. We're heading out to Anniesland.'

It didn't take long. The questions I had to ask Edward Leggat – also known as Eddy McCausland, also known as Ted Cuthbert – were straightforward, didn't seem to incriminate anyone and, in any case, Eddy Leggat would tell me anything to keep his already broken body from Twinkletoes's clutches.

The address for Leggat that Franks had given me was in Anniesland on the wrong side of Great Western Road. It was a pretty standard tenement flat. The only thing exceptional about it was that there wasn't much inside it other than Leggat himself: Hammer Murphy and his associates had emptied the place of anything of any value, Leggat told us in way of explanation for the lack of places for us to sit.

When he answered the door to us, the forcibly-retired con man was dressed in suit trousers and slippers, with a pyjama top on instead of a shirt, obviously because it was cheaper to ruin a pyjama top rather than a shirt by cutting it to accommodate the plaster cast that encased his right arm and shoulder. The cast held his arm hooked out from his body, as if he had it around the shoulder of an invisible buddy. Leggat had expensively cut blond hair, was tallish, and I guessed that he had been reasonably good-looking – a description that now looked like it would remain past tense. Someone had danced the fandango on his face and his swollen and blackened nose now had more angles in it than a trigonometry textbook.

'Hammer Murphy?' I asked.

'I fell down the stairs,' he explained. I didn't labour the point by asking him why, having fallen down the stairs once, he had obviously kept climbing back up and throwing himself down them again and again.

'How bad's the arm?' I asked, and a tearful bitterness filled his eyes.

'The elbow's shattered. They put pins and wires and shite in it, but I've been told I won't be able to bend it or straighten it fully again. It hurts like fuck all the time. Even with the painkillers.'

'Too bad,' I said. Hammer Murphy, whose dear old aunt Leggat had unknowingly ripped off, had gotten his nickname because of his – often deadly – handiness with a lead-headed builder's mallet. The word was that, now he had risen to be one of the Three Kings, Murphy didn't wield his hammer himself anymore. Instead he had minions to take over the more onerous bone-breaking duties. But when it involved family, I could imagine Murphy dipping into the old toolbox personally.

'What is it you want?' Leggat asked, eyeing Twinkletoes suspiciously.

'May we come in?' I asked. Twinkletoes rendered the question redundant by putting his massive paw over Leggat's bruised face and pushing him into the hallway, clearing the path for me.

'Listen . . .' a terrified Leggat said after McBride took his hand from his face. 'I already told Mr Murphy I'm going to leave Glasgow for good, just as soon as I get out of this plaster cast. And I'm sorry for what I done . . .'

I decided not to disabuse him of the idea that we were connected to Murphy. 'Listen, Eddie, this doesn't have to be unpleasant. We're not interested in you, but someone in the same line of business.'

'Who?'

'Dennis Annan.'

He looked at me, then McBride, then back to me.

'I don't know anything about him.'

'Twinkle?' I said and McBride stepped forward and grabbed a corner of the plaster cast, hauling the injured man towards him. Leggat yelled out, more in pain than fear. And he was very frightened.

'I swear . . . I don't know anything about him. No one does. He's a big time operator. I swear to you on my life that I don't know where you can find him.'

'Okay, Twinkle,' I said, and McBride let Leggat go.

'That's fine, I didn't say I wanted you to tell me where to find him. I have a funny idea I already know.'

Leggat looked at me, puzzled. But puzzled in a frightened

way, as if his failure to understand could have painful consequences.

'You've met Annan though, haven't you?' I asked.

'Aye . . . aye, well, a long time ago.' He nodded furiously. 'Years back.'

I took the photograph that Lynch and Connelly had given me of Frank Lang.

'This him?'

Leggat looked at the photograph closely, eager to please.

'No,' he said. 'That's no' him. I'm sorry.'

'It's all right, Eddie. I already knew that. I just wanted to hear it from you. Now, I'm going to describe someone to you. I'm going to describe them in as much detail as I can, because I don't have a photograph to show you. When I'm finished, I want you to tell me if my description matches Dennis Annan. I want you to understand that there are no right or wrong answers. No one is going to hurt you if you just answer a hundred percent honestly. You got that?'

He nodded.

I ran through my description and an expression of concentration tried to establish itself on Leggat's bruised face.

'Does that sound like Dennis Annan?' I asked when I was finished.

'Well, obviously that description could fit a lot of people. An awful lot of people. But that was Annan's thing you see?'

'What was?'

'He had this forgettable face. Really ordinary *general* kind of face. That's what gave him his advantage.'

'So does that description fit Annan or not?'

Leggat nodded. 'Aye. It does.'

I took a ten-pound banknote from my wallet and stuffed it in the corner of his plaster cast.

'Thanks. Buy yourself a back scratcher.' I turned to McBride. 'Come on, Twinkle, it's time you got some exercise.'

CHAPTER FORTY

I couldn't simply walk into the union's headquarters, and sending Twinkletoes in with a message was going to be less than low key, so I decided to 'phone Lynch from a call box. I was lucky and got him.

'You do know the police are looking for you?' asked Lynch. 'And I mean looking for you as in wanted fugitive looking for you. Our union cannot have anything more to do with you.'

'Listen, Lynch, I've only run into this shitstorm because your information about Frank Lang was so vague it led me to someone totally unconnected but very, very dangerous. We don't have time for this. I know who Frank Lang is. Or at least I'm pretty sure I do, and my description of him has rung the right bells. I think I can deliver him to you.'

'Are you sure?'

'As sure as I can be, but I need you. You were Lang's contact at the union. He kept it like that to cut down the number of people who could identify him. And that's what I need you to do. Identify him for me.'

There was a pause. I imagined Lynch at the other end of the line. His beady eyes. His lipless mouth.

'All right. When?'

'Now. Right now. Where's your car parked?'

'In Park Circus. Just around from the union.'

'I'll meet you there in five minutes,' I said, and hung up.

I was waiting for him by his car. When we had met in the working men's club, I had asked him what kind of car he drove and his was the only model of its type parked in Park Circus. I watched him approach, bare-headed, wearing the kind of slacks intellectuals and beatniks had a taste for, an open-collar shirt and a pale grey raincoat. Everything about Lynch annoyed me. Even his wardrobe.

'What's this all about?' he asked when he reached the car. 'I should be telling the police where you are, you know.'

'But you haven't.'

'No, I haven't.'

'Let's take your car,' I said. I let Lynch get in first, then nodded across to where Twinkletoes was parked; my pre-arranged signal that he should follow us.

'Where are we going?' Lynch turned those beady little eyes on me. I could tell he was uneasy.

'Don't worry,' I said. 'I'm not going to force you into any big confrontation. I just need you to eyeball Lang and confirm I'm right. I can take it all from there. Head south. Out through Rutherglen.'

We drove through the city, mainly in silence, and the land-scape around us changed from commercial and residential to purely industrial: dark, grimy walls lining the streets, smoke stacks black against the grey sky. I directed him turn by turn, occasionally checking over my shoulder to make sure Twinkle was keeping up.

'What are we doing out here?' he asked.

'You'll see.'

It started to rain and he switched on the wipers to clear the split screen of the windshield.

'Next left ...' I said. We had entered a warren of narrow streets. Most of the factories and yards around us were now derelict, apart from the occasional scrap yard where vicious-looking dogs bellowed and snarled at the car as it passed.

'Stop here.'

I got out and ran through the chill, greasy rain and unhooked a chain from the gate. Directing Lynch through, I beckoned for Twinkletoes to bring the Cresta in behind. When they were both through, I closed the gate behind him. It was as if the Luftwaffe had used this whole area for target practice. Ten acres or so of flat, empty, black landscape, punctuated by occasional piles of rubble yet to be trucked away. A single tenement remained, pointing a black finger into the sky.

'I've been working on this other case,' I explained when Lynch got out of the car. 'The guy who got killed in my office. He was in the demolition business and this was one of the sites he was clearing. Flattening slum tenements. That's the last to go ...' I said, pointing to the tall, black slum standing all on its own. 'I thought it was the ideal place to do this.'

'In there?' Lynch said incredulously.

'Trust me.'

'And who's that in the car behind? Is that Lang?'

'No, that's a business associate of mine. He has a special role to play in getting the truth from Lang. But the less you know about that, the better.'

We got out and Lynch cast nervous glances at Twinkletoes.

'Come on,' I said. 'Follow me.'

The tenements here had been the worst kind of slums. Crowded, filthy, insanitary. They had crammed in on each other, squeezed tight to allow the maximum occupancy in the minimum of space. Now, with all of its neighbours razed, this solitary tenement had a strange, brooding presence, like some siege-blackened mediaeval tower dominating its landscape.

I led Lynch through the china-tiled entry close and up the communal stairs, McBride bringing up the rear. When we reached the second floor apartment, I turned to Lynch and smiled.

'I'll just get the key ...' With that I kicked the door hard with the flat of my foot and it flew open, smashing against the wall inside. 'After you ...' I said, stepping back and extending my arm to indicate he should enter the flat.

Lynch stepped into the flat, along the hall and into the living room, which had been one of only two rooms, probably for a family of six or seven. There was no furniture other than a single kitchen chair sitting in the middle of the room on the bare, black-painted floorboards. There were two bed recesses in the wall, both empty of any palliasses or bedding. One wall was dominated by a fireplace and its mantel, the mirror above it the only item, other than the kitchen chair, left by the previous owners.

'What the hell is all this about, Lennox? Where's Lang?'

'Don't you see him?' I asked, infusing my tone with puzzlement.

'There's NOBODY HERE!' Lynch yelled at me. 'Have you gone mad?'

With one hand, I grabbed a fistful of the back of Lynch's raincoat. With the other, I seized him by the nape of his neck and ran him forward, pushing his face close into the mirror.

'Don't you see him?' I screamed at him. 'Don't you see Lang there?'

I hauled Lynch back and threw him onto the floor. I reached

into my coat pocket and tossed over to McBride a length of rope I'd brought from the barge.

'Tie him up, Twinkle. To the chair. Good and tight.'

'Okey-doke Mr. L.,' said McBride.

'Why are you doing this?' yelled Lynch. He struggled uselessly in McBride's grip.

'Now, now ...' said Twinkletoes, slapping Lynch so hard on the side of the head I even felt my ears pop.

'Give it up, Annan,' I said. And with that I could see it in his eyes. His tiny, cold, swindler's eyes.

'Who's Annan?' he protested when he recovered himself. 'What the hell has this got to do with Frank Lang?'

'There never was any Frank Lang. There never really was any Paul Lynch. All there was was Dennis Annan.'

He looked at me dully. Even through his fear, I could see he was assessing the situation. Deciding whether to keep the denials and pretence up or to try to start doing a deal.

'I know who *you* are, Annan. Who Lynch and Lang really are. But my question is: so who the hell is this?' I held out the photograph he had given me of 'Frank Lang' when I'd met with him and Connelly.

He didn't answer, or was having difficulty remembering. So Twinkletoes started to jog his memory. I stepped out into the tenement stairwell and smoked a cigarette. I could still hear the sounds of Twinkletoes working Annan over and went back in before it went too far.

I nodded to Twinkletoes and he stood back. Lynch's face was red and swelling up, but I could see Twinkle had done exactly what I asked: a big show, but nothing too damaging. I had been forced back into this kind of shit, but there was a limit to how far I was going to let myself sink.

I showed Lynch the photograph again.

'His name really is Frank Lang,' Lynch sobbed. 'And he really does exist. He is a merchant seaman. We used to serve on the same ship, work the same galley.'

'But he knows nothing about your little game?'

Lynch shook his head. 'I bumped into him in a pub in Glasgow, a few years back. He was pished and started to give me his life story. So I took it. He told me how he was getting out of the merchant navy because he was married and they were about to emigrate to Australia. I stole his wallet but made him think he'd lost it. I got his union and identity cards, as well as some other personal photographs.'

'So you set up this phoney identity and background, rent the house in his name, and use the position in the union to fabricate a working history for him.'

'Everybody is so worried about someone stealing their money or their stuff. The real big steal is if you can rob them of their name. Their identity. That's what I do. No one else does it.'

'Yeah,' I said. 'You're a real trailblazer . . . But the real effort has been put into the other identity – establishing Paul Lynch as a committed and unimpeachable union official. That right?'

I could see the small dark eyes working. 'Listen, Lennox,' he said, 'you're in a bit of a bind. In trouble to your neck. I can help you get out of all of —'

'Never mind the wriggling, Annan,' I said. 'Just tell me how you pulled it all off.'

'Okay, okay . . . I've been working on the Paul Lynch identity for years. I picked someone born around the same time as me but died when they were three years old. It's mad, but births and deaths are kept in different sections of the General Register House in Edinburgh. There's no connection between them, so you can take a dead kid and build a new life for it. That's what I did with Paul Lynch. To start with I didn't know what I'd use the identity for, and I just added details over time and then when the union job came up, I applied for it as Paul Lynch, with all kinds of testimonials and references and memberships of different labour mobs. It was tough going ... much more difficult than ripping off a company. Union people are like aristos, they really are a closed shop. Everyone knows everybody and I had to be seen in the right places with the right people before getting the job.' He looked up at me. 'You want to know the funny thing? I was good at it ... my job at the union, I mean. You see, in this game, you have to *become* what you're pretending to be.'

I looked at Annan. Or Lynch. Or Lang. Three people mixed up in one body. He was a con man, and good at his crooked craft, but there was something wrong with him. Anyone with such a tenuous grip on their own identity was missing something.

'So Connelly wasn't in on it?' I asked.

'No.'

'I don't believe you. You think you're a cut above the average embezzler but you're not. Every con man needs someone on the inside – some unwilling dupe or willing accomplice. My money's on Connelly either way.'

'But don't you see?' said Annan, his flushed, bruised face suddenly illuminated with workman pride, 'You're absolutely right. I *did* need a man on the inside. But *I* was the man on the inside. Or at least me as Paul Lynch. That was the beauty of it. No one would be looking for me. They would be looking for someone who never existed.'

'And that was where I came in ...' I said darkly. Annan fell silent, sensing another storm coming his way.

'You hired me . . . not Connelly, but you,' I continued. 'You had it all worked out. You put me on the trail of a non-existent go-between whose work needed him to stay elusive, and fed me just enough to stumble along and too little to find out anything substantive. No one would suspect you of having anything to do with the fraud, because it was you who hired me. The only problem I have with it all is this . . . you – or at least you as Paul Lynch – would have to disappear eventually. Wouldn't that point the finger? Or were you going to stay on at the union until you collected your pension?'

'A year, maybe. Maybe less, depending on how things worked out. I was going to arrange some kind of muddle or mess to do with records. Maybe a small fire. Something where my records and any photographs could go missing but be lost with everyone else's. There had to be time enough between the money going missing and that.'

I gave a small laugh with something like grudging respect in it. He had had it all worked out.

'Where's all the money you took from the union?'

'All over. Several accounts at different banks. Listen, Lennox, let me go and I'll take a powder. I'll give you half of the take. No . . . three-quarters. You want to piss off back to Canada, and you've got problems with the police here . . . there's enough money to get you free and clear. I can even set you up with a new identity. A new passport.'

'Yeah? That would be convenient for you, wouldn't it? I recently got a really interesting lecture from the police about circum-stantial evidence. Apparently, evidence of flight is part of it. If I disappear from sight, then the coppers assume they were looking in the right direction and don't bother to look anywhere else.'

'What are you talking about?'

'About Sylvia Dewar.'

'I don't want to talk about that . . .' he said.

I took a step towards him and grabbed his shirt front.

'Maybe I can get Twinkletoes here to make you feel a little more loquacious,' I hissed into his face.

'*Low-qway-shus* . . .' muttered McBride behind me. I turned to see him reach for his notebook, his brow furrowed.

'Not now, Twinkle,' I said, shaking my head. I turned back to Annan. 'Let's get one thing straight. This is not the time for you to try to wriggle out of what's coming to you from the law. This is the time for you to talk your way into staying in one piece. And I'm not talking in metaphors. Twinkle . . . go get your stuff.'

While McBride was out at the car, I put a cigarette between Annan's lips and lit it for him.

'I'll tell you something about Twinkletoes,' I said. 'He's a good bloke. Not too bright at times, but a good bloke. But I've never really seen him at his worst. A lot of other people have had a very different perspective on Twinkletoes, but they've never really put it into words, mainly because they've been too busy screaming and begging or losing consciousness through lack of blood. Do you know why he's called Twinkletoes?'

Annan shook his head vigorously, seeming to have lost the power of speech.

'Well, you're about to find out . . .' Taking the cigarette from his lips, I dropped it on the floorboards and crushed it out. Then I knelt down and with one hand untied the laces on his right shoe, holding his struggling ankle in place with the other. I slipped off the shoe and sock. Then repeated the process with the other foot.

'What are you going to do?' Annan's voice was loud and shrill and crackled with fear.

McBride came back. A long-handled pair of bolt cutters, fetched from the Cresta's trunk, hung from his beefy grip. Seeing him come into the room, filling it like an ocean tide filling a bay, even I felt scared. The high-pitched, barely audible sound I heard coming from Annan was somewhere between a whimper and a squeal.

'Do you want me to do his big toes as well, Mr. Lennox?' Twinkle asked matter-of-factly, as if he was a jobbing gardener enquiring about which hedges to trim.

'What do you want me to DO?' Annan screamed at me. 'Just tell me, for fuck's sake. Please ... please get that fucking ape away from me!'

Twinkletoes moved forward, silent. He crouched down at Annan's feet. Annan's small toe looked tiny between Twinkle's forefinger and thumb. He started to struggle furiously but fruitlessly against his bonds.

'I know you killed Sylvia Dewar,' I said. 'You thought you were free and clear when Tom Dewar killed himself after finding her. Even I thought it was a murder-suicide. But the pathologist's times of death didn't fit. And I know that when you were playing your occasional bit part of Frank Lang, Sylvia played a supporting role. What was the deal? Was she part of your set-up? I know she had previous for dishonesty.'

'STOP HIM!' Annan screamed, his pale, small toe now in the black jaws of Twinkletoes's bolt cutters.

'Just a minute, Twinkle. Let's hear what he has to say.'

'It wasn't like that,' said Annan, his eyes still wild. 'She wasn't part of it. I didn't even know who she was to start with ... just this married tart who kept coming to the door whenever I was there. I wasn't interested. The whole set up with the house was just to have an address for Lang. The only reason I made regular visits was to keep up the pretence.'

'But that meant showing your face.'

'People don't remember me, don't recognize me. And I kept my visits to the minimum.'

'So what happened with Sylvia Dewar?'

'I thought she was just some randy housewife who kept pestering me, so I gave her what she wanted. Just a couple of times. Then she hit me with it. She remembered me but I had forgotten her. She knew me from this shitty job I'd done when I'd first got into the business. She knew my name wasn't Lang and she asked what scam I was working. I made up some shite about an insurance company. She said she wanted a cut or she would tell the police I was renting the place under a false name and that I was a confidence trickster. We both knew that the coppers would never get me, but it would fuck up my cover story, meaning it would fuck up the job and the score.'

'So you played along. Screwing her and promising her a cash payout.'

'Don't make it sound like I was taking advantage. She shagged anything in trousers. She was a whore and she treated her husband like shite. I felt sorry for him, but I was just one of many.'

'But then you smashed her skull in with an ashtray.'

'She started saying she wanted away from her husband and if I didn't give her a cut, she'd tell the police everything. I knew Tom Dewar was going nuts and I reckoned he'd get the blame, but they wouldn't hang him or anything. I mean, they'd find it difficult to panel a fucking jury in Glasgow that she hadn't shagged at least one of them. I didn't think he'd kill himself, I swear I didn't . . .'

'Dead men and broken hearts . . .' I said, more to myself than Annan.

'What?'

'Something someone said to me recently.'

'Listen . . .' he said, glancing anxiously at Twinkletoes who was still patiently poised. 'We can do a deal here. You can end up rich. Really fucking rich. You can keep all the money – all of it – just give me a chance to get away.'

I turned to Twinkletoes. 'Untie him.'

'What about . . . ?' McBride nodded to the toe.

'Untie him, Twinkle.'

Annan twisted his lipless mouth in a smile that made me want to hit him again. 'You won't regret this,' he said as McBride laid the bolt cutters aside and set to loosening his bonds. I took two blank sheets of foolscap I had brought in my jacket pocket and unfolded them. I laid the sheets on his lap and handed him my fountain pen.

Annan looked nervously over his shoulder at Twinkletoes, then to me, trying to work out what I was going to do, and I could see a glimmer of hope in his eyes.

'On the first sheet, I want you to write down all of the account numbers and the corresponding bank details for every account you've set up. And don't think about flannelling me. If I for one second think that there is a single figure or account number that's bogus, then I'll let Twinkle get back to work on your pedicure . . .'

'You won't regret this, Lennox. I promise you . . . you can have it all.'

'Well, I want a little insurance. You're going to write down a full confession to the murder of Sylvia Dewar. Everything you've told me, but also all of the specifics about times and dates. Oh, and I want your fingerprint in ink next to the signature. Again, no lies or bending the truth, or you'll never tiptoe through the tulips again.'

'Wait a minute . . . I can't do that . . . they'll hang me.'

'Only if I give it to the police. If everything goes well with making withdrawals from the accounts, then you've nothing to worry about. And, anyway, a confession under duress isn't admissible in court.'

'So . . .' said Annan, still rat-clever and cautious despite his situation, 'what you're saying is if you get the money, you burn that?'

'Is it a deal?'

'How do I know you'll burn the confession?'

'You don't. You'll just have to trust me. I'm Canadian after all. The clean living and maple syrup makes us grow up straight and true.'

Rubbing his raw, untied wrists, Annan's little rat eyes darted about, as if looking for an escape route. Eventually, he started to write. Half way through he asked for a small red notebook from the pocket of his coat. Leaving him guarded by McBride, I got it for him, flicking through the pages and seeing rows of letters and numbers. It was some kind of cypher. Referring to the notebook, he scribbled down the details I needed.

He handed the sheet to me.

'Now the confession. And I want all the details of the union scam in it as well.'

It was clear he saw no way out of it and he started to write. Every now and then I checked over his shoulder to make sure he was telling it how it was. When he was finished, both sides of the sheet were filled with handwriting. I got him to rub ink on the tips of his thumb and forefinger and pressed them down on the paper.

'Sign it and date it,' I said. And he did.

He stood up slowly and painfully, handing me both pieces of paper. I checked them over again.

'There you go, Lennox. You've got it all. Happy?' A raw hatred peeked through the curtain of his fear.

'I'm a cheerful kind of guy.'

Annan put his socks and shoes back on, each movement slow and stiff except for his fingers, which shook almost uncontrollably. Twinkle had scared him good, all right.

He straightened up and started to walk past me. I stopped him with a hand on his chest.

'What's wrong?' he asked.

'Where are you going?'

'I'm not going to hang around. Or do you want me to come with you when you pick up the money . . . is that it? You've got the confession. You don't need me any more.'

'Oh, I think we do, Dennis.'

He looked from me to Twinkletoes. 'What is this? I thought we had a deal . . .'

'Well, that just goes to show you, you can't trust anyone. You've been conned, Annan. We're going to tie you up again, nice and tight, and tell the coppers where to find you. And we'll give them the bank details and your confession.'

'But that confession's not admissible, like you said . . .'

'True. But it points the police in the right direction to get evidence that they can use.'

'You bastard!' Annan looked like he wanted to hit me, but he was too yellow.

'Yep, Dennis,' I said, in a calm, conversational tone, 'I'm going to give the police everything you've given me. You maybe won't swing for Sylvia's murder, but you're going to spend a long, long time sleeping lightly in an eight-by-four cell with someone called Big Boabie who's hung like a mule and gets frisky after his cocoa.'

I thought of Sylvia Dewar with her head smashed in, of her husband's lonely walk up the stairs with a length of electrical cable. And I thought about all of the crap I'd been through. How chasing a ghost Frank Lang had involved me with a very-much-alive Ferenc Lang. Annan had no direct involvement with the Hungarian thing, but there would have been no Hungarian thing without him.

I wanted to give him a beating. One that he'd never forget. Instead I shoved him backwards and onto the chair.

'Tie him up good and tight, Twinkle,' I said.

Turned out I wasn't that person any more, after all.

CHAPTER FORTY-ONE

After we left Annan tied up again in his chair, I sat in the car, quiet for a moment, letting myself calm down. Twinkletoes sat silently beside me. When it came to the etiquette of violence, Twinkle was the equivalent of Barbara Cartland. After a while I turned to him and smiled.

'Thanks, Twinkle, you did great in there.'

He beamed at me.

'And I've got to hand it to you,' I said, 'your *psychological* approach with the bolt cutters really works. For a moment there even I thought you were going to start cutting off his toes.'

McBride looked at me vaguely for a moment, uncertainty in the childlike eyes beneath the Neanderthal brow.

'You know . . . the way we were bluffing in there . . .' I explained

'Oh aye . . .' he said eventually, slowly. 'Bluffing . . . That's right, the *piss-eye-co-logical* approach. That's what we was doing.'

I smiled again and started the car up, making a mental note to be clearer in my intentions in future.

I asked Twinkletoes if I could hang on to the Cresta for another day or so and he said it was no problem. I dropped him off at his house. Before he got out of the car, he paused and turned his huge Easter Island face towards me.

'Are you gonna be all right, Mr. L?'

'Sure, Twinkle. Everything's going to be fine. You've helped me clear up the Frank Lang thing. I don't know what I'd have done without you. All I have to do now is sort out this other business.'

'After that, is that you going to be in the clear and that?'

'It is.'

'And will you still want me to do jobs for you?'

'Of course. You can count on it.'

'Mr. Lennox ... there won't be any other stuff like today, will there? You know, with the bolt cutters? I'm sorry and that, but it's just I'm kinda trying to put all of that shite behind me ...'

'Trust me, Twinkle, I know the feeling. And no, it's not going to be like that again.'

He grinned and got out of the car.

I drove off, shaking my head in disbelief. An ex-gangland torturer, possible killer and all round thug had just expressed concern that I was perhaps the wrong company to be keeping.

After I dropped Twinkletoes, I stopped at a pay 'phone and called Jock Ferguson at his home. I waited while he bombarded me with curses, threats and then instructions about handing myself in.

'I will,' I said. 'But I've still got unfinished business. And that's what I'm 'phoning about. I've left a package for you. I'll give you the address in a minute. It's a long-firm fraud specialist called Dennis Annan, but you'll know him as ... well, as a matter of fact, you'll know him by a couple of names. The first is Frank Lang, neighbour to the recently deceased Mr and Mrs Thomas Dewar. Except there never was any Frank Lang. It was all set up by Annan as part of his scam. The second name you know him by is Paul Lynch, Connelly's deputy.'

'Lynch and Lang are the same person?'

'Yep. They're both Dennis Annan.'

'What was the scam?'

'Frank Lang was supposed to be a shadowy go-between hired to deliver cash from a special fund on behalf of Joe Connelly's Amalgamated Union of Industrial Trades – providing relief funds for labour and trades union organizations in oppressed countries. Except the labour organizations were bogus and the cash was being diverted to accounts for the non-existent Frank Lang.'

'You have proof of this?'

'The ledger with all of the details in it is waiting for you with Annan, who's all trussed up for you like a Thanksgiving turkey. Oh, and his car is parked outside. It's a green Morris Traveller, one of those jobs that looks half-car, half-garden-shed. If you show it to Maisie McCardle she'll confirm it was the car she saw being used by the neighbour she knew as Frank Lang. By the way, Lang killed Sylvia Dewar. He's signed a confession and that's waiting for you too.'

'Tell me where he is and I'll meet you there,' said Ferguson.

'No can do, Jock,' I said. 'Not when Dunlop still has me in his sights for Andrew Ellis's murder. You deal with Annan, I'll deal with Ellis's killers.'

'You're going to get yourself killed, Lennox. Come in and we can sort this all out.'

'I've told you Jock, can't do it. But if you want to do me a favour, there's a guy called Larry Franks being held in the Newton Mearns cells for police assault. Get him out. And I don't mean bail. He clobbered a copper to get himself arrested deliberately because ... well, let's just say if the story gets out it's going to reflect badly on the City of Glasgow Police. I need this as a favour and you owe me one. And you're going to owe me plenty more when I'm finished. I know who killed Andrew Ellis and I'm going to find them.'

Ferguson started to protest, but I silenced him.

'Everybody has been trying to cut out a piece of me, the police as well, and I'm too tired and too pissed off to argue. In the meantime, you go and pick up Annan.' I gave Ferguson the address.

'Lennox,' he said, 'if it's any consolation, I've been trying to keep the heat off.'

'I know, Jock, and it is. I have to go. I'll talk to you later. But listen, when you pick Annan up, everything you need will be there with him, but I have to tell you he's not looking any too pretty.'

'Okay . . .' he said. I could hear him take a breath to say something else, so I hung up.

CHAPTER FORTY-TWO

I was still a hunted man. I had given Ferguson everything he needed to clear up Sylvia Dewar's death, but no one had seriously been looking at me for that. They were after me for killing Andrew Ellis and – until I could find out what or where Tanglewood was and who Ferenc Lang was – I would remain the number one suspect for Ellis's murder.

I headed back to the barge and cleaned up. I made up some sandwiches from the stuff McBride had brought me and ate them slowly, thinking through what I was going to do next.

I folded out Ellis's map again, calculating times and distances. From his home in Bearsden, which was on the right side of the city, to the mark on the map and back, allowing for an hour's meeting, the timings fitted with those given to me by Pamela Ellis. This was the regular rendezvous, not somewhere in Garnethill. They had changed venue the night I found Ellis with 'Magda' simply because of the smog, I guessed. Or maybe he had picked her up at the translation bureau to go on together to some other location. But this place on the map was their principal trysting point. I would have bet all my money on it.

The thought of money made me set to my next task. I took the wax-paper-wrapped bundles of cash in three denominations and gave them a second wrapping in newspaper. I took the brown paper shopping bag McBride had brought the groceries in and cut it up to improvise wrapping paper. Before I wrapped the money up and addressed the package, I wrote a brief note.

Dear Mrs Ellis,
The enclosed money was placed in my trust by your husband to be given to you in the case of his death or disappearance. His primary concern was always that you be catered for should something happen to him. He instructed me to tell you that under no circumstances were you to inform the police or anyone else about this money.
Nothing can make up for the loss of your husband, but the enclosed was his way of ensuring some comfort in the future.
Yours,
A Wellwisher

I folded the note and placed it in the parcel before wrapping it up, writing the address and securing the package with string.

Then, after washing the dishes, I fell into bed. It was going to be a big day tomorrow.

My moustache was coming in well, and again I complemented the tweed and flannel outfit with the navy duffle coat before heading out to a camping store I knew about in the West End of the city. It was the kind of place that catered for the serious canvas-shelterer and I picked up a good quality bivouac, a camping stove and gas canister, a trenching tool, sleeping bag, as well as a kitbag and canteen. From the outdoor clothing section, I picked out the kind of pullover anorak favoured by Sir Edmund Hillary, archaeology field-trip students and secondary modern geography teachers. My biggest expense, more than the tent, was a pair of heavy walking boots.

The salesman insisted I try them on with a pair of heavy socks and walk around the store with the boots on. I appreciated his professionalism: I already knew from my army days that the wrong size of boots could end up crippling you. In the army your boots, after your gun, were your most important piece of kit. What was more, my feet were still painful from my sock-soled flight across Glasgow and needed the best protection I could give them.

Adding three pairs of heavy socks to wear with the boots and an oiled wool turtleneck that would have stood up on its own, I picked out a pair of waterproof trousers and another flat cap, something I would normally not be seen dead in. I really was pushing my luck, making the salesman's day by buying the whole camping caboodle. In November. And that meant he would remember me.

I fed him some baloney about buying the tent as a Christmas present for my nephew, and I was getting myself kitted out because, although I'd never been camping before, I had promised to take my nephew on a trip to the Trossachs in the spring, as soon as the weather improved. It was all a strain, because I went through the whole process putting on a vaguely Glaswegian accent. Or at least what I thought would sound like a Glasgow accent, but somehow came out more Boston Irish than anything else.

He'd probably remember that too.

When he took me to the cash desk to pay for the gear. I thought I caught the girl at the desk eyeing the bruises on my face, despite me doing my best to present everyone with my unblemished side as much as possible. The salesman was so pleased with my custom that he insisted on helping me out with the stuff, ignoring my repeated assurances that I could manage myself by making a couple of trips to the car. I had deliberately parked the Cresta out of sight of the shop, but my continued insistence on carrying the stuff myself would soon become in itself suspicious.

Piling the clothing into the back seat, I got the salesman to place the tent and the rest of the hardware in the trunk of the car. I'd forgotten that the bolt cutters were in there, but my overly helpful assistant seemed to pay them no heed, pushing them to the back as he carefully organized my purchases in the trunk.

I repeated my act in a grocer's in Milngavie, on the way out of the city, picking up some extra provisions. It was getting better. The trick, I learned, was not to work at it too hard. So instead of trying to do an impersonation of a Glaswegian, which always turned out bizarre, I used my natural voice but bent the Canadian a little and rolled the r's more. If there was one thing I could say for the fugitive lifestyle, it was that it exposed talents and abilities you didn't know you possessed. Music Hall now beckoned along with the laundry business as a possible post-prison career.

The grocer's was one of a small knot of shops in the centre of Milngavie, so I called into the newsagent-cum-tobacconist kiosk in the middle of the small square. The hunch-shouldered kiosk man tucked behind the counter with his paraffin heater was small and mean-looking and eyed me with suspicious loathing. I tried not to read too much into it, because that, I had found, was one of the two standard customer service ethics in Scotland: you were served either with intense hostility or embarrassing servility, with no middle ground between the two extremes. But, again, I thought he had examined the bruising on my face just that little bit too closely. I asked for four packs of cigarettes, two boxes of matches and a local newspaper.

It was all over the front page.

The police, the headline stated, were investigating the murder of Andrew Ellis, who was found dead from stab wounds in a city centre office. Ellis, who was a prominent member of the city's business community, had left a widow but no issue. Police were now keen to ascertain the whereabouts of . . .

And there it was. My name. The fact that I was a Canadian national. And a pretty damned good description. The only thing I was grateful for was that there was no mention of my bearing any marks or bruises on my face.

I folded the paper under my arm and paid the newsagent as matter-of-factly as I could. Then, looking behind him, I saw a rack of pipes. As if acting on a whim, I asked him for the most expensive of the pipes and a tin of ready-rub. It would go with my new image of the Scottish outdoorsman, I thought.

Maybe I was being paranoid – or more paranoid, as that had become more or less my permanent state of mind – but I was pretty sure that the little, hostile tobacconist was watching me from his kiosk as I walked back to the car. Fortunately, I had again taken the precaution of parking out of sight.

Heading first west to Dumbarton, then north to Loch Lomond, I pulled up in a lay-by off the road once I was out of town. This was one of the main routes north from Glasgow and there was a fair amount of traffic passing in both directions, so I couldn't very well step out of the car, peel off my clothes and change. Instead, I struggled in the confines of the Cresta, wriggling into the waterproof trousers over my flannels.

Sliding over to the passenger side, I opened the door and

swung my legs out, out of sight of the traffic. I slipped a heavy pair of socks over the silk ones I already had on and laced up the hiking boots. After my barefoot experiences, it felt good to have something so solid on my feet. I took off my jacket, slipped on the oiled wool turtleneck and planted the waxed flat cap on my head. I left the smock-anorak for the moment. My new outfit opened up the opportunity to be worn with either the duffle coat or the tweed jacket, as well as the anorak, depending on the particular rugged dash I was trying to cut.

The main thing, though, was that my new outfit and equipment had been chosen for purely practical reasons. Scotland – this *real* Scotland – in November could be lethally unforgiving.

My main hope was that the bivouac in the trunk would not have to be pressed into service, but if my mission lasted longer than I hoped, then I was going to have to take care of my own accommodations. And, anyway, I had in my time spent plenty of nights under canvas with more than the inclement weather to worry about.

I drove up the side of Loch Lomond, a massive expanse of water and the biggest lake in Britain. There wasn't a cloud in the sky, but I had to drive carefully as the roadway sparkled white with frost. After the gloom and grime of Glasgow, it made everything look fresh and crisp and clean. It was funny, I thought, how any sun – even hard, warmth-less sun – lifted your mood.

Halfway up the loch, I stopped at a roadside tearoom with a view out over the water and ordered some cheese sandwiches with coffee. The woman who served me was in her early forties, with fresh, pale skin and dark blonde hair. She was slim but sexy and I promised myself a return visit in happier times; but there was something about her nagged at my gut. I realized that she reminded me, in an odd way, of Fiona White. She had only one other guest in the place and I had to dance around her questions about where I had come from, where I was going, what I was going to do there . . . the routine building blocks of conversation she must have used with every guest she chatted with. I had given up on trying to sound Glaswegian or Scottish and simply sought to neuter my speech to a standard English.

She had probably seen the way I had looked at her and it was obvious she didn't mind at all and we chatted about nothing, all the time laying out our stalls in the indirect and abstract way you do before you seal the deal.

What the hell, Lennox, I suddenly said to myself, do you think you are doing?

I paid her and left.

I may have been picking up many of the skills of the fugitive; making myself forgettable was not one of them.

I cleared the top end of Loch Lomond and was well into the Highlands by the time the sun started to play peek-a-boo behind the mountains.

I stopped a couple of times to check Ellis's map and make sure I didn't miss my turning, but in the event I did. In the gloaming the landscape had started to melt into soft shapes and splashes of dull red light and shadows, and I drove past the exit and had to drive farther along the ribbon of lakeside road before I found a spot safe enough to execute a three-point turn.

It wasn't really surprising that I had missed it – a narrow, bush-flanked mouth that led off the main highway and up and away from the loch. I turned and followed it up a steep hillside and across an empty, darkening landscape of umbrous hills and deep gorge. There was one thing that was for sure: I wasn't being tailed. This was the Scotland of glens empty of anything other than sheep, wildcats, adders and eagles, and I would have spotted other headlights ten miles away.

After the adventures of father-and-son Catholic pretenders to the British throne, the lairds and lords of the Highlands had followed, with enthusiasm and vigour, the Hanoverian edict that the Highlands had to be cleared of troublemakers. Scotland's loss had been North America's gain, with whole Gaelic families of every generation being driven to the sea, then across it, to the colonies of what was now Canada and the US.

The Scots, I knew, liked to paint this pretty episode in their history as English domination and cruelty. The truth was that the conflict had been primarily Scot against Scot: Protestant against Catholic, Lowlander against Highlander. And the lairds and landowners who had driven the masses from their crofts had been their own kind. And often the Chiefs of the clans they belonged to.

Every now and again, I would pass evidence of the purge: roofless croft cottages, more like piles of roughly assembled stones, standing empty and barely perceptible in the gloom, in the middle of a trackless landscape or looming suddenly at the roadside.

The sky turned violet and the stars sparkled like the frost in my headlights. Up here, there was no city streetlight glow to obscure the stars, and the night remained bright and sharp and cold. Again, I had to stop a couple of times to fix my bearings with the map I had taken from Ellis's shed. The road here was only wide enough for one car to pass and was intermittently blistered with marked passing places, just wide enough to fit a car or tractor in to allow oncoming vehicles to pass. Some passing places came perilously close to where the edge dropped away steeply and suddenly into a gorge which, in the growing dark, turned into a bottomless chasm.

The narrow ribbon of road ahead of me became reduced to a frost-edged pool of light from my headlamps, and I found that bends would appear without warning. Some were unexpectedly sharp. Driving here in the daylight would be challenge enough, but in the dark it was a nightmare.

I just didn't see it coming. The road had been perfectly straight for half a mile, then took an almost right-angular twist. I slammed on the brakes, but the Cresta simply skated along the road, not responding to anything I did with the steering wheel.

The world slowed down. I took my foot off the brake, reapplied it gently, took it off, reapplied it.

Nothing worked.

Straight ahead of me was darkness, the road gone.

It was the strangest thing: to feel nothing beneath the wheels. To know you were in a motor car suspended in space. Another weird thing was that all that went through my head was McBride's pride in his car. The way it had been polished and cherished.

'Sorry, Twinkle . . .' I said out loud, and waited for the impact.

CHAPTER FORTY-THREE

When it came, the first impact, I felt it in every bone in my body. The Cresta had come down hard, but not nose first, instead landing not quite squarely on all four wheels. I was thrown upwards and collided with the roof. The car bounced and jolted, each impact crushing and tearing metal, tossing me around its inside. Every now and then I would see a flashbulb image of grass and rock in the headlights. More noise. Sound that seemed to fill the universe.

The windscreen shattered and showered me with glass.

Silence.

The engine had died. Or been killed by the crash. There was no more light from the headlamps and I guessed they too had been smashed by the impact.

I tried to work out where I was hurt. Which was difficult, because I hurt all over. Sprawled on the bench seat, I lay still, drinking in the silence and the dark. I was pretty sure I was alive, and I was going to stay that way. Or at least stay alive until I had to tell Twinkletoes what I'd done to his precious Cresta.

I slowly reconnected with my body. I made two fists and then flexed my fingers. Worked my elbows. Rotated my shoulders, getting a jab of pain from the right but not enough to indicate anything more serious than a strain. Tilting myself up slowly, using the steering wheel as a lever, I eased up into a sitting position before running my hands down each leg, rotating each booted foot at the ankle.

I took a long, slow breath. I knew that within a few hours I was really going to start hurting and I'd be as stiff as a board, but I didn't care. I was alive. I sat in the dark, behind the wheel, as if patiently waiting in a queue of traffic. It was weird. I couldn't see a thing in the pitch darkness and for a panicked moment wondered if I'd been blinded by a head injury. I ran my fingers over my face and through my hair. No blood. No lacerations. No duck egg bumps.

I felt around for the glove compartment, opening it to get some light into the cabin of the car, but none came on. The electrics must have been shot. I couldn't find my penlight in my pocket and spent ten minutes fumbling around on the seat and the floor trying to find it, without success. It would be hours before daylight – a full night, in fact – and I couldn't hang around till then. I decided to get out of the car, but the driver's door was jammed tight in its twisted frame. I slid over and kicked the passenger door open and crawled out.

It didn't do me much good. The only light was coming from the moon and stars, and even that was shaded by the brooding black shoulder of the hill above me. What I could see was that I hadn't come that far: maybe twenty yards from the road, but most of that had been downwards. I stumbled about and moved to the front of the car. More from what I could feel rather than see, it became clear that my continued descent down the slope had been halted by a thicket of brush and tangled wood. I allowed myself a smile at the irony. I looked up at where the road was, most of my journey back to it hidden in the deepest shadow.

It would be difficult enough to get back up in the daylight and there was no way I could make it in the dark. Anyway, I had all of my gear still in the car. There was nothing for it: I was going to have to spend the night in the car.

Somehow, without the aid of my penlight, I was able to open the boot and feel around for the sleeping bag. I took it into the back seat, shoving the scattered clothing onto the floor and, still wearing trousers, waterproofs and boots, climbed into it.

With my aches and pains, and with the adrenalin from the accident still coursing through my veins, I knew there was no way I would get to sleep.

As usual, I was wrong.

The sound of a car, up above on the single track road, woke me. By the time I was fully conscious, the engine sound was already fading into the distance. Not that it made much odds: there was no way I could flag down a motorist and cadge a lift.

The pain from being buffeted about in the crash was now localized – to the space between my toenails and the top of my skull. Just like the night before, everything hurt. It just hurt more. I took a minute to gather my senses, then unzipped myself from the sleeping bag and crawled out. The grey morning outside nipped at my hands and face as soon as I got out of the car. The sky was clear, but the morning was still busying itself with the uplands, and would take some time before getting down here. Still, I had a good view all around me. Looking up to the road, I could see where the car had dropped a good five feet before careering down the steep slope, leaving a scar where it had scored through the thin layer of earth that covered the rock. I blessed the five-foot drop for not being a fifty-foot drop, which it would have been if I had come off the road around the corner.

The Cresta had plunged through one thicket and into a second. I worked out that it would be difficult to see from the road, but I would have to get back up there before I could see for sure. The one thing I didn't want was someone knocking on McBride's door and telling him that his car had been found trashed and dumped in the middle of nowhere. I knew he would never give me up deliberately, but Twinkle was Twinkle and didn't sparkle the brightest.

It took me a good half hour to collect all of the stuff from the car, roll up the sleeping bag and pack everything into the rucksack. The only thing I couldn't fit in was the bivouac, but I lashed that to the back of the rucksack. All in all, with the anorak, the backpack and the professional mountain gear, I would really look the part of the serious mountain rambler. Given that it was November and freezing, it was probably more the part of the seriously deranged mountain rambler.

I decided to get the lay of the land. Leaving my pack by the car, I tried to find my way through the tangle of branches the Cresta had become caught up in. I couldn't, so I edged my way along it and stepped around the side.

Instinct, that strange old thing the nature of which I had debated, saved me. As soon as I felt the ground go from beneath my feet, I grabbed two fistfuls of branch. My feet scrabbled on the loose gravel, trying to get purchase and get me back from the edge of the cliff that dropped below me.

Scrambling back from the edge, I dropped down onto my backside, that good old instinct telling me to get as much of my body as possible in contact with solid ground, as soon as possible.

When I got my breath back, I inched forward again and peered down into the gully. Thirty feet below me, a river frothed angrily over rock as it surged along the valley bottom. I turned to look along the length of the cliff edge: the bonnet of the Cresta, projected over the edge by a few inches where it had burst through the tangle of bush, root and branch.

I had just slept through the night, like a baby, in a car being held back from a deadly plunge by a mess of dead vegetation. I suddenly felt sick and started to shake, as if the realization had triggered the delayed shock of the crash.

I stayed where I was, sitting on the cold, frosty earth, took the pack from the bib pocket of the anorak, lit a cigarette and smoked it to calm my nerves.

Then I smoked a couple more.

There was no point in trying to get back up to the road at that point. In fact, it was probably a bad idea to be visible, even if the chances of a car or truck passing were remote.

Instead, I decided to walk along the shelf edge that ran parallel to the road, but was low enough down for me to keep out of sight. Checking Ellis's map before setting out, I reckoned I hadn't that far to go, and the walking, while rocky, wasn't that arduous.

I had guessed that the shelf I was walking along would eventually come up to the road level, but it didn't, instead declining sharply into the valley bottom. After half-an-hour's walk, I found myself at the river's edge. I took the opportunity to fill a billycan and heat it on the small gas stove, tossing in some loose tea. I sat watching the river while I drank the tea. The odd thing was that, because of what I was wearing and the body heat from my exertions being trapped in their layers, I didn't feel at all cold other than on my cheeks – and my hands, whenever I removed my gloves. I looked around me at the heather-dressed mountains whose hues changed constantly, depending on the light and the occasional passing shadow of a cloud in the unforgivingly cold, blue sky.

There was no denying it. Scotland could be breathtakingly beautiful.

But so could Cape Breton Island or British Columbia. I rinsed out the billycan, packed up my gear and headed onward.

Despite it being a tiny mark on the map, there was a lot of give and take in the area it indicated, but eventually I caught sight of a pale grey wisp of smoke rising from some kind of settlement up ahead. The valley floor had been rising for some time and I guessed that the handful of houses indicated on the map at the head of the valley were the source of the smoke.

I found my way up the side of the mountain on the far side from the road and walked along a ridge, approaching the village from what I hoped would be an unconventional and unexpected direction. But the ridge became a path that again started to take me up the mountainside and away from my target and I realized I would have to retrace my steps. I changed my mind when I saw what I thought was an abandoned croft. It would give me a good view of the settlement, I guessed, so I headed for it.

It turned out not to be an abandoned croft but a bothy in a full state of repair. Bothies were small buildings maintained to provide shelter for hill walkers and mountaineers.

A notice board by the door instructed me in the etiquette of using the bothy's facilities. Basically, you were expected to leave the shelter how you found it, and if you took a dump you did it outside away from a watercourse; no trash to be left in the bothy when you left, that kind of thing.

The building itself was a rectangle of two-foot thick stone walls, divided into two rooms, each accessed from a separate door and not connected internally. The first room was the accommodations: a basic box of a room of naked, unplastered stone with a large fireplace and chimney breast in the soot-stained back wall. A robust table of some dense wood that was unidentifiable under several layers of lacquer sat beneath the single, square window. The second room was a storeroom containing a shovel for latrine digging, a box of candles and a couple of brooms. There was even a pile of firewood, which the notice on the wall advised had to be replaced if used.

The bothy was a godsend. I reckoned that at this time of year there wouldn't be many walkers up in the hills, although I knew it was a fraternity not noted for its common sense when it came to the weather, and the bothy was closer to a settlement, albeit a small one, than most were. If I were stuck, I could camp down here overnight.

I had been wrong about having a view of the village from it, however. A thicket of trees and a swell in the hillside obscured the view, meaning I would have to head back down the trail a little to see it; but that also meant that the bothy could not be easily seen from the village or its approach road.

I left my stuff in the bothy and walked back down the trail to where I could get a good view of the village, using my new binoculars to watch any activity. There was none. The village consisted of a clutch of cottages arranged on either side of the road, two larger houses and an inn. There was the massive shoulder of a mountain behind the village and I could see a second clutch of buildings higher up, about a half-mile from the village on the far side, and I recognized it as a farmhouse and outbuildings. But it was the second house that interested me. It was a grander sort of place and more like something you would see in town. A big, solid villa, with two wings to it and a separate stable block. I guessed that the farm was a tenancy of the big house.

Being on the other side of the village, the big house was too far away for me to keep tabs on from where I was. I needed to get closer.

I went back to the bothy and brewed up some tea with the gas canister stove, not wanting to light a fire and make smoke, despite the fact that the bothy was pretty much hidden from the village. I stretched out Ellis's map on the table and took the automatic from my backpack, checked the magazine and safety, and tucked it into the waistband of my flannels, obscured from view by the waterproofs, the heavy turtleneck sweater and the anorak. No one would see the gun, all right, but I sure wasn't going to win any fast-draw contests.

I leaned over the table and examined the map. Ellis's mark corresponded to my current location. What I was looking for was somewhere in the village, the farm or the large house I had seen.

This was where Ellis had come the night his wife had heard him on the telephone. I knew that for sure. I'd known it ever since I'd examined the mark on the map more closely at the barge's window. The mark wasn't a cross after all.

It was a 'T'. 'T' for Tanglewood.

CHAPTER FORTY-FOUR

It was, I reckoned, time for lunch.

I walked down the hillside, and along the valley towards the village. My destination was the inn and I wore my rucksack to convince anyone who cared that I was one of the more hardy, or foolhardy, of Scotland's wilderness wanderers.

The inn was a long, low jumble of stonework and small, irregular windows. It was one of those places you came across every now and then in Scotland: inns and taverns that had offered rest and nourishment to the weary and hungry traveller continuously since the days of Bonnie Prince Charlie or before.

In fact, the mutton pie they served me with a pint of room-temperature beer tasted like it had been in the pantry since the last visit of the Young Pretender – probably when, during one of Scotland's more dignified historical moments, the Prince had stopped by for a snack before slipping into women's clothing and skipping town.

The welcome I got from the barkeep reminded me that *dour* is indeed a Scottish word, and I was tempted to ask him if he had a brother in Milngavie, in the newsagent business. Instead I smiled and took the tepid beer over to a table.

The only other customers were a pair of old boys at the bar who watched me expressionlessly but constantly from the moment I came in. They had obviously run out of conversation sometime around the Boer War and the lack of animation in their expressions would have made Archie McClelland look like Danny Kaye. They could have been twins, I thought, their white, wrinkled, leathery faces identical under matching flat caps. They probably weren't twins, though: this was rural Scotland where everybody unrelated probably was.

I had once visited Fifeshire, because I had had to – which was the only reason anyone ever visited Fifeshire. Everyone in the ancient Pictish kingdom had shared the same dull-coloured hair and had had the kind of big, long face you would usually associate with a favourite for the one-thirty steeplechase at Chepstow. The look here was different but still familial and I reckoned that, as in Fifeshire, the wedding vows in this part of the world probably included the wording 'do you take this woman as your lawfully-wedded sister?'

I sat at a table in the corner of the taproom near the fireplace and picked at the mutton pie. Even in the hiker get-up, I felt hugely conspicuous. I guessed they didn't get a lot of outsiders here. As I had walked along the village main street – basically the road through it – I had seen only one vehicle, and that had been an ex-army Land Rover whose mud-splattered flanks told me that the driver was probably a local farmer. I took some solace in the fact that there was probably a direct ratio between the number of policemen in any given area and the overall population, making my chances of running into the bicycle-clipped forces of law and order pretty remote.

I was still pushing the pie around the plate, wondering if fossilisation was a cooking process, when two men came in and sat at the opposite end of the bar from the two old not-twins in caps. From the way the geriatrics shifted their gloomy attention from me to the two new customers, I guessed that the recent arrivals were, like me, strangers.

I checked them over without making it obvious. They were both dressed in ordinary suits beneath raincoats and one of them, the one with the curly dark hair and beard, was built like a house on legs, while the other was lean and more athletic-looking. Despite his less impressive build, it was the thinner of the two that had the look of a hard and dangerous man. When he took off his hat and hung it up on the rack by the door, his blond hair was skull-clingingly oiled and combed back from his brow and the skin on his hard-featured face was pock-marked.

I didn't recognize either man. But that didn't mean that they hadn't been part of the crew who had turned up outside Larry Franks's place. Despite everything having happened as a blur, the two guys who had left Ellis dying in my office and with whom I'd exchanged pleasantries on the stairs had made a big enough impression on me to remember their faces. These guys definitely weren't them.

Nevertheless, their presence bothered me. It was not as if they had paid me any attention when they had arrived; it was that they had gone out of their way *not* to pay me attention, or even look in my direction.

But the truth was my little trip into the village had been as much to show the dogs the hare as anything else.

I contemplatively swirled the last quarter of my tepid pint sluggishly around the glass, then I took the pipe out of my pocket and filled it, inexpertly, with tobacco, before quietly smoking it as I sat. Or at least sat quietly struggling to stop the pipe from going out while the two newcomers at the bar studiously avoiding looking in my direction.

I didn't think they were policemen but, coppers or not, it made no sense that the two heavies at the bar were there on my account. Whatever the connection between Ellis and this part of the world, there was no way anyone could have known I was on my way up here. Unless, of course, mine host at the bar had been told to make a call if anyone out of the ordinary called in at his establishment. Maybe that would explain why it had taken so long for my mutton pie to arrive, lukewarm, in front of me.

Or maybe I was just letting my paranoia run away with me again.

I decided to put them to the test. I downed the last of the pint, got up and left. Again the only eyes on me were the geriatrics at the bar.

I walked to the bridge over the river and leaned on the stone parapet, smoking my pipe while really waiting to see how long it would take for the two burly types to come out of the inn. They didn't.

A false alarm, clearly. If you're going to get through this, Lennox, I thought to myself, then you're going to have to calm down. Nothing gets a wanted man caught like panic. Or self-doubt.

I found my way to the far side of the village and started to hike uphill. The byway I was on was obviously used by occasional traffic, but was unmetalled and more like a farm track than anything. It took me up past the farm and its outbuildings, but it became clear there must have been a second, parallel route up to the large manor. I guessed that would be a better maintained way than the one I was on. As I passed the farm, I was aware of two men in the yard stopping whatever it was they were doing to watch me pass. I made sure I kept going, my pace unbroken and determined, like some wintertime nature lover striking out resolutely to attain the hilltop.

After a while, when I'd climbed a hundred feet or so, the path thinned out to little more than a trail or bridleway. I guessed I had reached the upper limit of the farm's land and the path was now only for hill walkers. It took a turn behind an isolated copse before continuing up the hillside and I ducked into the trees. Tree cover was rare in Scotland. The entire country had originally been dense with the Great Caledonian Forest, in turn populated with bear, wolf, lynx and elk. Stone Age Scots, a breed still evident in parts of Glasgow, had eradicated more than ninety percent of the forest, with subsequent generations reducing it even more. Now there were only these odd clumps of ancient woodland. The bears, wolves, lynxes and elks had long ago gotten eviction orders.

I used the trees as cover while I checked out the farm through the binoculars. It had been a good fifteen minutes since I had passed it, but the two men in the yard had been joined by a third, and they were still looking up the path I had taken, as if they were waiting for me to re-emerge from behind the trees. There was a lot of discussion, then, eventually, they went back to their work, the third man returning to the farmhouse.

From this position, I could see not just the farm down and to my right, but also the manor-type house. I had been right about the approach to it: I saw a wider, metalled way leading down to the village, but coming out onto the main road on the other side of the inn, near the edge of the settlement. My guess was that this had been the historical route for the local laird to take, avoiding having to pass through the forelock-tugging riff-raff of the village.

I watched both locations alternately. There was no activity

at the main house that I could see, and what there was at the farm was the expected drudgery of agricultural winter maintenance.

It was about an hour later when I saw the farmer – or at least the man I had seen coming out of the farmhouse to talk to the two workers – walk out through the farm gates and cross the fields, taking a direct route to the big house. There was no way of knowing if his visit was provoked by the presence of a stranger, or if he was simply the farm's manager reporting to its owner in the laird's house.

He certainly knew his place, going around to the back door before disappearing inside. He came out again half-an-hour later and strode back across the fields to the farm, never once looking in my direction.

Whatever the purpose of his visit, it didn't provoke any activity and, after another hour, by which time the chill had succeeded in penetrating my clothing, I decided to strike off across country and down onto the road that ended at the gates of the big house.

By now, and given everything that had happened to me over the last few days, I didn't care about being provocative. I *wanted* something to happen. Anything.

I slowed down as I passed the house. There it was: a name embossed on the gate capital. The name of the house. I was aware of my pulse in my ears as I passed it. This would confirm whether I had, after all of this time, found Tanglewood.

Collieluth House. I muttered a curse.

This name of the villa was Collieluth House. The farm over the way had been Collieluth Farm and, I guessed, the hamlet was called Collieluth.

I scanned the house, or as much of it as I could see through the gates. There was nothing unusual or untoward. No Hungarian heavies, no heavies of any denomination. No one on look-out. As far as I could see, I was passing by unnoticed and unremarked.

I tried not to panic. I was stuck up here in the middle of nowhere, another winter night closing in, without transport, having wrecked McBride's prized Cresta. I had wasted time I could ill afford, money, and effort in chasing after ghosts, based on the flimsy evidence that a cross on a map looked like a T. And now, I was stuck here. To get transport back to Glasgow would attract a whole lot of attention, even if I just started walking and sticking my thumb out when the rare car, truck or tractor passed by.

I reached the road, walked all the way back through the village, across the bridge and headed back up the hillside to the bothy. I needed time to think everything through. I'd spend the night in the bothy. Something would come to me.

It would have to.

CHAPTER FORTY-FIVE

Back in the bothy, I lit a fire with some of the wood from the store. I was no longer worried about attracting the attention of Ellis's Hungarian chums, but I was mindful that I was still a man on the run.

The only thing that stuck with me was the two men I had seen in the inn. It was a hell of a coincidence that they happened along just at the same time I had, tourists in a season that was as off-season as it was possible to be.

The bread I had brought with me was stale and hard, but I toasted it at the fire and heated up some beans from a tin on the billycan. Another mug of tea, swimming in leaves that I had to pick off my lips and from my teeth, warmed me up.

It was only seven p.m. but pitch dark outside. My feet and right shoulder were aching, so I piled up the fire, unrolled the sleeping bag and went to sleep.

I woke up twice through the night. The first time was when I heard a desperate screaming. I sat bolt upright, trying to work out if I'd dreamt the scream. Then I heard it again. And again. It took me a while to realize that it wasn't human. A fox, it sounded like to me.

I settled back down and tried to calm my heartbeat and nerves.

Eventually my exhaustion reclaimed me and I fell back into another dream about card games and how many people there really were at the table.

The second awakening was less rude, and took place just as grey fingers of daylight were beginning to probe the bothy through the small, square window.

'Mr Lennox?' a voice asked. A hand shook my shoulder. 'Wake up, please, Mr Lennox . . .'

Remembering where I was and what I was doing there fell into my brain at the same time as the realization that there shouldn't be anyone there with me, especially someone who knew my name. I spun around and sat up, my movements restricted by the sleeping bag. A hand steadily but forcibly pushed me back down. I heard the click of a hammer being pulled back on a gun.

I saw the gun. And the face. It was a hard, cruel, pockmarked face with blond hair combed back and plastered to his skull with macassar. The leaner of the two men I had seen in the bar. He eased back, keeping the gun on me.

'Please, Mr Lennox, get up and gather your stuff. You need to come with us now.' The quiet, polite tone didn't fit with the face, or the situation. The accent sounded more English to me than anything else. Not a foreigner, unless you considered anyone from south of Carlisle an alien.

'And if I don't?'

He smiled and shrugged. 'Then that could make things unpleasant. Now, if you don't mind . . .'

I lay there, considering my options. One of them was jabbing painfully into my waist. I had slept, deliberately, with the Femaru-Frommer automatic stuck in my waistband. But my polite chum had caught me unawares, and – like I said – I was in no position to enter a fast-draw contest. The question was whether Blondy knew I was armed or not. From his relaxed manner, I guessed not. I just hoped he wasn't going to search me when I got out of the sleeping bag.

I winced as I struggled to extricate myself from the sleeping bag, a sharp jab stabbing into my strained right shoulder.

'Bit tender?' the blond thug asked. 'We found the car. You were lucky to walk away from that, I'll tell you.'

'The question is, am I going to walk away from this?'

'That's up to you . . . Please, gather your stuff together.'

At that, the door opened behind him and his pal appeared; the one with the curly hair, beard and a build to put the bothy to shame.

'Go back and tell them we've found him,' the blond guy said.

'Will you be all right here?' asked Curly.

'We'll just get ready to go, won't we, Mr Lennox?'

'You're the one making the decisions,' I said, nodding to the gun in his hand.

'Get them to send a car as close as they can get it. No need to attract more attention than we need to.'

Curly disappeared and Blondy leaned against the wall, watching me while I packed up my stuff, coiling the sleeping bag back up into a roll. The only time he looked less than relaxed was when I reached for my camp knife, which sat on the table.

'Leave the knife . . .' he said sharply. 'I'll get that for you when we go.'

When I was packed, he told me to sit cross-legged on the floor, with my hands where he could see them. Other than that, he seemed perfectly relaxed and in control. He hadn't searched me. They obviously didn't know that Ellis's gun had gone missing.

Or didn't consider me enough of an operator to come along heavy.

'So ...' I said conversationally. 'How's the world of international post-war fascism?'

He stared at me blankly.

'You don't sound like some Budapest Blackshirt – so, unless I've got my wires, or my arrows, crossed, I'm guessing you're the local help. Or relatively local ... it's clear that you *ain't frum arrund thees paarts* ...'

My humour failed to work its magic on him. I fell silent. I had no moves. He was across the room from me, I was sitting with my legs crossed and, despite his relaxed demeanour, the barrel of his gun stayed locked onto me. Rushing him now would be fatal.

'So what now?' I asked.

'You've been getting in the way, Mr Lennox. My job is to take you out of the way. Simple as that.'

'I see,' I said.

We sat in silence for half-an-hour and my legs began to protest at being permanently crossed. I winced and wriggled.

'You can stand up and stretch your legs,' he said, straightening up from the wall. 'But nice and slow.'

I did as he said, surprised by his consideration. After I had stretched the knots out of my muscles, he told me to sit again, but said I didn't need to cross my legs, if I stayed very still and kept my hands in sight.

His architecturally-built friend arrived at the doorway again, red-faced from exertion and sweating in his heavy coat. Both men were dressed for the weather, but not the terrain, and both, I noticed, were wearing ordinary town shoes.

'I've got the car as close as I can. We're to take him straight there,' he said.

'Fine.' Blondy turned to me. 'Time to go, sport. And let's keep this nice and civilized. No monkey business.'

'I'm too tired and sore for that,' I said dully.

'Pick up your pack and let's go.'

I didn't put the rucksack on, instead swinging it over one shoulder. They made me walk ahead of them, Blondy cool and focused, keeping the automatic on me, Curly puffing away with the exertion.

'I take it you're not the outdoor type . . .' I said over my shoulder as we descended the trail back into the glen.

'Shut the fuck up and walk,' said Curly bad-temperedly. He clearly hadn't been to the same finishing school as Blondy.

As we walked, I could hear them both occasionally skidding on the gravel, their smooth-soled shoes failing to gain purchase on the loose, gravelly path. If I had an opportunity anywhere, that was where it would lie.

I made a show of stumbling over a rock myself, struggling to steady myself under the weight of my rucksack. When we made the turn that took the path towards the village, I could see where they had parked their car, on some rough ground beside the roadway. What's more, I recognized the car, or at least I was pretty sure I did. It was the same model and colour as the car that had been parked outside Larry Franks's that night. If we had been in the corresponding spot on the opposite side of the valley, they would have been able to drive the car along to a spot just below the bothy. As it was, we had another five to ten-minute walk to reach the car.

I stumbled again and I sensed Blondy tensing behind me.

'Damned boots,' I said. 'They're the wrong size. I had to pick them up in a hurry.'

'That right?' he said. 'That's a relief. Because here was I beginning to think that your little pantomime was you getting ready to make some kind of move ... And that wouldn't end at all well. And slow down a little. Don't try taking advantage of the rough going.'

Yep. He was the brains of the two all right. And experienced at this kind of thing, whatever this kind of thing was.

'You're not going to shoot me because of a bad choice of footwear?' I said.

'People have been shot for less.'

Yeah, I thought. But it's not me that's made the bad choice of footwear.

The world dimmed a little. And not because of my mood. The Highlands of Scotland were notoriously mercurial. A bright, sunny day could turn into a deadly snowstorm, a blinding fog or rain to make your head bleed without any warning. I could see a dark seething of clouds and the dark shafts of heavy rain rolling in from the far end of the valley, moving up in the direction of the village. Even where we were, a milky sheet of high cloud suffused and dulled the winter sun. The rain would have been a huge advantage to me, but I'd be in the car and long gone before it got this far up the valley.

I was running out of options. I scanned as much of the valley as I could without moving my head: measuring the distance to the car, the narrow, rough path leading to it, the steep flank of the valley rising up to my right, impossible to scale in any haste, and the equally steep slope on the left, down into the river. However I looked at it, I was a sitting duck.

But if I got into that car, I'd be a dead one.

I saw a vehicle on the other side of the valley, quite a ways back, heading towards the village. I kept walking. Then I decided to see how far Blondy's obliging nature would extend.

'Listen,' I said over my shoulder. 'Could you do me a favour?'

'What?' he asked, neither patient or impatient.

'Could you grab hold of this?'

I spun round, swinging the rucksack and let it go so that it flew hard in his direction. Instinct told him to protect himself rather than take aim, but only for the tiniest shaving of a second. I used that tiny moment well. I made no attempt to run. Instead I half-dropped, half-threw myself forwards and sideways, my injured shoulder thumping painfully onto the grass. Then I rolled. After the first couple of rolls Isaac Newton did the rest and I bounced and tumbled down the slope towards the valley bottom. I slowed with the decreasing incline and somehow found myself running, my feet splashing in shallow water, then deeper water up to my knees, my boots slipping on the current-smoothed rocks on the river bed. I didn't even take the time to look over my shoulder.

I heard Blondy shout for me to stop, which, even in my panic, struck me as one of the most redundant and stupid commands to issue, other than to ask me to stand still so he could get a better shot. I heard two cracks in quick succession and then the sound of bullets hitting the water and ricocheting off the rocks. But they were some way off.

He shouted again, and again two rounds zipped harmlessly into the river. I was splashing my way through fast-flowing, knee-deep water which slowed me to walking pace. The next rounds, I guessed, were going to hit me. But he didn't fire again.

I allowed myself one desperate look behind me. Blondy was coming down the slope towards the river – I guessed to get a better shot at me – but his smooth leather soles were causing him to skid and slip all over the place. Curly was lumbering behind him – far behind him – and didn't represent any danger.

A third man had gotten out of the car and was charging towards the river. He was tall and in a dark coat and even from this distance I recognized him as the boss of the men at Larry Franks's place.

I kept running. I was out of the river, racing across the river's edge and then scrambling up the bank to the road, grabbing handfuls of turf to haul myself up.

I made it onto the roadway just as the car I had seen drew close. I recognized it as the mud-splattered Land Rover I saw the day before. The driver was a man in his fifties. He stared at me, shocked.

'Did I see these men *shoot* at you?' he said.

'I need your help. Can you get me out of here?'

'Get in . . .' he said. And I did.

CHAPTER FORTY-SIX

'What the hell is going on?' the Land Rover driver asked, looking across me and down into the valley.

'It's a long story,' I said. 'The most important thing is we get out of here.'

'It's a long story for the police,' he said. 'As soon as I get you to my place, that's exactly who I'm calling.'

'Sounds like a good idea,' I said. I was too shaken up to argue or spin some line to cover why I couldn't have any dealings with the Stirlingshire Constabulary or the Highland Cow Squad or whoever the hell ran law and order around here. The important thing was I was in a car and my pursuers weren't.

'You maybe want to turn around,' I said. 'They're parked at the other side of the village. If we keep going this way we'll run into them.'

'Leave this to me, young man,' he said. We headed straight for the village, then suddenly swung to the right at an almost concealed entrance and up a narrow tarmacked lane.

I laughed.

'What is it?' he asked.

'Do you live in the big house?'

'Yes I do, as a matter of fact. Why? What's so funny about that?'

'Not so much funny as ironic. I thought you were the Apaches but turns out you're the cavalry.'

'I'm afraid I don't—'

'Never mind, sir,' I said. 'I can't tell you how relieved I am to get your help.' I twisted round in my seat, bounced along by the minimal suspension of the Land Rover, checking out of the rear window.

'No one there?' my benefactor asked.

'No one there. But I have to tell you, in a place as small as this, it isn't going to take them long to find us.'

'Like I said, you leave this all to me.'

We pulled in through the gates of Collieluth House and the Land Rover ground to a halt on the stone-chipped driveway.

'Come on ...' he said urgently and led me into the house, the front door of which had been left unlocked.

We entered a huge entrance hallway, walnut-lined and smelling of leather, polished wood and feudalism. He bustled me into what I guessed was the drawing room. Again 'baronial' wasn't a style, it was the reality of the place. This was the hub and tiller of a whole rural community.

'Wait here ...' he commanded. Commanding seemed to come naturally to him.

He went back out into the hall, leaving the drawing room door open, picked up the telephone and dialled two numbers.

'It's the Major,' he said. 'Get over here with two of the men. Tell them to bring their shotguns and shells ...'

He listened to the person on the other end for a second, his face clouded with impatience.

'Just do it ... I have a man here and his life appears to be in danger ... yes, from the strangers we saw in the village. Get over here now. I'm going to telephone the police in Crianlarich and get help.'

I wanted to stop him calling the police, but I couldn't for the life of me come up with a credible reason why he shouldn't. I'd have to play it all by ear.

I heard him dial again. Three numbers this time. I heard him tell the police about the attempt on my life, that there were men roaming the countryside with small arms, and to get people over here as soon as possible.

'All right . . .' he said, smiling, when he came back into the drawing room and making his way to the window to check outside. 'The cavalry, as you put it, are on their way. My men are on their way from the farm and the police will be here as soon as they can.'

I thanked him again. I had my first chance to examine him. He was a handsome man with greying temples and deepening creases on his face. He had the kind of face you trusted and had a quiet authority about him. He wore country clothes, but of the more expensive and stylish look that Hopkins had gone for.

'Please . . .' he indicated a leather chair. 'Sit down.'

'I'm afraid I'm rather wet . . .' I said in apology, looking down at my waterproof trousers. What he couldn't see was that the flannels beneath them were soaked through.

'Don't worry about that,' he said, almost irritated. 'We'll deal with your clothes in a minute. Please sit down and tell me what this is all about.' As he spoke, he went over to a large mahogany desk that was set against one wall, beneath a huge portrait of some Victorian whom I assumed was my benefactor's ancestor, despite the lack of any familial similarity I could see. He went into the drawer and pulled out an Enfield revolver and a box of shells. He looked at me inquisitively, breaking the revolver open and filling the chambers from the box, as matter-of-factly as if he had been filling his pipe.

I told him about being surprised in the bothy by the blond man whom he had seen taking potshots at me, how they had frogmarched me down into the valley and how I had made my escape.

He snapped shut the revolver and placed it on the burnished surface of the desk, going to the window once more and checking.

'That's all good and well . . .' he said. 'You have explained the *what* but not the *why*. Why did these men try to abduct you?'

I explained that I was an enquiry agent and I believed these men were responsible for the murder of Andrew Ellis, a Glasgow businessman. I explained that they believed I knew the where-abouts of funds Ellis had withheld.

'Funds for what?'

'A Hungarian émigré group. Ellis was Hungarian by birth and had patriotic leanings. He was helping – illegally – refugees get out of Hungary and into the West.'

'But there is no need, surely, to do so illegally. Great Britain has offered hundreds asylum.'

'Yes, but not the numbers and not the type that Ellis was helping.'

'What do you mean?'

'Ellis was a straightforward kind of guy. Not a lefty, but no rabid nationalist either. He thought he was helping liberals and intellectuals get out of Hungary – even a few dissident commu-nists.'

'But he wasn't?'

'No. I don't know what happened – maybe he saw a face in a photograph, or a name he recognized – but something must have made him realize that he was actually helping former members of the Arrow Cross.'

'Arrow Cross?'

'Hungarian Nazis. Many of them were executed for war crimes at the end of the war. Hungary had a breed of Nazi all of its own that started while Adolf was still a corporal. Rabid anti-Semites and Magyar racial purists. The communists had a lot of them locked up and others reduced to life in menial positions and under constant surveillance. The Hungarian Uprising was the ideal cover for getting them out and into the West.'

He shook his head. 'This is all very interesting, but what has this to do with us up here. Listen . . . sorry, what's your name?'

'Lennox,' I said, too tired to lie. The truth I was giving him was incredible enough without adding any fiction to it.

'Listen, Mr Lennox, we are as far removed from international politics as it is possible to be. The only border disputes we have are over fences and grazing rights. I can't see why the devil we have men rampaging over our countryside firing shots at each other because of events in Moscow and Budapest.'

'Because there is something up here . . . or around here . . . I don't know what . . . A meeting place.'

'I see . . .' he said contemplatively. There was an urgent knock at the door and he checked through the window before going out into the hall, leaving the revolver on the desk. I heard him open the door and issue orders.

'That's three men from the farm, armed with shotguns,' he said when he got back. 'They will keep guard until the police get here. What you said about this meeting place . . . when we were in the Land Rover you said you had thought I represented the Apaches when I was really the cavalry. I take it by that you thought this house was this group's meeting place?'

'I did. At least it made most sense.'

He froze for a moment, something troubling him.

'These men who are chasing you, the men from this Hungarian group . . . you didn't mention your suspicions about this house to them?'

'No, why?'

'Because they might then have worked out that this is where you would head, with or without my help.'

'Of course,' I said.

'But you still haven't explained why you found your way here, of all places. Why you thought the meeting place would be anywhere around here?'

I told him about Ellis's map and the T marking the location.

'And what it the significance of the T?' he asked.

'It stands for Tanglewood, which is the code word for their meeting place. The significance of it escapes me, I'm afraid,' I said.

He picked up the Enfield from the desk and pointed it at me. I made a start but he shook his head.

'Don't be silly, Mr Lennox. It's really very simple,' he said. 'You're sitting in Tanglewood . . . without boring you with etymologies, the name of this house, Collieluth, is an anglicization of the Gaelic *Choille Thiugh Dhlùth*. It means "the crowded, dark wood". Tanglewood.'

'And you are what?' I asked. 'Some British Arrow-Cross fellow traveller? Or do you have deep Hungarian roots.'

'You have no idea who or what I am. And I have absolutely no interest in or intention of telling you . . .'

'Actually,' I said, 'I know exactly who you are. I know the name you've been using and I know how long you have been in Scotland.'

'I really don't care . . .' He started to move towards the door. 'Now, just stay exactly where you are . . .'

'Or what?' I said, standing up. He brought his aim up, straight-armed, to my head.

'Don't be stupid . . .' he said.

'Well, you see, I have a habit of being stupid. I've gotten just about everything wrong, every step of the way. But you I didn't buy. Not for a minute. That's why I emptied your gun when you were at the door . . .'

I held out my hand and let the shells fall onto the floor. He squeezed the trigger and when he heard the click he made a rush for the door, but I was already on him. I swiped him across the throat with the blade edge of my hand, just like they'd taught me in training. It shut off his air supply immediately. When you can't breathe, you can't do anything, can't think of anything else. I pulled out the Femaru-Frommer automatic from under my anorak and, hauling him back by the collar, threw him down on the floor.

'I've been looking for you for a long time, Mr Lang. This is for Andrew Ellis . . .'

I slashed the barrel of the automatic across his temple and the skin burst, blood flowing into his hair. Beneath his desperate gasping, he made some kind of noise. I hauled him to his feet. And jabbed the muzzle of the pistol into the small of his back.

'Now, Ferenc, we are going to take a walk out to the Land Rover. You are going to tell your monkeys out there to pile their shotguns into the back of the Land Rover, then lie face down on the ground. If you don't, or if they don't do as they're told, I'll blow your spine through your belly. You got that?'

He nodded.

'Because I want you to understand something, Ferenc, I really want to kill you. Just give me an excuse and I'll do it in a heartbeat. You got that, too?'

'Yes . . .' he said, his voice hoarse.

I led him out into the hall. My plan was to get as far as I could as quickly as I could. I just hoped that the Land Rover had enough gas in it to get us to Glasgow and St Andrew's Square.

The tricky part was getting out of the drive.

I swung open the door and pushed Lang through, lifting the gun and pushing the barrel into his cheek to show his men that I meant business.

Except they weren't there.

Blondy and Curly stood next to the Land Rover. And they weren't alone.

'Well, well . . .' I said. 'Mr Hopkins, the disappearing intelligence man.' I pushed Lang down the steps and he fell onto the gravel. Curly hauled him up to his feet and dragged him off to a waiting car. A second car had Lang's hired help bundled in the back. I gave them both a cheery wave: after all, I hadn't seen them since we met on the stairwell of my office.

Hopkins was wearing the same dark coat I'd seen him in earlier, at the car, and before that, outside Larry Franks's apartment. The warrant cards hadn't been fake, after all.

'If you don't mind,' said Blondy, 'I'll take that.'

'Certainly, constable,' I said and handed him the automatic. 'By the way, I'm glad you're such a lousy shot. That was when I worked out which was the side of the angels.'

'You've caused us a lot of extra work,' he said.

'Have I? I kind of thought I'd cleared the whole thing up for you. By the way, if I can give you a tip . . . try not to be so ambiguous. When you said I was getting in the way and it was your job to take me out of the way, I started to get the wrong idea.'

'I think you're being paranoid,' he said.

'Oh I am that. I've been paranoid for over a week now. And it's getting worse. I've even been getting this crazy idea that you didn't identify yourselves as police officers because you wanted me to make a break for it and flush out your little Hungarian network. It's got nothing to do with expatriates, has it?'

'It has and it hasn't,' answered Hopkins. 'I think I'd better explain.'

And he did.

CHAPTER FORTY-SEVEN

I was driven back to Glasgow in a grey Rover with red leather seats that, after everything I'd been through, felt better than a woman's touch. Hopkins explained about Lang and how he had infiltrated the Mátyás Network, as the Hungarian émigré organization was known.

Ferenc Lang had skipped out of Hungary at the end of the war and before the Iron Curtain had closed around him. If he hadn't got out, Hopkins explained, Lang would have faced awkward questions about his Arrow Cross party membership. Then, when the Uprising had started to take shape, Lang had seen an opportunity to cash in on the situation in Hungary and get some of his cronies out amongst the others fleeing the coming Russian crackdown.

'Does Jock Ferguson know any of this?' I asked. My voice was drunk-slurry with tiredness.

'Don't be naïve,' said Hopkins. 'Do you really think that you were able to escape police custody without some collaboration?'

'As a matter of fact, I didn't. So Jock knew you wouldn't be in the building in Ingram Street?'

'I told you when we met that it was only a temporary arrangement. By the way, your associate Archie McClelland is in police custody. He assaulted the estate agent, Mr Collins, who is responsible for the building. I don't know what it is about you, Mr Lennox, but you seem to inspire great loyalty. I just wish the Crown had the same gift.'

'The charges against Archie . . . I take it you can make them go away.'

'I can, and I will. But only if you drop out of sight for a while. And forget what you've seen. There's more going on here than you can begin to understand.'

'I don't know,' I said. 'I'm a very understanding person. Let's start with Mátyás. Why did he side with Ferenc Lang?'

'He didn't. Mátyás, whom you met, is the genuine article. But his network became infiltrated with Lang's people.'

'The chaff in the wheat,' I said, recalling our conversation in Ingram Street. 'But Mátyás set me up. Him and the girl.'

'No they didn't. That day at the station, the day Ellis was murdered in your office, they genuinely thought they were arranging for you to meet Ferenc Lang. Just like Ellis believed he had been summoned to an urgent meeting with you because you had found out what was going on and wanted to help him.'

'So Magda and Mátyás really did get a call at the last minute to tell them Lang couldn't make it?'

'Yes. And asking that Magda meet with you to explain. I'm afraid the Mátyás network comprises writers and intellectuals. Lang had them believing he was a champion of Hungarian democracy and freedom. I'm afraid they're simply not equipped for this kind of subterfuge. Nor, frankly, are you.'

'I did all right,' I said.

'With the greatest respect, Lennox, you're an amateur and you have no idea what is really going on.'

'Really? Like Lang maybe not being a Hungarian fascist at all but really a Soviet intelligence agent?'

Hopkins smiled. 'Now why would you think that?'

'Because I don't know that Andrew Ellis would have been too perturbed about rabid Hungarian fascists. He had a tough time getting into the army because of his membership of a Hungarian youth organization before the war. My guess is the army wouldn't worry if he'd been a Boy Scout.'

'So why, then, was he so opposed to Lang, if your theory is right?'

I fumbled about in my pockets until I found the corner from Ellis's desk blotter. I handed it to Hopkins. 'It's got something to do with this, I think. NTS.'

Hopkins looked at the paper and shrugged. 'Doesn't mean anything,' he said, rolling the window down and tossing the paper out.

'If you say so . . .' I said. I closed my eyes and let the motion of the car rock me to sleep.

EPILOGUE

Dead Men and Broken Hearts.

Hopkins could not have put it better. He had been right when he said that was what men like me seemed to leave behind.

There were two murder trials that year.

Dennis Annan stood trial for the murder of Sylvia Dewar. His defence lawyer pointed out that much of the evidence came from dubious sources. I just happened to be in the witness box when he pointed it out.

The judge told the jury that they were dealing with one death, that of Sylvia Dewar. He instructed them not to allow themselves to be influenced by the fact that the murder of Sylvia Dewar had driven her husband to commit suicide. The fact that he pointed this out immediately before they retired to consider their verdict perhaps had something to do with them returning before the Jury Room tea had cooled in the pot.

They didn't bother trying Annan for the union fraud. He took the eight a.m. short walk to a long drop in Barlinnie jail just as the leaves were beginning to fall in Fifty-seven.

Joe Connelly somehow managed to come out of the whole thing squeaky clean and actually appeared as a witness for the prosecution. Whatever he was, Connelly wasn't simply a political animal, he was an apex political predator. Shortly after, he switched his allegiance from the Communist Party to Labour; and a couple of years after that actually got himself elected MP in some Ayrshire constituency where a mentally retarded donkey could have won, provided it wore a red rosette. His parliamentary career was, however, spectacularly short. It turned out that his heart had been as livid and puffy as his face, and he died of a massive heart attack a month after making his maiden speech.

The second trial was for the murder, in my office, of Andrew Ellis. Obviously, I appeared as a witness in that case, too. I had been prepared to describe, from the stand, my dramatic flight through the heather, my tussles with foreign agents and smouldering Hungarian brunettes. I would, I had predicted, stand heroically upright, pointing my resolutely accusing finger at Ferenc Lang and the two men I'd struggled with in the stairwell of my office building, immediately before finding Ellis dying.

I didn't get a chance. A Hungarian national, an absconded merchant seaman, was arrested and tried for the murder of Andrew Ellis. He admitted the killing, but with a plea of diminished responsibility, and provided details that only the killer could know. He was a small, dark, unprepossessing man in his thirties. And I'd never seen him before in my life. He was about as guilty of Ellis's murder as I was.

One of Hopkins's innocents to the slaughter.

Except he didn't go to the slaughter. His plea was accepted and he was declared unfit for trial and committed to the secure mental hospital in Carstairs. Case closed. No one asked me even to identify him, which I wouldn't have. My guess was that he wouldn't spend long weaving baskets and finger-painting: he would probably soon be repatriated to a Hungarian hospital 'on compassionate grounds'.

No one mentioned Ferenc Lang, Mátyás, Magda, Tanglewood or any putative émigré group. Deals, no doubt, were being done, intelligence traded, lives bought and sold. Or maybe he had been sold back to the Soviets.

I asked a friend of mine who knew about such things what NTS could have stood for. The best he could come up with was *Narodny Trudovoi Soyuz*. He explained it was a Russian anti-communist organization that had worked with Hungarian insurgents, encouraging them to revolt. But the rumour was that the NTS was actually a double-blind Kremlin outfit, placing communist agents in the West in the guise of right-wing refugees.

There was a rumour, my friend told me, that the NTS had encouraged Hungarian dissident groups to act sooner, rather than later, so that the Soviets could crush the Uprising while the West squabbled over who owned a canal.

Maybe I was still being paranoid.

I had to put my return to Canada on hold, until after the trials. In the meantime, the Iron Curtain had once more been drawn around Hungary, saving the West the embarrassment of having to look at the consequences of its inaction and deafness to the desperate, final broadcast pleas for help while Hungary's brief flame of freedom was snuffed out under tank tracks.

In the meantime, Suez emasculated Britain. Eisenhower flexed the US's economic power and, faced with bankruptcy without American support, Britain caved in over Suez and Anthony Eden's head rolled. Overnight, the great imperial power became just a little grey island off the coast of Europe.

What Hopkins didn't know – or probably did – was that I helped Mátyás's network over the next couple of months. Pamela Ellis met with me after the trial: she said she was sorry and I said it was okay and how I understood that Lang had put the frighteners on her. We talked about the Mátyás network and I put her in touch with it. She had, it appeared, some money she wanted to put to work helping Hungarian refugees.

Over the months after the Uprising, the Mátyás network succeeded in getting a great many Hungarians into Britain, France, Canada and the US. Some were geniuses, just as Hopkins had described in his Hungarian Brain Drain theory, but there were a lot of plumbers and sailors, mechanics and goulash cooks in there too. Oppression, contrary to the beliefs of some, is something the ordinary want to escape from every bit as much as the extraordinary do.

At least I made one person happy: I went back to the car lot on Great Western Road and made Kenny the salesman's month by trading the Atlantic in for the Talbot – after all, I didn't have anyone else to spend my money on. Well, I had one person, and Kenny came close to ecstasy when I told him I also wanted to buy the six-month old, low-mileage Vauxhall Cresta he had on the forecourt.

'For a friend,' I had explained.

Kenny probably blew the commission on hair oil and breath mints.

Jonny Cohen was never charged with the Argyle Arcade robbery. No one was. But one of his 'known associates', as the coppers were wont to say, met with a tragic accident. Drowning. They fished him out of the Clyde not far from the Queen's Dock, where I'd met with Jonny that day.

There was another, unexpected twist to my tale of dead men and broken hearts. I thought I'd heard the last of Sheriff Pete, the pale-faced loudmouth with the phoney American accent, the strange dark eyes and the mop of black hair.

I'd done exactly what Jock Ferguson had asked and kept out of whatever it was that was going on with him. After all, I had had a lot on my plate and Sheriff Pete had been the least of my concerns. I hadn't seen the little creep since I'd given him the slapping for harassing the girl from the dance hall. But I had thought about him. I had thought about him a lot. About the earnest look on Jock Ferguson's face. About Sheriff Pete's boast that no one would forget his face or his name.

He had been right.

I looked again into those coal-black eyes; every time his face appeared on the TV news; every time I passed a news vendor's stand.

They hanged him too.

The small, insignificant loser and Walter Mitty fantasist who'd been the butt of so many jokes in the Horsehead Bar had lived up to his promise of becoming a big name. Just like he said: a name no one would ever forget, in Scotland at least.

He'd managed that all right.

What I hadn't known, but Jock Ferguson had suspected, was that that night I'd met him, Pete had already murdered four women. And he had gone on to become the most notorious multiple rapist and murderer in Scottish legal history. They hanged him in Fifty-eight for the eight murders they tried him for. Eight out of maybe as many as eighteen or nineteen killings.

The small man got the big name he had craved.

Peter Manuel.

The Beast of Birkenshaw.

Over the next six months, I 'phoned Fiona White three times. The first two calls had been made drunk and she hung up on me. I was sober the third time and we spoke for three or four politely dry minutes. Her voice had been small and quiet and fragile on the 'phone, as if her fading out of my life was literal. I had had a list of things I wanted to say to her, promises I wanted to make, meetings I wanted to arrange, but somehow they too, faded to nothing.

It was in the summer of Fifty-seven that he came to the door of my new flat in Kelvin Court. James White. The last person I expected ever to see again. He asked quietly and politely if he could come in and talk to me. I decided to be very civilized and Canadian about it all and was polite back. He declined my offer of a drink and set down to business.

As soon as I had seen him on the doorstep, I'd guessed the reason for his visit. I could almost have saved him the effort of explaining that he and Fiona would be getting married and how that would be best for the girls and how he knew all about my past with her and they just wanted to put that behind them, they didn't want any trouble and she didn't want anything more to do with me . . .

Thing is, it wasn't that. It wasn't that at all.

He handed me a letter and I could see my name in Fiona's handwriting on the envelope. White told me not to open it until he explained a few things, which he did, and something deep, deep inside me froze, then snapped.

Turned out I'd got it all wrong; turned out I wasn't so expert on looking in on the lives of others as I had thought I was.

That night – the night after James White had been to see me; the night after I had sat alone in my flat when he had gone and read and reread the letter Fiona had written – that night I went out to get as drunk as it was possible to get, but somehow I couldn't. It was as if I'd been inoculated against alcohol, against all other feeling except the searing pain in my gut and chest. But I guess I was drunk after all without feeling it.

I picked up a girl. Or she picked me up. She was about ten years younger than me and pretty in a bottle-blonde, hard-faced sort of way. She told me all about her stupid life, her stupid job and her stupid friends and told me stupid things about me looking like the movie star Jack Palance and asked me what I did and was I married or did I have a girlfriend.

'There was someone,' I said, turning to her.

'Did you break up with her,' she asked.

'Yes . . .' Then I shook my head irritatedly. 'No . . .'

I thought of the letter; of what Fiona had told me about how she had felt about me; how I'd changed while I'd known her and how I wasn't to let *this* ruin that; how she wanted me to go back to Canada and find someone new, someone nice and start all over.

'No,' I repeated to the girl next to me. 'We didn't break up. She got sick. She died.'

'Oh . . .' The girl's expression changed, as if suddenly she wanted to be somewhere else. I couldn't blame her: she was just a girl looking for a good time, for fun, and the pony she had backed had turned out lame.

'She was sick and I didn't know it,' I explained and could hear something like pleading in my own voice. 'You see, all those times she went with him – all those times I thought she was *with* him . . . The hospital. He was taking her to the hospital and it should have been me taking her. She didn't want me to know. I got it all wrong. All wrong.'

I took the letter from my pocket and stared at it, a crumpled ball in my hand. I felt my face wet.

I sat for a while saying nothing and when I next looked the

girl was gone. I stuffed the letter back in my pocket, went through to the public bar and drank some more, a lot more.

Then, in the best Celtic tradition, I looked around for someone to fight.

ACKNOWLEDGEMENTS

My thanks go to the following people for their support: Wendy, Jonathan and Sophie Russell; Jane Wood, Ron Beard, Katie Gordon, Robyn Karney and all at Quercus; Andrew Gordon, Georgina Ruffhead, Tine Nielsen and Ania Corless at David Higham Associates; Ali and Al Muirden at Creative Content; Colin Black, Chris Martin, Larry Sellyn and Elaine Dyer.